PRAISE FOR *HAPPILY EVER AFTER*

"Susie writes a delightful story. I fell in love with this couple. Pursuing a dream, learning to trust each other, falling in love . . . a few hours of reading doesn't get better. The Footstep of Heaven Bookstore is a wonderful place to linger. Great job, Susie! I enjoyed every minute."

› **DEE HENDERSON** ›
author of the O'Malley series

"*Happily Ever After* is chock-full of humor and the reminder of God's everlasting grace. Susan Warren is an author sure to be around for a long time."

› **LORI COPELAND** ›
author of the Brides of the West series and Stranded in Paradise

"Perfect! Susan May Warren's tender tale of love and forgiveness delights the senses and warms the heart. With its vividly drawn characters and lush lakeside setting, *Happily Ever After* blends humor and deep emotion with a wonderful surprise that will keep readers eagerly turning pages."

› **CATHERINE PALMER** ›
author of English Ivy *and Christy Award–winner* A Touch of Betrayal

"Warren weaves a tapestry of life so real you breathe with her characters! Vivid descriptions . . . an intriguing story . . . a powerful message of betrayal and forgiveness . . . all combine to make you wish your visit to the lakeside town of Deep Haven would never end."

› **CHRISTINE LYNXWILER** ›
President of American Christian Romance Writers

"A prince of a guy . . . a damsel in distress . . . and a villain intent on doing them both in . . . Susan Warren's *Happily Ever After* spins all the elements of a much-loved fairy tale into this delightful modern-day story of suspense and romance. As fulfilling as the 'Happily Ever After' part proved to be, I found myself wishing this delightful tale never had to end."

› **SUSAN DOWNS** ›
novelist and editor

Susan May Warren

Happily Ever After

Romance fiction from
Tyndale House Publishers, Inc., Wheaton, Illinois

romance the way it's meant to be

HeartQuest brings you romantic fiction
with a foundation of biblical truth.
Adventure, mystery, intrigue, and suspense
mingle in these heartwarming stories of
men and women of faith striving to build
a love that will last a lifetime.

May HeartQuest books sweep you
into the arms of God, who longs for you
and pursues you always.

To my Lord
and Savior, Jesus Christ,
the giver of grace,
the author of dreams.
Thank You for reaching out
of heaven to gather me
into Your arms.

To my husband, Andrew.
You are my happily ever after.

Acknowledgments

Writing *Happily Ever After* has shown me again God's great provision for every dream. I am so thankful—and blessed—to be surrounded by a supportive cast of angels who have helped me in every stage of this story.

My deepest gratitude and appreciation go to:

Ellen Tarver, Sue Fuller, and Tanka, who devoted an entire Saturday to helping me plot a story about a woman who wanted to open a bookstore. Thank you for listening and for your steadfast enthusiasm.

Christine Lynxwiler, who expertly critiqued each chapter. Your excellent comments made this story sing.

Andrea Boeshaar, faithful friend who told me to keep dreaming. Your friendship has blessed me.

Yvonne Howard, who read this story so many times she could recite it. What would I do without you? Thank you for the many hugs, for the kind and perfect words, and for serving the Lord with such devotion and sacrifice. We love you, Auntie Vonnie!

Dee Henderson and Susan Downs, two authors I

admire, kept my chin up and fueled my hopes. Thank you for your friendship and encouragement.

Joyce Hart, my tireless agent who confirms that God knows our needs—and our hearts. Thank you for your wise words and your hard work.

Anne Goldsmith, for your support and encouragement. Your suggestions not only strengthened this story but strengthened me as a writer. I will forever be in your debt.

Lorie Popp—I'm so blessed to have you as my editor. What a joy to work with someone so talented. You put the polish on this story!

Curt and Mary Ann Lund, who helped me fall in love with the North Shore. Thank you for every summer we spent there and for printing out this manuscript over and over again. God's love for me started with you.

Finally, thank you, Drewski, for reading a mushy book and giving me your male opinion. You're living proof that God is a fulfiller of dreams. I would never have written one word if you hadn't sent me to my room.

O my people,
trust in Him at all times.
Pour out your heart
to Him, for God is
our refuge.

Psalm 62:8

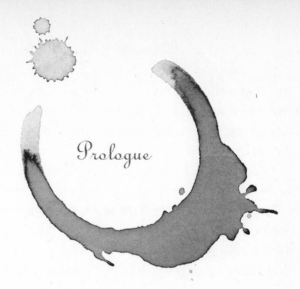

Prologue

He barely escaped with his shirt.

"I am *never* signing another book as long as I live." Reese Clark's voice echoed like a gunshot through the five-story Mall of America parking garage. He swept off his black Stetson and dragged a hand through his unruly, shoulder-scraping brown hair. He grimaced at the layer of sweat that came off in his hand.

The book signing had disintegrated into chaos, just as he'd expected. After two hours of orderly lines, with women breathing in his face and fawning over him as if he were a teenage movie idol, the peace had evaporated. Normal, law-abiding women began to push and argue.

He'd climbed on his chair, waved to the back, and assured the crowd he would sign every copy of *Siberian Runaway*. Yet they still fought for space in the line that curved past Macy's, snaked down West Market, and probably ended around the far corner of Nordstrom, another block farther. Despite ample bookstore security and two well-muscled mall uniforms barking orders, the crowd erupted. The noise and confusion resurrected enough ugly memories to send him looking for escape in the concrete parking labyrinth.

"Reese, come back here!" Jacqueline Saint marched up behind him, her spike heels echoing in monstrous volumes against the cement floor. "If you want to sell books, you'll wipe that pout off your face and march back inside."

He scowled at his publicist. "Back off, Jacqueline. You saw them in there." He made a show of shuddering. "I'm done. I'm not doing this anymore. One more fanatic reader and I'm going over the edge." Reese drew a deep breath. The smell of motor oil, cement, and dusty ceilings twisted his empty stomach. "I need some air."

Jacqueline dug her ruby red manicured fingernails into his arm. "You've got to loosen up, Reese. This isn't Chicago. No one is lurking in the men's room. I've made sure security is on you like glue. You're fine."

He stiffened. "Maybe I just have a better memory than you do."

He heard her clucking, a habit that could shred his nerves to rags. "The price one pays for fame," she said, not gently.

He tried not to rise to that. She was the closest thing he had to a real friend right now, and that thought turned like a knife.

"Listen, you're almost done," she soothed in false tones. "One more week on the morning-news circuit, then you can disappear and cultivate that 'mystery man of the mountains' image you love." Her voice hardened. "Until then, baby, you sign books."

Reese jerked out of her grip. "Give me five minutes . . . at least."

Jacqueline raised a thin eyebrow and ran her cool gray eyes over him as if evaluating prey. Checking the time on her gold watch, she nodded crisply. "Five minutes. Clock starts now."

Reese tightened his jaw and stalked away. Jacqueline might be the best publicist his editor had to offer, but after three months of her nonstop company, he was ready to topple her off those lizard-skin spikes.

He exhaled a hot, uneven breath. One week left. Then he would have nine peaceful months before the release of his next book. Soon he'd be off to the mountains—good riddance civilization. Not that he itched to shoulder a pack or climb inside his worn, polar sleeping bag again, but a multihued mountain sky, the threat of a storm, and even mosquitoes the size of his fist seemed a more welcoming atmosphere than a crowded mall bookstore. More welcoming—and safer. He'd take a face-to-face encounter with a grizzly over a lovesick fan any day, month, or year. He'd seen enough of crazed women up close and personal to make his blood turn cold.

The book tour served its purpose, however—funds to explore the planet. His books sold millions. Why, he still didn't understand. He wrote them because they called to be written, but women hungered after them, buying them in hardback, hot off the presses. Jacqueline reasoned it was because his hero never found the woman he sought, and his readers all fantasized they could be the one.

Reese wandered between a Lexus and a grimy blue

Chevette and leaned on the edge of the railing to peer down onto the highway, a spiraling mess of noise and exhaust. Beyond the concrete, the red-and-orange autumn foliage shimmered in the trees lining the Mississippi River. An errant breeze drifted toward him, carrying the tinge of drying leaves and the crisp anticipation of fall. They beckoned to him, and he never felt more trapped. Yes, he loved the writing, the traveling . . . it was the invasion of his privacy that pushed him to his last nerve. He was already plotting his escape. As traffic hummed below, Reese sunk his head in his arms.

The car behind him coughed and sputtered. It wasn't the Lexus. Reese whirled, intending to scuttle between the two vehicles. He made it as far as the front driver's door. It swung open, crashed into his knees, and swiped dirt across his tailored suit pants. As the driver barreled out of the Chevette, he jumped back, frowning, and dusted off his knees. "Watch it!" he growled.

He heard an offended gasp and immediately regretted his tone. Rudeness wasn't his standard.

"You watch it. My car can't move; you can!" The spitfire comeback didn't match the petite blonde steaming before him. Shoulder height and dressed in a black skirt and a white cashmere sweater, she didn't look the type to drive such a clunker or to meet her problems head-on. He blinked at her.

She clamped her hands on her hips, her eyes blazing. "What are you doing next to my car, anyway?"

He raised his brows. "Well, I certainly wasn't going to steal it."

Her mouth flew open a second before she harrumphed and shook her head. With one swift move she reached

down beside the seat and popped the hood. When she stepped back and slammed the door, the sound clamored along the low-hanging ceiling.

Silence passed between them as she stared at him. "Well, are you going to move, or are you paid to block traffic?"

"Sorry," he mumbled as he raised his hands in surrender. He scooted back to the railing.

The woman brushed past him, widely avoiding the scum on her car. She slid two fingers under the hood and heaved it open. As she propped it up, she shot Reese a sidelong look. Her eyes seemed to soften. "Sorry," she muttered. "I'm having a rotten day. First I lock myself out of the house, then I rip my skirt climbing through the window, then Macy's computer eats my layaway. And now, old Noah here won't start."

He bit his lip to stifle an unexpected grin. "Noah?"

She tucked a chunk of golden hair behind her ear. "Don't ask."

Still warring with a smirk, he stuck his hands into his pockets and leaned back against the cement wall, intrigued by a woman in fancy duds jiggling cables, adjusting the oil cap, and fingering the connections to her car battery. Remarkably, she had only a light coating of grease on her fingers when she turned back to him.

She chewed her delicate lip for a moment. Her forlorn gaze shifted past him, as if the answer lay in the bronzed hills. Then abruptly, she pinned him with a tentative look. "Know anything about cars?"

Reese rubbed his chin. He wasn't interested in getting dirty. Especially since he had to return to a crowd of cheering women in the bookstore. . . . "Yep, I know a few things." He stepped up to the car and leaned over the engine compartment.

Beside him, she peered into the blackness. "What do you see?" Her hair fell over her face, and she flipped it back.

Reese glanced at her and stifled another snigger. She had wiped a dash of oil across her cheek, like a football player. She *was* having a bad day.

Pinching his lips together, Reese examined the black hole of her car. Rusty wires merged with fraying cables, and sticky muck layered the corroded battery. After a moment of perusal, during which the odor of oil seeped over him like a fog, he reached in and tweaked the spark-plug wires. "Give her a try," he said, slapping his hands together.

"Really? That's all?" Her mouth opened in amazement when he nodded.

"Loose spark-plug wires will stop you cold every time."

Her green eyes glowed with sudden delight, and for the first time he noticed they were the color of finely cut emeralds, with magical golden flecks. They reached out and held him until he blew out a breath and broke away. "Give her a try," he repeated hoarsely and looked for a place to wipe his blackened fingers.

"Righto!" She sprang toward the driver's door.

Reese fished around in his back pocket and found a handkerchief. So much for his starched appearance. He worked the grease off his fingers.

The motor roared to life, and with it, inner snapshots of Reese's high school days. The hum of a Chevy could never be forgotten, especially the sweet melody of his Corvette, shined and stored on blocks in a place he was trying to forget.

With a sheepish grin, the blonde climbed out of her car. "It looks like you saved me." Her face brightened into a genuine smile. "Thank you so much." She reached over the open door. "Mona Reynolds."

Reese took her grip. "Clark."

Her eyes shone, and didn't she have the most beautiful smattering of freckles dotting her high cheekbones when she grinned?

"I suppose I should buy you a cup of coffee, huh?"

He handed her the handkerchief. "Nah, I happened to be in the right place at the right time." She frowned at the handkerchief, confused. He pointed to her face. "You've got a dab of war paint there."

She wrinkled her nose and ducked into the car, adjusting her rearview mirror.

Reese snared the moment to gather his senses. Coffee suddenly sounded nice. An escape with a pretty, sincere woman who didn't fawn over him might be just the breath of air he needed.

She turned around, a line of red where the oil had been. "Thanks." She handed the handkerchief back to him.

"About coffee . . . ," he began.

"Oh, I would really love to treat you. Give me your card, and I'll call you."

His hope deflated. "Uh, well, I don't have one on me."

"Oh." She appeared stymied, her lips puckering into an intriguing pout. "Well, maybe you could give me your number or your e-mail address?"

Reese pulled off his hat and rubbed a hand along the brim. His vision of a quiet coffee date with him safely disguised as an out-of-town business executive named Clark disintegrated under the glare of reality.

This was getting too complicated, especially with a crowd of fans waiting inside. It would only take running into the media and things would turn ugly. He shook his head. "Actually, I'm just passing through town."

She looked crestfallen, and he nearly changed his mind. After a silent moment, she sighed. "Well, thanks again. You were my hero today."

He smiled at that. Playing the part, he snuggled the Stetson back on his head and pulled the brim like a courteous cowboy.

She shut the car door, waved once as she backed out, then disappeared in a fog of exhaust.

Reese scowled against the acrid smell, and disapointment pinched his heart. For a second there, he thought Mona might have turned out to be more than just a fan. He'd never find a woman who would be able to see beneath the Reese Clark veneer. It was painfully clear he and women just weren't meant to be.

"Reese!"

He and Jacqueline weren't meant to be either. Reese trudged back to the skyway and his book tour.

Applebee's parking lot seemed fairly crowded for the predinner hour. Enormously late, Mona found a spot in the back and hustled to the entrance.

Stopping at the hostess booth, she craned her neck and spotted Liza Beaumont waving crazily at a high table in the middle section. "Excuse me, my party is

here," she said to the annoyed hostess and hurried toward Liza before her roommate made a scene and started hollering her name.

"Well, look how she's grown!"

Mona skidded to a stop, cringing as Edith Draper rose from her seat at Liza's table. The older woman headed toward Mona, her wide manicured hands reaching for Mona's face. Her mother's best friend thought she was still twelve years old.

"Hello, Mrs. Draper," Mona said weakly.

"I just wish your mother was here to see you take this big step. Imagine, owning your own business. I couldn't be prouder of you if you were my own child!" Edith's eyes glistened.

Mona surrendered to a hug. "Thanks, Mrs. Draper."

She drew back and waggled a finger in Mona's face. "Oh no. I'm Edith now. I'm going to be your neighbor."

Mona smiled warmly. She couldn't help but be drawn in by Edith's enthusiasm. "Okay . . . Edith."

"I ordered you a coffee," Liza announced as Mona slid onto a high stool and hooked her heels on the bottom bar.

"You look harried, dear." Edith put a wrinkled hand onto Mona's arm.

"I've had a horrible day," Mona replied. "I don't want to talk about it." She scanned the restaurant before returning her gaze to Edith. "Where's Chuck?"

The older woman waved her hand and shrugged. "You know how men are—have to use the bathroom wherever they go."

Mona smirked and spied Chuck Parson emerging from the men's room. Hitching his black jeans around his basketball stomach, he looked uncomfortable in his own skin. Poor guy. He was out of his element.

"Mona!" he called out from halfway across the room. Mona saw a waitress glare at him. Sliding off her stool, Mona met him two steps from the table. He wrapped her in a bear hug. "You're looking better than ever."

She sighed. She had them all fooled. Her insides were in knots, and her knees wanted to give out. If this thing really happened, her dreams were just a skip away. She kept pinching herself, waiting to wake up. God was so good to her to give her this miracle. She planned to grab on tightly to this chance and never let go. Now—to remain calm and focused. She had her heavenly favor, and God expected her best effort to make it happen. One shouldn't look lightly on the Lord's grace. Besides, God helped those who helped themselves.

She untangled herself from Chuck's embrace, and they climbed onto the stools. A waitress approached, balancing sodas and a steamy coffee. Mona didn't bother to look at the menu. "Chinese chicken salad and a side of plain toast."

Liza also ordered her regular—double-bacon cheese-burger and curly fries. Mona shook her head. It wasn't fair. Liza had legs that reached to her chin. The woman didn't know what it was like to just look at a Twinkie and see it appear on your thighs. Mona monitored her every bite with precision. She couldn't afford to buy new clothes. But she and Liza had been roommates for nearly a decade, and Mona had learned to live with the envy.

"I brought the layout and some pictures." Chuck hauled up a vinyl briefcase dated from the seventies. "Now don't get discouraged. It has potential. You just

need eyes to see it." He dealt the photos on the table like playing cards. "The porch might need a little hiking up here and there, but the foundation is good. There's a cozy apartment above the garage and an outbuilding, just like you wanted." He paused and scanned Mona's face with unmasked anticipation.

She picked up a photograph. It was perfect. The two-story Victorian answered both her prayers and her wildest dreams. "I'll take it."

Edith clutched her arm. "Dear, are you sure?"

Mona nodded and glanced at Liza. Liza's black eyes sparkled as she grinned wildly. Mona read the look. "Yep. I know what I've been waiting for, and this is it."

Edith sat back in the chair, a smile of satisfaction on her face. "I can't wait to tell your mother."

Mona fought the urge to roll her eyes. The last thing she needed was Edith Draper giving her mother in Arizona a chapter-by-chapter chronicle of her life.

Liza leaned close, her exotic perfume running over Mona like a wave. "This is it, Mone. The place where dreams come true."

Mona felt fear ripen in her stomach. *Please let Liza be right.*

"Oh!" Edith cried, clapping her hands together. "You have to see what I picked up today at the Mall of America."

Mona crossed her arms over her cashmere-clad chest and sighted a smudge of oil still staining her fingers. She grimaced. "I have to wash my hands."

"No, wait." Edith snared a bag at her feet. "I caught a book signing today."

"Who was it?" Mona grabbed a napkin and attempted recovery.

"I forget his name. He's that really famous writer
. . ." Edith snapped her fingers as if she were a genie,
waiting for the answer to poof.

"John Grisham?" Mona offered.

"Tom Clancy?" Chuck suggested.

"No, he's that one that was attacked a couple of years
ago . . . in Chicago, I think. I read about it in *USA
Today*. Some article about dangers to celebrities.
Reminded me of something out of a Stephen King novel.
A fan cornered him in the men's room and robbed him
. . . stole his boots or his hat. . . . I think he even ended
up in the hospital." Edith dug into her bag and pulled
out a hardcover. She cocked her head as she examined
the cover. "Not a bad-looking fella, either, the author.
Even if he does need a good haircut." She plunked the
book on the table, front cover down. "Reese Clark!"

Strikingly handsome in a forest green, plaid flannel
shirt, a smiling man in a black Stetson stared back at her
from the back cover. His brown curly hair dragged on
his shoulders, and his blue eyes spoke of some hidden
mystique. Reese Clark, Mona's favorite author. *Authors
aren't supposed to be that good-looking,* Mona thought
as she squinted at it. She wasn't great at remembering
faces, but it seemed she had seen that one before.

Suddenly the memory hit her, and she cried out in shock.

"What is it?" Edith went ashen and put a hand to her
throat.

Mona pinched the bridge of her nose and squeezed
her eyes shut. "I'm a complete idiot."

Liza leaned forward. "Well, besides the fact you just
painted your nose black, why?"

Mona looked at her fingers and grimaced. "My car

broke down at the mall. The guy who put it back together was Reese Clark."

She could have buried herself inside any one of the three astonished gapes.

"And you didn't get his autograph?" Edith looked at her as if she had sinned.

Mona shrugged. "I didn't recognize him."

Liza stifled hysterics. "Mona, you wouldn't know your own dog if it came up and bit you."

She made a face at Liza. But her roommate couldn't have said it better. Despite Mona's infatuation with his ongoing hero, Jonah, Reese Clark could have popped her a fairy-tale kiss and she wouldn't have known it was him. She groaned. "I actually invited him out for coffee. He probably thought I was some goggle-eyed fan trying to invade his privacy." After Edith's story, it was no wonder he had backed away from her at the speed of light.

"Oh, well," Mona murmured, heading for the ladies' room, "some things just aren't meant to be."

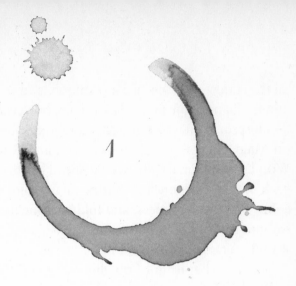

1

Μona leaned over the steering wheel of her Chevette and gunned the hatchback up the shoreline climb. The car nearly sailed over the top of the hill overlooking Deep Haven, but Mona didn't care if she touched down right into a speed trap. Delight drove her foot into the floorboards as she spied the town spread out before her like a red carpet—the place where years of dreaming and planning would reach their vivid finale. After ten long years she'd made it back. Finally, she would find peace. *Thank You, God.*

Mona stomped her brakes as she entered the forty-mile-per-hour zone and narrowly missed a pale-haired grandmother pumping her arms on a morning power walk. The woman glared at her. Mona returned an apologetic look.

As she motored along Main Street, Mona decided Deep Haven had changed little over the years. The lighthouse on the craggy point needed a paint job, and she noticed a number of new gift shops. Essentially, however, the population seemed intact—tourists and retirees. She turned off Main, clung to the shoreline drive, and headed for World's Best Donuts. She would spend her first moments back in this slice of heaven sitting on a boulder, propping coffee between her knees, and folding a sugary elephant ear into her mouth. It was an adolescent treat, but Mona wasn't quite ready to give it up.

She parked in front of the dime store and trotted over to World's Best. Squeezing into the packed bakery, she got in line and fifteen minutes later emerged with a crispy ear wrapped in a grease-dotted napkin.

Mona headed straight for a jagged outcropping on the shore of Lake Superior. Settling herself on a rock, she inhaled deeply, losing herself in the crisp, pine-laced lake air. Indeed, peace could be had in Deep Haven. She only had to inhale the fresh aroma of the forest and hear the scrape of waves on the beach to revive her father's memory in her heart. Finally, she could live the dream she'd waited a decade for already. Finally, nothing stood in her way.

She hoped her business instincts hadn't betrayed her. Although only a microdot on the Minnesota map, Deep Haven represented the only place to wrestle away a few days of privacy and calm from the stress of life in Minneapolis or St. Paul. When traveling the five hours north on I-35, tourists set their cars on cruise and started their holiday in the driver's seat, enjoying the jeweled countryside. Following the crisp Superior breeze, most vehicles found their own way to the tiny village nestled among the birch and maple trees, Norway pine, and balsam fir.

Very few people actually lived in Deep Haven. The town functioned like a large outside mall, where everyone met to slug down coffee and a donut, swap tales, and bemoan the horrors of life in the city. A few homes dotted the hillside, but Deep Haven had outlawed private building permits anywhere along the shore, except by approval of the local planning committee: Edith Draper.

Mona sipped her coffee—black, no sugar—and said a prayer of thanks to the good Lord for giving her mother, Verona, the sense to become Edith's friend thirty years ago. Mona checked her watch. Thirty minutes until Chuck's Real Estate opened and she picked up the keys to her future. It was all clicking together according to plan—from Edith's approval of her living quarters above the shop; to the down payment the size of her nest egg; to the agreement of her roommate, Liza Beaumont, to be her business partner.

Mona watched dawn spill across the water, turning the lake a sparkling indigo. Lake Superior's waves lapped easily a stone's toss from her feet. Oh, how her father would have loved it. He would have been beside her, swilling his own java—two creams, no sugar—and gesturing with a half-eaten chocolate cake donut at the seagulls dipping about on the waves. "Mona," he would have said, "there's a little bit of heaven to be found here. We just gotta keep our eyes out for it."

I'm looking, Pop. A gull, brave and cocky, landed near her and waddled close, its white head bobbing and its beady eyes fixed on the scrap of elephant ear. Mona tossed it to the scavenger, and the bird caught it before it hit the ground. She brushed off her sugared fingers and picked her way back toward the street.

"You all set?" Chuck sat behind his desk, a corduroy jacket over his plaid flannel shirt, appearing infinitely more at ease than he had eight months ago. Sunlight skimmed off his shiny head from the side window, and he had the gentle eyes of a man who'd spent his life serving people. The roller chair creaked as he leaned back.

"I think so." Mona smiled and held out her hand, palm up.

"Not so fast." Chuck stood and rubbed a chubby hand over his balding head. "I know you're excited, and frankly, it is a good idea, this bookstore thing. But I know how much it means to you, and I just want to make sure you know what you're in for."

Mona lowered her hand. "And what's that, Chuck?"

He met her eyes with a fatherly gaze. "The house is in rough shape, Mona, rougher than I thought. You have a lot of work ahead of you to be ready by tourist season."

Mona flexed her arm. "I've got Norwegian blood in me!"

Chuck smirked. "That you do. Okay. If you need some help, give me a call." He yanked out the drawer of his metal desk and rustled around until he found a long silver key. He held it out to Mona.

The Footstep of Heaven Bookstore and Coffee Shop. She had known that would be the name since the day she had sat on the beach with her father. Wrapped up in a best-selling hardcover, he had glanced up at the gathering fire on the horizon and said, "This place is the footstep of heaven." Somehow that phrase wound around Mona's heart and strengthened her during his funeral and over the past ten years.

Mona stood on the wide steps of the two-story Victorian, heart pounding, and knew this place was perfect.

She could see it clearly in her mind: the wide porch would be filled with intimate round tables covered with lacy tablecloths that fluttered in a fresh lakeside breeze. Sitting at them would be a handful of contented tourists, drinking freshly brewed coffee out of Liza's handcrafted mugs, eating gourmet muffins, and diving into classics they had unearthed in Mona's bookstore. Strains of Brahms or Chopin, as gentle as a whisper, would drift from the house and float along the street, and all of Deep Haven would bless her for bringing a little bit of heaven to their shores.

Mona hummed as she bounded up the steps of the house. She leveled off in a high-pitched scream as her foot sliced through the top step and sent her sprawling. She heard a car door slam, then laughter. She winced.

"Some place, Mona!" Liza Beaumont caught Mona under the arms and hoisted her to her feet. "Glad I made it for the grand tour."

Mona wrinkled her nose at her best friend. "Just one step, Liza. That can be fixed."

Liza propped her hands on her hips and nodded, brows arched. At least she clamped those ruby lips together.

Mona dusted herself off and stepped up to the door. The key worked, and she pushed the door open. A shaft of sunlight flooded in over their shoulders and lit a dusty hallway. Mona made a face and shivered when she spotted a wide spiderweb stretched from banister to ceiling. Liza pushed her into the house, whistling approval.

Once inside, the place looked cleaner. The hardwood floors suggested a silky amber glow if polished, and a magnificent chandelier in the dining room refracted the sun in a kaleidoscope of colors. A wide staircase ran up from the foyer. Down the hall, two leaded-glass doors opened into a fairly modernized kitchen. Or so Chuck had said. Poking her head into the room, Mona decided Chuck's description had been generous. Perhaps lime green cupboards and lemon countertops had been modern in his time . . .

"Our rooms are upstairs?" Liza asked.

Mona whirled, and the smile on her roommate's face bolstered her sagging enthusiasm. She nodded and held her breath as Liza raced up the steps two at a time. Thankfully, they didn't break.

Mona wandered to the family room on the first floor, envisioning floral arrangements on the oak mantel and a cushion on the bay window seat. Over there, in the dining nook off the family room, she would install her coffee bar, where patrons could belly up with a frothy mocha and swap quotes from their favorite literature. Mona would set up Liza's pottery in the other side of the house, in the parlor, with the two windows that seemed gateways to the sun. Liza's trademark bold colors would sparkle and draw customers like bears to honey.

A sense of gratitude filled her. So the place needed some elbow grease. It was still the only property along the shore to be offered that year, and she had been fortunate to land it. And soon, with Edith's help on the zoning papers, the lakeside home would become a legitimate business. *Her* business.

"Come up, Mona!" Liza leaned over the banister. "There's a bathroom for each of us!"

"Finally!" Mona answered with a playful laugh. She climbed the stairs, registering the squeaks for future notice, and found Liza lying spread eagle on a bright orange shag carpet in the master bedroom.

"What are you doing?" Mona leaned against the frame of the French doors and folded her arms across her chest.

"Dreaming of furniture," Liza said, sighing. Mona's roommate looked the part of a French Indian princess, with her black hair splayed out, loopy gold earrings glinting in the sunlight, and her fuchsia, fake-leather jacket akin to a brilliant royal robe. Mona shook her head teasingly and grinned.

The other room upstairs included two dormer windows that overlooked the slanting verandah roof, with a window seat built into each alcove. "This is my room," Mona declared, delighted.

Liza poked her head in. "You sure? The other room's bigger."

"Yeah, but the other room has a bathroom built onto it—perfect for cleaning all that clay off your body." Mona wrinkled her nose in disgust.

Liza's eyes narrowed in mock suspicion. "You just don't want to clean up the gigantic water stain I found under the sink."

That night, as the birch trees hurled shadows into the furnitureless bedroom, Mona and Liza huddled in their sleeping bags and counted the Victorian's casualties.

"Two broken windowpanes, a leaky kitchen sink, that big water stain on the dining-room ceiling, and the rotted floor under the fridge," listed Mona.

Liza buried her head into her folded arms and continued where Mona left off, her voice muffled from the
folds of fluffy down. "A broken front step, three rotten
boards on the verandah, two useless electrical outlets in
the parlor, and did you notice my bathroom door won't
close?"

Mona groaned in reply.

"But—" Liza popped her head up like a jack-in-the-
box—"the good news is that most of the problems are
cosmetic. And we can work around the rest." She flopped
over onto her back. "I hope you know how to hammer
because I'm doing the painting!"

Mona grinned at a cobweb on the ceiling and tried to
ignore the idea that a spider winked back. Six weeks 'til
opening day. Six weeks to remodel, paint, buy furniture,
and assemble her lifelong dream.

But it would be all right. A little spit and polish was
all they needed to turn the place into the Footstep of
Heaven.

Two days later, Mona was ready to blame Chuck for
selling her a Victorian from nowhere but south of its
heavenly name. Two shutters had fallen off, another
front step splintered when the movers arrived with the
industrial oven, and an entire section of plaster cracked
around the stain in the dining room. Liza heard it, and
like Henny-Penny, she flew out of the room screaming,
"The sky is falling!" A minute later the section gave
way and littered the floor with chunks of rotted plaster.

If that weren't enough, Mona created a miniature Old

Faithful in her kitchen when she stripped the nut on the faucet in an attempt to stop a leak. She managed to dam it up with some plumber's putty, but the plug looked iffy at best.

Then Liza walked in with the zinger. "You got a parking ticket, my unlucky friend." She tossed the offensive yellow slip at Mona. It drifted toward Mona's feet, and she stomped it to the planked floor.

That night, as the sun slid beyond a platinum lake, Mona sat on the porch and cradled her first decent cup of coffee. A half-eaten elephant ear lay soggy and cold in a donut bag crumpled beside her. It wasn't much of a supper. Liza had brought home a frozen pizza from the Red Rooster and had already wrapped up like a mummy in her bag. Perhaps tomorrow their furniture would show up, and they could sleep in their own rooms, off the pumpkin-colored carpet.

Mona sipped slowly, considering the repairs and the days remaining until opening day. Discouragement hit her like a cold Superior wave. *Lord, I wanted so much to build the perfect place. A place where people could enjoy the simple pleasures in life.* She squeezed her eyes shut and fought the lump forming in her throat. *I just want to do something right, something good and lasting.* The Footstep of Heaven seemed like such a good idea—even a God-ordained one. The goal had kept her forging ahead through a series of mindless jobs. Even the stint she had done as a Whopper flopper during college seemed worth it with Heaven in view. Now her one, God-given chance was slipping through her fingers. *Please, Lord, just a little more help?*

Mona set her empty mug next to the crumpled donut bag and sank her face into her hands.

Joe Michaels ran his hand over the dented hood of the Ford pickup. The paint job was even, except for a few rust spots over the wheel wells, and the black vinyl dashboard gleamed like a piece of onyx.

"She's a good runner," commented a ponytailed salesman in an ill-fitting tweed blazer. He looked and smelled like he had spent a few lifetimes under the hood of a hot rod, smoking something foul while he did it.

Joe grimaced. "Well, she's not a beauty queen, but her engine seems clean, and she hums like a song. How much?"

"Three grand."

"For this clunker?"

The salesman backed up, a hand out as if to push away the comment. "Okay, okay. Two and a half."

Joe examined the dirt and kicked a stone with his dusty boots. Money wasn't the issue—he just liked to run 'em around a bit. He made a face. "How about two?"

The salesman reacted like he had been shot. "You're killin' me, man." He paused for effect. Joe knew the salesman hoped he would recant, but he held his ground. There were other used-car lots, and he didn't need anything in particular. Just a change of pace. "Oh, okay," the salesman finally huffed. "I guess I gotta move her. Come inside; we'll sign the papers."

Joe bit back a grin. He loved winning.

They sealed the deal inside a ramshackle trailer. Joe

peeled crisp one hundreds from a worn leather wallet
and slapped them on the faded desk.

The salesman handed him the keys. "Stay light on the
gas; she's got an itchy accelerator."

Joe hiked out to the pickup. The sunlight glinted off
her polished forest green hood, and she twinkled like a
Christmas bulb. Joe flung his army duffel in the back
and climbed into the cab. He liked stick shifts, especially
those on the early models that groaned and wheezed as
you wrestled them into gear. They seemed nostalgic, and
he preferred them to the computerized SUVs of today.
Simplicity had its merits. No computer to bog down this
engine. Just an old-fashioned carburetor he could take
apart on the side of the road and rebuild if he needed to.

Joe saluted the salesman and roared out of the lot.
Where to next? North. To Deep Haven. He knew his
destination as if it had been whispered into his ear. It
was time to visit Gabe.

He had been shirking the responsibility for over a
decade, appeasing his brother with letters, presents, and
the occasional phone call. But he knew he couldn't
procrastinate a day longer. After fifteen years of avoiding the backwoods smudge on the map, God was forcing him to return. Last week's visit to his mother's
grassy grave site had revived her last words to him:
Take care of Gabe. He'd tried to protest, to reason away
the shame. He *had* kept his part of the deal. But the
excuses tasted bitter in his throat, and guilt, a heavy-
handed motivator, sealed his fate.

He owed it to his mother to visit, if not love, the son
she had sacrificed so much for. After all, Joe was the
only family Gabe had left. God kept pointing that out

until Joe surrendered. His goal: to stop in, say hi, make sure the kid was being well taken care of, and ditch town before the dust settled beneath his feet. And, if God intervened, he might also figure out how to untangle the mess he'd woven during his past eight months of fruitless roaming. A trek along the western seaboard and through northern Canada had left him with nothing to show for his time, something his boss didn't need to know—yet. It wouldn't take much for the wrong people to find him in Deep Haven, but he was one step ahead, and he still had weeks before his promises came due.

Maybe, if he kept his eyes open, a brief stopover in a sleepy tourist town just might provide the opportunity he needed to make good on his promises. At the least he might be able to scrape up a tidbit to throw to the wolves that ran his life.

Joe cracked open his window as he drove north up I-35. A road sign flew by. Duluth—thirty miles ahead. He would never forget his first trip north, the first time he had ever seen Lake Superior. He had been eleven, on a church camping trip heading toward the Boundary Waters Canoe Area, and when he smelled the crisp lake air for the first time, he was intoxicated by it. The smell of pine mingling with fresh water and a ripe amount of mossy undergrowth had so overwhelmed him, it had changed the course of his life forever.

Eau Claire, Wisconsin, had suddenly seemed claustrophobic. He strained at its borders. His mother must have sensed it, for on his eighteenth birthday, she let him go without a fight.

He had spent his first summer alone, hiking the Boundary Waters Border Trail, catching lake trout, eating wild

berries, and letting the love of nature embrace his soul. That summer he came to know God as his best friend, his Savior, his Creator, his Lord. For fifteen years, he'd carried that summer with him all over the world.

As Joe topped the hill overlooking Duluth, caught the rich smell of pine, and beheld the vast Superior spread out like an endless blue blanket, his heart swelled and quickened in his chest. For a moment he wondered if returning to the North Shore might again change his life, pull him out of the dead-end rut he'd wallowed in for so long. Something had to change—and fast, or his days of freedom were numbered.

Joe threaded the pickup through Duluth and stopped for lunch at the harbor park. Throwing the remnant of his chili dog to the seagulls waddling over the grassy knoll in front of the museum, he watched an oceangoing iron-ore tanker skid under the massive aerial bridge, headed out into Lake Superior and beyond. He waved to an assembly of sailors working the deck. A few returned the gesture. He felt sorry for them. He knew too well the life and the loneliness of months at sea.

He was back on the road by midafternoon, his windows at half-mast, a violent wind skimming through his short-cropped tawny brown hair. He stretched out an arm along the top of the bench seat and whistled an old tune, trying to ignore the squeeze in his chest as he ate up miles toward Deep Haven. Would Gabe even know him? Joe wouldn't blame his kid brother if he gave Joe one look and tossed him out on his ear. The yearly cards, gifts, and the occasional phone call didn't fill the gap left by their mother's death.

Gabe never gave any indication of offense, however.

All his letters, carefully etched out, proclaimed a feeling of open arms, inviting Joe to his home. At least Gabe had a home to invite him to. Joe hadn't had a home since he packed his bags fifteen years ago and left his mother's two-bedroom ranch on Linner Lane.

Lost in the past, Joe nearly broadsided a dog. He glimpsed a brown blur dart into the road and, going sixty-five plus, only had time to crunch his brakes and swerve madly. Thankfully, traffic was sparse on this sunny stretch of road. Joe angled the truck into the ditch and buried his head into his forearms. His heart had rammed into his throat, and it took some seconds for him to swallow it back into place.

Then dread roiled through him. Had he hit it? He jumped out of the cab. "Hey, pooch!" he hollered.

No sign of the mutt. The road behind him curled around the far-off jagged cliffs like a black ribbon. He scanned the other stretch of highway. Again, empty. Joe put two fingers in his mouth and whistled. No blur of brown, no whining lump in the ditch. Relief crested over him. The dog must have headed home.

Joe climbed back in the cab and had just shifted into drive when something banged against his passenger door. Joe glimpsed two muddy paws smearing his not-so-clean-anyway window, and a long pink tongue dangled sideways out of a grinning canine mouth.

"Howdy, boy," Joe said to the lop-eared dog as he leaned over and opened the door. A large, dark chocolate Labrador retriever scrambled inside and stared at him with droopy, nut brown eyes. The dog panted in heavy gusts, and drool dripped from its mouth.

"You're messing up the truck," Joe said with a mock

frown. He reached out a tentative hand. The dog watched, clamped his snout shut, and sniffed. Joe obviously passed inspection, for the mutt laid his muzzle into Joe's palm. With his other hand, Joe found the soft spot behind the dog's ears and rubbed vigorously. The Lab groaned happily.

"Well, you're not a stray," Joe said. "You're somebody's pal. What'cha doin' out here?"

The dog had hunger in those glassy, sad eyes.

"Stay put." Joe climbed out of the cab. Cupping his hands around his mouth, he yelled into the woods, "Anybody lose a dog?" The wind devoured his words; the trees hissed in reply. Joe pushed a hand through his short hair. Well, he couldn't just leave the animal in the woods. He climbed back in the truck.

"It's not much farther to Deep Haven. We'll see if anybody there knows you."

The dog settled down on the seat, laying his massive head on grimy paws. He sighed deeply.

"Feeling lost, bud?" Joe pulled out and gunned the truck to sixty-five, laying a hand on the dog's matted fur. "Aren't we all?"

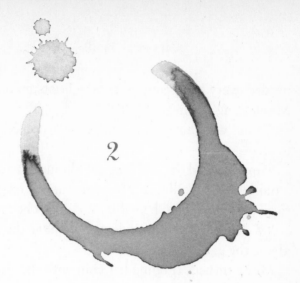

2

No way!" Mona's sharp tone wiped the eager smile off Liza's face, and even Chuck frowned, as if she'd used foul language. She softened her voice. "I'm sorry. I just don't want anybody here, meddling in our plans."

"A handyman is hardly a meddler, Mona," Chuck soothed. "You need help. You can't possibly finish all these repairs by Memorial Day, and as much as I would like to help, it's over my head. You have to hire someone."

Mona walked to the bay window. The sun dappled the buds of the jasmine bush in the front yard in sparkles of white, and a spring breeze filtered through the cracked window, mingling with the pungent odor of the drying varnish on the oak stair rail. Maybe they were right. She and Liza needed more than their four hands to get the place spruced up in less than six weeks. Why hadn't she quit work sooner and moved here in January?

Money. The answer burned in her chest. Because she

needed every last penny to get the Footstep on its feet. Mona hung her head. "Okay."

"What was that?" A teasing edge accompanied Liza's tone.

Mona peeked at Liza over her shoulder and sent her a half glare. "We'll hire a handyman. But only temporarily, and he has to be willing to work cheap."

"We could offer him lodging. We have the apartment above the garage."

Mona turned, rubbing her chin with the back of her hand. "That's a good idea." The one-room efficiency had a quaint round window that peered over the front yard and a kitchen nook just big enough for the sink, stove, counter, and fridge. Equipped with a pullout sofa and a table, it could be the perfect pad for a college student or a nanny. Or a handyman.

Liza beamed in victory and stuck a hand out to Chuck. He grabbed it and pumped, and Mona realized they had been in cahoots.

"You double-teamed me," Mona growled.

Chuck clamped a wide, gentle hand on her shoulder. "It was the only way to win." His eyes crinkled when he smiled, and her anger couldn't help but dissolve. Mona rolled her eyes.

"Don't worry, Mone. We'll make sure the ad says *No opinions allowed,*" Liza quipped.

Joe hung his head over the lumpy motel bed, stared at the mint green carpet, and conceded he was a coward.

Groaning above the whine of *Mayberry R.F.D.* reruns

on the television, he flopped back against two ancient, orange macramé pillows, clasped his hands behind his head, and looked at the dusty ceiling.

He'd been in town for two agonizing days, pitching stones into the cold lake, and he had yet to muster the courage to knock on his brother's door. Who knew it would be so hard to face your own flesh and blood? Maybe if he had a job or something that made his visit less . . . needy. Something to fill his time while he moseyed around, working up the guts to face the family he'd abandoned.

No, not abandoned. He would never abandon.

Anyway, he had nowhere else to go. He'd run out of options and ideas. That thought had hit him more than a few times over the past eight months. Nowhere to go, but certainly nowhere he could call home either. Even in this topographical castoff, his days were numbered, and that deadline loomed like a guillotine with each passing day.

Joe blew out a long, pained breath, rolled onto his side, and propped his head on his hand. He studied the chocolate brown Lab in the opposite bed. He'd smuggled the mutt in, feeling it was his civic duty to give the pooch a meal and a decent night's sleep. Besides, those pitiful eyes spoke to a lonely place in his heart.

The dog turned out to be a good guest, knowing to lie low and sleep late. He'd cleaned up well in the motel tub, his hide turning glossy milk chocolate. Joe appreciated his lean strong lines, despite the row of ribs that rippled along his sides. Although hungry, the animal hadn't been maltreated. He was probably lost.

Since arriving in town, Joe had photographed the dog and distributed "lost dog" posters to a few local businesses. Unfortunately, there had been no calls about his vagrant friend. Abandoning the search for the dog's master wasn't an entirely abhorrent prospect, however. Joe rather enjoyed the silent, steadfast company of the Lab in the opposite double bed.

"I guess I should name you, huh?" In one smooth movement, Joe leaped off his bed and straddled the Lab. The dog's ears perked. Joe rubbed him ferociously down his long back. The dog groaned with pleasure, rolling over. Joe scratched his underbelly.

"I better find us something worthwhile to do while I figure this Gabe thing out." He sat back, hands on his knees, scowling at the seventies-era motel room. He'd be more comfortable in a tent, but a camping trip through northern Minnesota wouldn't bring him any closer to his younger brother. No, he had to find something in town to stretch his muscles while he figured out how to be a brother. Nothing permanent, just a distraction to fill his thoughts with something more than memories. Maybe a distraction that would lead to ideas, answers— and an escape plan. And, hopefully, he'd find someplace to stay that didn't smell like three-day-old laundry.

Joe gave the dog a last rubdown, then rose, heading to the television to click it off. He felt the rip before he heard it as teeth latched onto his jeans pocket. Playing teeth, he hoped as he turned. The dog hung his head, looking sheepish with a swatch of denim caught in his incisors.

"Not done wrestling, huh?" Joe patted him. "You just earned your name, Rip."

Joe untangled the fabric from sharp white teeth and gave the dog a teasing glower. "No more pants for

breakfast. Only dog chow for you. It took me three long years and two mountains to get these to the shade and texture I like. Now I'm gonna have to find a seamstress." He craned his neck, looked behind him, and scowled. "Well, maybe the change will add character." Joe glared again, and Rip scuttled to a place by the door and ducked his eyes. Laughing, Joe kicked himself out of the pants, dug into the duffel, and found another pair, equally well worn.

"On to breakfast," he announced, pulling on a jean jacket. He'd spotted what could be a decent donut shop only a couple of blocks away. Rip's tail swished the floor.

Joe cracked open the door and squinted against the bright sun glinting off his truck and onto an empty, grass-lined, gravel parking lot. The wind skimmed the pine scent from nearby trees, and he inhaled deeply. The smell of a forest was nearly as effective as fresh-brewed coffee for an early morning jolt to the senses. He had to admit, Deep Haven wasn't a terrible place to hole up while he wrestled with his past . . . or his future.

Joe strode to his pickup, opened the door, and whistled. Rip shot toward him and leaped into the cab. Joe shut the door. "Stay put," he ordered, then grinned. It was hard to be stern to a pair of candy eyes. He headed to the motel office.

A thin clerk, with blond hair slowly giving over to white, greeted him. "Ya staying on?"

Joe plunked down a wad of bills. "Not sure yet. Book me, anyway."

"You bet."

"That today's paper?" Joe pointed to a stack of *Superior Times* overflowing a thin wire rack.

"Yup."

Joe fished into his pockets and produced three quarters. "That about right?"

The clerk eyed the change. "Yup."

Joe swiped a copy. The top headline of the thin paper read "Seagulls Damage Lighthouse with Droppings." Joe chuckled, folded the big news, and tucked it under his arm.

"See you got an old Ford out there. Quite the beauty. Had her long?"

Joe raised his brows. It was the longest sentence he'd heard the clerk speak since his arrival. "No. About a week."

"Well, I had me one of those a few years back. Couldn't find a better runner than a Ford. Keeps on going in the dead of winter, lives forever. I bought my first one back in sixty-eight, fresh off the line. She hummed like a baby for twenty-five years. I felt like I buried my best girl when she finally gave in. . . ." The clerk was polishing the oak counter, and his voice trailed off as he worked a shiny, dark spot. He continued to mumble, lost in a memory.

Joe shifted awkwardly for a moment, then slipped out, unsure if he was being rude or acting on cue. The clerk didn't glance up as the door swung shut.

Joe ambled to the truck and freed Rip. The dog licked him as if he'd been gone for days. As they sauntered to the donut shop, he flipped through the paper. Maybe he'd find something of value in this forgotten town.

Cl

The antique walnut table had taken Mona's breath away. From the minute she saw it, she knew it would

shine like ebony if she could only scrape off the lacquer. She counted her blessings to have been one of the first to discover it at a local estate sale.

Mona was leaning over it, sweat beading on her forehead, grunting and digging into the black, sticky stain, when he showed up.

"I know a special stain remover that'll practically melt that stuff off." The voice drawled the words out, smug and irritating.

Mona shot him a cool look. "You're dripping mud in my dining room."

The man examined his hiking boots, obviously shocked.

Mona straightened and wiped back a chunk of hair with her arm. She held her arms away from her and squinted at the man. He had given his boots the once-over and obviously decided they were presentable because he stood there, all six feet of him, and grinned at her like a long-lost brother.

"Excuse me, but who are you?" Mona asked.

A reddish grizzle layered his chin, an interesting contrast to his short, tawny brown hair. He wore a jean jacket over a blue sweatshirt, the type her father used to wear in fall, and his faded Levi's gapped with the comfort of wear. "I'm your new handyman."

Mona raised an eyebrow. "You think so?" She snapped off her rubber gloves. "We'll see." She crooked a finger at him. "Follow me." First stop was Hoover Dam, plugging the geyser in the kitchen sink.

"No problem," he said, shrugging.

Mona narrowed her eyes. She showed him the rot under the refrigerator. He rubbed his chin, tipped the fridge back, and shrugged again. "Yep. Can do."

Mona's irritation grew as she pointed out every broken hinge, splintered window, burnt socket, and cracked wall. He shrugged and nodded easily at each earth-shattering problem, and she couldn't help but feel foolish she'd even asked for help.

The tour ended at the black hole in the dining-room ceiling. The man inspected it, hands dug into his jeans pockets, swaying from heel to toe to unheard music. "I hope y'all ducked when this came down."

A muscle pinched in Mona's neck. "Can you fix it?"

He turned and studied her, his deep blue eyes looking right through her. She couldn't help but notice that they twinkled with some unknown humor, and he had a kind smile that made her want to like him. Then his smile vanished, and in its place came a look of sincerity that spoke to her heart. "I can fix it, ma'am."

Mona scrutinized her potential handyman. He seemed eager, if a bit rumpled and way too smug. Was he a freeloader, hoping to paint a wall in order to live rent-free? Mona chewed her lip. Still, he seemed genuine in his willingness to throw himself into her repairs. And she'd had no other calls. . . . Maybe Edith could ask around for her, find out his origins. In the meantime he could get started on the kitchen geyser.

Mona stuck out her hand. "Mona Reynolds."

"Joe Michaels." He shook her hand.

His hand was warm and somewhat calloused, perking her confidence in his handyman ability. "Great to meet you. The pay isn't great, and it isn't a permanent position. We need some help getting on our feet, that's all."

"That's why I'm here." His warm grin went right to her bones.

"You do get a room, however," she continued, tearing her gaze away and ignoring the tingle racing up her spine. "It's nice. Small but clean."

"Swell."

Perhaps he'd fit in just fine. Not too pushy, do what he's told, leave when it's done. No complications. No invasion of her privacy. Just the little help she'd asked for from God.

"Are you from around here?" Mona noticed how his eyes stayed on her, as if transfixed, and she looked down, suddenly aware of her disheveled appearance. She must look lovely, her hair in chunks over her face, dressed to kill in her best ragged sweatshirt and painted jeans.

He shook his head, eyes not leaving her face. "Just passing through."

Perfect. She liked him even more. "Not staying long then."

"Nope."

She had a sudden flare of doubt. "You're not . . . um . . ." She giggled nervously, feeling like an idiot. ". . . running from the law or anything, are you?"

He actually blushed. Fear leaped through Mona, and she wanted to cringe. Sure, he was just aching to confess he'd murdered three women in the last town. She gave another small, hideous giggle. . . .

His smile made her laugh die in her throat. "No, Mona. I'm safe. I promise."

She wiped her sweaty palms on her jeans. "Of course, I'm sorry."

He held up a hand. "No, I understand. You can't be too safe, even in Deep Haven."

No, Deep Haven is the one place where I finally am safe. "I think you'll do fine here," Mona said.

"Great." He circled the room. "What are you building here?"

"A bookstore. Well, at least this half is. The other half is a pottery shop."

Was it her imagination or did the color wash from his face? "A bookstore?" He looked as if reading was an approved method of torture. He probably hadn't read anything but a vehicle fix-it manual since high school.

"It's been a dream my entire life." Why did she tell him that? Now his horrified look had turned to confusion. "Let me show you the apartment, okay?"

"Right." He nodded, and she noticed how he swallowed, apparently relieved not to have to comment on how she'd taken out her heart and pinned it on her sleeve.

She followed as he led the way to the street and a rusty, tortoise green pickup. From the bed of the truck, he retrieved a bulging army duffel . . . and a dog. Mona guessed a Labrador. Chocolate eyes considered Mona for a moment; then the animal kissed her, juicy and full on the face.

"Whoa, Rip! Take it easy on the first date, bud!" Joe grabbed the dog by a frayed collar and pulled him away from Mona. She scowled, wiping her face on her already grimy sweatshirt.

"The ad didn't say 'no pets,' so I figured it'd be okay." Joe raised his eyebrows hopefully.

Mona reached out and rubbed Rip tentatively behind the ear. The dog groaned and leaned into her hand.

"He likes you." Joe said it in a singsong way, and Mona couldn't help but smile.

"Okay," she agreed.

Her new handyman flung the duffel easily over his shoulder and followed Mona to the backyard and up the stairs to the apartment over the unattached garage. She had devoted half an afternoon to cleaning it, windows included. When she opened the door, the sharp smell of ammonia seeped out in greeting.

Joe whistled low. "Swanky."

Mona rolled her eyes.

Joe dropped the duffel on the floor and sat on it. "Guess I'll need to invest in a davenport."

Mona tucked a chunk of hair behind her ear. "I'm sorry. We don't have much next door either."

Joe grinned. "No problem. Rip and I can sleep anywhere." He grabbed the dog and wrestled him to the floor, then held him down as he rubbed Rip's belly.

I can imagine. "We'll see what we can scrounge up for you, Mr. Michaels." Mona turned for the door.

"It's Joe, Mona." Something in his tone—the way her name seemed to sound almost like a melody when he said it—made her stop. She turned back, frowning.

Joe was playing with his dog—she, obviously, already a wisp of memory. He didn't even glance in her direction as she backed out of the room.

Cee

"Is she gone, Rip?" Joe croaked.

He'd felt like a fool, answering her questions in monosyllables, but it was the best he could manage after she fixed him with that startled, doe-eyed gaze. She'd been so intent on her table, she hadn't heard his knock or sensed his presence as he watched her scrub. Disarmingly gorgeous in a pair of faded jeans and a University of Minnesota sweatshirt, she touched his heart with her linebacker grunts and bulldog determination. He'd had to fight an urge to push back the golden lock of hair falling over her face. It was her eyes, however, that had sent his heartbeat into overdrive—deep, luminescent, and the rich color of emeralds.

He blew out a breath. *Stop it.* He let Rip up and walked to the little round window, overlooking the front yard. The grass looked like a forest, the front porch peeled in layers, and the roof appeared as watertight as a sieve. Inside, Mona's repairs had nightmare proportions. He felt swamped, but the challenge strummed a chord in his masculine heart. Desperation had been written on her face, and it called to him. She needed him, although he had a gut feeling she'd die before admitting it.

Joe scraped a hand through his cropped hair. *Focus.* He was here because of Gabe. He didn't really want to be embroiled in an endless pit of projects. Nor did he have room in his life for a woman. He depended on his freedom to allow Gabe to live the life he needed. Putting down roots would only mean courting trouble for himself, not to mention Gabe. And letting a woman in his life would complicate things, maybe unravel everything he'd spent the years struggling to create. At the least, it would mean setting himself up for the heartache he'd been trying to dodge most of his life.

God, what have You gotten me into this time? When he'd prayed over the want ads, this one had jumped out at him like heavenly neon. He expected a grandmother

to open the door, however, not a lady who could throw his pulse into turbo with a sheepish smile.

He tightened his jaw. It would do him well to remember it was a temporary assignment. His new boss had made it clear that he had six weeks to finish the job and clear out. Hopefully, he'd be long gone before then. And with some careful sleuthing, he'd have just what he needed to keep his future from crumbling. Meanwhile, he would maintain a safe distance from her and her magical green eyes.

Joe turned from the window, unsure whether to unpack or throw the duffel in the truck and make for the hills. He knew only one thing for certain: he'd have to tread in stockinged feet or his haphazardly constructed plan would crash down on his head like Mona's cracked dining-room ceiling.

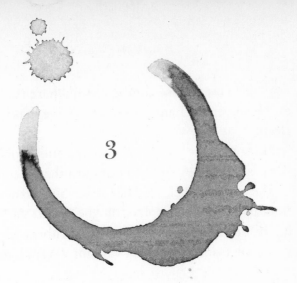

3

Liza bounced into the house just as Mona finished scraping off a second layer of stain remover. The smug look on her friend's face alerted Mona to mischief a second before a handsome stranger strolled in at Liza's heels.

"Mona, I'd like you to meet Brian Whitney. He's in charge of zoning down at city hall."

Mona wondered what other information Liza had gleaned about the man with wavy ebony hair, stunning green eyes, and a muscled body unsuccessfully hidden in a charcoal gray suit.

Mona cringed, feeling like a bedraggled schoolgirl in her ripped Levi's and stained sweatshirt. An unsightly hair drifted over her face, and she blew at it.

"Glad to meet you, Mona," Brian said in a honeyed voice and offered his hand.

Mona ripped off her gloves. His hands were clammy, but his grip strong as he crunched her hand. "Let's go outside." She nodded feebly toward the front door,

hoping to escape the dining room where the fumes—
and his overwhelming presence—were making her head
cloud.

"Liza tells me you are having parking problems,"
Brian said as they stepped out onto the verandah.

The cool wind cleared her head, but it reaped the
fragrance of Brian's spicy cologne. Mona gathered up
her disobedient hair and snapped a rubber band around
it, feeling even more like a vagrant. "Yep, I got a
ticket."

Brian had his gaze on Liza, who busily twirled her
long ebony hair between two fingers. Mona recognized
his appreciative look toward her leggy roommate.

"We'll see what we can do about getting this area
approved for a parking lot," he said, breaking his stare
and turning back to Mona.

Mona smiled gratefully, and he shot her a flawless
white smile to go with the rest of his perfection. Spying
Liza's enthusiastic grin, Mona's jaw grew tight. Mona
had found Joe, a rumpled drifter. Liza had dug up Brian,
the local jewel.

"Would you two like to catch a bite to eat?" Brian
asked. "I know this great place up the shore that serves
fresh lake trout that will melt in your mouth."

She suddenly realized how long it had been since
she'd last eaten. "Sounds good."

"I'll wait while you change."

Mona looked down at her sloppy attire, and her
appetite died. "No, on second thought, you and Liza go.
I have to finish my table."

Brian flared his brows, as if shocked at someone turning him down. "You sure?"

Mona nodded, but a tiny knot clenched in her chest as the two drove off together in his sleek, two-door black Honda that seemed out of character for Deep Haven. Well, so was Liza. They were a matched set.

Mona returned to her table, wiping away the last bits of lacquer. The walnut grain gleamed. With a coat of varnish, the table would be perfect for displaying muffins.

She heard steps down the walk, the truck door slam, and the growl of an old motor. Her new handyman roared off down the street. It seemed everyone had a social life but her. Mona polished furiously.

The table glistened with sticky varnish by the time Liza returned. Showered, with a peanut butter sandwich hardening in the pit of her stomach, Mona lay in bed and let exhaustion sweep over her in gentle waves. The slam of a car door and Liza's infectious laughter jolted her into consciousness. She flipped on her light and groped for a book as Brian's sultry tenor floated up from the porch.

When she heard the Honda drive away, she fixed her eyes on the book, trying to absorb the words. She was rereading the first sentence for the third time when Liza poked her head into Mona's room.

"You really should have gone. The fish was fabulous, and you know how I hate fish." Liza padded inside, uninvited. Mona's brass bed squeaked as she sat on it.

Mona turned her book facedown over her blanketed knees, folded her hands on top, and stared at Liza.

"You're mad," Liza stated.

"I'm not mad. I didn't want to go."

Liza shot Mona a dubious look. "You did want to go. I know. So why not?"

Because I don't have time to run after a perfect smile just so he can take over my life and tell me, sooner or later, that I am not perfect for him. Besides, he had eyes for only one woman on the porch. "I was tired."

Liza arched her plucked brows. "Not too tired to finish the table. It looks fabulous."

Mona managed a half grin.

Liza touched Mona's hands. "Next time, go."

"We have six weeks before opening day. I don't have time to go."

Liza leaned close and peered at her. "You're just afraid he might get under your skin, and you'll like him."

The only person that had gotten under her skin lately was Mr. Smug-is-my-middle-name Michaels, her new handyman, and that felt more like a case of the hives. Mona chewed her lower lip, debating Liza's words, then gave in to her wacky expression and smiled. "Did you have a good time?"

Liza swung her legs up onto the bed. "Marvelous. But he's not for me."

"What do you mean, 'marvelous but he's not for me'? You're nuts."

Liza shrugged. "He's real nice and funny. But he doesn't make me go all tingly inside."

Mona rolled her eyes. "If you're waiting for tingly, you ought to get one of those new neck massagers we saw in the mall."

Liza grinned. "All I know is the tingly thing is what made my mama's marriage go thirty years. She told me early on not to settle for humdrum."

Mona shook her head. "I'd settle for a nervous ripple."

The two laughed until the bed squealed in protest.

"Okay, Miss Picky, tell me who your dream man is. If it isn't Brian Whitney, who is it?" Liza asked.

Mona grew serious. "There isn't any such man. At least in the flesh."

Liza gave her a dubious look.

"Okay, my list is long and detailed, but here's the shorthand. He has to be patient, hardworking, willing to put others before himself, a Christian of course, kind, and able to be vulnerable. He has to be intelligent, a reader, must love coffee, and his favorite pizza can only be Canadian bacon with mushrooms and green peppers." Her tone lost its teasing quality. "Most of all, he must be able to commit to this place and living here." She held out her hands, palms up. "See, my dream man doesn't exist."

"I didn't know you were holding out for Jonah."

"Jonah?"

"Sure, Reese Clark's Jonah, as in *Siberian Runaway*." Liza reached over and tapped the cover of Mona's book. Mona gave her a sheepish look. "With the exception of the pizza toppings, I think you have Jonah nailed."

"What about commitment to place?" Mona stabbed a finger into the air. "Jonah hardly spends a month in one location."

Liza waggled a finger at her in return. "He would stick around if he found the right girl."

Mona wrinkled her nose.

Liza licked her finger and drew an imaginary line in the air. "One point for me. Don't tell me I don't know my best friend." She leaned close. "At least it gives me some guidelines to pray for."

Mona shot her a fake glare. "Don't hold your breath. I'm not looking."

Liza nodded, her dark eyes swimming with mischief. "Right."

Mona sat on the window seat, watching the moon splice the lake in one silver stream. She sighed and hugged her legs to her chest. Her conversation with Liza an hour ago replayed like a scratched record in her head. Unfortunately, her friend was right—she was picky and scared. For those reasons she had been avoiding anything close and personal with a fella for years.

The ugly truth was, despite any tingle, no man could compare to her dream. All she wanted was the Footstep of Heaven Bookstore and Coffee Shop. God had saved her life, forgiven her sins, and given her the Footstep. It was so much more than she deserved. "God saved you by His special favor when you believed. And you can't take credit for this; it is a gift from God." God certainly knew her heart when Paul wrote *that* in Ephesians. Yes, she'd be grateful for God's grace 'til her dying day. She didn't want a man—she had her hands full making sure her plans didn't turn to mush.

Not that the desire for a husband to hold her didn't rear its desperate head on an occasional starlit night, but love was just too intimate, too exposing. The last thing she needed was a man scrutinizing her heart or running roughshod over her dreams. Only God knew her deepest desires, and that was terrifying enough.

No, Mona didn't need anyone—not a rumpled know-it-all handyman and certainly not perfect Mr. Whitney.

She padded back to bed, picked up *Siberian Runaway,* and placed it on the nightstand. Surely she should be content with all God had given her—her bookstore and her imaginary dream man, Jonah.

Cle

"There's a man downstairs!" Liza's voice scrambled up the stairs just seconds before her feet. Mona covered her head with her pillow and groaned. She'd forgotten to mention their new handyman to her roommate.

Liza threw open Mona's door, breathing hard from her sprint upstairs. "I found a guy in the backyard," she wheezed. Mona peeked out from under the pillow. An impish grin lit up Liza's face. She scampered to Mona's bedside, plunking her chin down on the mattress, her eyes level with Mona's. "And he's cute."

Mona threw the pillow at her and climbed out of bed, reaching for her robe. "He's our new handyman." Slipping the robe on, she tied the belt and gave Liza a stern look. "Don't get attached; he's not staying long."

Liza produced a dramatic pout. "He could serve coffee?"

"Don't bet on it. Just what I need, a third partner. I have enough problems with you and your mud."

Liza threw the pillow back. "It's called pottery."

"Yeah, whatever. I used to dig up the stuff at construction sites in our old neighborhood. I made some great pots too. Only mine didn't sell for thirty bucks a shot."

Liza wiggled her fingers. "Gotta have the touch."

Mona rolled her eyes. "Go entertain our new handyman. His name is Joe. I'll be down in a jiffy."

"With pleasure." Liza waltzed out the door.

Mona sat on the bed and worked a strand of hair into a knot. *Lord, please make him a hard worker. Help me get this place in shape. . . .*

The sound of a motor roaring to life disintegrated the rest of her prayer. Mona leaped to her feet and raced to the window. The sun had cleared the horizon, and the house stretched out in a languorous shadow across the dark green lawn. Mona's heart pulsed with joy as she watched her new handyman run a lawn mower over the crisp, calf-high grass. Wearing a faded red sweatshirt and a royal blue baseball cap backwards, he was hunched over, pushing the mower hard through the jungle. Warmth spread through her. She hadn't even thought of the outside appearance yet. Maybe he would be some help, after all, in making her dreams come true.

Liza sat on the yellow kitchen counter, cradling a mug of coffee in her hands when Mona came into the kitchen. "Come help me dig out the stuff in the shed. I found some definite keepers yesterday."

Mona hummed in response. She bent over the counter, grabbed the crumpled remains of a donut bag, and began to scribble madly.

"What are you doing?" Liza asked.

"Making a to-do list."

"That's a novel."

Mona glanced up and smiled slyly. "He's mowing the lawn. I didn't even know we had a mower."

"It was in the shed. Along with a great many other useful items, like an old rolltop desk and a wicker chair."

Mona hummed again, this time in interest. "Okay. I'll be out in a second." She bent back over the list.

When Mona stepped outside, the day greeted her with golden sunshine breaking through a cirrus-scattered sky and the heady fragrance of fresh-cut grass. A spring breeze sang in the lilac tree next to the garage, and a grouping of fir that shaded the back shed replied in melody. Mona drank deeply and tasted peace.

A crash shattered the air.

Mona ran toward the shed and spotted Liza stumbling from the building, covered in soot. "Found an old woodstove," Liza muttered.

Mona bit her lip to stifle a laugh. It didn't work. She swaddled her stomach with her arms. "You're a chimney sweep!" she howled.

Liza glared at her. Then she swept Mona into a hug.

"Get away from me!" Mona sputtered.

Liza grinned, her white teeth a striking contrast to her soot-covered skin. "Just trying to share the happiness."

Mona examined her formerly clean pink flannel shirt and winced. "Okay, wiseacre, let's get to work."

Inside, the shed smelled of cinders, dust, and old lawn clippings. Mona wrinkled her nose in disgust. "I thought they cleaned this out."

"Not a chance. But lucky for us. Look at this." Liza held up a frayed blanket, revealing a very old, chipped, pool-hall piano.

Mona's eyes widened. "It's gorgeous."

"And it's ours!" Liza exclaimed triumphantly.

"Yeah, but how're we going to get it in the house?"

Liza made a wry face. "We need muscles."

"Somebody call me?"

Mona whirled. Joe Michaels held on to the upper frame of the door, leaning into the shed and grinning like a Cheshire cat. A fine layer of perspiration added to his rumpled, masculine appearance. His hair spiked around the baseball cap, his blue eyes teased, and Mona felt something inside her give way. She forcibly gathered her composure. "Well, Mr. Handy, we're gonna need more than your brute force to wrestle this inside."

"How about Brian?" Liza offered. "I'll ask him tonight when he comes over."

Mona's jaw dropped. "I thought you said . . . "

Liza's piercing gaze silenced her. "Some things I don't do for myself."

Irritation hissed through Mona. Liza had invited him over for her! She turned away.

"Well, surely you ladies aren't going to let all this brawn go to waste." Joe stepped between the two women. "Give me something to carry."

Mona didn't know whether to thank him for peace-making or throttle him for interfering. She wanted to let her best friend have it with both barrels. Then a dusty, wooden box set upon a pile of red bricks diverted her attention from her frustration. "What's this?" She climbed over a rusty wheelbarrow.

Joe met her in the corner. "Looks like an old phonograph."

"Really?" Mona reached to pick it up.

Joe leaned past her, grabbing the case. "Let me earn my keep."

Mona scowled. "I can carry this just fine. I think if I can muscle a canoe onto my shoulders, I can handle this."

Joe's eyes darkened, and his smile faded slightly.

"Sorry to interfere with your feminist moment. Here."
He dropped the box into her outstretched arms.

It weighed more than she'd imagined. Mona stifled a
grunt and lugged the phonograph out of the shed. She
set it down carefully onto the grass, ignored Joe's presence behind her, and worked the rusty latches. When
she pried open the box, the sight rocked her back onto
her heels. The RCA, complete with a record changer,
appeared in mint condition, despite the battered case.
"What a treasure," she gasped.

"I think there are a lot of treasures to be found here
if we keep searching," Joe commented softly.

Mona met Joe's blue eyes and saw his sincerity. Her
fury dissipated. He was just trying to help, and she
wasn't giving him the chance. He smiled. It drew her in
like an embrace. Then the sun moved out from behind
a cloud, and his shadow grew long and covered her.
Funny how she felt so comfortable inside it.

"Sorry I got angry."

He shrugged. "I shouldn't have assumed. You hired
me to help, not take over." His relaxed posture and the
crooked grin on his handsome face spoke forgiveness.

She returned his smile, friendship taking root in her
heart. Perhaps he was right. There were treasures all
around her—she just needed to keep her eyes open.

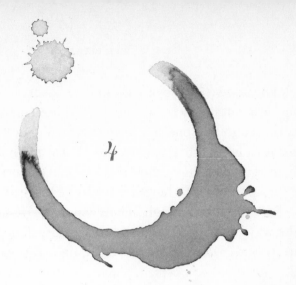

4

Joe sat in the round attic windowsill, a book open in
his lap, watching Mona dig a trench for flowers along
the front walk. She was hard at it, had been all day.
Looking beyond her, he noticed the low red sun turning
Lake Superior into copper. Weariness seeped through
his bones. Mona's little dream pushed his abilities to the
edge, although he'd patched roofs, reworked plumbing,
and built homes all over the world.

Joe forked a hand through his stubby hair and closed
the journal he'd been writing in. He took solace in
recording his daily activities, as if penning them onto
paper gave his thoughts and travels coherency. Purpose.
Sometimes they even offered hints at solutions for the
trouble that dogged him. But today he found no peace in
scribing his jumbled thoughts. Rip sprawled in a streak
of sunlight on the wood floor, sides heaving in largo
rhythm. "Tired from all the squirrel chasing today, huh?"

The dog's ears perked, but his eyes remained shut.

Joe tossed the journal on top of the refrigerator, then

plopped down on the orange-and-black sofa he'd picked up earlier at the local Goodwill. He'd been mildly surprised to find one in a town this small, but he'd chosen the least lumpy sofa, paid twenty bucks, and hauled it home in the pickup. Remembering Mona's horrified expression when he lugged it home, he laughed.

She would be a tough one to win over. He saw it in the way she quickly hooded her feelings, snatching them in whenever they wandered. She didn't trust easily and depended only on herself. She had a story to tell, evident from the haunted look that flickered in her eyes every time she stared at the house. Something would reach out and entwine itself around her, and she had to forcibly shake herself free. In the residue of her gaze, pain prowled so vividly he knew she'd lived with it a long, desperate season.

Yes, God's hand had surely directed him to this ramshackle Victorian. The place met his needs. He could stay in shape, pay up on the debt he owed, and be honest when he told his brother he had a job in town. And maybe he could help Mona and her roommate in the bargain. Joe chuckled, remembering the spark that lit between the two ladies. Obviously they had a tightly knotted friendship, but he'd walked into a powder keg today, judging by Mona's face.

He couldn't help but admire Mona for putting action to her dreams, even if her feisty independence did ignite all his protective instincts, something he'd have to learn to douse. She reminded him of a lady he'd met not so long ago, someone whose sassy demeanor lit a spark in his masculine heart. He'd have to keep on his toes if he was going to dodge the grip of her delightful zeal. He

would stay just long enough to make amends with Gabe and a dent in their repairs. Then he'd mosey on down the road.

Gabe. He couldn't escape it. It was time to see his brother. Now that he had something to occupy his time, he could honestly say he was just dropping in. No strings, no pressure to stay the night, the weekend, the month, forever. Just a quick, painless brotherly visit. He'd get it over with, and then maybe God would ease up on the guilt.

"Ready?" Joe asked the sleeping mutt.

Rip moaned in his dreams.

"I know how you feel." He headed for the shower, dreading the next few hours.

Nearly two miles separated the Garden from the main road. Joe followed the map imprinted on the back of a brochure Gabe had sent him a few years back when they'd changed the name. When Joe and his ailing mother had first checked out the place, it had been simply referred to as the Residence. He liked the Garden better, like they were cultivating something special.

Spotting a carved sign, he turned onto an unpaved road and followed the scent of pine through towering blue spruce and birch. Through a thinning of trees, he sighted a log home, recently built. The pale, skinned logs gleamed with sealant. It looked rustic, but from the pictures in the brochure, he knew otherwise. Plush and expensive, the institution had a long waiting list. He'd had to pull a fistful of strings to get Gabe admitted.

He drove under a wooden entrance gate, noticing *The Garden* elegantly carved into the wooden plaque attached to the top crossbar. Rip barked, balancing on the bench seat. Joe placed a hand on his back. "Calm down, bud." He spoke to himself as well.

They weren't expecting him, of course. He hadn't called, had never personally talked with the new director. Just sent the monthly dues. He slowed, approaching the main lodge. In the circle drive, he stopped next to a long porch. An assembly of residents, apparently gathered for after-dinner air, fixed their eyes on him.

"Stay," he commanded Rip, who clambered over him to get to the door. He scowled, spying a fresh paw print on the leg of his khakis. Quickly, he opened the door, slipped out, whirled, and slammed it in Rip's face before the dog had a chance to protest.

Joe felt the residents' eyes on him, but no one spoke, and he heard only the wind whistling through the trees. Fighting the urge to dive back into the cab, Joe brushed off his pants, straightened his tweed blazer, and pasted on a smile. He skirted his truck and made for the wide center porch steps. Not a word of greeting came from the dozen or so spectators.

He thudded up the steps and stood on the porch. "I'm looking for Gabriel Michaels." His voice didn't sound like his own.

"Gabe's inside, working on the dishes." A lean, middle-aged woman with stern eyes stepped from behind a screen door. A man with thinning gray hair and almond-shaped eyes peered from behind her.

Joe returned her stoic gaze. "I'm his brother."

Defense dropped from her face, leaving surprise

behind. She smiled, and warmth broke through her
hazel eyes. "Glad to meet you, Joe. My name is Ruby
Miller. I'm the director."

He shook her hand, curious that she knew his name.
"We didn't know you were coming."

He scrubbed a hand through his hair, then cupped
the back of his neck. "I didn't either. It just sort of
happened."

She pinched her lips. "In between trips?"

Inquisitive ears edged in on their conversation. He
flicked a nervous glance at the closing horde. "Yes and
no."

Her eyebrows flared in surprise, and he wondered
how much she knew.

"Where did you go last, Joe?"

Joe turned and found the owner of the voice, a young
woman in her mid-thirties. Her brown hair curled gently
around full cheeks and smiling eyes.

"Um, here and there. Saw Mount Hood in Oregon
State."

"I have a poster of that," another voice said from
behind him.

"Gabe reads us all your letters," announced a plump
girl with straight blonde hair.

"And your pictures are all over his room," added a
young man, whiskers sprouting over his face.

Joe felt surrounded. They knew his world, his life.
And he knew nothing about them. His mouth seemed
filled with cotton.

"Come on, Joe." Ruby's voice parted the crowd with
the effectiveness of a shepherd's crook. "I'll take you to
Gabe."

Joe followed Ruby inside, hearing the group file in behind him. Obviously, they didn't get many visitors.

They walked through a large family room. Navy and forest green accented the overstuffed sofas, and paneled tabbed curtains hung from skinned, shellacked tree branches—the latest in woodsy decor. The smell of oiled wood reminded him of Mona and the table she'd been scrubbing. It tugged at the knot in his chest. Under different circumstances, it felt like a place he could call home.

He found Gabe in the kitchen, dish towel in hand, wiping a baking pan. His brother chatted with a young redheaded woman who was elbow deep in sudsy water.

"Gabe?" Ruby tiptoed into the kitchen. "You have a visitor."

Gabe turned, and Joe went weak with shock. His younger brother had developed into a man, with whiskers, wide shoulders, and a tan. He appeared grown-up and tailored in a green polo shirt and khakis. Joe squinted at him, the effects of time and distance hitting him hard.

Gabe, too, stared blankly. Then, like a cloud moving from the sun, joy broke through. "Is that you, Joe?" He formed the words slowly, enunciating with difficulty, but the expression on his round face and the shine in his almond-shaped eyes shouted his delight with eloquence.

Joe's feet told him to run, but he planted them, masked his emotions, and grinned. "Yep. In the flesh."

In two quick steps Gabe closed in and threw his arms around Joe. He crushed his face into Joe's chest. Joe felt fear flush out of him, and he put his arms around his brother. Shame crawled into his bones the longer Gabe held him, and Joe realized what a fool he'd been to stay

away so long. "How are you doing, buddy?" His voice cracked.

Gabe leaned back, happiness making his blue eyes shine like jewels. "Great!"

Ruby patted Gabe on the back. "Why don't you show him your room, Gabe? Daniel will finish the dishes."

Gabe handed the towel to the gray-haired observer behind Ruby, then tugged on Joe's jacket. "C'mon."

Joe shot a look at Ruby, who smiled broadly. He must have had a help-me expression on his face, for her eyes took on a motherly texture. "Go on, Joe. It's okay."

He raised his brows, then followed Gabe from the room.

Gabe's large second-story bedroom faced the back of the property. Smooth, white-pine walls were dotted with posters from around the world, giving his brother's place a well-traveled aura. He eased into the room behind Gabe, crushing carpet so thick he could bury himself in it and not be found for a year.

"Did you fix this up yourself?" Joe asked.

Gabe stood in the middle of the bedroom, arms wide. "Yep. I love the color red."

Joe chuckled, digging a foot into the strawberry-colored carpet. "Well, it's bold."

Gabe laughed, the sound of it warm and accepting.

Joe dug his hands into his pockets and surveyed the room. A single bed, with a cherry red Indian blanket thrown over the top, lined one wall. He recognized the spread. He'd sent it to Gabe during his stint at a dude ranch in Texas. On the other side of the room a vinyl La-Z-Boy with peeling arms squatted in the corner. Joe felt a twinge. "That was Mom's."

Gabe plopped down in it. "She left it to me."

Joe remembered going through her things and wondering where the chair had gone. She must have brought it up on her last visit. He was glad she'd given it to Gabe.

Joe stepped toward the desk and the bookshelf next to it. Photographs in a myriad of frames were stacked arm deep. His own face smiled back in more than half. On the full bookshelf he spied a number of best-sellers, as well as a stack of Superman comic books. He picked up one. "Still in love with Lois Lane?"

"Superman has to be," Gabe said and flexed an arm.

Joe laughed. Despite his appearance, Gabe hadn't changed much. Yet, as Joe surveyed the room again, he realized his error. This wasn't the same brother he'd left behind in Eau Claire some fifteen years back or even the one he'd settled in the old dorm that used to occupy this land four years ago. Then Gabe had cried, their mother had sobbed, and Joe had felt like the evil doctor institutionalizing his brother. Guilt, which until that time had been a persistent wolf, bit hard when he signed the commitment papers and tenaciously hung on despite his moves to dodge it.

Joe berated himself for not staying and shouldering his mother's burden. Yet he knew if he had, he would have shattered. He had to leave. In the end, his mother seemed to understand. She'd even suggested that her eldest son had done the best thing. But Gabe was different. Would he ever forgive Joe for not sticking with them through the hard times?

The question would have to wait for another day. He couldn't tackle it quite yet. One hurdle at a time. He

was glad he'd made it this far and had Mona's place to hustle back to and regroup. Joe rolled the comic book. "Can I borrow this?"

Gabe smiled, his angled eyes lighting up. "Bring it back with a new one."

Joe grinned. Nope, different Gabe. More confident. Full of fun, perhaps even forgiveness. "No problem."

"Are you in town for a long time?" Gabe's smile dimmed.

"We'll see." He avoided Gabe's face when he said it.

"Where ya stayin'?"

Joe stared past him, out the window. The last thing he needed was Gabe or Ruby tracking him down and forcing a sticky face-to-face with his new boss. The less Mona knew about his little brother tucked in the woods, the better for them all. "Is that a strawberry patch?"

Gabe jumped to his feet. "Yes. That's our business. We sell strawberries."

Joe grinned and shook his head in amazement. Ruby was from the same stock as Mona—ambitious. "Well, maybe I'll stick around long enough to taste one," he said, peeking at Gabe. Gabe lit up like a Christmas tree. Joe couldn't help but smile in the face of his brother's intoxicating enthusiasm.

"Come and meet the others," Gabe said in a rush. "They know all about you."

Joe slapped his knee with the comic book. "That's what I'm afraid of," he muttered as he followed his brother from the room.

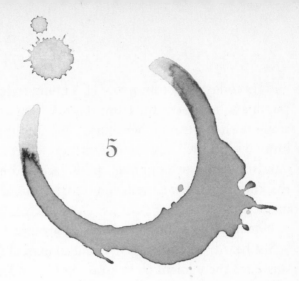

5

$\mathcal{M}$ona licked an escaping trail of chocolate chip ice cream sliding down the side of her waffle cone and fielded Brian Whitney's next question.

"So then you went to the University of Minnesota?" His green eyes, searing her with focused intensity, made her squirm, but his interest in her life seemed genuine. She tried to relax.

"I graduated in five years with an English major." She caught another drip off the end of her cone. "I always wanted to teach or maybe write. Then I realized my true love was reading and sharing the joy of literature. So I swapped my teaching certificate for a glitzy higher-paying job as a law secretary, saved every dime I made, and poof! Ten years later I'm fixing up the money pit on Route 65."

"Five weeks left. Think you'll open on time?"

Mona conceded defeat and surrendered her cone to the trash. "I hope so. I hired a handyman, and he seems to know what he's doing. He straightened the gutters today, and tomorrow he's going to jack up the porch and recement the front posts." Joe's crooked smile flashed through her mind. That and the way he'd hung on her shed door, looking rumpled yet impossibly handsome, his grin lighting up his face and unraveling the knot in her heart with some sort of masculine magic.

"Sounds like a good man to have around."

She heard Joe's voice, gentle and so masculine, as he suggested there might be treasures hidden in Deep Haven, and it sent a soft smile to her face even now. Mona nodded in agreement. "So, you have family here?"

Brian suddenly focused on his ice-cream cone. "Nope. Had some once but they all moved south. I'm the remnant, holding down the family homestead."

Mona watched his long fingers turn his cone. Elegant fingers. Unaccustomed to labor. The image of Joe's rough-hewn hands flashed through her mind, and she blinked to focus on the man she *should* be thinking about. "Not such a bad place to hold down."

Brian studied her with a peculiar expression. "No, not such a bad place," he echoed, but his agreement sounded hollow.

Mona folded her hands together, propping her elbows on the table. "Where did you go to school?"

Brian shook his head. "Didn't. Went straight to work driving trucks for the city. Worked my way up into management."

Mona raised her brows, remembering his sleek black Honda. "You've done okay."

"What, for a small-town boy?" His aggressive comeback startled her.

"N-no," she stammered. "I just meant they probably don't pay well here. You must be a good budgeter. Probably why you work for the city." She forced the words through a suddenly dry mouth.

"Right. Well, I have my sources. And—" he smiled broadly, as if to restore their friendship—"I am a very good budgeter."

"So what do you hear about my parking permit?" Mona folded a paper napkin into tiny squares.

"Soon. I'm processing the paperwork."

"You mean you can't just snap your fingers and make it happen? I thought all you city officials have ultimate power." Mona threw tease into her voice.

Brian leaned close, his cologne washing over her, his breath in her face. "We do."

He probably meant it to be alluring, but she felt a cold fist land in her stomach and recoiled. "Oh, that's good to know," she said and forced a smile.

Brian sat back, beaming. "Too bad Liza couldn't join us."

Mona couldn't agree more.

He stretched a hand across the back of the seat. Mona stared out the window of the Tastee Treat. The waves scraped the shore, calling to her, and at that moment she needed the silver-dotted sky. "Can we go?"

The question appeared to startle him. His face darkened. "Sure."

They stepped out onto the sidewalk. A stinging breeze whipped off the lake, raising gooseflesh on her arms. She wore a light windbreaker over a cotton sweatshirt, but cold seeped through the layers. They didn't talk. She must have offended him, for his face was taut, his pace quick. Mona heard only the scuff of her high-top tennis shoes against the pavement.

She was going to murder Liza when she got home. She had told her roommate she wasn't interested in Brian Whitney, and now she knew why. He was too glitzy, too smooth. Not her type. Again, reality proved her dream man a figment of her imagination. The perfect man didn't exist, and she had been a fool to accept Brian's offer to go out for ice cream. And an even bigger fool to fall for Liza's I-have-a-headache routine. She gritted her teeth and pounded out the last steps to the house.

Brian stopped her with a hand on her arm, two feet before her front walk. His dark eyes glinted concern. "Did I do something?" His tone turned a furrow of shame in her heart.

Mona stared at the pavement. "No. I'm just tired."

She felt his hand under her chin, lifting it. "Maybe we can start over? Rewind the tape and record over this evening? I'd sure like a chance to show you around Deep Haven."

Mona squinted up at him. He smiled, a five-o'clock shadow blanketing his chin. His shoulders were wide, and he cut a dashing pose in his tailored pants and V-neck sweater. Perhaps she had judged him too severely. She shouldn't compare a man like Brian to a drifter like Joe. Joe was intrigue and passing fancy. Brian was commitment and future. She'd do well to remember the difference. She nodded and gave an apologetic smile.

Her answer lit a fire in his eyes. "Great. I'll be by in a couple of days. I have to go to Duluth for some business. When I get back, I'll take you out someplace nice. No more slurps and licks."

Mona forced a smile. She rather liked Tastee Treat, with the right company. "Thanks for the ice cream," she said, turning.

He caught her hand in one swift movement. She turned just as he pressed his lips against it. "No, thank you, Mona," he said, grinning at her startled expression.

He left her reeling, desperately trying to untangle her welling confusion.

Joe pulled away from the darkened window. What was Brian up to? He hadn't liked the man from the moment he'd shaken his sweaty palm earlier that afternoon when the city official had stopped in and arranged the ice-cream date. Joe's defenses turned on high when he'd caught the look in the guy's eyes—like a tiger prowling. Then Joe had arrived home from the Garden to discover Mona out alone with the predator. He entwined his fingers and clasped them behind his neck, battling irritation. It wasn't his business, he reminded himself. He didn't live here; Brian did. Mona had a future with Brian Whitney, not with Joe Michaels.

Joe stalked to his closet, where he'd piled all the wrinkled clothes from his duffel, hanging the most important on three lonely hangers. He unearthed a pair of black athletic pants, running shoes, and a red Wisconsin sweatshirt. He needed a run, and the beach was just the place to unwind the mess of emotions from the day.

The moist night air, smelling of the lake and budding birch trees, cleared his mind and seeped calm into his soul. No wonder tourists considered Deep Haven, with the waves singing from shore and seagulls calling in harmony, the perfect getaway. He agreed that he'd like to dump his problems outside city limits and enjoy the sanctuary from life that Deep Haven offered. However, he couldn't afford to take a vacation from the choices he'd made that dictated his life. There was too much at stake.

Joe stretched briefly against the back steps, then lit out in a brisk run down the sidewalk. Lights from distant houses pushed back the darkness in uneven patterns. A dog barked. Rip answered but stayed at Joe's heels. Joe checked for traffic, then veered out across the street, angling down a short grassy incline to the rocky beach. He dodged waves crashing against a jagged shore, running so awkwardly he didn't even break a sweat. But Rip loved dancing into the spray, and it gave Joe the opportunity to behold the sky and praise the majesty of the Almighty.

Why am I here, Lord? The answer seemed clear—to get right with Gabe. But God often worked a mosaic, blending lives and purposes. Like when He'd sent Joe to wrestle salmon on a fishing boat in Alaska. The work had been short-lived and excruciating, even dangerous. But he'd seen a shipmate find salvation, saved a fella from washing overboard, and in the end, the adventure had opened countless doors and kept his boss in the black.

God directed every move he made, inhabited every place he lived. Through his mother's last plea, God had directed him to Deep Haven, and Joe knew, just as he knew he'd take another breath, that God had a bigger plan for him here in this town. Bigger, perhaps, than saving his own bacon, although the Almighty had come through on more than a few occasions.

Maybe he was here to help Mona. That idea had flitted through his mind various times over the past twenty-four hours. She'd seeded a soft spot in his heart when he watched her lug out the phonograph, gritting her teeth and grunting. He'd politely stifled his laughter when she wiped soot across her face, but he couldn't help but erupt when she fought with the rolltop desk. She had looked so perturbed, her face reddening with bottled frustration when it wouldn't surrender to her prodding. To say she was tenacious was an understatement. Maybe she really would whip her bookstore into shape. She had Napoleon dreams, to say the least.

God's plan definitely included Gabe. Warmth enveloped Joe, thinking of his little brother. The accepting smile, the exuberant embrace, and the eagerness with which Gabe had unveiled his life, his friends—all were an exhilarating contradiction to what Joe had expected. When he heard the word *institution,* it replayed an ancient nightmare in his head. He'd never been able to produce the term in his own speech. Somehow to say it admitted that his father had been right, that he'd been justified in abandoning the family. That having a son— or a brother—who had Down syndrome was a disease or a curse. Especially after seeing Gabe today, Joe would never agree.

He sat on the beach and prayed aloud. "Lord, I'm sorry for ignoring Gabe for so long. He's my brother and I should have paid attention." The image of Gabe's laughing face impaled him. Joe hung his head and dug both hands into his scalp. "What a fool I've been."

"What sort of fool?" Mona walked up beside him. "Thinking you agreed to too much and contemplating making a run for it?" Her fragrance settled over him as she sat down and so unraveled him he could only blink at her. "Sorry," she said, looking worried. "Am I bothering you?"

He quickly shook his head, his heart galloping in odd rhythm. "Hey," he finally croaked, "what brings you out here?"

"Stars," Mona stated in a dreamy voice. She settled next to him on the rocks. "What are *you* doing out here?"

Joe gave her a sidelong appraisal, taking in her sweet smile, her buttery hair dancing in the wind, her sculptured cheekbones, and the moon twinkling in her eyes. She seemed so calm it made his own erratic heartbeat that much more profound. He struggled to answer. "Praying, actually."

"Really? You're a Christian?"

"Yep. Since I was a teen. I found the Lord one night on a solo camping trip. Counting the stars, I was overwhelmed that He'd made every one of them and yet also knew every hair on my head, as it says in Matthew 10. What was even more awesome was that Jesus, God in the flesh, left those magnificent heavens, came to earth, and paid for my sins so that I could know this incredible God. Since then, whenever I pray, it seems easier when I am staring at the sky, at His glorious cosmos."

"I know what you mean." Mona hugged her knees. "There's something majestic about the North Shore. I can clearly see God's handiwork. The rhythm of the waves as they reach for my toes, the seagulls riding over the lumps in the water, the smell of the fir and birch trees. God made all this for us to enjoy. It always

gives me peace to sit under the stars, surrounded by His creation."

Her words lit a glow inside him. He couldn't have said it better himself.

"So, Joe, who are you? I know you can fix gutters, and you drive a mean mower, but what are you doing here? Do you have family in town?"

Joe raised his eyes to the sky, fastening on the dippers and wondering why the air suddenly seemed nippy. "Not really." Guilt stabbed at him. But he wasn't about to bring his little brother into the picture, dragging with it dozens of questions and not a little bit of pity. That was the last thing he wanted from this beautiful woman digging through the rocks beside him. Besides, some things were private.

"Are you a handyman by trade?" She tucked her hands into her sweatshirt cuffs, kneading them together, as if chilly. He wanted to put his arm around her, but the image of Brian kissing her hand hit him like a cold spray.

"Off and on. I saw your ad and thought I could help." That was true enough and sufficiently vague to keep curiosity tamed. The last thing he needed was to spark her interest and start her poking around his privacy. Worst-case scenario would have her asking the police to do some sleuthing, and it then it would only be a matter of time before his life—and Gabe's—would take an ugly turn.

"Hmmm . . . lucky for me, I guess."

Joe fished around at his feet and unearthed the perfect skipping rock. Winging it sideways into the water, he counted five skips. "I don't believe in luck or chance," he said quietly.

Mona turned her head, her cheek resting on her knees. "No, I don't suppose I do, either. But the other side is sometimes hard to accept."

The waves scraped the shore in syncopation. A seagull waddled near and ogled them with beady eyes.

"Other side?" Joe asked, shooting a glance at her.

"That God causes all things to happen, that everything filters through His hands."

Joe saw pain flash through her green eyes. Hers wasn't a throwaway comment. "The mystery of free will versus predestination. You're going to tie yourself up with that one, Mona. Either God is in charge or He's not. We can go round and round about the origin of evil, but the buck stops at God. The question isn't who causes something to happen, but rather, whether you see the outcome with His eyes or yours. Whether or not you trust He's got it all in His hands."

Mona rested her chin on her knees and gazed out into the dark lake. "Romans 8:28. 'We know that God causes everything to work together for the good of those who love God and are called according to His purpose for them.' See, I know it by heart, and I know He does take the bad and turn it into good. But you're forgetting God also holds us accountable for our actions. If it is Him doing it all, then by justice, He can't hold us accountable."

Joe smiled. Beauty and theological smarts too. Wow. "We are accountable because we are sinful. The unfortunate truth is that Adam chose to sin, and so do we. But the good news is that God gives us a way out, through Christ. Accountability and forgiveness in one shot. All we have to do is accept it. It's pretty easy."

"Or the hardest thing in the world," Mona murmured.

Her words hung between them. Joe threw another stone in the water, feeling personal indictment take root in his heart. She'd given him a glimpse behind the curtain of her pain and instead of measuring his words, he'd given her a nickel answer. *It's pretty easy.* He knew better, and he wanted to snatch back his quip and try again. Silence thickened between them. Rip ran by and scared a seagull.

When Mona sighed and climbed to her feet, Joe's heart fell slightly. "Good night, Joe." She trudged toward the road, leaving a stinging wind in her wake.

Joe felt as if he somehow shouldered the unnamed burden she'd carried out to the beach. The desire to ease her suffering washed over him, burning his eyes. He lifted his eyes to the winking stars. *Lord, please give me another chance to be a blessing to her.*

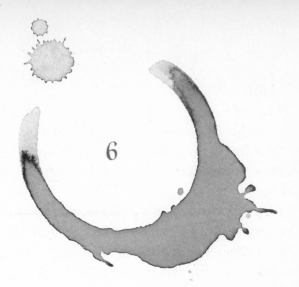

6

Can you put a new plug in the corner?" Liza asked.

Joe's gaze followed Liza's pointing finger as he rubbed the handle of a screwdriver between his shoulder blades. "Yeah, I reckon I can do that, but the wire will have to be external, unless you want me to open up the wall."

"No, I just want a lamp on my desk. This corner is way too creepy. I can't figure out why they'd put only one outlet in this room."

"'Cause this house was built before the advent of electricity?"

Liza hit him with her paint rag. "You're probably right." Laughing, she added, "But you have to admit, it does have character."

"If you call a rotting roof and a saggy porch character, then I'll agree."

Liza scowled. "Think positively. Close your eyes and imagine what this place can be. It's more than an old house. It's a dream come true."

"How so?"

Liza bit her lip, her dark eyes running over him. "If you can keep a secret, I'll let you in on a bit of history."

"My lips are sealed." He bit back a smile at her earnest expression and held up three fingers, like a Boy Scout.

Liza squinted at him a moment, then smiled conspiratorially. "Mona's been saving for years for this place. It's her dream, more than anything else in the entire world. And it just has to happen. If it doesn't, I'm not sure what it will do to her."

Joe frowned. "Why?"

Liza shook her head. "You'll have to ask her that, Joe. Suffice it to say this dream goes back a long way."

Joe mulled over her words while walking to the window. The front lawn shone rich jade in the sun. Across the road, the lake rolled against the shore in gentle rhythm. Seagulls waddled over the rocks, and the blue sky was smeared with wispy cirrus. Determination swept through him like a wildfire. It must have shown in his face, for when he turned, Liza gaped at him. "Then we better make sure her dreams come true, huh?"

Liza nodded.

A car door slammed. Joe glanced outside and spied Mona unlocking the hatch to a tiny blue Chevette. He'd seen the car on the street yesterday but didn't connect the ownership dots. Now, watching her lug something from the back, revived a memory so profound, he gasped.

"What's wrong?"

He turned to Liza, forcing a casual smile. "Nothin'. Just Mona."

Liza raised one of her thin black eyebrows and

smirked. Joe ignored her, slipped the screwdriver into his back pocket, and walked toward the front door.

Mona had pulled a stump of wood from her car and was rolling it on one edge up the front walk. Her blonde hair fell over her face, and her jaw was set.

"Need some help?" Joe hollered.

Mona looked up at him, two hands balancing the stump. "Nope, I got it."

"Okay." Joe stuck his hands in his front pockets, rocked back and forth on the porch, and watched her wrestle the stump toward the front steps. He had to bite the inside of his mouth to keep from repeating the question as she let the stump rock back, sat on it, and rested her arms on her knees, slouching. Sweat beaded her forehead, and her chest rose and fell with exertion. The stump did look heavy. It was nearly a foot and a half in diameter and two feet high. A nice piece of oak, from what he could see.

"Where'd you get it?" Joe asked.

Mona gave him a sidelong gaze, and he felt a jolt ripple through him. Why did her fir green sweatshirt have to make her eyes sparkle so? He blew out an unsteady breath.

"Holland's Sawmill. I plan on using it for an end table. What do you think?" She stood, gesturing at it like it was a prize and she was Vanna White. "With a little sanding and a coat of varnish, it could be pretty."

"You have vision, Mona. I'll give you that."

She beamed. "Well, I like to be original. I ordered an overstuffed sofa in a navy-and-green plaid for the dining room. I wanted a place where folks could drop their worries for a moment, kick back, and bury themselves in a book."

"It wouldn't hurt if they bought the book, either."

She chuckled. "Nope, nor a cup of cappuccino." She motioned to the stump. "I thought it would give the store a rustic, at-home feel."

"Like bringing the wilderness inside."

"Yup." Mona squatted, wrapped her arms around the log, and strained.

"You aren't serious, are you?" Joe leaped all five porch steps and landed at her side. "Let me help you."

"Back off," Mona growled through gritted teeth.

Joe recoiled. "Calm down, Mona. I don't want you to spend the next month in the chiropractor's office, that's all. Let me give you a hand."

"No!" Mona dropped the stump and pounced to her feet, her face red. "I don't want your help. I can do this."

Joe eyed the stump. Fifty pounds, at least. "Mona. Don't be silly. That thing is heavy."

Mona swiped her hands together. Sawdust and chips of wood broke free. She sighed. "I'm sorry, Joe. I shouldn't have barked at you." Her tone softened. "I don't want to get used to your help. I have to be able to do this on my own."

"I'm not offering to marry you. I just want to help you lift the stump."

Mona flinched. "You may not agree, but if I start depending on you, you'll begin to think you're indispensable."

Joe squinted at her. "And what's so bad about that?"

Mona pressed her lips together as if holding back a reply, one he all at once dearly wanted to hear. Sighing, she squatted and wrapped her arms around the stump again. Joe watched, shaking his head as she rocked it

into her embrace then began to mount the stairs with it.
Her legs quivered. He tiptoed behind her, ready for a
swift catch. She made it to the third step, groaned, then
finally plunked the stump onto the porch. Slapping her
hands together, she sprinted to the landing and whirled,
beaming. "See?"

He'd never had to war with the idea of pulling someone into his arms to silence a victory dance. But, as
Mona grinned at him, her hands clamped on her hips,
wood shavings layering her sweatshirt, and hair flopping
over her face, that was exactly what happened. Perhaps
it was relief, frustration, or admiration, but suddenly he
fought a barrage of furious impulses.

"Were you born stubborn?" he demanded. As her
mouth opened in shock, he stalked past her into the
house.

♈

Mona hummed as she sanded the top of her oak stump.
She heard Joe, tucked under the kitchen sink, attacking
the drippy faucet. Liza had mentioned something about
painting the inside of her newly emptied potter's shed.
Mona blew on the dust, scattering it into the wood-
tinged air, and admired her stump. The wood grain
wound in thick, brown circles. Alton Holland had
already set aside another stump for her, one with the
remnants of root still stretching from the base like thick
fingers. They would be beautiful. Mona felt hope surge
through her. What had Joe said? *You have vision.*
Perhaps. But mostly she had dreams.

Mona stood up and stretched, surveying the two rooms

that would be her bookstore and coffee shop. The ceiling had yet to be patched, the floors sanded and varnished, the windowsills painted, and the walls papered. But she had four and a half weeks, and it was doable. Finally, nothing stood in her way. The late-afternoon sun lit a path of orange along the wood floor, swirls of dust waltzing in the tangible rays. Mona inhaled, feeling peace enter like a fragrance.

"Arrgh!" Joe's cry from the kitchen shattered her serene moment.

"What is it?" Mona raced to the kitchen. The scene that greeted her scattered the lingering aroma floating about her heart with the effectiveness of a stink bomb. Roaches, as thick and deep as a moving carpet, scrambled over her lemon-colored counters, seeking refuge from Joe's shoe. Mona stood paralyzed, watching roaches climb out of the depths of her house and envisioning one of the monsters tiptoeing over a coffee mug. Worse yet, perhaps it would nestle into someone's shirt collar and she could invite the entire health department over to finish off the muffins as they shut her down.

"W-where'd they come from?" she stammered.

Joe shot her a sorry look and pointed to a gaping hole under the sink. Rotting drywall littered the floor around the open cabinet doors. "You have a slight plumbing problem."

Mona's heart sank. She gripped the counter, crouched, and surveyed the black hole at the base of the pipes. "How bad is it?"

The sensation of movement scuttling across her hand eclipsed his answer. Mona leaped to her feet in time to spy a confused roach heading toward her shirt cuff.

Screaming and shaking her hand, she danced into the center of the room, all her feminine instincts boiling over. Then she spotted Joe grinning so widely, it seemed his cheeks would pop. She glowered at him. Great, just what she needed after her triumphant performance with the tree stump. Now he'd conjure up all sorts of maiden-in-distress images. Mona sucked a calming breath, peeled off a shoe, and began to whack at the odious insects, feeling a strange satisfaction as she squashed them.

The screen door whined open, and Liza popped her head in. "What's all the ruckus about in here?"

They didn't need to answer. Liza screamed and beat a trail through the kitchen. Her boots crashed up the stairs. Mona caught Joe's bemused expression and flattened another bug with a satisfying smack! Then, to her amazement, Joe leaned over, took off his boot, gripped it with his right hand, and began to parry and thrust, whacking the roaches like a fencer. Mona flicked an eyebrow. Did he think this was funny?

To add injury to her horror, his filthy dog, Rip, scrambled into the kitchen through the open screen door, dragging the forest with him, and went wild. He barked and growled at the intruders, hair spiking along the back of his neck. Mona groaned. These two jokers were a pair of overkill soldiers invading her poor kitchen. It was a wonder they hadn't attracted the entire neighborhood.

Liza dashed into the kitchen, armed with a can of Raid and the yellow pages. "I'm calling the exterminator," she declared, as if it were a novel idea.

Mona escaped into the front room, sat down on the walnut table, and stared at the hole in her ceiling. Just what a kitchen needed, a mafioso family of roaches, extended relatives included. As exterminator charges totaled in her mind, despair gripped her in a neck spasm.

Then Joe moseyed out of the kitchen, gripping the can of Raid like a six-gun. "I'm gonna git those varmints yet," he drawled. He had tied a blue bandana over his mouth, bandit-style, and his eyes twinkled under a masked grin. He seemed so hopeful, so eager to help that she couldn't help it—she laughed.

Joe lay on the sofa, his hands behind his head, watching shadows of the front-yard birch trees chase each other across the ceiling, and letting the echo of Mona's laughter fill his heart with delight. It was so unexpected, so hard earned, everything he'd hoped it would be and more. Her laughter and the warm acquiescing smile that followed had seeded an unfamiliar longing deep in his heart, and now he lay cultivating healthy sprouts of tenderness toward his new boss.

Despite Mona's almost antagonistic response to his help, the need buried in her jeweled eyes called to him. She was afraid. He could sense it in the way she burrowed into projects and focused like a sniper on her goals. It looked like determination, but it could also be escape.

Was Mona running from something? She had all but admitted it last night on the beach. *Forgiveness is the hardest thing in the world to accept.* What horrific, unforgivable load was she carrying?

Joe sighed and laid a hand on Rip, who was breathing

in rich slumber on the floor next to the sofa. *Lord, what can I do to help her?*

Make her bookstore come to life.

The yearning was so profound, he knew it was his answer. Mona's dreams would come true if he had anything to do with it. He just hoped it wouldn't cost him the one thing he needed to bail his way out of trouble.

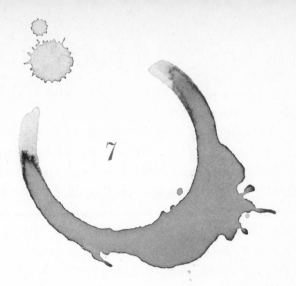

7

Okay, Mona, you're on jack duty. Make sure it doesn't slip, and if it starts to move, you holler."

Mona nodded and wrapped both gloved hands around the jack handle. "Will this work?"

"Yep," Joe said, without glancing at her.

She watched him retrieve two cinder blocks from the pile on her walk. He was different this morning. Somehow, after yesterday's horrible roach party, he seemed more serious, even driven. Although he couldn't seem to quell his quips and spurts of craziness, she had to give him credit—he was a hard worker. She'd spied him in the backyard late last night, painting Liza's workshop by the glow of an electric light. She'd lingered, watching him from her bedroom window, grinning when he wrestled Rip to the grass for a paint rag. The mutt wasn't so bad. He did have the saddest eyes she'd ever seen. And yesterday, when she'd claimed a quiet place on the porch to sort out her frustration, Rip had flopped down next to her, resting his muzzle on her foot, as if he understood and wanted to comfort her.

This morning, she'd glimpsed her handyman driving away in a fog of exhaust, and when he returned, he had a bed full of cinder blocks, exterior paint, and roofing materials. She scowled, spotting the price on the cans of paint, but she supposed the higher price would guarantee she wouldn't have to repaint soon. "I'll tack the amount on to your pay if you'll give me the receipt," she said, after bounding up to him, arms outstretched to help carry supplies.

He gave her a look that made her shrivel. "Nothing doing. Consider it a gift."

Mona's fury rose like a flood. "I don't need your help. Haven't we been through this?"

"Yep." He loaded her arms with a bag of cement. "Just put it by the porch." Mona gaped, but Joe didn't spare her a glance as he crossed to the tailgate. Opening it, he hauled out two cinder blocks. "Hurry up. We have a big day ahead of us."

Mona clamped her mouth shut, muscled the bag up the front walk, and dropped it down in front of the porch. Joe sprinted as he unloaded the truck, and Mona helped in mute amazement. *All right, Lord, I asked him to be a good worker, but this is too much!* Nevertheless, she had warmed to his exuberance as the morning grew long.

"Okay, Mona," Joe said, his voice alerting her to the job at hand. "I'm going to slide the blocks in. Then you ease up on the jack ever so slightly, and we'll see how they settle."

He layered the blocks on top of one another in a

smoothed spot. At his nod, Mona pressed the jack handle. The porch moaned, the blocks scraped, and the corner of her porch leveled out.

Joe beamed in triumph. "Now let's jack her back up and I'll cement it in." He stood and gripped the handle, laying his hands next to hers. His presence was close, and he smelled unnervingly masculine—sweat and flannel and wood chips.

"I got it," he whispered.

She looked up and was captured by his magnetic blue eyes. They entranced her, holding her in some sort of magical grip. Mona felt an unfamiliar tingle ripple up her spine. She jumped back, but his eyes stayed on hers, penetrating, peeling away her toughened layers until she felt as if he could see into her soul. Frowning, she turned away. She heard him grunt as he jacked up the porch.

What was different about him? Mona chewed her lip. He acted as if the house were his and he was taking ownership of her dreams.

"Can you hold the jack again?"

Mona turned and gripped the jack, noticing he withdrew his hands the instant hers took over. He walked to the bucket and began mixing and stirring the cement.

Mona shivered in her flannel shirt. The cool air didn't seem to bother Joe, however. He'd stripped off his blue sweatshirt, and his wide chest and thick arms stretched over a gray army T-shirt. Fit and strong, he carried himself like a man used to manual labor. Joe straightened, snared the bucket, and turned to face her.

His blue eyes shimmered deep indigo against the navy bandana he'd tied on his head, and the brightness of them caught her like a gust of wind. Her mouth went dry, and she realized he had eyes like her father's. Rich, discerning, pensive. And, at times, laughing. Mona struggled to collect her composure.

She numbly watched him trowel cement over the blocks. Then he eased them into place again. "Okay, let her down."

Mona lowered the jack. The cinder blocks held. "Well, now the muffins won't tumble off the plates," she commented, forcing a carefree tone into her voice.

Joe grinned. "Poor Rip. He was counting on the extra tidbits."

Mona laughed and rolled her eyes but couldn't ignore the implication that he might be staying. What was worse, for the first time the idea seemed oddly pleasing.

Joe gripped the steering wheel, felt the warmth of Rip's head on his lap, and watched the forest envelop him. The lush undergrowth along the dirt road to the Garden effectively blotted out the sun, yet the creamy birch trees gleamed white like bones.

With the wind singing through the trees and the pine scenting the truck cab, Joe knew it had been wise to obey Mona and take the day off. He'd fought the impulse for a moment, as he stood beside his truck and watched her attack her newly leveled porch with white paint. It was a daunting task. Still, she seemed so content, happily humming, and it balmed the shard of guilt piercing his heart. He finally surrendered to the urge that burned in his chest—to go see Gabe.

The Garden lodge seemed deserted, the handful of

wicker rocking chairs on the porch empty and unmoving. As Joe climbed out of the truck, Rip squeezed past him and, with a jubilant bark, took off after a pair of startled squirrels.

"Anybody here?" Joe called, unwilling to walk into the lodge unannounced.

The screen door squealed. Ruby emerged, wearing a welcome smile, a pair of baggy jeans, and a floral-print flannel shirt rolled up past her elbows. She held a ledger and had tucked a pencil above one ear. "Hello, Joe. Gabe was hoping you'd stop by."

"Hi, Ruby. Is he around?"

"Sure. He's out back with the others. Go behind the lodge."

Joe heard voices as he trudged around the building—someone shouting orders, other voices singing. Although they sounded like a busy bunch, he didn't expect the sight that greeted him. The Garden occupants—some gripping hoes, others kneeling—were working the soil around hundreds of green plants. Gabe stood on the bed of a wheelbarrow and barked orders like an army sergeant. Amazement rooted Joe to the spot.

"Put the mulch on that section near the back!" Gabe gestured with a hand trowel to a portion of the garden. Gabe was an uncanny mirror of himself—clad in a pair of old army pants, a gray sweatshirt, and a red Bulls baseball cap. Joe had received it from a friend in Chicago, and seeing it on Gabe's head warmed him inside.

"Hey, Gabe, doing a little gardening?" Joe tucked his hands in his pockets and sauntered up to his brother.

Gabe's eyes registered delight. "Joe! Where have you been?"

Joe shrugged. "I got a job in town helping remodel a house."

"A job?" Gabe hopped down from the wheelbarrow. "Why? You have a job."

Dodging the question and the countless others that would follow, Joe motioned toward the endless beds of sprouts. "Wow, are all those strawberries?"

Gabe grinned, his oval eyes dancing. "Yep. The Garden's fresh strawberries are famous. Don't you remember?" He frowned. "I wrote you about it."

Joe felt like a cad. When Gabe mentioned in his letters that he liked to grow strawberries, Joe had thought his brother had been inflating their success by his overactive imagination. But as Joe's mouth hung open and he gazed at the garden, he estimated over two acres of strawberry field. "This is amazing."

Gabe's chest puffed out, and he wiggled the brim of his cap. "We won a prize too."

"I'm impressed. I had no idea."

"C'mon, I'll show you what we do." Gabe grabbed him by the arm and gave him a walking tour of the field. "These plants are about five years old. We'll dig them up this year, but they'll put out runners. We'll replant them over there, in the bed Daniel and Melissa are digging up."

Joe squinted, making out two workers turning over soil on the south end of the field. Gabe pulled him between rows of rich black dirt, and they walked on wooden planks between the beds.

"We replanted these last September. They won't give much this year, but by next season their berries will be the best." Gabe pointed to a large bed covered in

chicken wire. "That's a special berry we're trying to produce. We want the Garden to have their own special type." His words slowed as he struggled to explain their plans, but his eyes shone with delight.

Words deserted Joe. He never imagined Gabe to be involved in such a project. His brother was full of interesting surprises, to say the least. But then again, most people had something tucked into dark corners of their lives. Something that could surprise, even shatter, everything others believed about them.

Take Mona, for example. The spitfire had secrets hidden behind those luminous eyes. He saw them—and the fear—yesterday as she'd nearly leaped away from him while jacking up the porch. What had frightened her? He'd felt fear himself as a streak of warmth shuddered through him when they'd stood a mere breath apart. She smelled so . . . feminine. Some sort of lilac soap on her skin, fresh and clean and delicate.

He'd wondered later at his reaction, as the moonlight traced the grooves of his wooden apartment floor. Never had a woman wound herself into his heart so quickly. Never had he allowed it. Was it Mona's need that softened all the rough places inside him? Or rather her determination, the way she bit into her projects with the persistence of a beaver? Something about Mona definitely made him ponder the ramifications of letting down his guard, crossing the invisible picket line, and sweeping her into his life.

And what good would that do him? Secrets. His own would ambush any hint of romance like a bandit. Imagine Mona finding out about the Garden and the brother Joe had hidden away. It would take only one look at Gabe for her to wonder what a future with Joe might hold. A second look might turn her on her heel and send her striding out of his life, the slam of the door on his heart as crushing as the one his father had left in his memory. Joe didn't even want to think of what his other mysteries might do to Mona's planned-to-the-nth-degree life.

No, it was better to leave his secrets, and hers, carefully locked up where they couldn't spring free and sabotage anyone's future. And he better keep his eyes open and those warm moments beside her at a minimum if he wanted any kind of future at all.

"Hey, want a lemonade?" Gabe asked.

"Sure," Joe said, aware suddenly that he'd been blindly gazing at the gardeners while the sun dribbled sweat down his face.

Gabe waved his arm to the others. "Let's take a break!"

Joe watched twenty people drop their hoes, rakes, and trowels and run toward the house. "Quite a group you have here," he remarked. "Does everybody help with the garden?"

"Of course. We're a family. Everybody works."

Joe put a hand on his brother's shoulder. "But you don't have to work. Everything is paid for."

Gabe shot him a puzzled look. "Of course I have to work. Everybody has to do something. This is my job."

Joe turned away. "I don't get it."

Gabe sprinted toward the house. Joe trudged after him. He'd have to corner Ruby and figure out what was going on. His monthly payments more than covered Gabe's living costs. So if Gabe's words were accurate, where was

all the cash from their prizewinning strawberries? Was this just a dream cooked up by Ruby to keep the residents busy? Either way, she was obviously manipulating her easily fooled charges. Angry, Joe let the screen door slam behind him and stalked into the kitchen.

At the sink, Gabe washed dirt from his hands. Ruby sat at the table, a sweating glass of lemonade in her grip. She glanced at Joe and her smile vanished. "What's the matter, Joe?"

"Can I speak to you privately?" He tried not to growl, but by the defensive scowl that appeared on Ruby's face, he realized he hadn't been successful.

"Sure," she said, rising. She walked to her office, leaving an assembly of astonished, muted workers in her wake. Joe turned to follow, feeling stares on his back.

Ruby shut the door behind him, then crossed her arms over her chest. "What's this all about?"

Joe walked stiffly to the window and kneaded the back of his neck with his hand. He swallowed and tried to keep his voice low. "I pay good money for Gabe to live here. I expect him to live a comfortable life without a care." He turned around. "Can you tell me why he's digging in the dirt? He seems to think he has to work to pay his way. But you and I both know that isn't true."

Ruby gave him a piercing look. "Sit down, Joe." She gestured to an overstuffed denim love seat. Joe considered the request, then acquiesced. Sitting across from him at her gleaming oak desk, she folded her hands on a neat blotter and looked every inch the stern housemother. Joe braced himself.

"You don't know much about Down syndrome, do you?" she asked.

The accusation hit him hard, and he clenched his jaw. Her stare nearly hurt.

"Let me help you out. Your brother and the others who live here are only one chromosome different from you. They think, have feelings, want to feel worth and the love of family. They may not think as fast on their feet as most folks, and they often struggle to reason things out. But they need to feel a part of God's world as much as the next person."

Joe looked away, unable to face her steely gaze.

Mercifully, her voice softened. "Gabe doesn't work because he has to for money; he works because he has to for his spirit. This is his home. He and the others are family. They depend on each other, and they want to build a life. Part of that life is creating and running a business. With their money, they take trips, add onto the lodge, even help other group homes less fortunate than ours. This garden is a way for them to depend on each other. They take turns running it. This summer, Gabe is the foreman."

Joe hung his head, feeling dressed down. "I'm sorry. I had no idea."

Ruby stood, walked around her desk, and sat next to him on the sofa. Her presence felt motherly, and Joe's anger dissipated. "Joe, Gabe is very proud of you and all you've done. He talks about you constantly. We know a lot about you."

A muscle in his jaw pulled slightly at her words. If she took what she knew and accidentally ran into Mona with it, his little stopover in Deep Haven, his desperate escape plan, and the chance to help Mona build her dreams would crumble into sawdust.

"But you don't know much about Gabe," she continued. "I don't know why you chose now to come to visit. But I think you should stick around and get to know your brother. He has much to teach if you are willing to learn."

"I should have visited more often," he murmured.

"Yes, you should have," she agreed. It hurt him to hear the truth spoken out loud. "But you're here now, and that's what matters. Besides, I think Gabe understood your long absence and why all your travels took you everywhere but here."

Joe frowned. "How's that?"

She shrugged. "Your mother must have explained it to him."

"Right." That made sense.

"Either her or your father."

Joe reeled, feeling like he'd been slugged. "My father?"

Ruby stood, seemingly unaware that she'd dropped news with the weight of an anvil on his chest. "Yes, he comes around a few times a year, writes regularly. Even calls."

"My father?" Joe felt weak and dazed. "I haven't heard from my father since he walked out on our family when Gabe was three years old."

This information seemed to catch Ruby by surprise. Confusion crossed her face. "Wayne Michaels has been coming to see Gabe for nearly four years."

Four years. Right about the time Mom passed away. Fury ripped through Joe, shredding his common sense. He pounced to his feet, breathing heavily. His expression must have scared Ruby, for she went ashen, gasped, and put a hand to her throat.

Throwing open her office door, Joe stormed through the house, barely hearing Gabe's voice over the fury that boiled in his soul. He hopped into his truck, started it with a roar, and peeled away from the Garden as quickly as his pickup could take him.

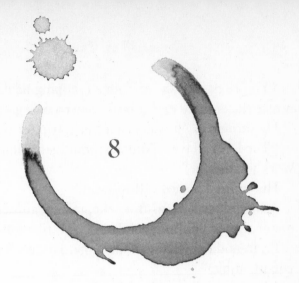

8

Mona heard the engine of a vehicle slow and pull up to the curb but forced herself not to look up as she dug a hole in the soil. She was thankful no one could hear the way her disobedient heart slammed against her rib cage. Joe had been gone for four hours, and her rebellious emotions acted as if it were half a century. She gritted her teeth and refused to turn at the scrape of feet on the sidewalk. The last thing she wanted was for Mr. Drifter Michaels to see the flush in her cheeks.

"Would you like to go out for pizza?"

Mona's pulse rate plummeted at the voice. She rocked back on her heels, wiped a hair from her face, and dredged up a smile. A well-dressed, slick-looking Brian Whitney marched across the grass, grinning. She tried not to compare him to the memory of a rumpled and dirt-streaked Joe. So the guy didn't have a lopsided smile—at least Brian didn't smell like hard work and sport a three-day growth of beard. She batted that delicious image away as well.

"You're back!" she exclaimed, hoping he didn't notice the enacted enthusiasm. She rose to greet him.

He shrugged. "It was just a quick trip for business."

"The Deep Haven Zoning Commission doing some work in Duluth?"

His smile vanished. "Research."

A breeze blew across the lake, raising gooseflesh on her arms. "Liza's out back," she said, filling the silence.

Brian nodded, then examined her garden. "What are you planting?"

"Peonies, dahlias, gladiolas. I'm putting in a hedge row of marigolds over there." She gestured to a spot of furrowed land edging the fence.

"Hope they bloom in four weeks," he commented wryly.

She frowned. "They will."

"Sure. Well, I know I said I'd take you out someplace nice, but I thought we could pop over to Pierre's Pizza for supper. I'll do the fancy dinner next week."

Mona tugged off her work gloves. "Pizza sounds great." She gave him a stern look. "But we go dutch."

"Right. We'll see."

Mona pointed a finger at him. "Dutch. I'll get Liza." She jogged around the house.

The sound of humming emanated from Liza's pottery shed. Mona leaned against the doorjamb, watching her best friend stacking unbaked pottery on her newly constructed shelves. Liza had a shipment of her finished, painted, and baked pottery due to arrive any day from her workshop in Minneapolis. But Mona knew Liza was itching to dive into a chunk of clay. It was a stress reliever as well as an occupation.

"Brian Whitney is here. He wants us to go out for pizza with him."

Liza turned, a teasing glint shimmering in her black eyes. "Are you sure he wants to take us both?" She had slicked her hair back into a bubblegum pink scrunchy and wore a fringed rhinestone-studded sweatshirt over black leggings.

"I'm sure—" Mona wrinkled her nose—"but we're not going anywhere until you change into something a little less . . . conspicuous."

Liza produced a mock-offended pose. "What, you don't like my new bangles?" She tilted her head and leaned her ear toward Mona. Mona peered at the earrings, then bit her lip to suppress her laughter. Only Liza could pull off a pair of hoops with rainbow trout dangling from them.

"I'm just trying to blend with the locals."

"By wearing fish?" Mona trembled with glee.

Liza beamed. "Listen, I'll save you from a night alone with Brian Whitney, but only if I can wear the trout."

Mona gave a start. "What do you mean, 'save me'? How do you know I don't want to have Brian all to myself?"

Liza pushed her out of the shed, then locked the door. "Because I know he's not your first choice of available men."

Shock nearly sent Mona sprawling. "What?"

Liza turned, linked her arm with Mona's, and led her toward the house. "You know exactly what I mean. You'd much rather build porches or swat roaches with our local handyman."

Mona went numb. "That is not true. Joe is nothing

more than a drifter, an intruder in my life. The sooner he fixes this place up and moseys on his way, the better."

"You don't know your dream man when you see him, honey."

"My dream man is certainly not a know-it-all jack-of-all-trades. My dream man has aspirations, dreams. He's intelligent, thoughtful, and well read. Have you seen one book in Joe's possession?"

Liza shook her head, her eyes glinting. "I haven't been in his apartment."

"I haven't either!"

"He might have an entire load of books in his duffel bag."

Mona rolled her eyes.

"'My dream man has to be patient, a hard worker, someone who considers others above himself and is a Christian,'" Liza quoted, her chin high.

"And be able to be vulnerable!" Mona spiked the air with a grimy finger. "Joe would rather tell a joke than be serious and reveal his true feelings. He's all puff and chuckles, the life of the party, but he guards his privacy like a secret treasure. I would take Brian I-am-the-greatest-thing-to-ever-come-out-of-Deep Haven over Mr. Private Michaels any day. At least Brian told me about his life. Joe won't even tell me where he's from."

Liza crooked an eyebrow. "I knew it," she said smugly.

Mona fumed and marched into the house behind her. She spotted Brian outside, inspecting her flowers. With his suit coat flung over his shoulder and groomed eyebrows furrowed in concentration, he appeared refined and stable, just the type of man who could fulfill her list of requirements. But as he squatted to survey the new

cinder-block posts, the image of Joe hit her hard—his short-cropped, tawny hair, his gray T-shirt pulling over thick arms and a muscled chest, and his liquid blue eyes that somehow skinned calloused layers from her heart.

Mona scampered up the stairs, wishing Liza wasn't always right.

Joe laced his fingers behind his neck and hung his head as he squatted on the beach. Every muscle tensed from the foolishness of not cooling down after his run. But he hadn't been running for exercise. Memories chased him along the beach, and he fought to escape the pain that seemed as vivid now as it had been fifteen years earlier. Ruby had ripped open his scars with her revelation, and the wound throbbed, fresh and gaping.

He'd spent the afternoon driving up the Superior coastline, searching for comfort in the rugged beauty that had so ministered to his soul in years past. He'd finally surrendered to the fruitlessness and returned to the Footstep, hoping to bury himself in manual labor.

He'd arrived in time to see Mona climbing into Brian Whitney's black-as-night Honda. He tried to ignore the stab of new pain as they drove off.

His chest heaved. Sweat ran in rivers down his back. Rage, like a separate being, roared about in his soul. Wayne Michaels—deserter, quitter, destroyer—back in Gabe's life. Just when Joe thought he'd buried the memories so deep they'd never be unearthed.

Joe jammed his fists into his eyes. The past revived, and he heard every angry, abusive word his father said echoing in the waves slamming onto shore. In the cold foamy spray, he again felt his tears, and the screams of the seagulls voiced his broken heart. Most of all, he felt the nip of blame in the stinging wind. Joe shuddered, burying his head into his drawn-up knees.

He would never forget the sound of his father's Mustang roaring away from the house or the image of his mother, crumpled in tears in the kitchen, pain etched into her face. She'd been so fragile after his father left, always exhausted from working late at the hospital while Joe cared for Gabe.

Gabe. The little brother he had always wanted. The paradox of both loving and hating his little brother had tied Joe in emotional knots. He didn't know where to pledge his allegiance. After his father left, he had felt tied to Gabe, forced to drag his abnormal little brother everywhere and defend him against the bullies of the world. When Joe was eighteen, he had broken the bonds and left. Just like his father. But, he always reasoned, he'd been better than the old man who'd given up on them. At least he'd provided, looked back, stopped in to check on Gabe now and then.

Why was his father back in Gabe's life? He had no business interfering after all these years. He didn't deserve the chance.

Joe groaned. What if Wayne Michaels had stepped back into Gabe's life to get at Joe? to twist the family purse strings and see if he could wring out something for himself? The thought made Joe nauseous. All his years of dusting the trail behind him could be obliterated by one well-placed phone call.

No, Wayne Michaels had been writing to Gabe for

four years. If he wanted to cause Joe trouble, he would have done so already.

Still, the urge to escape flooded over him and nearly put action to his feet. He had to move on. It was the only option he could see from his perch on the rocks, as he stared into the rapidly darkening sky. A few faint stars twinkled.

Regret formed a jagged lump in his throat. Leaving meant he would have to abandon Mona. And he didn't even want to think about what it would do to his future. His last chance for redemption slipping through his hands like jelly.

Both realities made his chest tighten.

"Joe?" Like an apparition, Mona appeared. Joe blinked at her, gaping. She smiled and put a gentle hand on his shoulder. "Are you okay? You look pale."

Joe couldn't speak, his tongue locked somewhere in his foundering heart. He shook his head.

She frowned, her green eyes flecking with concern. "Wanna talk about it?"

The tenderness in her voice threatened to make him cry. He shook his head again.

She considered him a moment, then settled next to him anyway. She began to flick through the rocks. "I saved you some pizza."

He swallowed, cleared his throat, forcing pleasantness through his agony. "What kind?"

"Canadian bacon, green peppers, and mushrooms."

"Thanks. That's my favorite."

Mona gave him a strange look. "Brian hates it. He and Liza got pepperoni." She continued her rock hunt for a moment, then stared at the sky. The wind pushed through the trees, sounding like a muted waterfall.

Joe didn't fill the gap with conversation; instead he searched for the words to tell her he had to leave.

"I told them I wanted to take a walk," she finally continued. "Stars calling, you know." She glanced at him, and Joe caught the sparkle in her eyes. He broke her gaze and looked woodenly across the lake. The sun had left a crimson fire simmering along the horizon, painting Lake Superior flame red.

He closed his eyes, fighting the pain stabbing at him. *Why, God? Why is life so difficult?* Now, just when he wanted to stay, when he'd let Mona and her dream into his heart, when he'd found the hope for his despair, self-preservation drove him away. But hadn't it always been that way? Joe Michaels, founder of the "save thyself" society? Expert at evasion, patent holder of "pack and run"? Why couldn't he, just once, summon the inner chutzpah to plant his feet in one place?

His one-word answer? Gabe. It all came back to his brother. Even now, Gabe was the reason the past had risen like a phantom, haunting. Joe felt tears forming and pressed his thumb and forefinger into his eyes to drive them back.

"The Footstep is shaping up," Mona said, oblivious to the emotional warfare being waged beside her. "I planted flowers today. Tomorrow I'm going to paint the windowsills. And Ernie down at the bowling alley said I could have his old bar. He's putting in a new one. I thought it would be a great place to serve coffee." As Mona's words rolled out, Joe found her presence oddly calming. He began to relax into her plans. The rushing urgency of retreat slowed.

"I'm renting a floor polisher on Monday. I'll buff the floor and then add a coat or two of varnish. My wallpaper order came in today also. I'll slap it up next week."

Her ideas bubbled over, and it was easy to crawl inside them. Her gentle voice, the way the wind played with her hair, and her subtle fragrance of lilac balmed his heart in a way that seemed natural and safe. She sat slightly in front of him, and he let his eyes skim over her fine profile. Smiling intermittently as her dreams tickled her, she occasionally peeked back at him. He met her eyes once, held them with his own, and felt her strength and kindness surround him like a blanket. His heart ached anew at her easy friendship. She was a lady who made him want to stay. Perhaps her dreams were large enough for both of them to hide inside.

Mona paused in her monologue to hurl a stone into the water. It skipped twice, then plunged into the calm waters.

Silently pushing through the rocks with his index finger, Joe unearthed a flat one and topped her throw by two skips.

She whirled and frowned at him, her eyes glinting. "You're messing with a master rock skipper."

A grin crept up his face. He found another rock, bounced to his feet, and let it fly. He heard the rocks tumble as Mona scrambled to her feet. He counted, his voice rising with each number. ". . . seven, eight, nine . . . ten!"

She shot him a playful glare. Then she crouched, hunting for a flat stone.

"Forget it, Mona. I'm the champ."

"Never. I have skipped more stones into this lake than you've even stumbled on."

"Ha!" Joe squatted beside her. The rocks gleamed opal, ruby, slate, and amber. He found a perfectly round, smooth, platinum-colored stone, made by God for skipping. Tossing it in his grip like a ball, he waited for her throw.

Mona sprang to her feet, gave him a predatory look, bent low, and flung the rock. Her count split the cries of the seagulls. ". . . fourteen . . . fifteen!" She raised her arms in triumph. "Beat that!"

Joe smiled, enjoying the delicious competitive expression on Mona's face. "Watch this," he teased. He flung the rock with such force, his wrist cracked. Cupping his hands over his eyes, he watched it splice the waves. ". . . ten, eleven, twelve . . ." It was still moving strong, but a whaler chugging in the distance had sent a series of waves to shore. Joe spotted a monster crest forming, preparing to gobble up his rock. "No, no!"

Mona picked up the count. ". . . thirteen . . . fourteen! It's a goner, and Mona Reynolds nabs the championship!" She twirled in victory.

Joe crossed his arms and fought the rising desire to take her into his embrace and dance to her melody. Joy lit her face and her eyes shone, igniting a warm glow inside him. He threw up his hands. "Okay, I concede defeat. But only on one condition."

Mona stopped and clamped her hands on her hips. "No conditions. I won fair and square."

"My skipper would have gone an easy twenty had it not been for interference."

"Them's the breaks. Timing is part of rock-skipping

skill. You have to know when to hold back and when
to throw."

"You have to give me a chance to even the score."

"How?" Mona jutted her jaw, her eyes blazing.

"I'll race you across the Devil's Kettle."

Mona gasped. "You've got to be kidding."

"Nope. I know a spot above the Kettle where you can
cross, if you're steady and have balance."

"*Balance* is my middle name," Mona quipped, spiking a golden eyebrow.

"Right, just like *steady* is mine."

The words hung in the air and seemed to hit her, just
as they hit him. She was hopelessly out of balance,
obsessed with her dream. He drifted like a vagabond,
dodging trouble from one town to the next, living a life
that was anything but steady. Her smile vanished, and
the light in her eyes flickered.

"Sorry," he mumbled.

Mona wrapped her arms around herself. "You're
right. I might be a little taken with my idea. But I have
to be. God's given me this one chance, and I've got to
give it my all. No one else is going to grab on and fight
for my dream." She turned away, poised to head
toward home. Joe caught her elbow. "Joe, listen, I
could wake up tomorrow and you'd be gone. I know
that—"

"I'm not going to leave, Mona. Not until you don't
need me anymore." His own words sucker punched
him, erupting from a place inside he'd yet to harness.
But what choice had she given him? He felt powerless
before her haunted green eyes. They reached out to a
place inside he didn't even know existed and extracted

promises he doubted he could fulfill. He spoke it again, as if to convince himself. "I'm not going to leave."

She spun, and the expression on her face told him exactly what he needed to see: hope, determination, and something else indiscernible. Then her eyes pinned his with a look so desperate, it tore a swath through his heart. Her voice was soft. "Don't make me depend on you, Joe. I can't take my heart breaking again." She turned and sprinted from the beach.

Joe watched her go and hoped that the promise he'd made didn't keep him in town long enough to let Wayne Michaels, or anyone else hanging around the fringes of his life, destroy this beautiful house of cards he was creating.

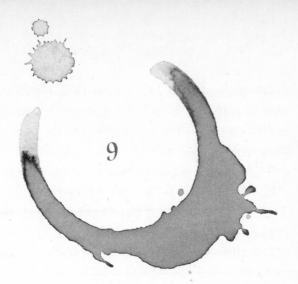

9

Joe opened his arms, and Rip tackled him in an exuberant bounce. Knocking Joe to the ground, the Lab smothered him with the kisses of a long-lost love. Joe laughed, pushed Rip away, and rolled to his feet. Gabe grinned like he was next in line. Joe reached out and hugged him. "Thanks again for taking care of Rip, Gabe."

Ruby stood, cross-armed and stoic, behind her charge. "Next time, don't run off so fast. You might find that your problems are better solved by sticking around."

Joe ignored the dig. Obviously she had yet to figure out that it was his so-called running that kept them out of trouble's grasp. He forced a smile. "Thanks for looking after things."

She fielded his loaded gratitude, responding with a curt nod. He hadn't made any friends with his stormy retreat yesterday, but his morning spent hoeing a section of the strawberry patch, along with a face-to-face chat with Gabe, had softened Ruby's attitude. Although he avoided the father subject, he managed to apologize with sincerity to Gabe, who forgave him with a smile and an embrace. The unconditional response made Joe burn with shame.

Ruby's voice warmed. "Come back soon, Joe."

Rip emitted a slow whine as they pulled out of the Garden. Joe rubbed his hand over the dog. "Finally found a place to call home, Rip?"

The affirming bark opened a festering wound in Joe's soul.

♈

Mona was watering her flowers when Joe pulled in. She grimaced and waved her hand in front of her nose, as if the fumes from his truck soured the air.

He grinned and sauntered up the walk, swinging his keys. "Let's go!" he called.

Mona frowned at him. "Go where?"

"Devil's Kettle, remember?"

"I thought you were kidding. No, I have far too much work to do. I have to paint the windowsills, and you still have to patch the hole in my ceiling." She turned away and dragged the hose to her poplar sapling.

Joe crossed the yard in two giant steps, wrapped one arm around her, and grabbed the hose with the other. "Nothing doing. You're a chicken."

She fit so well inside his casual embrace, the sudden urge to bury his face in her hair and smell her smooth skin made his pulse notch up. He took a calming breath and settled for the spark that lit in her green eyes.

"I'm not a chicken. I have work to do."

"Fine," he said mischievously, "concede me the winner."

He could have happily hid himself inside her furious gape for a year.

She raised her hands in surrender, releasing the hose into his grip. "Okay, smarty, I'll go to the Devil's Kettle, if you'll finish watering for me *and* promise to fix the hole in the ceiling tomorrow afternoon."

He bowed low. "As you wish, milady."

Mona rolled her eyes, but he saw a smile push at the corners of her mouth. She darted toward the house. "Let me change clothes."

He thought her faded jeans and University of Minnesota sweatshirt looked just fine.

She disappeared inside the house, and he turned to the sapling. She'd done a decent job, by herself of course, of planting the tree. Someday it would shade the yard, and she could put a garden table and chairs under its arms. Or he could build her a pair of Adirondack chairs and a picnic table.

Reality hit him like a cold gust. He wouldn't be here long enough to start sharing in her future. But maybe, if Gabe still lived at the Garden, he'd be back for a visit. That thought made him hum.

A car door slammed, slicing through his melody. Joe whirled, and the song died. Brian, dressed like a biker in a black leather jacket and matching jeans, swaggered toward the house, a sappy grin on his face. Joe wondered if he was wearing a black T-shirt to complete the ensemble. Brian saw Joe, and his smile dimmed. "Hey, Joe."

"Brian," Joe countered.

Brian entered the gate and ambled up to the sapling. "Nice maple."

"It's a poplar."

"Right." Brian stuck his hands in his pockets. "Have you seen Mona?"

Joe bristled. "She's going up to Devil's Kettle with me."

"Really? I haven't been up there for a long time. Maybe I'll tag along."

Joe's eyes narrowed. He was about to clip out a reason why Brian was not suitably dressed for a hike through the wilderness when he heard screams from the backyard. An earsplitting crash, then Rip's low barks merged with Liza's angry shouts.

"Sounds like you have trouble," Brian commented dryly.

Joe restrained the urge to turn the hose on him.

"You'd better see what's up."

Reluctantly, Joe dropped the hose at the roots. "Can you turn off the water for me?"

Brian nodded, humor glinting in his eyes. Joe gritted his teeth and sprinted toward the backyard.

Liza had Rip by the scruff of his neck. Her eyes blazed and he thought he saw actual fumes spiraling from her ears. "This mutt of yours just destroyed a day's work. Keep him out of my shed!"

Joe cringed and reached for Rip. "Sorry, Liza. I'll tie him up."

Her eyes flashed. "If I ever catch him in my shop again, I'll mold *him* into something!"

Joe nodded and dragged Rip to the porch door. He

threatened the dog with a low growl, then went in search of rope. Finding one in the pile of rubble and garbage next to the back steps, he tied it to the dog's collar, knotted it tightly, and attached the other end to the railing. "I'll get you a leash in the morning," he soothed. "Until then, you stay put." Rip sunk into the dirt and hid his muzzle under his front paw. Joe scratched him behind the ears.

"Now, c'mere and help me clean this up!" Liza ordered.

Joe trudged to the shed. Liza had swept the cement floor, where hardened shards of earthenware curled like ribbons of chocolate. She handed him a garbage bag. "Hold," she commanded, gathering the broken pieces in a dustpan and dumping them into the bag.

"How'd it happen?"

She shot him a withering look. "I had the bowls laid out on those sawhorses, and Rip charged in and upset the shelf."

Joe glanced at the sawhorses. "I'll make you a real shelf, Liza."

She stopped and considered him a moment, the dustpan on her hip. "Okay, buddy, you make me a shelf and I'll forgive your mutt."

Joe grinned. "Consider it done."

"And," she added, "I'll tell you what you have to do to make Mona's heart melt."

Joe nearly dropped the bag. "What did you say?"

Liza laughed at him, delight illuminating her face. "You two are a matched pair!"

Joe tied the corners of the bag and threw it over his shoulder, beating a hasty retreat.

Mona stood at the window, watching Joe lug trash from Liza's shed, still reeling from his quick embrace, if one could call it that. Something about his presence drew her in, threw her heart into overdrive, and turned her knees to jelly.

She sat on the bed and hung her head in her hands. She couldn't afford to take her eyes off her goal. She had a deadline and a mountain of work to accomplish. She didn't have time to dance about to the tune of love—especially with a man whose days with her were numbered.

Shaking his image away, she dug into her closet and unearthed a pair of clean Levi's, a white T-shirt, and a windbreaker. Under the bed, she located her hiking shoes next to a pair of grimy socks. She'd have to descend to the cellar and do laundry when she came home. She prayed the washer the previous owner left worked. If not, maybe Joe could fix it.

You're a chicken. The teasing echo of his voice made her cringe. His blue eyes did strange things to her common sense. What was she doing taking a day off to hike the Devil's Kettle?

She'd been up the Kettle trail on occasion in years past with her father. Once, they'd sent a log over the falls, watching it race downstream and finally disappear into the Kettle, a swirling teapot-shaped mass of rock and granite. The log never resurfaced; local legend suggested the Kettle swallowed everything that went in. The memory made her shiver. Perhaps this wasn't the wisest idea.

Glancing out the window at the marshmallow clouds billowed against an azure sky, she decided her fears were nonsense. A hike would be good for her soul. The breeze singing through the pines always had a peaceful effect on her, and she definitely needed some distance from her obsessive focus on the house. She had enough time, after all, to finish the repairs. A day in the woods, reminding herself of God's creativity, sounded like a pleasant balm to her overworked, worried heart.

But spend the day alone with Joe? The thought caused nervous ripples to stream up her spine. His smile was charming, his laughter intoxicating. Too much time with him might get addictive and distractive.

She tied her shoes, then flew down the stairs. "Liza!" she called from the landing. Trotting through the kitchen, she popped out the back door. Rip almost took her head off with an exuberant bounce toward her. Mona recoiled, then stepped out and crouched beside the dog. "What happened to you?" She examined the rope around his neck.

"He's in the doghouse." Joe clunked the top on the metal garbage can and strolled over. "He destroyed a bunch of Liza's pots."

"That's right! And now I have to spend a whole day remaking them." Liza stomped toward the house, dark eyes on Rip. "But I got Joe to agree to make me a drying rack, so it's not a complete loss." She waggled her eyebrows at Joe, and her eyes shone with mischief.

Mona glanced at Joe. Was he blushing? A strange feeling squeezed her heart. Jealousy? She dismissed it with a shake of her head and got to her feet. "Sorry, Liza. Not today. Joe and I are going hiking, and you're coming along!" She smiled hopefully at her friend, adding, "Please?"

Mona caught Joe's expression. He didn't seem happy. "Liza needs a break too, Joe."

He gripped the back of his neck. "Sure she does." He forced a smile. "Come with us, Liza," he said in a voice that lacked enthusiasm.

Liza surveyed the pair, her eyes narrowing. "I don't think so—"

"Let's go!" A smooth tenor interrupted her answer. Mona turned and saw Brian Whitney strutting toward them, his perfect white grin a vivid contrast to his black leather getup.

Mona didn't miss the delight coloring Liza's face, and an idea birthed. "Are you coming with us, Brian?" she asked sweetly.

Brian tucked his hands in his coat pockets. "I'd like to. I haven't been up to see the Kettle for a long time and never with such beautiful company."

Mona rolled her eyes. Liza beamed at him.

Joe cleared his throat. "Does that 'beautiful' description include me?" His grin teased, but Mona detected annoyance lurking in his eyes.

She turned to Brian. "You're definitely invited. Let's go." She peeked at her friend. "Liza?"

Liza nodded, her grin betraying her emotions. "I'll change." She bounded past Mona into the house.

Mona put a hand on Rip's head. His tail hit the side of the house in loud thumps. "Are we bringing the hoodlum along?"

Joe didn't meet her eyes but crouched beside the dog. "I need all the friends I can get," he murmured as he untied the rope.

The sun pushed through the heavy foliage of the forest like the rays of heaven. Mona marveled at the song of a pine and birch forest—the whisper of a gentle wind tickling the trees, the occasional drill of a woodpecker, and the chirp of a wren nesting high in a poplar. The scent of balsam and moss drew through her like a cleansing breath.

Mona stopped often as they treaded up the path, simply to inhale the forest fragrance. In the distance, the roar of the waterfall sang, beckoning, promising a breathtaking view of God's awesome creation. Ten paces in front of her, Joe weaved through the forest in silence, perhaps enjoying the peace as well.

Brian and Liza lingered together in the back, chatting. Joe had let Rip loose, his bark long ago swallowed by foliage. Mona climbed the last bit of a steep rise, breathing heavier than she would have liked. When she reached the top, the trail opened, and below her perhaps fifty feet, the Devil's Kettle roared in all its ferocity and potency.

Mona leaned on a rough-hewn safety rail and peered over the edge. There were other spectacular views, both from above the Kettle and from an extension bridge they'd passed on the climb up, but this view revealed the mouth of the Kettle, where the rutted granite swallowed the water and anything that swept along with it. Mona shivered, reliving the feelings of childhood.

"Awesome, huh?" Joe leaned on a pole, his arms crossed against his chest, wrinkling his navy-and-green-plaid flannel shirt. Mona turned, nodding. A layer of russet whiskers peeked from his cheeks, framing his warm smile, and joy swam in his eyes. The wilderness was definitely his element.

His smile dimmed, grew rueful. Eyes down, he toed the dirt with his scuffed hiking boots. "I was thinking, Mona . . . maybe today isn't the day to race across the river. It seems higher than normal, and it probably isn't safe."

"What?" Mona clamped her hands on her hips, looking indignant. "I plan on showing you women can not only skip rocks better than men, but we can also walk on water!"

She was rewarded with a crooked grin that made her stomach flip-flop.

"Right," he said. "Well, you can always change your mind. I'll take a rematch."

"Nothing doing," Mona countered. "I'll go swimming before I let you win."

His brows arched, and his eyes twinkled as if that idea pleased him. Mona sent him a fake glare. She hadn't had this much fun with a fella since . . . oh, truth be told, never.

"Who's going swimming?" Liza appeared, then leaned over and gripped her knees, breathing hard.

"Nobody," Joe answered, his eyes piercing Mona's. They'd dropped their teasing quality and taken on an edge of seriousness.

Mona turned back to the Kettle, wondering if it could swallow people and, if it did, where they'd end up.

"This is nothing! I thought you wanted me to do something dangerous." Mona hid a grin and saw Joe's eyes reflect a hint of annoyance.

She turned back to the bridge of stepping-stones, gauging their sturdiness. They were far above the Kettle, nearly a half mile, and the stones cut a path through what she guessed was a knee-deep portion of the river. Hissing twenty-five feet from her perch, a narrow waterfall dropped about fifteen feet into a pool below. The river picked up from the base of the falls, rushing with increasing intensity over boulders and juts until it spilled into the Kettle. The thought made her jaw tighten, but she wasn't going to let Joe win. Not after seeing him lose last night. His frustration was too precious.

Mona stood up. "So how do we play this?"

Joe rubbed his chin. "I don't know. I'm still not convinced this is safe."

"You're the chicken now."

Joe turned and considered her. She met his worried expression with a dour face. He shrugged. "Okay. You win. We'll race across. But I'm taking you at your word. No swimming." He smiled, but the worry remained in his eyes.

"No swimming, I promise." Mona held up three fingers.

"Okay. We count to twenty, slowly. You have to get across the river and back before we finish."

"Piece of cake!" Mona turned, rubbing her hands together.

"Wait. Let me go first so I can check the rocks. It's been a while since I've done this."

She stepped back, eyes narrowed.

"Please?"

She shrugged and held out her hands. "Be my guest."

Joe stooped, measuring out his trail. Liza sat down on the rocks, grinning. A stiff wind lifted Joe's baseball cap from his head, and he twisted erratically to clamp it back.

Mona laughed. "Is that a dance, Joe?"

He shot her a glare, but the crooked grin in its wake gave him away. Then he whirled and sprang for the first step. He landed on a large, rounded boulder, crouching to grip the edge and keep from falling backward.

"It's cold water!" Mona hollered.

He stood up, wobbling, and scrambled along the row of tiny rocks, barely skimming the top of the water. He resembled a ballerina dancing on his tiptoes over the water, and Mona clapped a hand over her mouth to keep from laughing aloud, completely forgetting to count. His last step was a giant leap to a long flat rock. He landed cleanly, doing a slight jig on its base.

"Okay, wiseacre, now come back," Mona called.

"Don't forget to count!"

"One!" Mona yelled over the river song. She raced through the numbers, fighting giggles.

Joe made the return dance easily before she reached ten. "Now, it's your turn," he said to Mona, his hands on his knees. His eyes sparkled with challenge, and it lit determination in her heart, not to mention what it did to her pulse.

"No!" Brian's voice brought them up short. "I'm next."

Before Mona could stop him, Brian jumped onto the first stone. His shiny black boots were a poor match for the slippery rocks, and Mona grimaced as she watched him dunk his feet into the water. He moved awkwardly over the stones and by the time he reached the other side, his pant legs were wet to his thighs. Undaunted, he climbed the flat rock and gave a movie-star wave. Mona noticed that Liza returned it like an ecstatic fan.

"I'm going to wait here till Mona comes!" Brian called. "Send her over."

Joe's concerned expression returned.

"C'mon, Joe. I grew up here. I'm not going to go in the drink."

"Have at it, Skipper," he said, forcing a breezy tone and doffing his hat.

Mona stepped up to the shore, rocked on her feet, then jumped for the rounded boulder. It was higher than she expected and she clawed the sides, fighting a momentary terror. Scrambling successfully aboard, she surveyed the remaining rocks. None of them appeared sturdy enough to hold her for long. The river skimmed over two of them, wetting their jagged edges like tiny black blades.

Hearing Joe yell, "Three," Mona gulped and leaped.

The river licked her feet as she danced across, but she kept going, and the other shore approached quickly. Two more rocks, then the final leap. She skipped across and hurled herself into the air, aiming for the long flat rock.

Just as she was about to land, a dark blur whizzed across her face. Wincing, she lost sight of the rock, fell against the hard edge, and landed in the water. The icy arms of the river pulled her down. Water crested over her head.

A million needles pierced her skin. Shocked, she inhaled and choked. A rock slammed into her hip. She pushed frantically against it, and her head broke the surface. "Help!"

The current grabbed her. She tumbled down the river, battling to get her feet ahead of her. The river fought back. It twisted her mercilessly. Hearing her name, she sought the shore. She spotted Joe racing over the rocks. He waved his arms, white-faced, frantic. She gritted her teeth, rolled over, and struggled to swim. The cold stole her strength.

Her hands scraped bottom. A stone ripped the flesh from her wrinkled fingers. Gasping, she drank more water. Then she felt the grip of the waterfall yank her toward its mouth. It hissed in her ears.

Joe's horrified expression was the last thing she saw before she went over.

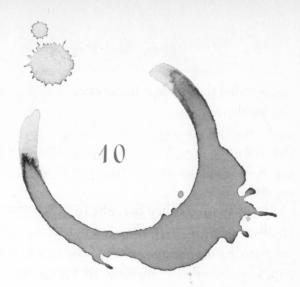

10

Terror grabbed Joe when he saw Mona fall into the water. He shot a dark look at Brian, who still had his hand outstretched. He'd seen the guy reach out to grab her, miss, and knock her off balance. It was all Brian's fault.

But as Joe raced downstream, yelling at Mona to grab a branch, a rock, anything, he knew the fault was his. She floundered about in the Kettle's icy grip because he had goaded her into playing his game. His pulse thundered as dread propelled him along the rocky shoreline. "Get your feet under you!"

Liza ran behind him, screaming.

He stumbled down the riverbank, praying he'd reach Mona before she was swept over the falls. Mona flailed in the water, fighting like a banshee, but the river tossed her at will. His foolishness whipped his heart when he glimpsed her panicked face. *Oh, God, please help her!*

He screamed her name one last time before she pitched over the falls. He didn't think beyond that, reacted on instinct. Racing to the top of the falls, he plunged into the pool several feet behind Mona. He came up, already digging into the current. From her pale, stricken face, he knew she'd swallowed a dangerous amount of water. She spotted him and called out weakly.

"Swim!" Joe lunged toward her, riding the swift current. He narrowed the gap between them, but they were eating up the mile toward the Kettle at a rapid clip. She slammed against the rocks; her face grimaced in pain.

"Fight, Mona!" He touched her jacket. The river yanked it away.

Bursting to life, she kicked toward the shore, reaching for low-hanging saplings and underbrush. Her grabs, while they didn't hold, slowed her down.

Joe tumbled past her and managed to snare a root jutting over the water. His feet swung around with the current. He propped them against a sturdy underwater boulder.

A second later Mona slammed into his chest. He curled a steel arm around her waist and pinned her frigid body against him. The river fought him, trying to wrench her from his grasp, but he refused surrender and gripped the root like a vise.

"Mona, turn around and grab the root." Although clearly exhausted, Mona groaned and reached out. He kept his arm around her body, and his legs were iron against the current, despite its fury. "Now, pull yourself up and climb onto shore."

She strained to break free of the current. He tried to help, lifting her as best he could. A spasm of coughing

ripped through her body. He winced, feeling her tremble, but her determination amazed him. She seized the
root while her legs scrambled for footing.

"C'mon, you can do it." His skin felt numb from the
icy lick of the river. Mona's lips were blue. Slipping on
the muddy, unstable rocks, she cried out in panic. Joe
steadied his footing and caught her as she tumbled backward. "I'm right here, Mona," he said into her ear. "I'm
not going anywhere."

He heard her moan as she grabbed again for shore.
Hand over hand, she climbed onto the mossy, rooted
bank.

Finally, she sank into an exhausted ball in the weeds.
Joe clambered up after her. Her teeth chattered and she
shivered violently. Joe wrapped his arms around her and
pulled her to him. "Are you hurt?" He feared the answer.

She shook her head. Joe closed his eyes, relief pouring
through him in fierce tremors. *Thank You, Lord.* He'd
caught sight of the Kettle opening a mere fifty yards
from their perch.

Mona settled her head on his chest. He heard her
hiccup, felt her shudder; then she began to weep. His
heart ripped open as he held her, burying his cheek in
her sodden hair.

Mona clung to Joe, fisting her hand in his soggy shirt,
and let her fear seep out in giant sobs. She hadn't known
terror like that for years. As she'd raced downriver, she
relived the horror of feeling life slip out of control and
hope slide through her grip. She'd been down her own

dark kettle, not the Devil's Kettle, but a terrifying place nonetheless, and she had no desire to repeat it.

As her sobs subsided, she became aware of Joe's arms around her, the tender, steady way he held her without comment. A husky male scent mingled with the smell of the river embedded in his soggy clothes. He rested his cheek against her head, and as she relaxed into his embrace, she felt his heartbeat thundering through his chest. His breath came in heavy gusts.

He'd risked his life to save her.

Locked safely in his grip, a sense of peace overwhelmed her, a feeling different from the tingle from his earlier embrace. This one comforted, protected. She didn't fight it, and for a brief moment she sank into it, grateful for his presence.

"Mona!" Liza's terrified voice sliced the air. Mona heard the echo of branches breaking on the other side of the river.

Pulling back, Mona glanced up at Joe. He caught her with his piercing blue-eyed gaze. Her mouth grew dry at the emotions written in his expression.

"Th-they're searching for us," she stammered.

Joe nodded but didn't loosen his hold. Biting her lip, she wiggled out of his arms. As she climbed to her feet, the world began to spin. She grabbed for a branch; her hand closed around air. She pitched forward.

Joe's strong arm snaked around her waist. He pulled her back into his arms. "Are you okay?"

She avoided his probing eyes. "Yes, just a bit dizzy, that's all."

She heard her name again, then spied Liza and a blurry Brian crashing through the woods on the oppo-

site side of the river. She waved, steadying herself on Joe's muscled arm. "Over here!"

Liza's relief was vivid, even from a distance. Brian emerged from the forest a step behind Liza, his face creased with worry. He waved to her. Liza cupped her hands around her mouth. "We'll meet you at the bridge!"

Mona gave her a thumbs-up. They would meet at the extension bridge that crossed the river below the Kettle. "Guess we're bushwhacking," she said to Joe as she stepped out of his arms. He wore a strange expression on his face but nodded. She felt his hand wrap gently around her elbow as they set off down the shore.

"Don't even say it," Mona muttered fifteen minutes later as she climbed over a fallen birch. She folded her arms across her chest, pressing back a violent chill. Goose bumps layered her skin, and it didn't help that the wind suddenly decided to whistle through the forest on a nippy lash of northern exposure. Her cold jeans chafed her skin, and her hair felt plastered in thick chunks to her head. *I must look adorable.*

"Don't say what?" Joe's voice was solemn, his face grim. He'd finally loosened his grip from her arm, yet walked close enough to steady her if the world should go Tilt-A-Whirl again. He'd said nothing as they passed by the Kettle. Her own fear—and the realization of what might have been—muted her into profound gratefulness.

"Don't say that you won."

Joe stopped, gripped her arm again, and turned her to face him. "I wouldn't even dream it." Guilt weighed in his eyes. "This is all my fault, Mona. I'm so sorry."

Mona blinked in surprise. She jutted her chin out.

"Hardly. I distinctly recall you trying to talk me out of crossing the river."

"I should have insisted."

"Like you could stop me? I have my own mind, and I remember turning of age a while back. I am perfectly capable of making my own decisions. I think I know what I can and cannot handle."

Joe's eyes flashed. "That's quite clear."

"Are you saying I don't know what I am doing?"

"I just think you let yourself get in over your head without realizing it. And I, being the one who *did* see it, should have stopped you."

Mona sighed. "Give up, Joe. I don't need you baby-sitting me. I'm a big girl—"

"—and you don't depend on anyone but yourself, I know!" He threw his hands up in surrender and turned his back to her.

Shock silenced her. She stared at him, saw him clasp his hands behind his neck, and pull deep breaths. Her anger dissolved, watching him wrestle with his own. She deliberately softened her voice. "I'm sorry, Joe. I know I tend to do things myself." She rubbed her hands over her arms. "But I will admit it—you saved me." She offered a rueful grin.

He peeked over his shoulder. "God saved you. I just played along."

She bit her lip, weighing his words. God *had* saved her. Again. Her eyes brimmed with tears at the knowledge. Another undeserved rescue by the Almighty. Somehow she dredged up her voice. "I can't believe you actually jumped into the falls."

He turned, a begrudging smile curling his lips. "Well,

that was the only way to keep up with you. I didn't know you were serious about going swimming today."

Mona laughed, and it was easy to find comfort in his teasing expression. It made her want to play along. His friendship suddenly felt warm, a safe refuge for her battered emotions. "I don't suppose you want to race to the bridge?" she suggested in a roguish tone.

Joe shook his head. "I've had enough racing for today."

A woodpecker drilled not far away, and the thick foliage whispered as the breeze stirred it. Her whole body tingled when he took her hand and led her through the forest. She decided it was due to the fresh river wind.

Liza was leaning over the bridge, scanning the other side of the river with pensive dark eyes, when Mona and Joe finally emerged from the trail. Tears accompanied her exclamations of relief as she ran to Mona and embraced her. Joe released Mona's hand, feeling well the absence of its warmth. He ran a hand through his wet hair. Civilization never seemed so attractive.

Brian walked up behind Liza and gave Joe a piercing look. "Good thing you caught her," he said, his voice sharp.

Joe bit back accusing words. It wouldn't do any good to attack the guy in front of Mona and Liza. But he had to swat away visions of wrapping Brian's smug smile backward around his face. He'd tried to shy away from brawls since his schoolyard days when he'd gotten enough practice defending Gabe. Joe blew out a hot breath and turned away.

"Get me out of these wet clothes," Mona moaned.

"I don't know. The drenched-puppy look becomes you." Liza's cheery voice teased, easing the horror of the afternoon's near tragedy.

Joe spun around. "Where's Rip?"

Liza gave him a blank look. Brian shrugged.

Joe walked to the center of the bridge, cupped both hands around his mouth, and called Rip's name. The river roared in reply. He whistled, called again. No answering bark. Great. He'd left his dog in the woods. Some owner he was. Indictment screamed inside him—he was always abandoning someone.

Mona came up beside him. "He'll show up, Joe. Keep calling." She must have read his desperation, for she turned upriver and called Rip's name. The action warmed him. So, she secretly liked Rip.

They hollered for Rip as they hiked the rest of the way down the trail, but Joe's hope sank lower with each step. In the Kettle parking lot, Brian's black Honda cooked in the low afternoon sun, and Joe couldn't help but notice his truck looked like the wreck of the *Hesperus* next to it. For some reason, the comparison made him grimace. He'd been proud of the forest green clunker until now.

Trudging toward his wheels, he wondered if Mona would be riding back with him. She and Liza had ridden up with Brian. The refined hoodlum in black threads had forbidden the Lab to ride in his car, so Joe had followed in his truck. He wasn't relishing the thought of a long, quiet ride home to relive the mistakes of the day.

He stalked to the cab, paused, and was about to holler for Rip a final time, when a pool of brown fur in

the bed of the truck caught his attention. Relief washed
through him seeing Rip, deep in slumber. Joe scratched
him behind his ear, and the Lab instantly sprang to his
feet, bathing his master in liquid kisses.

"You found him!" Mona exclaimed.

Joe appreciated the relief in her eyes. "The guy wore
himself out, I guess."

"Too many squirrels in this forest."

Joe nodded and reached for the door handle.

"Can I ride with you?"

Do birds fly? "Sure."

Joe caught Liza's smirk as Mona climbed into the
truck. He chose to ignore her.

The ride home was long. The warm truck cab magni-
fied his weariness, and sleep lay like sandbags on Joe's
eyelids. The river had sucked the strength from his
bones.

Mona lay slumped against the door, eyes closed. She
looked exhausted and beautiful, with her hair drying in
golden tendrils around her face. Her windbreaker was
glued to her arms and torso, and she had to be uncomfortable in her sodden jeans. But a slight smile played
on her lips, belying her misery. Something turned in his
heart. The trip wasn't a total loss. He had that smile as
a keepsake—and the delicious memory of her nestled in
his arms, unloading her fear into his chest. He wanted to
hold her forever and decided he would, no matter where
he went.

By the time they rolled into Deep Haven, the sun was
a steadily falling crimson ball flecked with orange. It lit
the clouds over Lake Superior red-gold, and they seemed
tufted against the sky. The energetic lake was throwing

itself in mighty white heaves against the jagged shoreline, and seagulls layered the far lighthouse like a gray-
and-white blanket. Someone had tossed a box of meat
scraps on shore, and another gang of greedy gulls
screamed and fought each other for the morsels.

Joe drove slowly along Main Street. The gas line at
Mom and Pop's gas and groceries stretched a half mile
as pickups with trawler boats and camping gear, headed
for the northern lakes, filled up their extra tanks. The
convenience store would be sporting a full till this
evening, by the looks of the patrons lugging out bulging
bags of supplies, gas cans, and boxes of live bait. Joe
realized with a start that fishing season had opened.
Maybe he should ask Gabe if he would like to catch
some walleye with him. Would his brother know how?
If not, maybe he could teach him and be the big brother
he should have been.

World's Best Donuts had closed for the day. The dime
store, however, pushed back the approaching twilight
with a pale yellow light, holding out for the last few
anglers. Joe wondered what it would be like living in
this slow, sleepy tourist town during the winter, when
the boom of vacation season died. He envisioned sitting
with Mona in the Footstep, warming their feet in front
of a wood-burning stove, cups of coffee perched on the
stumps she had varnished. The idea embraced him, and
he was afraid of how much he liked it.

Mona stirred next to him, rubbed her eyes, and sat up.

"Almost home," he said. *Home.* He hadn't had a
home in fifteen years, and now he was calling the Footstep home? A sense of panic hit him. What was he
thinking? He had a life to live outside Deep Haven,

a world to experience. His home had no borders, and until now, he'd been perfectly content with that. He wasn't searching for a place to live. He had his back-pack, and now Rip. That was the only home and family he needed.

Joe gritted his teeth and pulled up to the drive. "Back to your place."

An hour later Joe had peeled off his wet clothes, taken a hot shower, and changed into his Rip-torn jeans, wool socks, and a Texas A & M sweatshirt. All his other clothes were filthy. He'd have to find the local Laundro-mat tomorrow.

Armed with a hot cup of decaf and a ham sandwich, he set the plate on a backless caned chair and settled into the sofa. He knew he should be fleshing out ideas for what he'd seen today—opportunities to get back into the good graces of his employers, tidbits that could pan out into treasures. But something about the way Mona had clung to him, trusting him with her pain as if he were already a part of her life and her world, gave him pause.

Perhaps this wasn't the right place, the right time. Maybe he'd chance going back empty-handed, and if he paid the price, then perhaps Mona wouldn't have to. Maybe she'd never have to answer probing questions or wonder at his motives. Maybe he could leave in his wake just the memory of a man who'd rescued her from the Devil's Kettle and helped her scrape together her dreams.

He rather liked the idea of being, rather than play-acting, a hero. He rifled through his backpack and dug out a creased paperback. He'd read Louis L'Amour's

Last of the Breed at least a dozen times, but he never tired of reading the story of a fighter pilot lost in the Siberian wilds.

Joe was somewhere in the Yablonovy Mountains when a loud rap jerked him back to reality. "Enter," he called, laying a thumb over his last sentence.

The door opened and Mona leaned in on the knob. "I'm doing laundry. If you want, you can do a load after I'm finished."

"Just in time. I thought I might have to wear my long johns to church tomorrow."

Mona rested her shoulder against the doorjamb and folded her arms across her chest. "Going to church?"

Joe nodded.

"Where?"

Caught. He fell into the snare without a thought. He'd been invited by Ruby to worship at the Garden. "Um, at a church north of here."

"Up the Gunflint Trail?"

Joe calculated his answer. The road leading to the Garden strayed off the old, half-paved logging trail that stretched north from Deep Haven to the shores of Minnesota's boundary lakes. "Yes. It's off the Gunflint."

"Oh, you must mean Gunflint Chapel," she said. "We've worshiped there a few times. Cute chapel and the pastor is really nice." She paused. "At least the pastor who served there ten years ago. I liked how he led worship in his moccasins."

Joe raised his eyebrows. That sounded like a church he might enjoy. He hadn't spent much time in formal fellowship, preferring to spend his Sundays with his Bible open in nature's lap, listening to the birds sing

their praises and letting his heart hum along. But actual voices raised in praise had a joyous effect on him, and on occasion he longed for the oneness of corporate worship.

"Well," Mona continued, "I attend Grace Church, just up the road. You're welcome to join me if you'd like."

Joe folded his book on his lap, dog-earing the page. "Thanks, maybe some other time."

Mona frowned. "Are you reading?"

Joe smirked at her expression. "A man's been known to do that now and again. Don't tell anybody. I'd hate to let out our secret—that we're actually above primates in the evolutionary scale."

Mona giggled, and it cheered him to hear it, especially after the day's harrowing events. "What are you reading?"

Joe flexed an arm muscle. "A *man's* book." He held it up, and she made a sour face. "What, you don't like Louis L'Amour?"

She shrugged. "Let's just say I don't think a man has to wear a six-gun to be a hero."

"Well, what do you read?"

"Adventure, romance, intrigue. I love to read."

"Who's your favorite author?"

"Reese Clark."

The name knocked the wind out of him. "You like *him?*"

She wiggled her brows. "Actually, I'm in love with Jonah, his main character."

"Why?"

"Because he's a real man." She turned and shut the door, leaving him to restrain the strange leaping of his heart.

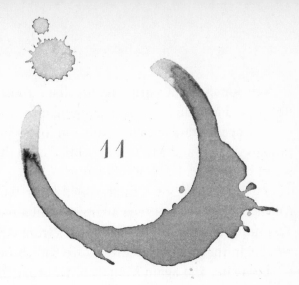

11

Mona hummed as she dug out the dirty clothes from her closet and tossed them into a laundry basket. She'd had to empty the basket of a stack of old books, and as she did, she couldn't help but open a few and dive into her favorite chapters. Thus, sorting laundry took over an hour.

She piled the stack of Reese Clark novels next to her bed, intending to reread them soon. Her words to Joe rung in her ears. *Jonah is a real man.* Not that Joe didn't have some of these utterly "real man" qualities—a tender streak that showed itself every time he wrestled with Rip and a protective nature that drove him into a frigid river to save her.

But Jonah was safer. Jonah always, without question, was honorable. He always let the heroine win, never stood in her way yet stood beside her. He never let his ladylove suffer, he never betrayed her heart, and he would never, ever leave her. It was always the women doing the leaving in the Reese Clark books.

Poor Jonah. It all started on his first adventure, when he worked as a dude rancher dodging unruly cattle and a nasty head wrangler. He'd fallen in love with the ranch's owner, and Mona had sobbed onto the pages when his love had died in his arms.

In Clark's next book, she traveled south with Jonah to Mexico, where he saved a family from a flash flood and stopped a ring of drug smugglers from destroying a village. In the end, his Mexican love had chosen another for her mate, and again Mona's heart broke for her favorite character.

In *Alaska Abyss,* which she bought in hardback, Jonah sailed ship north and hired onto a salmon-boat crew in Alaska. After weathering a gale-force storm, her favorite hero hiked Mount Denali and saved an Inuit woman from hypothermia. But when she left him behind for her village in the Arctic Circle, Mona was secretly delighted.

In *Berlin Crossing* she had devoured the story of Jonah in Germany, where he watched the Wall crumble and helped a lady from East Germany find her family and true love on the Western side, again leaving Jonah with his heart in his hands.

By the time Jonah herded reindeer in *Siberian Runaway,* Mona was openly thrilled he hadn't found a woman to win his love. That only meant more Jonah books—more adventures across the world, more opportunities to find the right lady.

Mona had preordered *Canadian Catastrophe* months ago and planned a prominent display space in her bookstore. It was due to hit the shelves in a month.

Mona sighed as she propped the laundry basket on

her hip and treaded down the stairs. Liza's accusation smacked of truth—Jonah was her dream man. In her mind's eye, she conjured up his description—short hair, delicious blue eyes, and an embracing smile.

Mona skidded to a halt in the kitchen. She'd just described Joe! Her heart tumbled through her chest, and she battled the thought. Joe was an irresponsible drifter with no real goals. So what that he acted as if her dreams mattered to him? He pushed her to her last nerve with his goofball antics and his I-can-do-anything-better-than-you-can smirk. Joe was anything but Jonah. Joe might be flesh and blood, but only Jonah could hold her heart without breaking it.

She closed her eyes, fighting the image of Joe as she prayed. *God, I know You've provided Joe for now, but please help me not to see more in him than what he is. Help me to look upward at Your plan for my life and not get entrapped by the petty longings of my heart.*

She opened her eyes and breathed deeply, feeling calm take root in her heart.

The rotting cellar door creaked when she opened it. The damp, dust-laden air filtered into her nose and Mona stifled a sneeze. These catacombs of her home made her flesh crawl. Groping the wall, she found a light switch and flicked it on. The grimy overhead bulb lit a dim orange trail down the stairs. Mona squinted into the shadows, gauging her steps. The floor seemed muddy in the hazy lighting, not quite solid. Frowning, Mona eased down the stairs.

Her confusion slowly metastasized into horror.

The floor of her home *was* mud.

A lake of water, ankle high, filled the basement.

Rotting wood, cement chips, dirt, and scum floated along the floor. Standing two steps from the bottom, she watched ripples lap at her feet and gripped the flimsy rail to keep from collapsing. Where was the flood coming from? Was the house built on a swamp? From her perch, she examined the murky cellar, searching for a leak. A dark gray swath in the far cement wall seemed suspicious. She focused on it and made out a thin waterfall skimming over the top.

Mona flew up the stairs. Throwing her basket into the kitchen, she rushed outside, flicked on the backyard light, and sprinted around the house.

What she saw nearly buckled her knees. The garden hose had been left running under her lilac tree, gurgling for hours as she'd bounced down the Kettle River.

The sopping wet lawn glistened in the moonlight, and the foundation of the house was saturated. Mona squished through the grass, wading to the faucet. The whine and rush of water stopped as she cranked it shut, but fury coursed through her in a ferocious torrent. Joe! He was completely irresponsible, and now his foolishness had cost her a gigantic water bill and who knew how much in home repairs!

Anger took possession of her as she scrambled, fell, and scurried up the stairs to his garage apartment. She didn't bother to knock; it wasn't his place anyway. Bursting through Joe's door, her frustration peaked. He lay relaxing on the sofa, calmly reading a book while her life sank in a quagmire.

The expression on her face must have betrayed her emotions, for he sat up and went white. "What?"

She shook, rage devouring coherent thought. She

pointed at him, her finger shaking. "You! You let the water run! My basement is completely flooded!"

Joe jumped to his feet. "What? No, I didn't."

"Don't deny it. When I let you water my tree, I didn't know you were out to drown me!" She threw her hands in the air. "What am I going to do now? The foundation is probably ruined, the cellar is a swamp, and I have four weeks until opening. There's no way I can repair this." She closed her eyes, willing her pulse to a slower beat, her voice to a normal pitch.

"Mona, calm down. It'll be okay. I'll help you fix it. I'll work round the clock. . . . I'll even pay for it."

Mona opened her eyes and glared at him. "I don't want your help. I don't want your money. You're fired! Pack your bag and your measly dog and get out of here *tonight!*"

She whirled, grabbed the door handle, and slammed the door behind her. The building shuddered. She got as far as the bottom step. Sinking onto the hard wood, she buried her face in her hands and wept.

Joe scraped his hands through his hair, searching through the events of the day, desperate to make sense of Mona's accusation. Had he left the hose on? He closed his eyes, blew out a shaky breath. He'd been watering the poplar tree. Brian had arrived, and Rip smashed Liza's pottery. . . .

His jaw clenched. Brian! He'd handed the hose to Brian and hadn't touched it again. The weasel had left it running under the lilac tree. Anger blew through him. He trembled and closed his fists, wanting to stalk down the culprit and sop up the basement with his fancy leather jacket while he was still wearing it. *Help me calm down, Lord.* Joe unclenched his fists and blew out a hot breath. It would do no good to attack Brian. It would just show Mona he couldn't accept responsibility and would rather cast blame.

He trudged to the sofa and sank into it, anguish swamping him. Fired. Mona wanted him to leave. But without his help, she'd never piece the Footstep back together. Just like her blind determination to jump across the river despite the obvious perils, she was going to fire him without another helper in sight. Even if she did find another handyman, she would probably spend all her time following him, ordering him around. Maybe she'd even wander down to the beach with him and challenge him to a rock-skipping contest.

The thought made him burn. He leaped to his feet. No, he had to reason with her. For her own good, he had to stay.

He marched to the door and whipped it open. Determination fueled his steps, but he skidded to a halt on the landing, and his pounding heart skipped a beat. Mona sat at the bottom in a crumpled mass, weeping, her agony audible. He stifled a moan and tiptoed down the stairs.

Wordlessly, he sat down next to her on the steps. She had her arms wrapped over her head, and her entire body shook. She tried to contain her sobs, but they hiccupped from her tiny frame. His heart wrenched, watching her emotions bleed. Tentatively, he curled an arm around her. After a moment, she leaned her head

against his chest. She sounded so broken, it brought
tears to his eyes. He wanted to soothe the pain away,
tame her fears, and hold her until she could smile again.
He rested his cheek on her hair, his eyes burning.

When he felt her body stop racking, he cupped a hand
under her chin so her swollen, red eyes lifted to his. He
caressed her cheek with his thumb, smearing her tears.
"I'm not leaving, Mona. I am so sorry this happened,
but I am not going to leave you to chip away at these
massive repairs and watch your dream die. I'll even
work for free. I don't care what you say. I'm staying."

He saw argument, albeit weak, gather in her eyes. He
put a finger over her lips to silence her.

She hung her head. "I'm sorry, Joe. I shouldn't have
lost my temper."

"I forgive you." He wove his fingers through her hair.

Her chin quivered, and he saw a fresh batch of tears
glisten in her eyes. "I don't know what to do."

"I don't either. But we can pray and ask God for help.
I know He can rescue you and the Footstep."

To his profound surprise, she shook her head. "No.
That would be asking too much. Maybe God doesn't
want this to happen. He's probably using all these
repairs, even this catastrophe, to tell me to give up."

Joe frowned. "Why would God do that?"

She didn't meet his eyes. "Because I don't deserve His
help. I don't deserve this dream to come true."

Joe gently drew her gaze to his again. Her eyes were
tortured, and he recognized the familiar pain prowling
in them. "You don't believe that, do you?"

She shrugged, tears spilling.

"Mona, God isn't the great saboteur of dreams. He

doesn't give us a dream just to make it fail. He puts that dream inside us for a reason, and He wants to help make it happen."

"You don't understand. I don't deserve any of God's goodness. I wouldn't blame Him a bit if He yanked it all away."

Her hopeless words made Joe ache. He caressed her face, reaching out to her with his eyes. "Listen, the character of God is full of mercy—*not* giving us what we *do* deserve—and grace—giving us what we *don't* deserve. You say you don't deserve God's help, but by your very words, you prove He isn't trying to destroy your dreams. Ask God for help. If you don't think you deserve it, then perhaps that is exactly what God wants to delight you with, to show how much He loves you."

She frowned at him, biting her lip. Joe searched her face and saw only doubt. "Mona, have you ever heard this verse: 'Take delight in the Lord, and He will give you your heart's desires'? When we delight in Him, He wants to fill our lives with His love, with our deepest longings."

Her eyes filled, and he saw in them desperation, as if she were trying to comprehend his words. *Lord, what is keeping Mona from accepting Your love, Your grace, in her life?*

Mona's expression abruptly changed. Flicking her tears with both hands, she squinted at him. "So you're staying?"

The way she said it, her eyes flecking with hope, trust pitching her voice, entwined his heart. Suddenly all the reasons he had for leaving, or staying, were muted by one thought: he was falling for this lady, hard and fast.

"I'm staying," he affirmed softly. She smiled, and he couldn't stop himself. She looked so beautiful and needy, and the vulnerable way she gazed at him, as if longing to believe his words . . . it reeled him in. Cradling her face in his hands, he gently kissed her. Her soft lips tasted of salt, and she trembled at his touch. Her response was everything he'd hoped for, tender and yielding. He longed to linger, to pull her into his arms, but self-control forced him to draw back. He studied her face. "As long as I'm not still fired."

Shock washed over her beautiful face. Her eyes widened and she shook her head.

"Good," he whispered, "'cause Rip and I weren't looking forward to sleeping in the truck."

"Mona?" Liza's voice called from the house.

Mona pulled out of Joe's grasp and scrambled hastily to her feet. "Out here!" she answered. She breathed out, a shaky breath that spoke volumes for both of them.

What had he just done? Looking at her as she smoothed her hair and straightened her sweatshirt, her eyes not meeting his, his mouth went dry.

He'd just kissed Mona.

It was by far the sweetest kiss he'd ever shared. And he'd enjoyed it way more than a man without a future in Deep Haven should.

Liza banged through the back door. "There you are. What are you up to?" She braked, eyeing them quizzically. "Not working on house repairs, I see."

Joe gave Mona a tender smile. "Nope, other kinds of repairs."

The silence between them was accentuated by the gentle wind singing through the trees and waves combing the shore. Liza scrutinized the couple on the steps, grinning suspiciously, then went back inside. Mona rubbed her arms and stared at Joe. He saw her confusion and offered a reassuring smile, one that might calm both their racing heartbeats. "Good night, Mona."

She stuttered her reply. "G-good night, Joe. See you tomorrow." Then she bolted toward the house.

He lingered on the steps, remembering the hope in her eyes, feeling the touch of her lips, and pushing back not just a little panic. He had no business kissing her. Yet being near her unraveled his common sense and pushed him into the realm of hope. Mona trusted him. That thought made something thick and warm spread through him.

He buried his face in his hands. *Lord, I'm in big trouble here. This could really hurt.* The memory of her tear-streaked, incredible green eyes staring up at him as she clung to his words of assurance made his chest burn. Yes, he was definitely here to help Mona, as long as he remembered what was best for all of them—keeping a tight lock on his privacy. If he kept Gabe and Mona in separate worlds and a low profile himself, he just might be able to forget that he had a deadline looming. And he could throw himself into Mona's dreams—not forever, but long enough to remind himself what it felt like to have a place to call home, a dream worth building.

Joe watched Mona's light flick on in her room. He would stay until the job was done, but he was going to need a little help.

And please, oh please, Lord, make Mona's dreams come true.

Mona slammed her fist into her pillow, hoping to fluff it into a more comfortable position. But when she plopped her head back on it, she knew sleep was no closer than it had been three hours ago. Moonlight spilled through her window, streaking across the wood floor. The wind tugged at the trees, and the branches moved in quick, stilted jerks across the window. By the sound of the waves lunging at the shore, Mona guessed that a storm front was breezing in. Or maybe the storm she sensed was only the turmoil in her heart.

She'd let Joe kiss her. So she'd been bereft, totally knocked off her feet by the horror in her basement. It didn't mean she had to go blubbering to her local handyman. He probably saw her for what she was— a desperately lonely woman who needed this dream more than anything in her life. He'd probably kissed her out of pity.

Except . . . it had been such a gentle, impossibly tender kiss, with his fingers lightly brushing the sides of her face and sending tingles down her spine. It didn't feel like a pity kiss—it felt more like what had been written in his eyes when he'd dragged her out of Devil's Kettle. Emotions she couldn't possibly put a name to if she wanted to keep her focus. Emotions that were building in her own heart. Ones she'd have to exorcise—and fast. This accident was a case in point. Joe had surprised her with his charm, and in a weak moment, she'd allowed herself to trust him and stopped hawking his every move.

Now, not only was her house floating on a virtual

lake, her heart was poised to be crushed. It would do her well to remember that Joe was a drifter. He was leaving in four weeks, if not sooner, and if she wasn't careful, he would be taking her heart with him.

Her throat grew raw. Did she want to destroy everything she had worked so hard for? Mona sat up, swung her legs off her bed, and let the cold floor jolt the soft image of Joe and his glistening blue eyes radiating concern from her mind.

The Joe Michaels package was definitely alluring. She couldn't deny she enjoyed his company, his teasing laughter, and his ocean-deep eyes. And she was profoundly grateful for his hard work. But she couldn't surrender to his charisma. God was giving her so much with the Footstep dream. She simply couldn't add love to her list of requests.

The desires of her heart. Joe had no idea the thoughts *those* words produced. She shuddered, reluctant to unlock her heart, her dreams, even for her own private investigation. Desires—like the success of her bookstore. Desires—like a man to share her home, her dream with. Or how about her craziest dream—that Jonah would walk off the pages of Reese Clark's books and into her arms? She chuckled ruefully. Some desires were beyond even God.

Still, Joe's words stung. Not because he wasn't right but because they would never, ever be for her. Why would the Almighty grant even one, let alone three dreams for a woman who'd killed someone she loved?

Forgiveness was enough. It would always be enough. Her desires would stay safely locked away where they wouldn't hurt a soul.

Her throat closed and she padded to the window seat, curled inside, and buried her face in her knees. *Oh, Lord, I'm sorry I let this happen—I should have watched Joe better. Please forgive me. You've given me this house, and I know it's a gift from You. Please give me another chance to make the Footstep happen. I promise to keep far away from Joe if You'll just help me pull this house together. Don't let it all crumble, please.*

Cold tears swabbed her face, and hair clung to her wet cheeks. The storm breakers hurtled onto shore as Mona rocked herself, reliving years of grief and wondering if she would ever break the bonds of sorrow.

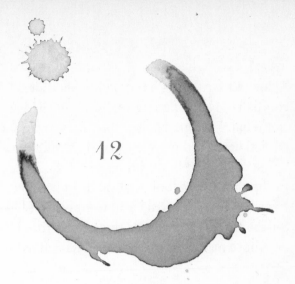

12

$\mathcal{J}$oe found Mona in her rumpled church dress, sitting cross-legged in the hallway. The phone lay in her lap, and she wore the most mournful expression he had ever seen. He hunkered down beside her. "What's the matter?"

Mona bit her trembling lip and shook her head.

Joe's heart twisted. She looked brutal this morning—puffy red eyes, sallow face. And when he'd greeted her with a smile, she merely offered a grimace in return. Obviously she'd had a hard night. He measured out a soft tone. "Please, tell me."

Mona's voice sounded weak. "The insurance company can't come until next week. Why did I have to find a company with the nearest branch office in Minneapolis?" She covered her face with her hands.

Joe pinched his lips together, debating whether or not to reveal his morning's activities. The yawning rumble behind him in the front yard made his decision.

Mona jerked her head up. "What's that?"

Joe put a calming hand on her shoulder. "The septic company. They're going to clean out the basement."

"What?" Mona banged the phone onto the floor and hauled herself to her feet. "I didn't call them."

Joe stood and braced himself. "I did."

She shot him a look that made him wince. "I can't afford it, Joe, especially a weekend call. I have to wait for the insurance adjuster to arrive before I can spend one more nickel on this place." She stalked toward the door.

He followed her, keeping his voice low-key. "I'm paying for it."

She whirled; if she had fur and claws he would have thought her a grizzly. "Oh no you're not. I already owe you more than I can ever repay. You're working for peanuts, and I don't need your charity."

Joe buried his hands in his pockets and examined his scuffed shoes. How to make her understand? "Well, maybe this whole thing is my fault. Maybe I *did* leave the hose on." He offered an apologetic grin. "The least I could do is pay for it."

She glowered at him, but her fury lost steam. He saw her turning over the words in her mind, and her eyes flickered with an unknown emotion. Relief? Thankfulness? Anger? Joe didn't want to know. He took a step closer to her. "Please let me help you, Mona. I don't want to see your dreams crumble."

She went white, and in her eyes rose a desperation so vivid it masked all other emotions. He wanted to hold her then, like he had last night on the porch, and like he did in his dreams. He wanted to smooth her hair and surround her with reassurance. At that moment he

didn't care if his heart might be stripped in the process. The longing for her to reach out to him, to trust him with her hopes, made his chest ache. What had happened to all that trust that had budded last night on his steps? Not a trace of it remained in those tortured eyes. Couldn't she just let him help, a little bit, without making it seem like a federal crime?

Her next words drove a cold fist through those thoughts. "It's a loan. I'll pay you back if I have to wash dishes in some greasy truck stop for the rest of my life." Then she hustled outside, putting distance between them like a wide receiver pulling away from the pack.

Cee

The sewer-truck hose snaked through the front foyer, along the wood floor that thankfully she hadn't polished yet, through the kitchen, and down the back stairs. Mona listened to the loud pumps slurp up water and scowled as the truck's tires plowed wide swaths into her front lawn.

The sight of a city septic truck at a Main Street business attracted a swarm of onlookers, and Mona spent most of the afternoon fielding mindless questions and meeting neighbors. It seemed everyone wanted to know why the old Victorian was leaking.

Edith Draper surveyed the scene like a general, standing on the porch with her arms folded across her chest, her nylon-clad legs pushed into sensible shoes under blue polyester stretch pants. Her eyes stayed pinned to the long plastic tube running across the porch. Mona stood next to her, thankful for her stalwart presence.

Edith muttered something under her breath. The truck's motor gobbled up the words.

"What did you say?"

Edith raised her voice and leaned close. "I said, no wonder Brian didn't want to pay much for this house. He must have known about the leak in the foundation."

Mona looked at Edith. "It wasn't a leak. Joe left the hose on. But back to the part about Brian paying for this place—what are you talking about?"

Edith adjusted the hem of her pink acrylic sweater. "Brian Whitney. This was his grandmother's house. When she died, her will instructed the family to sell it and divide it equally. Brian put in a bid for the entire house, but it couldn't match your bid, so he lost it. I'm sure he received a portion of the proceeds, however."

Mona felt sick. Why hadn't Brian mentioned anything? He must have been assaulted by memory every time he walked into her home. Pity pierced her heart. Poor man, losing his grandmother's home just because he couldn't top her offer. No wonder he always seemed slightly jumpy when he was around her, always trying to impress her with his slick car and fancy duds, as if trying to keep his dignity. At least he was making the attempt to befriend her.

Her gaze traveled to Joe, and she watched him talk to a maintenance man. His hands were in his back pockets, and he rocked back and forth from heel to toe. He'd done a kind thing for her, and she'd treated him with all the warmth of a porcupine. If only he didn't have eyes that reached right into her soul or words that found the soft spot in her heart, where they could twist and rip and scar.

After this morning, she longed to trust him with her dreams. But how could she count on a man whose worldly possessions consisted of a ratty duffel bag and a sad mutt? The man looked poised to bolt every time he returned from one of his mysterious outings. She often wondered if the roar of his rattletrap truck leaving the Footstep would be the last thing she ever heard from him.

Brian might have all the charm of a largemouth bass, but he was sticking around for the long haul, despite his pain. He was a friend she could count on. Joe, however, was a supernova in her life—dazzling her blind for a moment before he fizzled out and all went dark.

The air smelled wet, and along the dark horizon something sinister gathered in the black rolling clouds. The choppy lake water peaked white, and angry waves threw foam high onto shore. A greedy wind tugged at Joe's baseball cap. He scraped it off his head and threw it onto his sweatshirt, heaped on the sidewalk. Repositioning the shovel, he spaded another chunk of matted grass, chopped it up, and turned it over. The welts in the grass where the truck had settled for most of the day appeared fatal. But if he dug them up tonight and the approaching storm worked the soil, the ground would be fertile and ready for new sod in the morning. He wanted Mona's grass to be a beautiful, unscathed carpet by opening day.

Joe heard the front door open and glanced toward the house. Liza stood on the porch and held out a cup of coffee. Joe smiled and waved. "Just a second. I'll be right up." He had to admit, Liza's quirky humor and ready smile had softened all the rough, hard moments of the day. Joe was thankful for her calming presence.

For some unknown reason, Mona had spent the day dodging him. When they did talk, her remarks were clipped and cold, and he couldn't help wonder where the delightful, teasing Mona had gone. Had he been blind, living in a dream the past week? She hadn't even mentioned their kiss, avoided him like he had leprosy, and made it plain she wasn't going to get close enough to let him wrap his arms around her again.

Well, he couldn't blame her. And it was probably for the best—for both of them. A sour ball of regret settled in his chest. It hurt that she thought he had flooded her basement. But it was nice of her to let him stay on, even if he did pay for the sewage services. He knew she'd repay him if she had to sell the shirt off her back or her rusty Chevette, Noah. Why did she call it that? And why would a woman nearly thirty years old drive a beater she probably bought in high school? He couldn't believe the clunker still puttered along, although on the occasions he heard her drive it, he recognized the death coughs and fatal ticks of a car headed toward the junk heap.

Sacrifice. The Chevette screamed it. Mona was sacrificing everything to make her dream come true. Liza's words replayed in his head. *If it doesn't happen, I don't know what she'll do.* Why was this bookstore so important to her? What drove her?

Joe turned over the last shovel of grass, chopped it into chunks, and smoothed it out. He would rake it in

the morning. Shouldering the shovel, he swiped up his hat, plunked it on his head, grabbed his sweatshirt, and headed for the porch.

Liza sat on the top step, cradling a coffee mug. A wisp of steam curled off the surface. His stomach growled at the rich scent. Hearing it, Liza cracked a grin. "I don't think coffee's going to silence that monster."

Joe returned the smile and plopped down next to her. She handed him the warm mug. The drink soothed his tired bones. "Thanks, Liza."

She shrugged. "Actually—and don't tell Mona I told you—she made it and suggested I bring it out here."

"Really? I thought I rated lower than pond scum. I've been chilly all day from her frigid looks."

Liza laced a strand of her long black hair between her fingers, examining it. "I know she can be cold when she's frustrated and hurting. Give her a chance to get her feet back under her. She'll warm up."

Joe took another sip of coffee. "I hope so. I can't handle two storm fronts." He gestured at the lake and the approaching thunderheads.

Liza hummed agreement.

"Can you tell me something, Liza?"

"Maybe."

"Why does Mona call her car Noah?"

"How did you know that?"

Joe stared at the lake. "She must have mentioned it."

Liza rolled the hair around her fingers. "It's a long story, but suffice it to say she drove her car into a pond."

"What?"

Liza grinned. "Okay, I'll tell you the story, but you

have to promise, even under the vise of torture, never to reveal how you found out."

Joe crossed his fingers and held them in a salute.

"Okay." Liza flicked her hair back and leaned back on both her hands. "I think she was a junior in college. She was dating this fella, who, in my opinion, was trouble with a giant letter *T*. His name was Terrance. All brawn, no brains, and even now she isn't sure what she ever saw in him. Anyway, his car was broken and he called her one night during a downpour and asked her for a lift home from work. Her father warned her not to go out, but she was stubborn and didn't listen.

"The way she tells it, she made a left turn onto what was normally a road and found herself afloat in an ark, drifting toward the curb. She climbed out of the window, pushed her car to high ground, and hiked to Terrance's office. Her father had to bail them both out. The next morning, the sun was high and bright and baked the car like a fish on shore. She said she couldn't ride with the windows closed for three months." Liza giggled and her eyes danced with glee.

Joe shook his head, smirking. "No wonder her car is frosted in rust. Why didn't she buy a new one? That beater must be over ten years old."

Liza shook her head. "I'm not sure. Her dad bought her Noah, and maybe she just can't part with it. And she's always trying to save money, you know."

Joe sipped his coffee. "Her father sounds like a wise man. I'd like to meet him."

The seagulls screamed from the shore, a loud cacophony with the charging waves. He shivered.

"You can't," Liza said quietly. "He was killed ten years ago."

Downed branches and torn leaves littered the road to the Garden, the legacy of the previous night's tempest. Joe swerved his pickup around bottomless puddles, trying not to eject a stiff-legged Rip from the bench seat. The forest breath blew a pine scent through the truck cab's open window, and when the wind stirred the trees, droplets covered the windshield.

Joe's eyes burned and weariness dragged his shoulders down, although not because he'd already put in a full day's work. Unraveling the mystery behind Mona's haunted eyes made him toss the night away in sleepless eternity. Did it have something to do with her father's death? The news had made him want to weep. Joe knew what it meant to lose a father.

Just as disturbing was the sudden freeze emanating from Mona's side of their friendship. She all but hid from him yesterday, and his frustration with her fear tied him into knots. So they'd shared a kiss, one that he knew he should never repeat despite the fact it never drifted far from his thoughts. It didn't mean he was going to take her in his arms their first moment alone. In fact, he was pretty sure he had the internal fortitude to make sure it never happened again. Pretty sure.

It hadn't escaped him that the woman had wrung him out in the matter of a week. She'd drawn him in with her mischievous smile, let him splash about in her liquid green eyes, then spit him out into the cold world of rejection. He was feeling about as skinned and raw as the birch trees.

He'd spent the night listening to the storm slam against his windows and watching battered trees lurch in shadows across his ceiling. Sometime during the gale, he realized why he had always avoided anything complicated with the female persuasion. He didn't have the strength to endure the wounds and scrapes it took to let someone crawl inside his heart. Love required vulnerability, sharing secrets.

Eventually it would mean revealing Gabe.

And wouldn't that just drive a woman into his arms?

If Joe had inherited any abnormal chromosomes, the type that caused Gabe's Down syndrome, the possibility of his having such a child was a reality. Could a relationship survive the stress of a handicapped child? His parents' hadn't. Even if it could, Mona in particular had no room in her dream for a child, especially a child with special needs. No, letting Mona sneak into his heart was a pivotal mistake. The memory of her sweet lips only turned the blade. He thanked God that she had made it clear he would be job hunting in four weeks. He'd dodge her like a case of the flu, then sever the strings and never look back at the Footstep of Heaven.

Joe drove up slowly, his wheels sluggish in the mud near the porch.

Ruby sat in a rocking chair, reading a book in her lap. She glanced up, and he was warmed by her welcoming smile. She trotted down the stairs as he stepped from the cab. Rip spent an entire two seconds greeting her, then scrambled toward the woods, in search of playmates. "We missed you yesterday."

"Yup," Joe acknowledged. "I got tied up with a problem in town."

"Doing some business in Deep Haven?"

"Sort of." He looked past her. "Is Gabe around?"

Ruby squinted at him, then nodded. "In his room."

Joe took the porch stairs two at a time. He felt Ruby's eyes on him as he disappeared into the house. She knew way too much for his own good.

Gabe was sprawled on his bed, running his finger under the neatly printed words of a letter. His mouth moved as he read. Joe watched him for a moment, then greeted him from the door.

Gabe looked up, delight lighting his features. "Joe!" Joe could never get over the way the day brightened with Gabe's smile.

"What are you reading?" Joe hooked his thumbs onto his belt loops. A shadow crossed Gabe's face. He sat up and swung his feet onto the floor, holding the letter in both hands. The big, bold writing seemed familiar to Joe, and a jolt of pain ripped through him.

"A letter." Gabe's eyes focused on the carpet.

Joe's voice cracked in his parched throat. "From whom?"

"Dad."

"Really?" He felt weak as reality hit him square on. Ruby was right. Dad had been writing to Gabe. It took everything in him not to swipe the letter and tear it into pieces.

Gabe held out the letter. "Want to read it?"

Joe shuffled back, reeling. "Nope. Thanks."

"Why not? It's from Dad. He misses you."

Joe turned from the hideous letter and stared out the

window. Why did his father have to come back now? He'd been gone long enough for the wounds to scab over. Joe closed his eyes, his emotions raw.

He didn't want to run. Despite Mona's cold shoulder, something pulsed inside him to stay, to forsake even the unfinished business deal throbbing at the fringes of his brain, and dive into this one final project. Besides, wouldn't turning tail and stalking out of Gabe's room shred every beautiful thread he'd woven into their new brotherhood? Perhaps Ruby was right. He might solve this problem better by sticking around. His father had run. Joe wouldn't. "Let me see the letter."

Joe's hands shook despite his resolve to stay calm. Even after eighteen years, he could hear his father's baritone as he read his words:

> Dear Gabriel,
> Thank you for the pictures of the strawberries. I see you have added a number of beds. Do you think you'll win another award this year?
> It is warm here. I was out near Lake Calhoun yesterday watching the sailboats. They look like swans gliding across the water. Do you remember the flamingos we saw at the zoo last summer? I saw a sailboat with a sail the exact color.
> My new company is going very well. We specialize in restorations now, and our reputation is growing. Although I am busy, I am planning on taking a vacation this summer. I will come to see you. Maybe we can go fishing, like we did last time.
> Have you heard from Joe? Where is he now? Did

*he write to you from Canada? I hope he is well.
I miss him. I miss you too.*
Love,
Dad

Joe closed his eyes and pushed back a wave of hurt. *He
misses me? Right. He misses me about as much as he
misses a case of lice.* His heart throbbed. *How dare he ask
about me? He hasn't given me a second thought since he
let the screen door slam behind him.* Joe saw himself, a boy
of fifteen, standing at the kitchen door, willing his father to
turn around, to simply say good-bye. But his father had left
without sparing a backward glance. Refusing to cry, he'd
watched his father's prize Ford Mustang peel out, its
perfectly tuned engine taking him to places far away.

Joe had felt something inside rip asunder. It had taken
him eighteen years to sew it back together. He'd run
before he had to face that kind of pain again.

His father had betrayed them all, and now he was
writing letters to Gabe. Bitterness seized Joe. He battled
an urge to crumple the letter. Instead, he handed it back
to Gabe. Gabe folded it and slipped it into a plain white
envelope. A thick silence wedged between them.

Gabe's eyes were red-rimmed, and Joe saw his
brother's question written on his face before he voiced
it. "Why don't you like Dad?"

Joe's voice was tight. "Why do you think?"

"Because he left us," Gabe softly answered. "He left
Mom and you."

"And you."

"I know." Gabe wrung his hands together. "But he's
sorry."

Joe folded his arms across his chest. "It doesn't matter. He ran out on us." His voice pinched. "He left us. He broke Mom's heart. It was his fault she died. She worked so hard; it was probably her ulcer that caused her stomach cancer."

"Mom didn't say that," Gabe retorted. "She said Dad was different. That he changed. Dad is a Christian now."

Joe frowned. "I don't believe it. He probably said that to worm back into our lives." *Into my life.* "Besides, how did Mom know?" A knot tightened in his stomach.

"They came here right before Mom died. That's when I met him. She told me."

Joe winced and drew in a painful breath. "He came back? How come Mom never told me?"

"She didn't have time. She got sick fast. When you came home, Dad was afraid to talk to you." Gabe's voice, straining to form the words, betrayed his fear in pitch and tone.

"They were together when she died, and she didn't tell me?"

Gabe nodded.

Joe's eyes stung. He gritted his teeth against the pain that threatened to shred him anew. Why had she kept it from him? He realized that to Gabe it was simple. Dad had been gone, and now he was back. But Joe wanted more thorough answers. Why had Dad left? And why had Mom kept the truth from him? He clutched his head with his hands, feeling her loss like a fresh blow. Even when she died, he'd found the truth hard to accept. He'd flown in, spent the day with Gabe, and escaped before the sun had set. He'd berated himself a thousand times for his callousness, but he'd done it to survive. If

he'd stayed, he would have shattered. And then who would have been there to pick up the pieces?

"Mom said she forgave him, Joe. And she wanted you to do it too."

Fury curdled Joe's composure. "No! How could I? He let her work herself to the bone, and he left *you.*"

"He left you too." Ruby stood at the door, her hands in her pockets.

Joe glared at her. "This is a private conversation."

"It's so private I can hear you down the hall."

Joe clenched his jaw and ran his gaze up to the ceiling. "You don't understand, Ruby. You haven't been here long enough. You don't know the history."

"I've met your father. I know he deeply regrets his actions. I know he's trying to make it up to Gabe. He would like to make it up to you too."

"He won't get the chance."

Ruby raised her eyebrows. "Why? Are you going someplace? Running out on Gabe, just like your father ran out on you?"

Joe tried to strangle her with a look, but Ruby didn't flinch. "You have no right."

"I call it like I see it, Joe. I see you running all over the world, afraid to turn around and face the past."

"I'm not afraid. And I'm not running. Somebody has to earn a living to pay for Gabe's room and board. Our no-account father isn't going to do it."

Ruby crooked a finger at him. "Follow me."

Joe cast a look at Gabe, who watched him with wide eyes. Why did his brother have to hear this? Hadn't he had enough pain? Joe drew a shuddering breath and stalked down the hall.

Ruby was in her office, flipping through a file. She held it out to Joe. He pasted her with a look of annoyance, then scanned the paper. It was the rundown of monthly services at the Garden. The total seemed significantly higher than his automatic monthly payment.

"Ever wonder why your payment hasn't been raised in four years? Look around you. This place has been completely overhauled. And you haven't paid one red cent more. Why? Because your father's been filling the gap."

Joe closed his eyes. Frustration boiled through him. Why was his father interfering with his responsibilities? Why couldn't his father leave Gabe and him alone? He opened his eyes and handed the file back to Ruby. He must have worn a wretched expression, for her anger dissolved and pity entered her face.

"Joe, don't you think it's time to forgive and be a family again? For yourself as much as for Gabe. You've made a good living these past years, and I know you're trying to help your brother, to tell him you love him. But he needs you, not your letters. Please consider staying."

"I can't," he rasped. "I have a brother who depends on what I do. And if I stuck around, someone could get hurt. We both know that." He challenged her to argue with the look in his eyes.

The wall clock ticked; the plush carpet gobbled the sound. In the kitchen, a group of residents laughed while wiping supper dishes. Joe felt Ruby's eyes on him, and he suddenly wanted to sink into the leather couch and hide.

"Joe, what would be harder for you? Forgiving your father, or staying and learning to forgive yourself?"

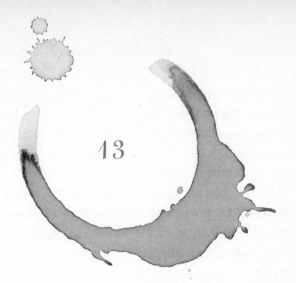

13

Joe ran until his lungs burned. Sweat dripped off his chin, and he bent over to gulp in the cool air.

But the physical pain pushed back the invasive echo of Ruby's voice: *Forgive yourself . . . stay.* The crazy woman thought since she looked after his brother she had the right to dissect his life as well. She couldn't be further from the truth. He had nothing to forgive himself for. He hadn't run away from Gabe or his responsibilities. He'd been the one who had stayed to pick up the pieces.

Joe straightened, clasped both hands behind his back, and walked slowly down the gravel road. In the woods across the drainage ditch, he could hear Rip joyfully tramping after some wildlife creature. The wind hissed through the birch, rustled the balsam, and scented the air evergreen. Joe glanced behind him at the sinking sun. It bled orange and red as it dissolved into the horizon. He sighed, knowing he was no closer to peace than when he'd arrived home, changed into his athletic pants and running shoes, and raced off down Main Street.

He whistled. Rip answered from the folds of the forest. Joe began to stroll the three miles back toward town.

Sweat dripped down his back, his heart pounded through his chest, and his legs trembled from exhaustion, but the physical exertion helped clear the fog from his mind, helped him focus. Wherever he ended up on the globe, running elevated him beyond the plane of the obvious, let him see the big picture and talk to his maker. His sneakers were worn to a nub from miles of conversations with God.

"God, You're making this trip a bit too personal. I want to help Mona with her bookstore dream, but why did You have to bring my father into the picture?"

Forgiveness. The word burned into his heart like coal. "Forgiveness, Lord?" Joe spoke into the wind and shook his head. "He doesn't deserve it."

"God showed His great love for us by sending Christ to die for us while we were still sinners." Romans 5:8 thundered in his head.

Joe scowled and started into a shallow jog. The voice followed him like a Sunday school teacher in a Bible drill, crying out Colossians 3:13: *"The Lord forgave you, so you must forgive others."*

Joe increased his pace, focused on his feet grinding against gravel.

"Why worry about a speck in your friend's eye when you have a log in your own?" Joe skidded to a halt. "That's not fair. I didn't do anything wrong. He's the one who left. He needs forgiveness, not me!"

The wind stirred the trees, but no voice replied. Joe clenched his fists and marched into town.

The clouds were streaked red as if painted across a gray palette. For a Monday night, the town rumbled with activity, belying the three weeks left until opening day of tourist season—Memorial Day. Pickups rolled by, tenting gear and fishing poles poking out of their beds. A string of gleaming Airstream motor homes blew exhaust at the only stoplight in town, drenching the fresh lake air with diesel fumes.

Joe had left Mona working like a machine, scrubbing old varnish off a bowling alley bar she'd picked up at Bowl-O-Rama just north of town. He'd also noticed the smell of fresh lacquer paint wafting from Liza's workshop as he'd descended his attic stairs. The ladies were waging a war against time, and as he counted the pickups loaded with bait and coolers, Joe wasn't so sure his employers were going to win. He hated to see them fail. It was hard enough to face his own defeat.

From a block away, Mona's bedroom light flickered like a beacon in an otherwise dark and gloomy Footstep of Heaven. An ominous shadow obscured the backyard and Liza's deserted workshop. Joe made a mental note to pick up some yard lights on his next hardware run.

He whistled for Rip, who had taken a side trip toward Pierre's Pizza. The dog bounded toward him, a prize in his mug. Joe scowled in disgust. "You have dog food, you know." The Labrador sat, raised his brows, and gave Joe a look that resembled something Mona would have produced if he'd offered her instant coffee.

"Right." Joe chuckled and laid his hand on Rip's

head. To his surprise, the dog dropped the pizza and growled.

Stunned, Joe snapped back his hand.

"You should muzzle your mutt in city limits, Michaels."

"Brian," Joe said stiffly. No wonder Rip had growled. Joe gave him points for taste.

Brian was casually dressed for a man who loved to show off his threads, wearing a pair of faded Levi's and a bulky windbreaker that seemed many sizes too large.

"Going camping?" Joe eyed the backpack slung over Brian's shoulder.

Brian chuckled, but his dark eyes flashed and held no humor. "Where've you been?"

Joe shrugged. "Here and there."

Brian's eyes pinched, and the pause between the two men grew pregnant with distaste. "Where do you run off to all the time? What's your business in my town?" Brian demanded.

Joe clenched his jaw. "Same as you, Whitney. Trying to eke out a living."

"No. I live here. You're a drifter, just passing through. For all I know, you're a parolee, searching for your next big heist, or—" he smiled wickedly—"maybe you're a serial killer waiting to prey on two innocent women."

Joe battled the image of sinking his fist into Brian's smug face and greased on a fake smile. "There's only one person in this town I'd murder, Brian."

Brian's smile dimmed.

"And that's the person who stands in the way of Mona's dreams."

Brian didn't even bother to disguise his glare. "Accord-

ing to Mona, that's you, Joe. Something about a hose left on, flooding the basement?"

All the fury that had been gathering inside him since he'd seen Brian knock Mona into the Kettle River, aided and abetted by Ruby's merciless comment, sent Joe into a full boil. He balled his fists, shaking. His voice was tight, his words clipped. "We both know who did that."

Brian acted surprised, but Joe plowed ahead. "I don't know if it was a mistake or on purpose. But I meant what I said. Don't try and sabotage Mona's dreams."

"Why would I do that?" Brian held out his hands, and Joe nearly slapped them away.

The question lingered between them until Joe had to acknowledge it. Why *would* Brian want to sabotage the Footstep? Confusion tangled his voice in his throat. He glared at Brian, wanting to strangle the arrogant smile from his tanned, chiseled face. The intensity of the feeling unnerved him.

"C'mon, Rip," Joe muttered, eyes still on Brian.

Brian chuckled as Joe strode past him. It rankled Joe, but he refused to turn back. Clenching and unclenching his fists, he strode toward the dark house.

The sky had bled out and only metal gray remained on the horizon. The wind sliced through his sweatshirt and raised gooseflesh on his skin. A faint, sour odor assaulted him as he turned up the front walk of the Footstep. It was most likely the aftereffect of his acrid meeting with Brian.

His resolve solidified as he stalked around the house and up his stairs. If he stuck around, it wouldn't be to forgive himself for leaving Gabe. It would be so he wouldn't have to fight the guilt of abandoning Mona.

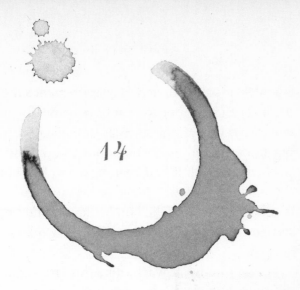

14

"No. Oh my. No. No!"

Early the next morning Mona's scream woke Joe
from a sound and dreamless sleep with the effectiveness
of a cold shower. He sputtered into consciousness. No,
she wasn't standing in the room, but she sounded as if
she were, her cry bouncing off his rafters.

Joe rolled, fell off the sofa onto the bare floor, scrambled to his feet, and tripped over to the window. He
couldn't see her, but gazing past the house toward the
front yard, he spied the reason for her horror—her lawn
was splotched in yellow and white patches.

Joe raked a hand through his hair. What now?

Yanking on a pair of rumpled jeans, he grabbed a
sweatshirt and leaped down the stairs. He ran barefoot
to the front yard and saw a distraught Mona and an
equally white-faced Liza on the front porch.

Mona didn't even bother to greet him. "Look at the
lawn! It has the measles!"

He didn't know whether to surrender to defeated

laughter or sob with her. Her assessment rang with truth. The lawn appeared to have come down with the worst case of German measles this side of the Atlantic. Big spots melded with small ones and the entire surface smelled tart, as if it had been baked in lemon juice.

"What happened?" Joe kept his face stoic. He walked to a large spot, crouched on his hands and knees, and sniffed the stain as if he were Rip. The odor assaulted his nose.

"I don't know. It wasn't like this last night."

Joe sat back on his haunches. "It smells like weed killer."

"Weed killer?"

Joe's chest tightened. He stood up and angled a sorry look at Mona. "Someone is trying to kill your grass."

Mona's jaw slowly fell open, and her face began to crumple.

"Why would someone do that?" Liza's voice shrilled in disbelief.

He didn't answer. Instead he walked through the grass, kicking through especially pale splotches. A seagull cried overhead. The waves lapped the shore in rhythm. The rich blue sky was nearly cloudless. It would have been a perfect day except for the bitter smell that hovered like the specter of death over the Footstep. Joe whirled and stalked toward the porch. Mona had sunk down on the top step, wrapping her arms around her knees.

"I don't know why," Joe finally answered, forcing himself not to take Mona into his arms. He'd have to find a different way to comfort her.

Mona hid her face in her arms. "Is it ruined?"

"We'll see."

Mona's head popped up. He met her eyes. They were red-rimmed and tortured. *Don't give up, Mona.*

"I'll be right back." Joe hopped off the step and dashed for the side of the house. The hose, curled like a snake, glistened slick and muddy from its adventure two nights before. Joe snared it and cranked open the squeaky faucet. Water spit from the rusty hose end. He turned it to full blast, then dragged the hose back to the front yard.

Mona met him at the corner, hands on her hips, eyes wide. "You planning to swamp the place?"

"Yep," Joe said, grinning. Mona's brow knit.

"You already tried that tactic, Joe," Liza called from the porch. "The insurance company won't buy it a second time."

Joe sent her a mock glare. "If you two skeptics would hold your tongues, I might be able to save your precious lawn. Drowning this stuff is exactly what I have in mind." He marched to the front edge of the lawn and stuck his thumb over the end of the hose. The water sprayed out at odd angles. He aimed it toward the grass. "Maybe I can wash it away before it settles into the soil."

The odor rose in a humid cloud around him, but he noticed the powder pool and foam and finally move in a mini-wave toward the curb. "I think it might work!" He turned and winked at Mona. The hopeful look she gave him made him want to dance.

"I'll make coffee." Mona headed toward the house. Liza was one step behind her, waggling her eyebrows at Joe.

"Hardworking, check." Liza sidled up to Mona, who stood at the parlor window, cradling an after-lunch cup of coffee. She leaned close and whispered in Mona's ear. "Patient, check."

"What are you talking about?"

"I'm simply pointing out the obvious. Joe's been showering the lawn for roughly four hours. The ground is saturated, his bare feet have to be ice cubes, and he's out there singing 'Amazing Grace.' If that doesn't fit your description of the perfect male, nothing will." Liza leaned against the window frame, looking smug.

"No, Liza," Mona countered. "You forgot, 'committed to family.' Joe's not committed to anything but his hobo lifestyle. It would take him all of twenty minutes to clear out of here. And he will. I can tell. He takes off every chance he gets. Where does he go, anyway?"

Liza shrugged.

Mona turned back to the sight of Joe cleansing her dusted yard. "He's hardworking, I'll give him that."

"And cute. That five-o'clock shadow only adds to his rugged appeal."

Mona rolled her eyes. But she couldn't deny the truth of Liza's assessment. Joe had flown to her aid so quickly this morning, he hadn't had the chance to shave. Since then, he'd been watering her lawn. She watched him aim the spray at her baby poplar. He was certainly thorough. And she had never been more thankful for his quick thinking. Except, of course, when he dove into the Kettle River after her. She had yet to contemplate, let alone accept, her profound relief when she found herself

rescued, safely nestled inside his strong arms. She had successfully refuted all memory of that moment, as well as the kiss he'd given her on the stairs. The horror of the flood, and now the damaged yard, had bowled her over, and she felt it was easier to drown in worry than surrender to the feelings that threatened to tug her under.

But those feelings were becoming harder to fight. *God, I am so weak—why couldn't You have sent a retiree to help me fix up the place? Someone married, with a passel of grandchildren and a sour disposition?* Yet God had sent Joe, and his presence at the Footstep buoyed her spirit. Despite her cold shoulder, he'd been warm and kind to her. She didn't deserve his accepting friendship. The acrid flavor of regret lined her thoughts. What if Liza was right? What if he was the perfect man and she was driving him away? But wasn't he the one who was leaving? She was only protecting her heart from the inevitable. *God, please make me strong. Help me not to lose my heart to a rootless drifter and forget everything I've worked so hard for. I've made You a promise—help me keep it!*

Mona examined her coffee. "He's leaving, Liza. There's no use in my getting involved with him. He's been more places than I can even dream of."

"Maybe he would stay if you asked him to," Liza said softly.

Mona bit her lower lip, shaking her head. "There's too much at stake. I have to get the Footstep up and running before I even *think* about a man. This isn't the right time. And he's not the right man."

"Still waiting for Jonah?"

Mona bristled. "Jonah doesn't exist. He's a character

in a book, a fairy tale. Just like my dream man." She smiled wryly at Liza.

"I'm starved!" Joe's voice announced his entrance and Mona jumped. Her handyman slopped into the room, damp and disheveled. His jean cuffs were wet and his short brown whiskers glistened. He'd pushed up his sweatshirt sleeves over tanned forearms and his cap, worn backward on his head, had done a miserable job of shielding his handsome face from the kiss of the sun. He looked positively . . . heartbreakingly handsome. Her words replayed in her head like a taunt: *He's not the right man.*

He shivered slightly. "Coffee! Oh, sustenance to a starving soul." His blue eyes twinkled, and Mona heard the echo of her words die in the face of his warm smile. His presence seemed to turn her brain to honey.

Liza leaned close to Mona. "Coffee lover, check," she whispered. Then she turned to Joe. "Cup of coffee coming right up for our local hero." She headed for the kitchen.

Joe turned to Mona, his eyes bright. "I think the grass will live. The sun's out, the sky is clear, and the swamp in your front yard will evaporate in no time. Maybe in a few days we can put fertilizer down, but I'll have to see. We don't want to burn it."

"Were you a landscaper in an earlier life?" Mona, painfully aware of her racing pulse, fought to make sure it didn't infect her voice.

Joe laughed. "No. I've tended a few gardens in my life, but no landscaping jobs. Just old-fashioned fix-it projects, a few stints as a ranch hand and reindeer herder."

"Reindeer?"

She thought she saw Joe color. His eyes lost their twinkle, and in a heartbeat his smile vanished, as if a door had slammed shut on his sunny disposition. "Forget I mentioned it." His cold tone hit her like a slap. Maybe she'd been mistaken about his warming presence.

"You brought it up." She studied her coffee, but out of the corner of her eye she saw him wince.

"Sorry. My mistake." He abruptly whirled and headed for the kitchen, nearly breaking the sound barrier.

Mona stood, reeling from his frosty exit. Well, *vulnerable* was certainly *not* on his list of attributes!

Joe's neck ached and his arm muscles screamed. He never knew plastering a ceiling could be so painful. Or perhaps the hurt came from the confused, even angry, glances Mona kept spiking his way from the next room. She scrubbed at the stain on the coffee bar with unequaled passion, the steam from her demeanor nearly peeling off the dark tar. Joe gritted his teeth and focused on smoothing the ceiling. Just when she was starting to warm to him again, he had to summon his defenses and stomp all over their tender friendship. He regretted his impulsive words.

"It's as smooth as frosting on a wedding cake."

Liza's voice startled him. He lost his balance, dancing as the step stool wiggled, then toppled over. He landed with a thump on the floor.

"Oh! Sorry, Joe! I didn't mean to scare you."

Joe waved his forgiveness as he climbed to his feet. Mona had stopped her scouring, and he caught her concerned expression. He returned a half smile, and she instantly hid her worry under a guise of vigorous scrubbing.

"Anyway, nice ceiling. Can't even tell it tried to kill me." Liza grinned widely.

"Who's trying to kill you, beautiful?"

Joe scowled, recognizing Brian's syrupy voice and abrasive cologne.

Liza whirled and delight lit her face. "Brian! We haven't seen you since Saturday! Where have you been?" She nearly skipped over to greet him.

Joe turned, glimpsed Mona's welcoming smile as she approached, and something inside him burned.

Brian hugged Liza with one arm and caught Mona in the other. Joe was glad to see Mona didn't relax into the embrace like Liza did.

"How are my girls?" Brian asked.

"Great," Liza replied. "We had a mishap this morning, but Joe saved us and I think we're back on schedule."

"Mishap?" Joe echoed incredulously.

Mona, too, appeared less than pleased at her roommate's choice of words. "I think *mishap* is a little too soft. Try *ambush.*"

Brian's smile dimmed and worry creased his face. "What happened?"

Joe took a step toward the trio, his eyes fixed on Brian. "Someone poured weed killer all over their front lawn last night."

He had to admit, if Brian was the culprit, he was the consummate actor. Surprise flooded Brian's expression. His jaw slacked and his eyes darkened appropriately in defense of Mona's property. "Did you report it to the police?"

Mona blinked at him. "No. I didn't even think of it. Joe immediately started washing it away."

Brian pinned a suspicious look on Joe. "I guess the evidence has been destroyed then, right?"

Joe's mouth gaped, and an unnerving anger rose in him. His knuckles turned white as he gripped the putty knife. "I did the first thing I thought of. I saved the lawn."

Brian's green eyes were icy. "Or you saved yourself."

Mona and Liza stared in horror at Brian.

"W-what are you talking about?" Mona stammered.

Brian's gaze on Joe never faltered. "It just seems you've had a number of so-called accidents around here since he showed up."

Mona went ashen. She looked at Joe, and written in her beautiful eyes he could see the signature of doubt. He shook his head, dumbfounded, heartsick.

Tears glistened in Liza's eyes. "That's not true, is it, Joe? You're not trying to wreck us, are you? I mean, flooding the basement was an accident, right?"

Joe winced. He glared at Brian, who returned a frosty smile.

Mona addressed Brian. "I'm sure Joe had nothing to do with this." Her voice was thin, however, and when she again met Joe's gaze, all the trust he'd so painstakingly built had eroded from her eyes.

Joe gave her a desperate look. "I didn't do this."

"Then why are you here, Michaels?" Brian narrowed his eyes at him. "Where do you go at night? Where do you spend your days off?"

Joe heard the silence of a thousand accusations, and fear rushed alongside anger to suffocate him. The last thing he needed was Brian Whitney getting wind of his brother. Mona would demand to meet him, and from there things would unravel faster than a cheap sweater in the washer. He shook his head, refusing to answer.

Mona looked as if she'd been slapped. White-faced, horrified. He could see the mishaps mounting like evidence in her eyes. If he could force words out past his clenching chest, maybe he'd be able scrape up something. He managed a feeble, "Mona, listen—"

"Please get back to work."

Her words stabbed his heart. "It's not what you think."

"And what do I think, Joe? Are you trying to destroy me?" Her eyes filled. She didn't wait for an answer. "Forget it. Please, just finish what I hired you to do."

"And you'd better hope nothing else happens around here," Brian added.

Joe ignored him. Gritting his teeth, he climbed back up the stool. In an instant, he'd gone from local hero to hired help. No, he'd gone back to pond scum.

"Show me what you're working on, Mona." Brian's sugary tone soured Joe's resolve not to practice an old football move on the liar. Joe focused on the ceiling, listening to Brian weave the ladies around his little finger. "You've done a miraculous job on this bar and also those darling coffee tables!"

What kind of man uses the word darling? Joe crouched and scooped up another slab of plaster.

"Do you think you'll be ready by opening day?"

Joe caught Mona's nod and saw the sparkle of hope in her eye. "I think so. If we can avoid any more 'accidents.'"

The conversation came to a crisp halt. Joe felt eyes on him. He forced himself to hum quietly.

"I came by to give you permission to build a side lot for parking, Mona. But I see my real job here is to persuade you to let me treat you girls to dinner. I know a new steak place about twenty miles down the lakeshore drive. It's not fancy, but the fare is tasty."

Joe could tell by the texture of Brian's chuckle that the ladies had agreed.

"I'll wait on the porch while you change."

Footsteps filed past Joe.

The next five minutes seemed like an eternity as Joe fought the urge to plaster all the open spaces on Brian Whitney's face, especially the gap that caused him the most grief. He breathed out in relief after the girls clambered down the stairs and the Honda roared away.

Joe sat on the stool and hung his head in his hands. Now Mona thought he was a saboteur. And who knew what fertilizing descriptions Brian was adding to their fledgling suspicions? Maybe he should leave. It would be simpler—and safer—than having to explain his presence in their town, and in their lives. And certainly easier than letting Mona inside his privacy, his past, his pain.

But what if the saboteur struck again? Mona would be left holding the broken pieces of her dream. Joe clenched his eyes shut. *Give me wisdom, Lord. Help me know what to do.*

The truth will set you free.

Joe opened his eyes. The truth. Which truth and how much? And he wasn't trapped. He had nothing to tie him down. No home, no responsibilities. He was the most free of them all.

If he didn't count the fact that he had a debt hovering over his head . . . a debt he hadn't figured out a way to pay. But over the past few days he'd all but abandoned the idea of escape. Yes, he'd pay the price, but weren't investing in Mona's dream and enjoying Gabe's friendship worth it? Plotting his redemption would sacrifice precious hours with both of them, stir up feelings of regret, even guilt. He was already going to leave the taste of deceit in his wake. That was painful enough.

Joe sighed and stood up. The best thing for him might indeed be a quick exit, but he'd made promises, and while he didn't have much in the way of earthly possessions, he did have his honor . . . well, at least he *wanted* to have honor. Yes, he was proud of all he'd accomplished in his life, but somewhere along the way, it had taken a southward turn. Somehow all his hard work and his dreams had morphed into a medieval monster, shaking off its tether and swelling to nightmarish proportions. His "career" had even landed him in the hospital. He longed to wrench free of its grasp and start down a different path. A simpler path. With his eyes wide open, aware of the limitations and the sacrifices of the life he'd chosen. He might not choose a different line of work, but he'd certainly redraw the blueprint to include a home and perhaps a family.

But then again, he couldn't very well redraw Gabe, could he? Maybe his hobo lifestyle was the best for everyone. And as long as he kept his eyes peeled for

trouble, no one would get hurt. Dreaming of a different life now was about as helpful as holding out a sieve in a rainstorm.

Joe found the lid to the plaster bucket and pounded it into place. Carrying the bucket outside, he put it next to the other construction items—paint, stain, varnish, and tools that he had piled near the side of the garage. Then he returned to the dining room, rolled up the plastic, and folded the step stool. After setting it in the hall, Joe retrieved the broom from the kitchen and began to sweep up the remnants of plaster that had fallen as he repaired the ceiling.

It would be much easier to rationalize the urge to ditch town if Mona didn't have a saboteur lurking in the shadows. Was the offender after Mona? Or did the so-called accidents have to do with the house? Was Liza the intended victim? Joe mulled over the horrific possibilities as he swept plaster into a dustpan.

He dumped the debris into a trash can, then wandered to Liza's side of the Victorian. Liza was certainly a breed apart from Mona. She'd painted her walls sky blue, and instead of polishing the floor, she'd stenciled an elaborate seascape on it. Her decorating finesse equaled Mona's, however. She made good use of the resources at hand. She'd constructed a tall wall shelf from five long, blue-painted boards and red bricks, and painted an old caned chair a creamy pumpkin color. The room felt like Liza—carefree, airy, and cheerful, even if it was a bit whimsical.

Mona's side had a more serious tone, yet the warm feeling of home and a pine forest drew him like a cozy fire. If only he could get the proprietor to warm up and trust him again. But after Brian's Oscar-winning performance, he'd be lucky to have a roof to sleep under when they returned home. Joe continued to sweep in wide strokes, and as the image of Brian's smile rankled him, he slid the broom roughly under Liza's shelf. A piece of paper floated into the air and settled in the dust. Joe picked it up and turned it over. It was a boarding-pass stub, dated a week ago, for a Northwest flight to Chicago from Duluth. Frowning, he stuck it in his pocket.

Joe swept the remaining dirt into the dustpan and flicked it into the garbage. Setting the broom aside, he strolled out onto the porch. The salmon-colored sun hung low beneath wispy clouds. He inhaled the wet, fragrant scent of the lawn, and relief drew through him. The acrid smell had been obliterated. He hummed as the image of Mona's relief, accentuated by her beautiful smile, swept through his mind. Yes, four hours standing barefoot in icy water had been a small price to pay for that smile. He hoped it wasn't too late to get back into her good graces.

Joe whistled. Rip bounded from the side of the house, appearing with an old rag hanging in his mouth. Joe met him at the bottom of the steps and reached for the rag. Rip growled playfully but surrendered his toy.

"Where'd you get this, buddy?" Joe's nose wrinkled against the dense odor of gas seeping from the stained rag.

Rip sat, his thick brown eyebrows wrinkling. Joe patted him on the head. "No more stalking other people's garbage." He wadded the rag in his hand. "C'mon, boy. I'll rustle us up some macaroni and cheese. That'll beat steak any day."

Joe tossed the rag in the trash pile beside the garage and climbed the stairs to his apartment, determined not to listen for the purr of Brian's slick Honda.

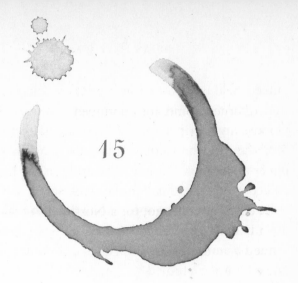

15

Mona saw his lips move and knew he was speaking, but no matter how hard she tried, she couldn't comprehend Brian Whitney's words. His voice simply couldn't breach the scream of horror in her heart.

How had she been so blind? Could Joe really be trying to sabotage her and her dreams? Why? Was he an ex-con, like Brian had suggested during the drive to Shoreline Steak House? The word *convict* had sent a chill through her, and since then she'd been numb to her bones. Her thoughts traveled back to that first day, when she'd asked Joe if he was a parolee on the lam. He'd blushed and assured her, in his charming I-am-your-hero tone, that she was safe with him. Safe! She felt sick.

She knew so little about her handyman. Yes, he could fix just about anything and skip rocks like a pro across a windblown lake. But his clandestine background and his answers to her questions about what he did in his off-hours had tangled her thoughts on more than one occasion. Unfortunately, judging from his nonverbal, stay-outta-my-life answer earlier today to Brian's accusations, Joe had no intention of even hinting at his secrets. He was mystery personified, and she had let him *kiss* her. The foolishness of that impulse made her stomach pitch as she stared at her plate and pushed her uneaten cold porterhouse through the steak sauce.

Liza's laughter snapped Mona back to reality and informed her she had missed a quip from their host. She offered a smile, but from Brian's disappointed face, she knew he wasn't fooled.

He considered her for a moment with an enigmatic expression. It soon melted into pity. "Now, Mona, don't worry. I'm sure everything will turn out all right." He cupped his hand over hers. It was oddly sweaty and added to her unease.

"Thanks, Brian," she said, pulling away her hand. She grabbed her napkin and dabbed it at the corners of her mouth, then tucked it beside her plate. There was no point in trying to finish the medium-rare steak, waffle fries, and spinach salad. It might have been the best meal she'd eaten all year, but it still turned to coal the minute it hit her tightening stomach. The urge to run back to the Footstep, not only to assure herself it still stood but also to confront the man who said he wasn't leaving her with that mess, was swelling to unruly proportions.

Or maybe, instead of running back to the Footstep, it would behoove her to run to the Deep Haven police station. She wondered what she'd have to do to get the local law to poke around in Joe's history . . . if Joe was even his real name. Tears pricked her eyes.

She leaned toward Liza, who was absorbed in Brian's

witty assessment of the local politics, and whispered, "Can we go?"

Liza angled her a frown. Mona must have looked pitiful, because Liza suddenly smiled gently. "I think we're ready to head home, Brian," Liza said sweetly, touching his arm.

Brian sat back in his chair, frowning. "Are you sure?"

Mona nodded stiffly. Brian was visibly disappointed. Guilt stabbed at Mona. He'd been so kind to them this evening, trying to distract her from the nightmarish truth that her handyman was trying to ruin her. She gave him a grateful smile. "Brian, thank you so much for this wonderful evening. We really appreciate your kindness."

Brian perked up. "My pleasure. Anything for my new neighbors. I just hope you stick around for a good long time."

Mona stood, gathering her purse. "That's my goal. Unless the Footstep crumbles around me, I plan on staying."

She couldn't help but notice the odd expression that crossed Brian's face at her bold words.

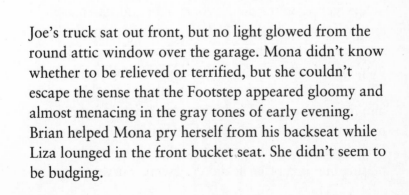

Joe's truck sat out front, but no light glowed from the round attic window over the garage. Mona didn't know whether to be relieved or terrified, but she couldn't escape the sense that the Footstep appeared gloomy and almost menacing in the gray tones of early evening. Brian helped Mona pry herself from his backseat while Liza lounged in the front bucket seat. She didn't seem to be budging.

"Thanks for a nice dinner, Brian." Mona eyed Liza suspiciously as Brian leaned on his car door.

"Anytime, Mona. I want to help you feel comfortable in Deep Haven."

Tears edged Mona's eyes. To think she'd thought ill of this man only two weeks earlier. She felt properly chastised. "Thanks, Brian," she repeated hoarsely. Glancing past him, she waved at Liza, who beamed back. Obviously Brian was doing all he could to make her feel as comfortable in Deep Haven as well.

Mona turned and studied the dark house, feeling her throat burn. Brian's car door slammed; then the Honda roared away from the curb, driving at NASCAR speed. Evidently, Brian wasn't wasting any of the lingering twilight he had with Liza.

The front door squealed, raising gooseflesh as she entered the dark corridor. What if Joe or some other saboteur was lurking in the shadows, just waiting to put the finishing touches on his handiwork? Mona shoved the thought away and fumbled for the hall light. The sudden brightness drove the shadows into oblivion, and Mona laughed nervously at her silly fears. Still, tension hovered as she crept through the house.

She flicked on the dining-room light and stared at the creamy white ceiling Joe had plastered. Tears pushed at her eyes again and this time slipped over the edge. She didn't know what to think about her faithful handyman. Was he a saboteur or a savior? Should she fire him or beg him for forgiveness? The look on his face when she'd ordered him back to work replayed vividly in her mind. Disbelief and not just a little hurt. She'd shamed him by putting him in a place he didn't deserve. He was a handy-

man, but he'd done so much more than simply plug up geysers and dark holes around her house. He'd believed in her dream; he'd promised to stick beside her. He'd dove into a rapids to save her. That didn't sound like the average convict. It sounded more like a gift from heaven.

Yet Brian was right. Problems did surface when Joe was around. The paradox tightened her jaw. Despite Joe's embracing smile and entrancing eyes, she'd have to hawk his every move. Or fire him.

But she had only three weeks left until opening day. She needed help. She needed Joe. If she wanted to see her dream come true, she'd have to trust that he was more than what he appeared at the moment. And she'd have to trust God to protect her from mishap.

Would the Almighty protect her dreams after what she had done? An evil voice whispered doubt into her heart. Protection? She didn't deserve protection. Closing her eyes, Mona hugged her waist. *God, help me to trust You and not give in to defeat. You* do *want this, don't You?*

Mona wiped the tears from her stained cheeks and jutted her chin. A blaze of determination ignited inside her. She would stay. There was no other choice. She'd invested her life into the bookstore. She couldn't consider failure. No, regardless of what Joe or an unknown saboteur did to her, she wasn't going to leave her Footstep of Heaven.

Mona headed to her room. Her bedside lamp pushed back the twilight, illuminating her stack of Jonah books and her leather Bible on the very bottom. How long had it been since she preferred time with God to moments with Jonah?

Liza's accusing words rose in her memory as Mona

changed into fleece sweatpants and a clean T-shirt. *Still waiting for Jonah?* The thought stung. She knew Jonah would never be darkening her doorstep. But was it a crime to dream about the perfect man?

She returned to the table, pushed aside the books, and tugged out her Bible. She ran her hand over the cover and felt her eyes burn. She'd been hoping for God's blessings, but had she truly enjoyed knowing Him? She'd been so focused on her goals for so long, the whisper of God in her heart seemed but an ancient echo.

As Mona flipped through the thin pages, her gaze fell on a verse in Psalm 37: "Take delight in the Lord, and He will give you your heart's desires."

What did it mean to delight herself in God? She winced. *Delight* was not the word she conjured up when thinking of the Almighty. *Gratefulness . . . awe . . .* definitely *fear.* But *delight?* No wonder she had a problem grasping the idea of God granting her wildest dreams. She'd hardly "delighted" in Him.

Mona put the Bible on the night table and picked up *Siberian Runaway,* unable to face her self-indictment. Tonight she needed Jonah's struggle against the wilderness in Russia. Struggle was something she could definitely relate to. Mona tucked the book under her arm, intending to whittle away the first chapter while she perked a cup of decaffeinated coffee.

Determined to conquer fear, Mona flicked off the hall light on the way to the kitchen. She deftly assembled the coffee in the pot, then leaned against the counter, reading to the dim blue light from the gas burner. Although she owned a coffeemaker, she preferred the enticing nip of freshly perked coffee to calm her ragged nerves.

Jonah's story ate the time, and only a heady coffee aroma successfully yanked her from a tiny village in northern Siberia. She could almost feel the arctic wind swirl in and curl around her bare feet.

Pouring herself a cup, she tucked the book under her arm and balanced a leftover donut on the rim of the mug. Then she padded up the stairs, ready for an evening of peace. She would tackle Joe and her problems with renewed vigor in the morning.

A tickle of wind betrayed the intruder just as Mona entered her room. She had enough time to gasp before a steel arm snaked around her neck. She caught a familiar scent of cologne; then a rough hand jammed a cloth against her nose and mouth. Mona tried to scream, but the rag ate the sound. She had the vague sense of burning as coffee coursed down her leg. Hot breath filled her ear. She clawed skin from his forearm and he yelped, then cursed. The rag crushed her teeth; her nose burned. Fear fogged her brain. *Help!* She thrashed. Her breath leaked out. She slammed her heel into his shin. Pain spurted up her leg. The room spun, began to turn gray.

The iron grip held her until her body turned to lead and her mind drowned in darkness.

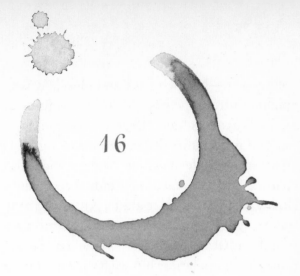

16

Joe sat on a ledge above a rocky outcropping in the shoreline, where the lake slapped the rugged surface and sprayed foam up the cliff face. Farther out, the waves crested white at full peak and glinted in mysterious beauty against the kiss of the rising moon.

Joe didn't know how long he had lingered here, watching the sunset, stroking Rip's smooth short hair, and mulling over saboteurs. His hair felt mussed from running his hands through it in frustration, and he knew he looked like something the dog dragged in, having abandoned the idea of shaving in lieu of an after-dinner beach stroll. He wasn't planning on running into anyone who mattered, anyway. Mona was out with Brian, Mr. Smooth and Sultry, and Joe was crouched alone on a cliff with Rip, his only friend in the world.

He sighed. He wasn't looking forward to facing Mona. Her doubts hurt like a fist in the gut. Still, he'd spent the better part of the evening mulling over Mona's "accidents." He knew all about saboteurs. He had one of his own—his own flesh and blood, Wayne Michaels, phantom from the past, haunting his future.

Joe's tenuous life in Deep Haven could unravel in a second if his father decided to make a grand entrance back into his life via Gabe. Wayne Michaels couldn't be trusted. He had failed their family completely. And Joe knew that even if he couldn't protect Gabe from the games his father played, he would protect himself.

His father had written to Gabe. His father, the traitor, cultivating a relationship with the only family Joe had left. Joe's chest burned as he remembered the letter and the carefully printed words, simple enough for his brother to comprehend. *Maybe we can go fishing . . .* Joe clenched his teeth and winced.

Fishing. A memory revived so clearly he could hear the water lap against the boat, taste the salt of a mouthful of sunflower seeds, and feel the cork of the pole handle rub against his hands. He'd been eleven years old. A golden time. His mother was pregnant with what he hoped was a baby brother, and his summer plans were wrapped around the hope of rebuilding, shoulder to shoulder with his old man, the Ford clunker his father had just purchased. The Friday before Memorial Day, his father had roared up to the school as students were whooping their way out of the building.

Joe recalled the thrill that had zipped through him as he spied the pickup packed with camping gear and bait. They'd headed north, found a remote lake, and fished from dawn to dusk the next day. He'd learned to fillet northern pike and cook a walleye shore lunch, while reveling in his father's love for what would be the last time. By the next Memorial Day, Gabe would be on the

scene, his father would be avoiding home, and Joe's life
would begin shredding in wide, painful swaths.

Joe moaned aloud. Memory burned through his
resolve to keep his father at arm's length. In truth, he
ached for the peaceful life before Gabe's birth. For years
after his father's disappearance, he told himself his
father would return. He'd hung on to hope . . . and his
fishing gear. Later, he went fishing again, finding the
exact lake, as if reliving the sound of his father's voice
mingling with the wind would bring him solace and help
bury his demons.

He never went again.

Joe watched the moonlight part the dark choppy
waters and forced the memory to oblivion. It did no
good to dwell on what would never be. His father had
sabotaged his life, then and now. Saboteurs. Joe had
one. Mona had one.

Joe suspected that Brian was the mastermind behind
the Footstep's inexhaustible repairs. His suspicions were
based on more than just the way his stomach lurched
every time he was near the man. It had to do with the
way Brian ogled Mona as if she were a prime-cut sirloin
for him to devour. Joe didn't trust Brian as far as he
could throw him.

And Mona was out with him.

Joe went cold. Brian wasn't aiming to hurt Mona,
was he? Like pushing her into a river . . .

Joe scrambled to his feet. Rip, up in a flash, broke
into a run beside his master.

The Footstep greeted him dark and silent, just as he'd
left it. Joe slowed his pace, still a block away, as sweat
dripped off his chin and into the hollow of his neck.

Clutching his knees and fighting for breath in the middle of Main Street, he realized with mortification he'd let panic ride and control him. Again. With his luck of late, Mona and her hot date would drive by any minute and spot him, looking like a hoodlum who'd just robbed a bank, and confirm their every suspicion.

Joe straightened, forcing his pace to a comfortable, innocent stroll. Perhaps he was jumping to conclusions by blaming Brian. After all, the man seemed eager to help.

Joe smelled the pungent odor two houses down from the Footstep. The sick, oily smell made his nose curl. Burning paint and plastic. Joe scanned the darkness for the offender—burning garbage within city limits was strictly banned. As he drew nearer the Victorian, the foul smell saturated the air. Rip trotted ahead, then scurried back to him and whined. Joe frowned. Rip barked, then tore off up the Footstep's walk, around the house, and toward the garage.

Joe watched his dog and in a moment made out the glow emanating from the backyard. He broke into a run. Surely Mona wasn't burning trash. Leaping the fence near the front corner, he nearly mowed down the poplar sapling and sprinted to the back of the house.

The size of the blaze made him gasp. Creeping up his stairs, growing and sparking high into the inky sky, the fire glowed orange and red, licking the garage and spitting embers. He ran for the hose. It was coiled where he'd left it. Joe cranked the water on full blast and raced back to the blaze, now chewing up his stairs. He aimed the water where the source appeared to be, next to the garage under the stairs—where he'd thrown the paint,

the gassy rag, and the drying grass clippings. Realization spread like tar through his chest.

His carelessness had started the fire.

The wind began licking up the sparks and blowing them toward the nearest available kindling . . . Mona's century-old roof. Joe's heart stopped at the sight of flames flickering out from under the eaves above Mona's bedroom window. Directing the spray, Joe aimed high, praying he could saturate the roof before it flamed like a haystack. Thank the Lord, Mona was still out with Brian and wasn't here to see her dreams burn.

"Mona!" Liza's voice came from the front yard.

Fear gripped Joe. "Liza?"

Liza appeared, screaming. "Where's Mona?"

Her expression told him all he needed to know. "Call 911!" he yelled and ran for the house.

The back door was locked, but two jams with his shoulder dismantled the flimsy doorframe. "Mona!" Smoke wisped through the lower floor. Joe's eyes watered. "Mona!" He raced toward the stairs, scrambling, falling, then scampering up on all fours. "Mona, where are you?"

He found her crumpled in her bedroom. Scooping her into his arms, he crushed her to his chest. His pulse roared and his eyes flooded, but he managed to find the stairs. Smoke twisted past him as he stumbled down the steps. When he hit the landing, sirens blared in his ears.

He burst through the front door, clutching Mona tight. The cool, clear air revived her, and her eyes jolted open when he jumped off the porch. Joe held her tighter, subduing her immediate struggles. "Don't look, honey."

Liza met him in the front yard. "Is she all right?" Tears glistened on her cheeks.

"I think so."

"Oh, thank You, Lord!" Liza's hand trembled as she covered her mouth.

Joe lowered Mona to the grass. Her green eyes gripped his with confusion and a growing terror. He ran a gentle hand over her ashen cheek, forcing himself to remain calm.

"I'll be back," he said in a voice that betrayed his emotions. Before she could protest, he sprinted toward the backyard.

The inferno attacked Mona's house without mercy. It inhaled the gutter, crawled down the siding, and roared like some ancient world dragon.

Joe wove a path through the hazy ground layer of smoke and unearthed the flimsy garden hose. He aimed it at the roof, praying that the spray would somehow halt the assault. But the flames only flickered, undaunted. As he gritted his teeth and edged closer, they mocked him and climbed higher, out of the reach of his feeble stream. Behind him, his back stairs cracked as the weight of the upper landing crumpled the charred posts.

Joe's heart fell to his knees as he watched the fire lap at his apartment door. Everything he owned, and more, was trapped in that apartment.

He turned back to Mona's house, trying to ignore the fact that a year of unfinished work—scraps really, of unworkable schemes—lay at the bottom of his rumpled duffel bag. Drenched in sweat and with tears stinging his eyes, he sprayed doggedly, hoping to stun the blaze. He

felt as if layers of his skin were peeling back in the face of the searing heat.

"Move!" The command was screamed into his left ear. Joe whirled, and a man in a face mask and helmet roughly shoved him aside.

Stumbling backward, Joe barely escaped the full force of a fire hose. The blast blanketed the house in a film of water, the hiss of steam adding to the commotion of the night as the volunteer fire department swarmed Mona's backyard.

"Anyone else in the house?" a fireman yelled.

Joe shook his head.

Staggering back to Liza's shed, he gulped deep breaths. The air grated his scorched lungs as he watched the firefighters battle the flames.

"Oh no! No, no!" Mona's voice wailed above the din. Joe spied her rushing toward the fire, a blanket falling off her shoulders. Horror constricted her beautiful face.

He sprinted and caught her tight. She struggled against him, beating at him with her fists. "What have you done?" she sobbed. "Why, Joe?"

Her words made him reel. "What?" He held her away from him.

Mona's eyes flooded. She shook her head and wrenched herself from his grasp. "Why? What did I ever do to you?"

Joe grabbed her forearms and held on, despite her struggles. "I didn't do this, Mona. Please, you have to believe me. I wouldn't hurt you!" The image of the pile of rags and clippings flashed through his mind, and he felt sick. Had his recklessness caused her dreams to explode?

Her green eyes bored into his, searching. His heart

wrung at her wretched, smoke-streaked expression. He began to pull her toward him, but she shook her head and tore away.

"Please, Mona!" he yelled, but she stumbled toward the front yard.

When he started after her, an iron grip on his arm stopped him. "This is the man, Chief."

Joe turned and anger coursed through him. He yanked his arm from Brian's grasp. Beside the weasel, a cop scowled at Joe like he was the local horse thief.

"Sam Watson, Chief of Police." The man offered his hand, but Joe knew he wasn't trying to be friendly. Joe caught Brian's dark smile. "You'd better come with me," the chief suggested.

Stone-faced, Joe followed the police chief to his squad car, parked prominently in front of the house where the entire neighborhood could watch. Joe leaned against the hood and folded his arms, intending to keep the house and Mona in sight.

It crushed him to see Mona sobbing into Liza's embrace. Even more horrifying was the sight of Brian joining the duo and taking Mona into his arms. White-hot anger seared through him.

"I didn't do this," he said tightly, meeting the police chief's steely appraisal. The man, perhaps in his late thirties, with a thick thatch of blond hair, had too few lines on his face to suggest experience. Joe surmised he didn't have a rough job defending tourist country. But from the set of the chief's jaw, Joe realized he took his job very seriously—at least tonight, when the newest business in town threatened to wipe out Main Street a month before tourist season.

"I had nothing to do with this," Joe repeated.

"We'll see about that," the chief retorted. "Why don't we start with you showing me some ID and telling me what you're doing in my town."

Cee

The fire roared in Mona's ears, snarling as it consumed her house. A moan escaped her lips, emanating from her soul, and all she could do was cover her head and weep. She felt Brian's arms around her, heard his soothing tones, but it couldn't ease her sorrow. Not only was her house crumbling to ashes, but it was her fault for hiring a drifter with criminal intent. Mona bit her lip and shuddered.

Brian's sweaty hand caressed her hair. "I know you're upset. But it will all work out. Insurance will cover the fire, and I am sure you can still sell the place."

Mona looked up at him, frowning through her tears. In his eyes she saw the same odd expression she'd seen in the restaurant.

"Some things just aren't meant to be," he continued. "You have to know when to throw in the towel."

Mona winced at Brian's well-meaning words.

"You'd have to agree that the Footstep of Heaven is turning out to be a nightmare. It's just over your head."

Gulping back the painful emotions that filled her throat, Mona pulled away from Brian. She had to gather her senses, focus, stay in control. Brian's words had the power to unravel her.

Mona clenched her fists and stared at her burning Victorian. A white spotlight from the fire truck illuminated the tragedy. The black smoke and the orange-red blaze made the house appear like a fright-night spook show.

Her chest constricted with the horrible truth: it was time to concede defeat. Gritting her teeth, she folded her arms, fought a violent tremble, and watched her dreams burn.

Ce

"So no one can vouch for you this evening, is that right?"

Joe ran a hand through his singed, dry hair and flinched. Rip. His dog was the only one who knew the truth. He reluctantly shook his head.

Chief Sam looked grim.

"C'mon, Chief. Think about it—the weed killer, the water in the basement. I'm not responsible for this. There's a saboteur out there." Joe held out his hands and gave a hopeful, pleading look.

Chief Sam scratched his chin. "I don't know, Joe. Considering your situation, I want to believe you, but it isn't looking good. Not unless you can find due cause and a reasonable perpetrator."

Joe stared at the chief, liking him despite the awkward situation. After a moment of disbelief, Chief Sam had easily accepted Joe's credentials, laughed ruefully, and put them on a first-name basis. Under different circumstances, Sam might be a guy Joe would seek out for a morning of angling or a quick game of hoops. He hoped the chief was a man who could keep secrets.

"Help! Get this mutt off me!" The cry pierced the murmuring crowd, the hiss of the water hoses, the

shouts of firefighters, and found Joe's ears. He frowned and scanned the darkness.

"Help me!"

Sam whirled, now hearing the desperate plea. He cast a glance at Joe. "Stay here," he ordered, but Joe was on his heels as Sam ran toward a man stumbling from a neighboring backyard. A small, milling crowd gasped and parted like the Red Sea. Joe skidded to a halt, horrified to see Rip attached to the man's calf. The Lab was growling and blood stained his lips.

Chief Sam steadied the man as Joe wrapped a hand under Rip's collar. "Let go, Rip!"

The dog responded with another growl.

Joe tightened his grip. "Let go!"

Rip grudgingly released his victim. He backed up, sat down, and whined. Joe ran a hand between the dog's ears. "Stay."

The man collapsed into a heap, clutching an ugly wound. He glared at Joe. "I'm gonna sue you into bankruptcy," he snarled. Joe surveyed the man's appearance and his gaze hardened. Besides the black coveralls and a ski mask pushed back on his head, the gassy odor seeping from his gloved hands cultivated a hearty suspicion.

"Who is he?" Joe asked as Sam crouched beside the man, giving him a stern once-over.

"Leo Simmons. He works for the City Park Department."

Joe glowered at the man and wrinkled his nose. "You stink." He glanced at Sam, who met his gaze and nodded. "Good work, Rip," Joe whispered.

Leo Simmons cursed his way to the police cruiser, threatening Rip, Joe, and quite a few people Joe didn't know. Joe followed him, battling the urge to free his steel hold on Rip's collar. Sam led Simmons into the passenger seat of a cruiser, retrieved a first-aid kit, and crouched beside him. Joe's immediate frustration dissolved into respect as Joe watched Chief Sam work his suspect with the savvy of an inner-city detective.

"Sorry about the dog bite, Leo. We'll get you fixed up in a second."

Leo's lined, sour face softened at Sam's words. He glared at Joe. "The mutt ought to be shot."

Sam nodded. "We'll talk about that later. Right now I want to know what you're doing here."

Leo responded with a grin of well-rehearsed surprise. "I'm just down pickin' up a few supplies for the wife, Chief. Ain't a man got a right to shop for his family?"

"Sure he does. But why the ski mask? It's early May."

Leo's face turned granite.

Chief Sam stood, surveying the fire as if he hadn't noticed Leo's expression. "I hate to add this, but you smell like you bathed in gasoline." He returned his gaze to Simmons. "It's not looking good."

Simmons studied his fingertips. "I'm not saying anything. I know my rights. I want a lawyer."

Joe watched the man and tightened his grip on Rip's collar, thinking how much he'd like to join his dog in a collective lunge at the saboteur. The fire hissed behind them as the Deep Haven VFD saturated the last rebellious flames on the house and the garage. The pungent smell of wet char fueled Joe's frustration. He shot a piercing glance at Sam, who answered him with a spiked eyebrow and a nearly indiscernible shake of his head.

Joe sent a prayer heavenward as Chief Sam knelt

before Simmons. "Tell you what, Leo. You tell me why you're in town, dressed in black, reeking of gas fumes and hanging around a house fire, and I might be inclined to help you out of this fix."

Leo's face colored slightly at the chief's words.

"I've known you a long time, Leo, and other than a few reckless-driving citations, you usually stay on the right side of the law. I'm inclined to believe your story, if you tell it to me straight." Chief Sam's eyes were gentle. Joe felt as if he were watching a wood-carver whittling away a man's hard shell to find the treasure inside.

Simmons buried his face in his hands.

"Cindy and the boys would sure like to see you back at home tonight."

Joe saw the man's shoulders begin to shake. He could barely make out Leo's ragged voice. "I didn't have a choice, Sam. It wasn't my idea."

"Tell me who's behind this, Leo," Sam prodded.

Simmons surrendered to sobs. Sam gave Joe a look that told him how he felt about seeing a man crumble. "You're free to go, Joe."

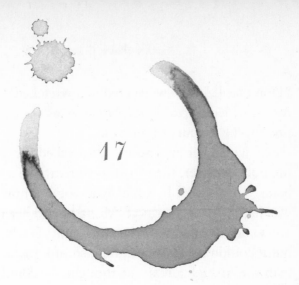

17

$\mathfrak{M}$ona shivered in the sopping grass as mud soaked into her fleece sweatpants, watching the smoky apparition gnaw on her dreams and consume her hope. The fire had crawled along the gutter and invaded her bedroom—where she had been unconscious earlier. If it weren't for Joe, she'd still be inside, unaware of the specter inhaling her lace curtains. For a fleeting moment, she wished she still lay blissfully unconscious on her bedroom floor. Smoke inhalation. How painful could that be? Certainly less so than waking up to find her future literally reduced to ashes.

Who had attacked her? She ached in places she didn't even know she had hurt during the struggle, but nowhere more than in her confused heart. Had Joe snuck up behind her, strangled her, then set fire to her home, only to drag her from the flames moments later? Doubt raged through her. She'd seen the pain in Joe's eyes when she'd accused him of starting the fire, pain she'd now inflicted twice in one day. Most of all, she remembered the sheer agony on his face as he dragged her from the house.

"Don't look," he'd whispered in a wretched tone. She was appalled to realize that, as soon as she caught her breath, she'd pounced on him.

She wiped her eyes now and searched the darkness for the police cruiser, then froze in horror. She'd seen Joe being interrogated by Chief Watson, and now the chief was handcuffing a suspect. Mona buried her head in her arms and shuddered—Brian was right! She bit her lip, but it couldn't restrain the anguish of knowing that a man she trusted, a man she thought she could even love, had betrayed her. She should have known better than to open her heart. At least she'd been wise to rebuff Joe the past few days . . . just think where she'd be if she'd let herself fall completely for his charming, deceitful smile.

Mona turned her attention back to the firefighters, watching them through a liquid haze. The fire, finally extinguished, sent a fog of steam into the night sky. The local volunteers, decked out in gray fire-retardant jackets and black rubber boots, were dousing the house, dragging hoses through her wild roses and trampling the hosta, drowning the porch and, with her luck, her polished coffee bar and sanded end tables. Thankfully, the new sofa had yet to arrive. She could cancel the order and save herself the hassle of returning it. A fine, airy mist settled over her. She lifted her face to it; the moisture mingled with her sorrow.

A crowd had gathered in the unpaved lot next to the house, a fistful of gawkers and speculators in bathrobes. She heard murmuring and some clucks of pity, but Mona refused to turn around and acknowledge the disaster to their faces. It was bad enough she'd lived down the appearance of the plumbing truck, the exterminator, and

the numerous deliveries from Frank's Hardware. They knew the truth as much as she: The Footstep of Heaven Bookstore and Coffee Shop was a failure.

She searched for Liza, thinking it strange her friend wasn't also sobbing beside her in the grass. When she spotted Liza nestled safely inside Brian's embrace, a shard of jealousy pierced her. Liza had chosen correctly. She had seen Brian's shining-knight character while Mona had picked a saboteur. Her gaze drifted back to Chief Watson, loading the culprit into the squad car. Well, at least Joe Michaels was out of her life. He wouldn't be around to do her, or her heart, any more damage.

"Are you all right?" A worried voice sliced through her despair. Mona lifted her gaze and gaped as Joe squatted beside her, his sooty arms hanging over his wet knees, his blue eyes studying her with palpable concern.

She glanced back at the police cruiser. "I thought . . ."

"I know what you thought." Mercifully, he looked away, but Mona's heart tore anyway.

"I-I don't understand," she stuttered.

Joe met her look with troubled eyes. "I'm not sure I do either. But I think Sam and I found your saboteur."

"Sam? Since when are you on such friendly terms with the local law?"

Joe shrugged, but his eyes glinted mysteriously, accompanied by a hint of a smile. Mona felt heat travel up her spine, and a warm glow spread out through her entire body. *Joe wasn't the saboteur.* The relief she felt at that realization was so profound, her eyes filled. "Who was it?"

"A guy from the park department."

"I don't know anyone from the park department." Her voice broke into a moan. "I don't understand."

"I don't either, but we'll figure it out." He smiled at her, and the *we* in his phrase embraced her heart. He was keeping his promise, despite her atrocious behavior. That insight tore open a thousand wounds.

"I'm sorry, Joe. I should have never let myself believe you would hurt me. I should have trusted you."

Joe looked away and ran a hand through his hair. When she saw a muscle pull in his jaw, she felt physically ill. She'd hurt him much more than she'd realized. He said nothing but remained hunkered down in the grass next to her.

Silence passed between them while shame colored Mona. Was it too late to repair the damage she'd done to their friendship? "I'm so sorry," she repeated weakly.

Joe finally met her eyes, and the tenderness in them made her want to cry all over again. "I forgive you."

She looked away, blinking back tears, letting his kind friendship comfort her. If only she had been able to hold on to her dream as well . . . perhaps she might have found a little touch of heaven in Deep Haven.

"Your dream isn't crushed, Mona. I think we caught it in time," Joe said gently, as if reading her tortured thoughts. "I'll have to sleep in the truck, but the house still appears structurally sound. We'll see in the morning. Please don't give up."

Her sweet moment turned bitter as she hung her head and mentally refuted his words.

He cupped her chin with a grimy hand and forced her to meet his gaze. "It's going to be all right." The compassion in his tender eyes made her long to climb inside his strong arms and hold on tight.

Mona closed her eyes. It wasn't all right. Joe's inno-

cence was the only good news in the tragic evening. She
had to face the brutal reality. God didn't want her to
have the Footstep of Heaven. She didn't want to know
why. She just wanted to stop fighting Him. Maybe there
were lessons to be learned in defeat.

"Nope. I give up. The Footstep of Heaven is gone."
She heard Joe sigh and she opened her eyes. The expression on his face baffled her . . . sorrow perhaps, or maybe
agreement. He frowned, as if he were about to argue, but
Mona shook her head. "I've had enough. God is trying to
tell me something—the Footstep of Heaven Bookstore
and Coffee Shop just isn't meant to be."

She turned her gaze back to the house. It looked so
wounded in the moonlight, the fire-engine spotlight adding
to its sickly pallor. In the backyard, the skeletal remains of
Joe's steps and his charred apartment reminded her that he
was homeless and now probably penniless. The odor of
melted plastic and charred wood turned her already soured
stomach. She spied some of the firefighters folding their
long gray hose into even sections; others wandered to the
scattered remnant of spectators, weaving tales of bravery
and exploits. The mob behind her began to disperse.

"By the way," Mona murmured into the watery
padding of midnight, "thank you for saving me."

Joe stared at the house, but out of the corner of her
eye, she saw his eyes fill with fierceness, a certain flicker
of determination she'd seen before, just before she'd
plunged over the waterfall.

Then Joe moved close and did what she was hoping
he'd do. He wrapped his arms around her and cocooned
her in an embrace she didn't have the strength or desire
to fight. She laid her head against his chest and wept.

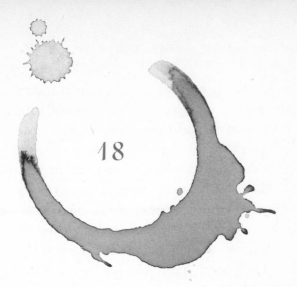

18

"You look like a pretzel," Mona commented, leaning over the bed of the pickup truck, where Joe was curled up clutching her extra motel pillow. Rip lay at his feet, looking profoundly more rested than his owner, although she had to admit, despite his soot-stained shirt and ripped jeans, her handyman looked amazingly handsome this morning.

Joe opened one eye and stretched his arms. "Beats a motel bed," he said, grinning.

"Sorry about booking the last room," she said. She'd offered her floor, but he insisted he preferred his truck. She suspected he also preferred a perch where he could monitor her securely locked motel door. It warmed her to know he wanted to protect her.

Liza appeared at the door of the room, looking bedraggled and drawn.

"Liza's looking unusually rough this morning," Joe commented, winking at Mona. She punched him playfully, in defense of her roommate.

Joe swung out of the bed of the truck and landed next to her. "I'll take you two out for breakfast. I know a great spot that sells deep-fried elephant ears guaranteed to chew through the lining of your stomach."

"Oh, yum," Mona said, touched by his offer.

The World's Best Donuts dining area was packed, all seven tables. Joe, Mona, and Liza stood at the door, toting their greasy bag of morning goodies and balancing coffee, creamer, and little red stir sticks.

"Over here!" Edith Draper stood, attracting the attention of every patron in the room, and waved the crew over to her table. Next to her, Chuck Parson, Mona's Realtor, sent them a sympathetic look. The trio found vacant chairs from around the room and scooted under the tiny orange Formica table.

Edith immediately covered Mona's hand with her own. "I'm so sorry about the fire, honey."

Mona blinked back tears. She thought she'd cried herself dry last night into the ratty motel pillow. "Thanks, Edith," she said in an unsteady voice.

"And don't worry; I won't mention a word to your mother. I am sure you'll be back on your feet in no time."

Mona started to reach for the bakery bag. She didn't want to discuss her plans within earshot of the town. Despite her cool composure, she was fragmenting quickly.

Joe handed her a napkin-wrapped elephant ear. Liza had chosen a chocolate-covered donut, and Joe folded his own gooey long john into his mouth.

Chuck sat next to Joe, whispering into his ear while Joe nodded. Mona narrowed her eyes, wondering at their conversation. Joe flashed her a wide, conspiratorial grin.

"Now, I suppose, Brian will get his wish," Edith blurted, scorn lacing her tone.

Mona frowned. "What are you talking about?"

Edith stirred her coffee. "I told you Brian wanted to buy your place. You are going to sell, aren't you?"

"I-I don't know yet," Mona stammered. Despair gathered in her chest.

"Fight for your dreams, sweetie." Edith patted her arm. "I would hate to see a Speedy Burger built over that cute little Victorian."

"What are you talking about, Mrs. Draper?" Joe leaned forward, an odd expression on his face.

Edith's gaze traveled around the group. "Oh, my goodness, did I forget to tell you?"

Everyone nodded.

"Brian bid on the house because he wanted to tear it down and build a Speedy Burger!"

"Speedy Burger?" Mona sputtered.

Edith shook her head. "Yes, can you believe it? A greasy fast-food joint right in the middle of our quaint Main Street. He even flew up the suits from the franchise headquarters in Chicago."

"Chicago?" Joe echoed.

Edith nodded. "But I thought he had abandoned the dream months ago when I told him Mona had outbid him on the house."

Joe made a face. "I don't think so." He fished around in his back pocket and pulled out a folded piece of thin paper stock. "This is a boarding-pass stub for a Northwest flight out of Duluth to Chicago. Last week. I picked it up at the house last night. . . ."

Mona's heart lodged in her throat.

"Liza, were you with Brian all evening?" Joe asked, eyes narrowed.

Liza appeared startled, then paled. "After we dropped off Mona, he took me to Tastee Treat. I went inside to wait for him while he parked the car. . . ." Her voice became stilted. "I didn't see him again until after you rescued Mona. I completely forgot—I took off for the house when I saw the orange glow from Tastee Treat . . ." Her voice trailed off again, and Mona saw Liza's eyes widen in shock.

Silence enfolded them and Mona felt slightly ill. "He's been behind this the entire time." Her voice shook. "Brian Whitney's been trying to drive me away!"

"Brian Whitney tried to kill you," Joe stated icily.

Mona saw the expression of rage gathering on his face, and her mouth went dry. He bounded to his feet. "Joe, no! Wait," she gasped.

"I'll be back."

Mona froze in horror as she watched him leave.

"I'd better call Sam," Edith said in a tight voice.

Cee

Brian Whitney should get an unlisted number if he's going to attempt murder, Joe thought as he floored the truck toward Brian's street. Clutching the torn page of the telephone book, he thanked the Lord that the Deep Haven population still trusted each other enough to print addresses. *Lord, please help me to stay calm, to apprehend Brian without killing him!*

Slowing as he turned onto Brian's street, he crawled along, scanning the mailboxes. He found Whitney's

name spelled out on a black tin box, and noticed the
weasel's Honda parked in the gravel drive.

"Quiet, Rip," he commanded as he turned off the
motor. He thought the dog actually glared at him. "I
know, but I need to solve this myself."

Joe climbed out of the truck, barely closing the door. He
had to admit, Brian's digs were nicer than he expected for
a small-town city official. The one-story ranch was well
groomed. Hosta edged a flagstone path leading up to a
long covered porch. A pot of blooming red geraniums
guarded the front door. Finding it unlocked, Joe opened it,
wincing when the door squeaked slightly. Every hair on his
neck raised, and his heart hammered in betraying pitches.

Heavy green polyester drapes darkened the room, and
the musty scent of a sixties-era orange shag carpet told
Joe that Brian hadn't done much updating to the inside
of his home.

The refrigerator clicked on and hummed as Joe tiptoed
through the shadowed kitchen, timing his steps with the
plink of a dripping faucet. In the dark windowless hall he
spied a light streaming from an open bedroom door.
Shuffling closer, he heard a muttering voice. Joe avoided
crossing the stream of light and instead lingered in the
shadows and watched around the doorframe as shirts,
pants, papers, and books landed in soft thumps in an
open suitcase on the bed.

Brian was running. He'd destroyed Mona's dreams,
and now he was escaping like a gutter rat. Anger ignited
Joe's adrenaline.

Joe stormed into the room, slamming the door against
the wall. "Whitney, what are you doing?" His voice was
not nearly as calm as he would have liked.

Brian whirled. His sweaty, red face, a sharp contrast to his crisp two-piece suit, betrayed panic. His expression instantly tightened into a glower. Joe saw his reflection in Brian's dark eyes and knew he wasn't dealing with a rational man. He instinctively balled his fists.

Brian exploded in fury. "Get out of here!" He lunged at Joe and smashed him into an oak wardrobe. Blinking, Joe saw a fist headed toward his face and ducked. Brian's fist landed in the wardrobe door. He cursed.

Joe hurled himself at Brian, hooked a foot around Brian's leg, and pushed. The two men crashed onto the floor. Joe threw an arm against Brian's neck and pressed down, crushing his Adam's apple. Fury shook him. Joe gulped in ragged breaths in an effort to remain focused. "Why! Why did you do it?"

Brian spat at him. Joe recoiled, and Brian's fist exploded into his temple. The room spun at odd angles. Brian easily knocked Joe off with a knee to his midsection. Joe groaned, but panic launched him off the floor. He tackled Brian as the schemer scrambled from the room. They fell into the hall with a shuddering thud. Joe wrapped his arm around Brian in a headlock, his knee lodged between Brian's shoulder blades, and yanked hard. Brian grunted.

Joe spoke through clenched teeth. "Tell me why! Why would you hurt Mona or Liza?"

"It didn't have anything to do with them," Brian rasped. "They ruined my life. I've been waiting years in this wretched town for my grandmother to die, sacrificed everything to save up the cash, and Mona had to sabotage my plans. That house is *mine*. She has no right to take it."

"Take it!" The burning pain in his gut made Joe tighten his grip. "She's poured her life out for that house, her dream. *You* are the saboteur!"

"That's enough, Joe. Let him go." Chief Sam's calm voice bathed Joe in reality.

Joe gritted his teeth. Brian's jagged breathing matched his own. The clock ticked out Joe's fury in tune with his thundering heartbeat.

"Let him go," Sam repeated.

Joe blew out a hot breath and reluctantly released his grip. Brian threw him off like a ratty blanket and clambered to his feet. Joe stood right behind him.

Instantly Brian transformed into a cool-demeanored man. "Hi, Chief. Glad you were in the neighborhood. This man was trying to kill me. He's trouble, just as I thought."

Chief Sam scanned past Brian to Joe, as if to give Brian's words merit. Then he shifted his gaze back to Brian. "Why don't you come down to police headquarters, Brian? You can file a complaint and tell me all about it."

Brian hesitated, shot a confused scowl at Joe, then narrowed his eyes at Sam. "I guess you think I'm a fool."

Sam shrugged. "I guess we're even then. C'mon, Brian. We have a few questions to ask you."

"We?" Brian stepped back and met Joe, an iron wall behind him.

"We. As in Leo Simmons and I. We want to know why you wanted lime from the city park department, the kind they use in the local outhouses. It's puzzling me, especially since you've had indoor plumbing all your life." His eyes darkened as he continued. "He told me about the money he stole and your threats. Frankly, Brian, I'm not sure what to charge you with first— blackmail, destruction of property, or attempted murder." He crossed his arms, motioning with his head to the deputies behind him. They moved toward Brian.

A muscle flickered in Brian's jaw. His face hardened and for a moment Joe thought he'd have to put him in a headlock again. Then Brian groaned. Just as the deputies reached him, he turned and stuck a wide, quivering finger in Joe's astonished face. "The house is cinder, Michaels. Even if you are the best handyman in the world, Mona will never get the place open in three weeks." His eyes glinted malice.

Joe glared at him, but a despairing voice inside confirmed every word.

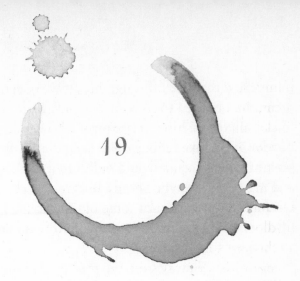

19

The Footstep of Heaven looked like the tongues of the underworld had licked it. Mona hugged herself and vainly attempted to calm a violent shudder.

The back of her house made her want to sob. Thankfully, the firemen's persistence in wetting down the roof saved the old roofing tiles from igniting like fireworks, but the back siding was charred from the rafters down to nearly the first floor. To augment the ghastly scene, the garage had become a soot-blackened shell. Even if his apartment were inhabitable, Joe would need a ladder to get home. The smell of creosote soaked the air, and mud flooded her shoes when she stepped in her previously lush grass.

From the front, the inferno's teeth marks weren't as visible. Only the soggy lawn, pools of water in recesses of uneven porch boards, and the smell of day-old smoke hinted at something amiss. Still, the place would take a small army and a sizable fortune to repair.

Mona bit the inside of her lip to keep her tears at bay,

but sorrow throbbed through her. It was over. Her dream had burned to a crisp. The only logical step was to sell. But she'd lose everything—who would want to buy an overcooked money pit? Brian had won. Whoever bought the Victorian would bulldoze it to the ground and start over. Maybe Speedy Burger was just what Deep Haven needed, not some old-fashioned bookstore filled with fancy. Bitterness wound around her heart. She'd been such a fool.

Mona turned away from the tragedy and shuffled back up the walk. Chuck was probably in his office. She could get the paperwork started immediately.

She plowed into Joe. "Where are you off to?" He caught her as she stumbled.

Mona couldn't look at him. Instead she stared at the poplar sapling, which seemed to have survived the onslaught of the rubber-booted soldiers and had bloomed tiny white-and-green buds. Mona sucked in a deep breath and her throat burned. She couldn't voice her decision. It was lodged in a painful place in her heart. She shook her head and worked free of his grasp.

Joe moved into her path. "Whoa, not so fast, Silver. I see it in your eyes. You've given up." He gripped her arm. "Well, not on my watch."

Mona's jaw tightened as she met Joe's piercing gaze. "I don't have a choice. Don't you see? This place was never meant to be. It's a silly dream. I'm sorry I wasted all your time on it."

Joe winced and glanced skyward. She saw his lips move, but no sound came out. Then he turned his compassionate blue eyes on her, reaching out with a look that made her tremble. "I'm not going to let you

give up, Mona. I'm here for a reason, and right now, it's to help you get back on your feet."

Mona closed her eyes. She couldn't give in to his kindness, the temptation to hope in him—or in her dream. It cost too much. She shook her head again, this time fiercely.

The urgency in his voice startled her. "Mona! Why? Why won't you believe it can work? After all you've sacrificed to make it happen, you're going to give up that easily? You're going to let Brian win?"

"It's not about Brian!" she shot back. "It's about me! I know I don't deserve this dream to come true, and the longer I play out the charade, the more it will hurt when it finally shatters." Her voice turned wretched. "My heart can't take it."

She didn't expect his powerful embrace. His arms went around her, pulling her to his wide, muscular chest. She resisted slightly, but when he put a hand on her head and tucked it under his chin, she gave in with a releasing shudder. His hug was firm yet gentle. She relaxed against him, smelling denim and the musky scent of soap mingled with perspiration. Why did it have to be so comforting?

"'If God is for us, who can ever be against us?'" Joe whispered.

Mona stiffened.

"He's the author of dreams. And He's not a trickster. He doesn't give us a dream only to yank it away and laugh."

Despair coursed through her. "I'm not sure God is for me."

Joe released her in an abrupt motion and held her

away from him. His gaze probed hers. "How can you believe that? You're His child! He loves you."

Mona looked away.

Joe cupped his hand under her chin and turned her face to his. "'Since God did not spare even His own Son but gave Him up for us all, won't God, who gave us Christ, also give us everything else?' How can you not expect the best from God, who loves you like a daughter?"

"I don't deserve the best." Mona's voice broke.

"None of us do. But while we were still sinners, God chose to give us His best, and He will do nothing less *after* we are adopted as His children. We don't deserve grace, but because of God's character, we can *expect* it! If this dream is from Him, then you can expect Him to make it come true."

Joe's blue eyes searched hers, and she felt his invasive gaze to her toes. It was intimate and tender, and something inside her wanted to reach out and reveal everything, to tell him her terrible secret, her deepest fears. But the intensity of his stare and the nakedness of the truth were so raw she closed her eyes and pushed the urge away. Tears streamed down her cheeks.

"Mona, don't judge God based on your understanding of people. God isn't just a really good guy up in the sky. He is *God*. He operates on an entirely different set of rules. We'll never deserve His love, but He knows that, and He's chosen to love us anyway. We can accept it or not. But that doesn't change who He is. He's a God who loves us more than we can imagine and desires to fulfill the dreams He gives His children."

His thumb ran along her check. "Nothing, not even

roaches, a flood in your basement, or a fire, can keep God's love, His best, from your life. Trust Him for this. Don't give up."

Mona closed her eyes and ached to accept Joe's words. She wanted to believe that God had His best in mind for her. She'd believed briefly when she'd stood on the steps of her Victorian the first day and seen it all materialize. Didn't she feel God's peace, His love in that moment, like a foretaste of what could be? And God had provided Joe. That had to mean something.

Mona opened her eyes and pulled away from Joe's grasp. She met his gaze. The look on her face must have given him hope, for his eyes began to shine. She smiled tentatively and whisked away her tears. "Okay."

"That's my Mona." He put his hand on her cheek. She didn't know if the warmth she felt was from his touch or was generated in her own heart by his words "my Mona."

Ce

"Break it up, you two!"

Joe grinned at Liza's playful words, but he kept his eyes on Mona. She seemed so delicate, so ready to let discouragement blow her away from Deep Haven and everything she held dear. He longed for her to hang on, to believe in God's love, to trust the Almighty to fulfill her dreams.

Liza strolled up and surveyed the couple. Mona scurried out of Joe's reach. Liza paused, a smile touching her lips; then she gestured toward the house. "It's not so bad, Mona. Come and see." Her voice was buoyant.

"The inner walls are fine, and your bedroom isn't a lake, despite your moaning." Liza winked at Joe. "I think our nifty handyman can fix it."

Joe smiled wide. He was so glad Liza had a half-full view of life, even if she was a bit flaky. She balanced out his half-empty Mona. "You must think I'm Bob Vila," he said.

"Yep." Liza wrapped her arm around Mona. "C'mon, girlfriend. Let's see what we have to do to salvage our dream."

Mona fell into step with Liza. Joe had to give the dark-haired beauty credit. She had recovered quickly from Brian's betrayal. Or maybe she was merely putting up a false front for her best friend. Nevertheless, he thanked the Lord for Liza as she led Mona toward the back.

In the light of the morning sun, the damage seemed ghastly, but not devastating. Remarkably, the needed repairs appeared to be mostly cosmetic. The stairs up to his apartment would need to be rebuilt, but aside from a blackened door, the place looked repairable. As for Mona's house, the back siding had been scorched, but if he concentrated on touching up the front of the house, he could repair the back and his apartment after the Footstep opened.

Joe stopped himself. What was he thinking? He couldn't stay. Even if Mona did decide to trust him just a little and keep him on after opening, he had a schedule to keep. His days of free roaming were drawing to a close. Joe scrubbed a hand through his hair and blew out a breath.

"Too much for you, Superman?" Liza's voice breezed through his thoughts.

Joe forced a nonchalant grin. "Nope." He didn't want to shatter Mona's fragile hope. He'd stay as long as he could and pray it was enough to turn Mona's scorched house back into the Footstep of Heaven.

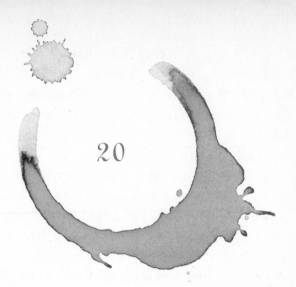

20

Joe's tenor filled the hallway as Mona turned off the floor sander. "'You are my sunshine, my only sunshine . . .'"

"Is that for me?" Mona peeked around the corner. She must have startled him. As he tore his attention from the overhead light in the hallway to look at her, he wobbled on the step stool.

"You're having a hard time staying on that thing," Mona commented, stifling a giggle.

"Only when a pretty lady catches me singing about her."

Mona's mouth went dry and she clamped it shut. It was Joe's turn to laugh. "I don't think I've ever seen you wear that shade of red."

Mona glared at him.

"So, what do you think of the light fixture?"

Mona folded her arms. "Get down. I can't see with your head in the way."

Joe jumped off the stool. She had to drag her eyes off him to examine his handiwork. He looked adorable in his faded blue jeans, navy-blue-and-hunter-green-plaid flannel shirt and tan work boots. His horribly tousled hair betrayed he'd been musing over something. It made her smile to know his personal vices.

"Looking good," Mona said, not necessarily meaning the light fixture. But the antique, wrought-iron, three-armed light with scalloped-edged globes suited the hallway perfectly. It was just the contrast she needed between Liza's place and hers.

"Thanks, Joe," she said, meeting his eyes. He shrugged. She wanted to go on, to tell him how his backbreaking labor the past week had turned her spark of hope into a living flame. He'd worked from dawn to midnight—painting the front porch, installing lights, tearing out charred siding, and helping her with miscellaneous odds and ends. And he'd done it all without a word of complaint or a bed to sleep in at night.

It made her muscles ache to think he'd spent five nights camped out in his truck, but when she'd offered to put him up at the local motel, he'd actually acted offended. "Brian may be behind bars, but I'm still on duty." She didn't allow herself to argue with that, preferring instead to be buoyed by his enthusiastic demeanor and warm grin. With two weeks left before her grand opening, she was starting to believe her dream would come true.

"Hey, I have an idea, Mona." Joe tucked his wire clippers into his back pocket. "Can I take you out for dinner tonight? I know this place up the trail I'd love to show you."

Mona stared at him dumbly. Was he asking her out on a date?

"Mona, you look like I just asked you to fly to Paris with me. Calm down."

Mona felt her breathing restart. She laughed nervously. "I'm sorry, Joe. You caught me off guard. Sure, I'll go out with you tonight." Her heart raced as she considered the implications of her words. A date. Her warning sirens blared, yet for some reason, she felt like dancing. A date. With Joe. She had to bite her lip to keep from grinning.

Joe wiped his hands on his pant legs. Then, to her shock, he held out his hand, as if they were making a deal. "Great. Now shake on it so you don't back out."

Mona frowned. "Why would I do that?"

"Because you don't know where I'm taking you." Mischief glinted in his blue eyes.

Mona tentatively shook his hand; all day she relived the tremor of excitement that rippled through her.

Mona shouldn't have spent so much time ironing the blue floral-printed skirt. "The city dump? This is your great place?"

She grimaced as they passed the green-and-white sign. The municipal dump was located far from scenic Deep Haven for good reason . . . it was about the most unattractive place within sixty miles. And this is where Joe had chosen to take her on their first date? Mona rolled her eyes. So much for culture. He personified the he-man he read about in his Louis L'Amour books.

Joe shot her a sly look. "Don't give up on me, Mona. Hold your judgment for a moment, okay?"

Mona crossed her arms over her white cashmere sweater. She'd probably have to soak it in lilac-scented detergent to get the stench out.

Joe maneuvered the pickup between the ruts in the road and found a flat place overlooking a valley littered with broken refrigerators, stoves, toilet seats, cans, newspapers, bottles, detergent boxes, tires, and a collection of other trash.

"Oh, this is picturesque," she commented dryly.

Joe's grin was undaunted. "Just you wait until the others get here. That's when the fun starts."

"Others? It's a party?"

"Sort of." Joe slid out of the truck. "Stay here."

She easily acquiesced. But Joe's happiness was contagious and her interest piqued. She watched him fiddle with a tarp in the back of the truck, then turned her attention to the pit. The city had dug out a long valley into which garbage was dumped. Someday, she supposed, the area would be filled in and another patch of wilderness would be furrowed out for humanity's litter. She wondered how much forest hid trash, new life covering the debris of the past. Oddly, she couldn't smell the refuse piled below. The pine surrounding the dump absorbed the odor and scented the air. A scant wind pushed through the trees, and the sun winked through the top branches on its downward slide. Perhaps the beautiful evening would soften the repulsive scenery.

"Okay, ready." Joe climbed back in the driver's seat.

"Are we leaving?" She couldn't hide the hope in her voice. Maybe this was a joke.

Joe laughed aloud. "Not quite." He put the truck into reverse, backed up, turned around, and backed into the

place where they'd just been parked. Then he cut the
engine, left the keys in the ignition, and turned on the
radio. As a crackly country station crooned a sorry, out-
of-date love song, he opened his door and stepped out.
"Your table is waiting, milady."

Mona gave him a suspicious look. He stretched out
his hand, and she took it. Pulling her across the bench
seat, he helped her out and led her around to the bed of
the truck.

Mona gasped, delight seizing her at the sight of her
"table." He'd spread out a Navaho blanket on the bed
of the truck and filled his duffel, rescued and cleaned
after the fire, to make a long pillow. A blue wicker
picnic basket sat in the center.

"My table?"

"The best in the house."

Mona cocked a grin. "With the best view, I suppose."

"And the best service." Joe's eyes danced with
tomfoolery. In one swift movement, he scooped Mona
up and deposited her on the Navaho blanket.

Mona giggled.

Joe climbed aboard. "Let's see what the chef
prepared." Opening the basket, he fished around for a
moment, then gave her a sneaky look. "You'd better
close your eyes."

She scowled.

"Please. The chef can't work when he's being
watched."

Mona suppressed another giggle and obeyed. She heard
ripping paper, the hiss of a soda bottle, and silverware
clinking. "Did you raid the local Colonel Sanders?"

"Eyes closed!"

Mona leaned against the army duffel. He may be poor, but Joe was certainly creative. But was he poor? He seemed to manage just fine, never asking for more than the measly wad she paid him. Where had he found the money to sop up her basement?

"Okay, open!"

When Mona opened her eyes, her heart swelled, and for some reason, she felt dangerously near tears. On a starched white linen napkin Joe had assembled a picnic of smoked lake trout, Ritz crackers, Gouda and Edam cheeses, and Concord grapes. Joe handed her a crystal glass filled with soda.

Mona was speechless. Taking a sip of the soda, she blinked furiously and struggled to find her voice.

"Mona, are you okay? I thought you'd like it." Joe sounded disappointed.

Mona gathered her composure and met his blue-eyed, gentle gaze. "It's more wonderful than I could have ever dreamed, Joe."

A slow smile reappeared on Joe's face, and in his eyes she saw his feelings clearly written. Her face flamed at the rush of unexpected emotions. She quickly took another sip. "W-where'd you get the finery?" she stammered, holding up the glass.

He looked so cute when he blushed. "You'd be surprised what the Goodwill sells."

She smiled, grateful to see that he, too, felt the awkward moment. "I guess I'll have to start shopping there."

"One man's garbage is another man's treasure," Joe quipped. He began peeling the golden-skinned lake trout with a fork. "Just have to look beyond the obvious." He raised his eyes to hers, and his words hung in the air.

Mona's heart thumped—hard. "So when do the 'others' show up?" she asked, shifting the topic.

Joe hesitated, then focused back on the fish. "Soon, I hope. It'll be hard to see them after the sun sets."

Mona frowned.

"But I'm sure this delicious fish smell will act as a dinner gong."

"Fish smell?" She began to feel sick.

"Yep, bears love it."

"Bears." Mona gulped the rest of her drink.

Joe grinned as he handed her a piece of fish nestled between two Ritz crackers. "Black bears. And maybe a brown one if we're lucky."

Mona's eyes widened. "And grizzlies?"

Joe laughed. "No. Minnesota isn't known for grizzlies. Wolves, maybe, but grizzlies are few and far between." His eyes twinkled. "Unless you count the one in the truck with you."

Mona bit back a smile. "You're looking remarkably less grizzly tonight." She eyed his indigo V-necked cotton sweater and black jeans. "I like your footwear; they match the music."

Joe lifted one of the shiny, midnight black cowboy boots. "Authentic Texas rawhide." Leaning back against the duffel, he winked at her. "It's not ev'ra girl who gits ta see maw c'ontra side," he drawled in a mock Southern twang.

Mona laughed until she hurt. Joe looked happy and relaxed sitting there, trying to catch all the crumbs from his fish sandwich. As she watched him, memory abruptly hit her hard. His easy smile, the way the wind played in his hair—she'd seen that look before. It was the way her father had looked while watching seagulls snap up the fishbones he tossed on shore. She'd forgotten the contented smile her father wore in that delicious, priceless moment. And Joe had captured the memory for her. Mona blinked back another rush of tears.

"Here they come!" Joe pointed to a remote corner of the distant forest, and Mona was profoundly thankful for the reprieve. She didn't need to spend the night blubbering down memory lane.

She searched the heavily shadowed forest and spied two black bears, one slightly bigger than the other, lumbering toward the dump valley. They were bigger than she imagined, even at this far distance. Gooseflesh dotted her skin. "Are we safe?"

Joe laughed. "Yes. They won't come over here. I was kidding about the fish. They'll stay on their side and paw through the trash. There's enough pickings in this dump to keep them happy 'til hibernation."

Mona blew out relief. "Well, we certainly have enough to share." She eyed the spread of food.

"Rip will be glad to hear that. He wasn't too happy when I locked him in the apartment tonight."

The sun was low and to their backs. Long shadows reached out from the pine and birch woods and slowly surrounded the truck. Mona ate her fill of fish, exotic cheese, and grapes, listened to country minstrels, and watched wildlife rummage through the discards of society.

At one point, after he'd packed up dinner, Joe leaned into the folds of the duffel and wrapped his arm around her shoulders. She was amazed at the ease she felt with him. As if they had always been together, knew each

other inside and out. Or maybe it was just the desire for
it that awakened within her. Joe was a man she wanted
to know, wanted to let inside her dreams.

But there was so much at stake. Could she let him
know the scream inside that drove her to perfection,
to sacrifice? And what about Joe? He was like the old
English poem *Beowulf*. Rustic yet charming. And
completely confusing. She didn't even know where he
was from. He had simply appeared in her life like an
angel and helped her build her dreams. And somehow
he'd broken through the carefully constructed walls of
her heart. Who was he? Was he destined to sneak in
like a thief, snare her heart, and steal it away? Would
he leave her empty and gasping in pain if he left?

When he left.

A chill rippled through her. It was too late. The pain
was inevitable. Joe would leave, and when he did, he'd
take her heart with him. She nestled herself deeper into
the nook under his arm. It was suddenly as plain as the
North Star winking through the lavender twilight.

Mona was falling in love with her handyman.

The Saturday morning sun was barely peeking above the
trees when Joe drove up to the Garden. The lodge emitted a peaceful stillness, and for a moment, Joe thought
he'd arrived too early. Then the porch door banged
open, and a pretty redhead grinned at him. "Hiya, Joe.
We're eating breakfast. Want some pancakes?"

Her pleasant smile warmed Joe, as did the way she
hunkered down and hugged an ecstatic Rip. The dog

bathed her face in kisses as she giggled. Joe grimaced. "C'mon, Rip. Settle down. I know you like this place, but you're overreacting."

The redhead giggled again, then stood and led them both to the kitchen. The residents looked up from their pancakes to greet him in a cheerful chorus. Joe waved sheepishly. Gabe jumped to his feet and wrapped Joe in a hug that left him unraveled. Their hospitality over-whelmed him, especially in the wake of his horrific behavior the last time he left the Garden. The memory of him slamming the screen door and roaring down the driveway in response to Ruby's probing words made his face flame.

Joe certainly didn't deserve the chair they dragged up to the table nor the plate of steaming flapjacks Ruby set in front of him. She must have guessed his shame, because the housemother leaned over his shoulder and spoke gently into his ear. "Welcome back, Joe. We missed you."

Joe's guilt eased into gratitude as he sat next to his grinning brother and listened to the Garden family tease one another and plan the work for the day. Joe scooped the hotcakes into his mouth, enjoyed the real maple syrup, and knew his brother had something special going at the Garden. This was his family, his brothers and sisters. Gabe had what Joe had never given him— total acceptance. Unconditional love. The pancakes began to stick to the lump in Joe's throat. He swilled a cup of coffee and asked for another.

"Where've you been, Joe?" Ruby asked as she filled his cup.

All eyes turned to Joe.

"I've been working in town as a handyman."

Ruby arched her eyebrows. "Really? You're a man full of surprises. It's amazing how you always seem to find a niche."

Her knowledge of his life piqued him. "What do you mean?"

Ruby gave him a knowing, kind look. "You're always filling a need, blessing people. That's how God uses you." She cleared her throat and smiled. "And it hasn't hurt you in the least, either, has it?"

Joe stared into his coffee, turning over her words. Was he blessing Mona? She seemed to have enjoyed their date last night. Slowly, she'd discarded her mantle of stress and relaxed. He warmed at the memory of the way she'd looked at him when he'd wrapped his arm around her. Her green eyes had filled with wariness, but the fear had dissolved as their evening unfurled. A jolt had rippled through him when she finally leaned her head on his chest. She'd hummed to a Statler Brothers' tune, poked fun at the garbage-picking bears, and let him charm her with a few stories. Never had he felt so alive, so willing to open his heart to a woman. She asked nothing from him, fiercely demanded to carry her own weight, and resented his intrusion into her life. Unfortunately, this only awakened all his protective impulses.

He had desperately wanted to kiss her. The feeling nearly overpowered him, but he fought the urge, as much for his sake as hers. He didn't want to lead her down a path he couldn't follow, and alarms blared when he nestled her close. He needed time to figure things out before he surrendered to the desire to touch those enchanting lips. His first kiss had been impulsive.

His second would be planned and offer them more than just a moment of delight.

For the first time in his life he was dreaming of putting down roots. He found his thoughts drifting into a life with Mona, wondering what it would be like to work side by side with her at the Footstep, to wake up to her beautiful emerald eyes each morning. The thought turned him to putty. There had to be a solution, a way to carve out a future.

Thankfully, he had time. The Footstep was on the mend, and no one expected him for a couple of weeks. Maybe God could work it out . . . maybe the Almighty's plan went beyond using Joe to bless Mona and help fulfill her dream. Joe smiled at Ruby and responded to her comment. "No, I can't say it's hurt me."

Ruby gave him an odd look, as if sifting through the meaning of his words.

"Joe's goin' fishing." The redhead piped into the conversation.

Joe shot her a quizzical look. "How do you know that?"

Her almond eyes curled when she smiled. "You have fishing poles in your truck."

Joe held up his hands in mock surrender. "Guilty. I was hoping Gabe could get some time off today to go fishing with his big brother."

Ruby crossed her arms. "Well, he is the foreman of the garden this year, and we have a full agenda today." She scanned the group with her gray eyes, as if to assess their opinion.

Joe's heart fell. He'd come upon the idea a few days back, and his excitement since then had built to a pinna-

cle. He'd be crushed if Gabe couldn't go, especially since he doubted they would get another chance in the near future.

"Let him go!" Joe recognized Daniel and gave the older man an appreciative smile. "I'll fill in for him today," Daniel added.

Ruby drummed her fingers on her arm. "Do you want to go, Gabe?"

Gabe nodded like his head was on springs.

Ruby waved at them, beaming. "Get out of here, you two."

Bearskin Lake was a sapphire. The sun skimmed it and refracted the blue in jeweled clarity. Observing the green backdrop of woods and the turquoise, cloud-scattered sky, Joe knew God had created a masterpiece when he made the Northern Minnesota Boundary Waters Canoe Area.

Joe deposited the tackle on the beach. "I'll be right back," he said to Gabe, who appeared every inch the hopeful fisherman with a thin-brimmed, floppy hat and a standard orange life preserver. Joe had tried to talk him out of the rain poncho, but Gabe was insistent. "I always bring it!" he'd said, as if he were a pro.

Joe rented a canoe from Bearskin Lodge and returned to the lake, canoe balancing on his shoulders. He flipped it easily against his thighs, then lowered it into the water. "Climb in." He held the canoe steady. "And make sure to balance yourself on both sides," he added, picturing Gabe flipping into the water and Ruby's subsequent fury. She'd pulled Joe aside as Gabe changed clothes and gave him a rundown of rules—life preserver at all times, no loud motors, and no handling hooks.

Gabe picked his way to the front of the canoe and sat down on the bow seat. Joe loaded in the tackle box and fishing rods, then eased the canoe into the glassy waters.

As Joe paddled, searching for the perfect patch of weedy shoreline, the song of a loon echoed across the watery landscape. The drip of water from his paddle as he drew it forth and the bump of the canoe splicing waves played in perfect harmony with the whisper of wind through the forest. The sun had cleared the tree-tops and winked full in their faces, promising a warm, clear day. With Gabe sitting expectantly in front holding the gunwales, Joe felt an unfamiliar swell of contentment.

Gabe cast him a glance over his shoulder. "Do you think it's a nice day, Joe?"

"I do, Gabe," Joe replied, his voice hoarse. He should have been here to do this with Gabe years earlier. The only thing missing from this near-perfect day was Mona sitting in the middle, laughing, enjoying the brother God had given him. Joe swallowed a lump that formed in his throat and pushed the thought away. Dreaming of more would only steal joy from the blessings he *did* have.

Joe guided the canoe toward a small, grass-lined inlet. Tucking the paddle inside, he grabbed a fishing pole. The drugstore in Deep Haven, stocked for the tourist trade, sold just about everything, including Navaho blankets and fishing tackle. Joe checked the fishing line for tangles one last time, then tied on a weight and a lure. Reaching into the minnow bucket, he snared a

slimy, finger-length fish. He hooked it on and handed the outfit to Gabe. "Can you cast?"

Gabe nodded, but when he nearly took off Joe's right ear with the first attempt, Joe decided he wanted to keep his appendages. So he took the pole from Gabe and landed the lure himself in a nice patch of clear water, several feet from the nearest weed.

Gabe grinned wide, eyes hopeful, as Joe handed back the rod and reel. "Catch me some supper," Joe said, winking.

Gabe hummed a familiar tune as Joe baited his own hook. Casting to the opposite side, Joe joined his brother's off-melody hum of "Amazing Grace." Bugs scurried across the surface of the water, and a fish jumped far from his line. "C'mon, smallmouth bass, I got something more delicious than a water bug," Joe purred to the cloudy water.

"Help!" Gabe's cry ripped him from his peaceful reverie. "Help, help!" Gabe's pole curled like a finger, dipping into the water. "I got something!"

"Hold tight!" Joe wedged his pole into the space in his seat and leaned forward on his knees to help Gabe set the hook. "Give me your rod."

Gabe surrendered the pole. Joe yanked it hard and felt the fish dig in for a fight. "I think you got a trophy. Reel her in!" He handed the pole back to Gabe, who set his jaw and began to reel. Joe watched with pride as his brother fought, grunted, and reeled in the monstrous fish. The catch played hard, sometimes swimming close, other times jerking until the tip of the pole disappeared into the water.

"Hold it up; keep the line tight," Joe coached.

Gabe followed his every instruction. He gritted his teeth and fought the fish.

Joe saw a silver gleam skim the surface of the water. "It's a walleye!" he whooped. "Maybe five pounds!" He scrambled for the net. "Bring him by again, and I'll net him."

Joe dipped the net low in the water. Gabe was laughing and straining to turn the reel. The fish swam close. Joe leaned out and scooped him into the net. The frame strained as he hauled it aboard. He let the fish flop in the bottom of the canoe, securely meshed in the net, as he hugged his brother. "You did it, Gabe! It's a beauty. I almost hate to eat it."

Gabe looked horrified. "Eat it? Why? Dad and I always throw them back."

Joe's jaw dropped. "You throw them back? You can't be serious." Gabe flinched at his words, and Joe immediately schooled his tone. "This is the best-tasting fish in the entire world, Gabe. Trust me, I know. You don't want to throw a walleye back."

But he saw the horror in Gabe's eyes. Gabe couldn't kill the fish.

"It's just a fish," Joe mumbled. Gabe stayed silent, his lip quivering as he stared at his catch. Joe quietly unhooked the fish, holding it down with his foot. He was careful not to rip the walleye's mouth as he eased out the hook. Then, with a moan, he dropped it back into the water. The fish swam away faster than a U-boat on nuclear thrust.

"Look at him go!" Gabe exclaimed, thrilled.

Joe rolled his eyes.

"Let's catch another one!" Gabe's eyes glowed.

Joe gave him an exasperated look. "Why? Just to throw them back? What's the use?"

Gabe's face fell. "To have fun?"

His answer was so simple, Joe couldn't deny its wisdom. Despite his dream of a batter-fried shore lunch, he was here to spend time with Gabe. To know his brother better . . . and maybe let him settle in a place inside his heart.

"Right." He grabbed Gabe's pole.

By his count, Joe caught five smallmouth bass, two crappies, a tiny northern he would have thrown back anyway, and a walleye that taunted him with its bulging black eyes the entire time Joe carefully unhooked him. He tossed the scoundrel back gently. "Go play with your brother," he growled to the escaping fish.

Gabe laughed. "It's nice to have a brother," he said.

His words were the best catch Joe had all day.

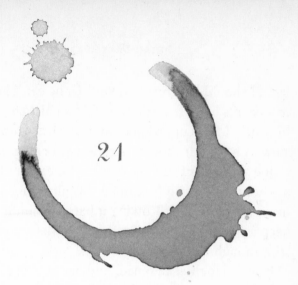

21

The fuzzy shadows of twilight crossed the dirt drive in front of the Garden as Joe and Gabe pulled in. Rip, an ardent but brief welcoming committee, tackled Joe as he got out of the car.

"Gabe looks tired," Ruby commented as her charge trudged past her into the house. Gabe still wore his silly rain poncho, despite the fact the sun had been a radiant umbrella all day.

The rain from the past week had revived the pine, and the scent perfuming the air made Joe linger on the front steps. He inhaled deeply, heard the wind comb the fir, and knew it had been a good—a very good—day.

"You don't look any worse for the wear." Ruby crossed her arms over her navy blue sweatshirt. "Did you have fun, by any chance?"

Joe pulled off his baseball cap and rubbed the saggy brim. "Did you know he throws back everything he catches, even the walleye?"

Ruby erupted in vivacious laughter and slapped her

leg. "I should have warned you! Gabe can't kill anything to save his life. He can't even skin a chicken. It makes him sick." She cupped her hands over her mouth. "I'm sorry. I'm sure it came as a rude awakening, huh?"

Joe shook his head and replaced the cap. "He caught a whopper of a fish first thing this morning, and my heart nearly broke throwing it back. Wouldn't let me keep a thing." He smiled at her. "It was a good fishing trip, though."

Ruby's laughter dimmed, and her gray eyes were piercing as she stared at him. "Felt good to accept your brother the way he is, didn't it?"

Joe considered her a moment, then shrugged. He looked away, preferring the pine landscape to her probing gaze.

Ruby walked over beside him. "That's how a family is, Joe. Everyone's different, yet they work together. They give and take and learn to forgive." She laid a hand on his arm. "I bet you were hoping for a nice fish dinner tonight, huh?"

Joe grunted in agreement.

"So you had to forgive him for wrecking your plans, stepping on your toes, and not letting you keep the fish, right?"

Joe eyed her suspiciously. "What are you getting at?"

Ruby faced the woods. The wind picked at her graying hair, and Joe saw wisdom edge her eyes. "Even though you had to surrender a decent shore lunch, you reached out to him and discovered it was worth the risk. Everyone, even within a family, is different. We all have different needs, different issues we struggle with. Part of being a family is learning to face those

differences, forgive, and accept so that you can move on to love."

"You're referring to my father, aren't you?"

"Not necessarily. I was thinking more about you realizing that you, too, had a hard time dealing with Gabe, and that he has accepted it and forgiven you. When you forgive someone, it gives you room in your heart to love them." She turned to him, and her voice was gentle, despite her iron-grip gaze. "But this does apply to your father, doesn't it? You might find, after a day of 'fishing,' you can forgive his mistakes and learn to live together as a family."

Joe met her stare, refusing to run this time. This woman just didn't understand. "You haven't had the experience of holding your sobbing mother or explaining to your little brother why Daddy didn't love him, why he left." His voice held a warning edge.

"No, but I have comforted your brother and explained to him why you don't visit, why you can't bother to come home for more than twelve hours for your mother's funeral, why you prefer strangers to the company of your own flesh and blood."

Joe winced and fury coursed through him in tremors. But Ruby's words, despite their sting, were accurate. He'd betrayed Gabe as much as his father had betrayed them all.

And Gabe had forgiven both of them.

The realization crippled Joe, and he shrank onto the top step. He cradled his face in his hands. "What have I done?"

Ruby settled beside him. "Coped. Ran. Survived." She touched his shoulder. "It's time to come home, Joe."

"I'll never have a home, Ruby. Not as long as—"

"Not as long as you wall people out."

"I was about to say not as long as I have contracts to fill, people to please. Not as long as people know who I am."

"No, that's not your biggest problem. You can find a way to deal with the invasion of your privacy. You just don't want to. It's a convenient excuse to hide the real reason you keep running."

"I don't think seventeen stitches and a broken shoulder are a convenient excuse."

Ruby was silent beside him.

"Anyway, I love what I do. And I love my freedom."

"Sure you do. But you wouldn't give it up for the right woman?"

Joe flinched.

"You have to stop walling people out. Gabe wants to love you, and he wants to be a family—that means you and your dad."

"I'm not letting Wayne Michaels within shouting distance."

"Then you'll never stop running."

He glared at her. "I am *not* running."

"Joe! You haven't lived in one place for over a decade. Running is exactly what you're doing. You'll barely slow down to take your brother fishing."

"That's not fair. I'm here because I love him."

"Of course you are. I'm not disputing your love for him. But you won't even consider sticking around."

He made a move to object. Oh, he'd considered sticking around. In fact, that very fantasy consumed his thoughts over the last week more often than he wanted to admit.

"Don't you see?" Ruby continued. "You were scared to let Gabe too close, scared to risk getting hurt. But today proved that yes, love comes with a cost, but it is also priceless. In order to truly love Gabe, you're going to have to learn to forgive. And it has to start with your father."

Joe gave a harsh laugh. "I've gone half my life without talking to him," he said. "Do you think forgiving him is going to revolutionize my life? maybe erase everything he's done? Suddenly we're going to start baking the Thanksgiving turkey and become the Norman Rockwell family?"

"No. But I do think forgiving him might give you a chance to really let someone inside that locked heart of yours. In fact, I think forgiving him is the first step to finding what you are searching for."

"And what's that?"

Ruby was silent.

"Forgiving him is just going to let him off the hook for completely shredding our family. Why should I forgive someone who ran at the first sign of trouble?" Joe's words stuck in his throat.

"Yes, why should you?" Ruby shook her head. "Why should you forgive someone who made a mistake? You've certainly never made any."

Joe sucked in a sharp breath. "You don't pull any punches, do you?"

"I'm sorry. I don't mean to hurt you."

"I never made the mistakes he did. He doesn't deserve forgiveness."

"Does anyone? That's not your place to decide. God's forgiven him. Can you do any less?"

Joe's eyes burned. "You don't know what you're asking."

"This might be difficult for you to believe right now, Joe, but God doesn't expect you to do this hard thing by yourself."

Joe frowned.

"God knows how tough it is to forgive, especially when someone has done you wrong. But He does expect you to do it. And He expects you to be patient and trust Him to work in others' lives. Psalm 37. It's one of my favorites, especially when I know God wants me to do something impossible, like forgive."

Ruby directed her gaze to the sunset hovering over the far pines. "'Be still in the presence of the Lord, and wait patiently for Him to act. Don't worry about evil people who prosper or fret about their wicked schemes.'"

"But God hasn't cut my dad off or punished him. He's *forgiven* him," Joe spat out.

"The story of the Prodigal Son is hardest for those in the shoes of the oldest son," Ruby responded. Her voice softened. "The baseline truth is, you don't want to forgive your father, despite the fact God already has. You think you have some righteous corner on pain that absolves you of obedience. But you must forgive and trust God to deal with your father. Wayne Michaels *has* been punished . . . he's lost you. But you've had Gabe's and the Lord's favor all this time. It's time to forgive and inherit all God has for your family."

Joe rubbed his forehead with his hand. "I don't know. I'll admit, I didn't realize how much I missed Gabe. But I'm not sure God wants us to be a family. It might be too late."

"Did it ever occur to you that God brought you back here precisely because He wants to save your family? I know you're afraid to really stick around and love Gabe. The more you love him, the more you stand to lose. The more you're reminded of exactly what your father did. Don't you see how the memory of how deeply he wounded you keeps you on the run? You hold people at a distance, afraid to let them know you.

"Perhaps, Joe, if you stood your ground, you might find the strength to forgive. Maybe you'd even find that it's easier than you expected to trust someone with your secrets." Her voice gentled. "Maybe, for you, hoping in the Lord means forgiving and finally finding a place to call home."

"I don't need a home."

"Everyone needs a home. But you'll never find it as long as you keep hiding. As long as you refuse to let people love the real Joe. You'll never know the joy of love unless you risk your heart. And you'll never be able to risk unless you learn to forgive."

Joe took off his cap and scrubbed a hand through his hair, wishing he could put distance between Ruby and her bluntness, but knowing it was the one thing she expected him to do. Yes, he was afraid to risk, but the risk was more than just letting someone inside his life, revealing his identity. Gabe was the biggest risk of all. However, jeopardizing his heart had nothing to do with forgiveness, did it?

He rubbed his eyes with his thumb and forefinger. "It's easier for Gabe to forgive, you know. He hardly remembered Dad. I lived with him for fifteen years. Then he was gone and my life . . . it just . . . hurts too much." He winced at the desperation in his voice, feeling like he'd just carved his heart out of his chest and tossed it flopping and bleeding in front of her.

"I know it hurts," Ruby said softly. "But I don't think it is easier for Gabe at all. He knew what your father did to you and your mother. And he still forgave. The difference is Gabe lets God fight his battles. He lets God work in people's lives, and he lets them be human. Trusting God protects him, gives him the courage to risk opening his heart and let out love. He knows he is safely in God's shelter. He won't crumble if your father, or even you, let him down. God will hold him up."

Her words tugged at Joe's spirit as he thought about all the times God, indeed, had held him up, given him strength, courage, answers to problems. Forgiving his father, however, had never been a problem he'd struggled with. In fact, he hadn't even considered it.

"I know about the woman in town, by the way," Ruby said. "I heard about the fire." She hesitated. "Joe, would you tell me about Mona?"

Joe's mouth went dry. "How do you know about her?"

"The fire made the *Superior Times*. I figured the rest out."

He pulled a deep, ragged breath. "Mona is . . . exasperating. Or maybe *determined* is a better word. She's definitely the most creative woman I've ever met. She's got this notion that she can transform an old house into a bookstore . . . and somehow she's doing it. She calls it the Footstep of Heaven. She works every daylight hour and then some, remodeling, ordering books and coffee supplies, and planning her future. She's amazing and fun

and smart, and she has these eyes that leave me speech-less—"

"Oh, Joe, you're in trouble." Ruby had a sly grin on her face. "Does she know who you are?"

Joe cringed. "No."

She obviously understood what his answer meant because she shook her head. "Then I take it she doesn't know about Gabe either?"

Joe's chest clenched. "I don't know how to tell her."

"Shame on you. I'd try the truth."

"How can I? You, better than anyone, know what the truth can do. Even if I told her who I am, Gabe just seals my fate. She's better off believing I'm a rootless handy-man."

"You ought to give her a chance. You might be surprised."

"What if I'm not?" His tone revived his childhood betrayal.

Ruby sighed. "Only you can decide to take that risk. But until you do, you'll never find peace. You can't run forever. She'll eventually find out, maybe not about Gabe, but your face will grace the newspapers in this little town the minute someone figures out who you are."

Softly he said, "Maybe I'll be gone by then." The sudden stinging in his eye made him clench his jaw. It was painfully clear that Ruby was right. Eventually the truth would blow sky-high, and it hurt him enough to imagine the shock written on Mona's face let alone her anger. He might as well open his chest and let her stomp his heart into a million jagged pieces. His throat burned.

"It'll be a lot easier if I just leave." He winced as the words rose up and nearly choked him. It wasn't hard to admit, even to himself, that his choices came with a stiff price. "I can't stay." He wanted simpler, easier answers, but there were none. "Even though she needs me."

"Or you need her," Ruby gently corrected.

Joe flinched.

Rip's sudden appearance soothed the moment. The Lab came bounding from the woods and roared into Joe's lap, bowling him over. Covered in burrs, Rip smelled like a three-day-old roadkill. "Yuck, get away from me."

Ruby laughed. "C'mon, you old dog." She grabbed his collar, made him sit, and began working the burrs from his fur. "You just need a good brushing and a bath."

Joe admired Ruby's way with dogs and people. Her direct, striking comments wounded, but her manner soothed the pain.

"It sounds like you have two very good reasons to want to put down roots in Deep Haven, Joe. I know Gabe would be thrilled."

Joe rubbed Rip behind the ear as Ruby worked with his fur. He didn't want to admit that the idea touched a desperate place inside him.

"God wants to be your shelter too, you know. Relax inside His protection. Ask Him to help you forgive and tell Mona the truth. God will take care of the rest." Ruby pulled out the last burr and tossed it off the porch. "It's either that or say good-bye to Mona and spend the rest of your life wishing you hadn't."

Cu

Twenty-four hours later, Joe rolled into Deep Haven, nearly gagging from the smell emanating from Rip's

body. The dog's odor had only ripened over a day. "You
need a bath and something stronger than Dial soap on
that coat of yours." He pulled up next to the local dime
store, thankful their summer hours had already started.
The over-the-door bell jangled as he entered.

A slim brunette in a brown smock, pushing back age
with too much makeup and cornrowed hair, looked up
from the cash register. "Ten minutes, pal."

Joe nodded and headed toward the shampoo section.

He'd been fighting Ruby's words the entire day. He
thought spending the night at the Garden would help him
come to peace with the thoughts she'd stirred up. Face his
past? He did that every day of his life. He was the one who
lived with the guilt and shame of abandoning his brother.
But how could Ruby suggest he put down roots, surrender
his freedom? Surrender his entire life, she meant. He'd been
living for the high of adventure for so many years, he'd
crash hard if he suddenly had a permanent address.

Maybe it wouldn't be quite as painful, however, if
Mona was there to catch him.

There he went thinking with his heart instead of his
brain. Obviously his gray matter had turned to mush over
the past four weeks. Yes, he'd spent much of this past
week harboring ideas—even dreams—of becoming at
least a semipermanent fixture at the Footstep. But if he
were to take a hard look at the truth, he'd notice that
Mona hadn't mentioned one word about him staying on.
Hadn't even breathed the thought, even if she did seem to
enjoy his company. Unfortunately, he'd allowed her
laughter to seed all sorts of delicious dreams he'd never
before acknowledged. Now they'd snowballed hopelessly
out of control.

He wasn't ready to chuck everything he'd built over the last ten years, was he? Freedom had a price tag . . . but staying put could be his death knell. Contrary to Ruby's smug presuppositions, his lifestyle wasn't a pitiful excuse to hide from love. The woman didn't have an inkling about what it felt like to be stalked, to be constantly glancing over your shoulder, poised for trouble. Even if he did satisfy Ruby's prerequisites and figure out a way to forgive his father—and the odds of that were slim—he'd still have to tell Mona the truth, and that would certainly obliterate his so-called privacy. Living in a glass house would be a thousand times worse than saying good-bye to a white-picket fence and little people in sleeper pajamas.

What, now he was thinking about children? He blew out a breath and tried to focus on dog shampoo. Maybe a stubborn daughter with green eyes and curly blonde hair whom he could delight with stories and tickles. Or a child with a cupid round face and almond eyes. He groaned aloud. Yes, that was exactly the type of child that would fit into Mona's ordered life. The Gabe problem only cemented the many reasons for him to keep his dreams safely leashed.

He'd thought that some time away from the Footstep might straighten out the jumble in his brain. Might tighten his focus and remind him of his liabilities. Unfortunately, as the day wore long, he only ached more to see Mona, despite the fact that he'd buried himself in hours of work at the Garden. He felt wrung out, dirty, strangely alive . . . and terrified.

He was crazy in love with Mona. His own description of his "boss" to Ruby reverberated in his head over and

over, and he'd finally admitted the truth to himself sometime in the middle of the night as he listened to the mantel clock tick out the hours. He loved Mona's laughter, her determination, her dreams. He felt a tinge of relief to finally put a name to that hot, explosive feeling that spread though his chest every time he thought of her luminous green eyes and the way the wind played with her hair. Maybe that feeling was just the thing he'd been searching for all his life. Maybe God had answered the one prayer he'd always been too ashamed to ask . . . to send him home.

Maybe Ruby was right. He needed Mona.

Oh boy, he *was* in trouble. Yes, he had to figure out a way to stay or his heart would take a serious beating.

"Closing up, mister. Did you want to get something?" The brunette stood before him, hands on her hips, eyeballing him like he was a shoplifter or the local hobo trying to find a place to park for the night. He certainly looked the part.

"Yes, dog shampoo."

"You're not going to find it standing next to cosmetics. Try third aisle down, next to the flea-and-tick medicine." Her condescending voice shrank him three sizes.

He slunk over to the pet aisle and grabbed the first bottle of shampoo he could find. The clerk was counting change at the front. He plunked the bottle down on the counter and reached for his wallet. Flipping it open, he paused for a moment at a picture of himself on a fishing boat, holding a coho salmon, surrounded by a group of grinning, grimy sailors. In the photo, his hair was long and tangled, and he had at least an inch of whisker growth on his face.

"Hey, great picture!" The clerk leaned over and studied it, actually grabbing the wallet to pull it closer. "You know, I've seen that photo somewhere before. . . ."

Joe stifled a groan. He pulled the wallet away. "How much for the shampoo?"

The clerk smiled as if she had a secret. "You're not—"

"No. How much?"

She licked her lips and scrutinized him. "You know, if you added the beard, you'd look just like—"

"I don't need the shampoo. Thanks anyway." Joe spun on his heel and darted through the door before the clerk could finish her thought.

His throat thickened as he stalked to the truck. A noose had banded around his chest—the very noose he'd been expecting for weeks. He unlocked the door, got in, and leaned his forehead against the steering wheel, breathing hard. Yes, he needed Mona. But *he* was the last thing *she* needed. She had her hands full building her life, and the Joe Michaels deluxe package, complete with handicapped brother and covert identity, did not fit into that reality. She needed a man who could hang up his backpack and invest in her dreams.

Instead he'd spent the past month knitting together a facade of white lies. Lies meant to keep him and Gabe safe. Lies that could unravel any moment.

No, he couldn't stay.

He closed his eyes and fought the urge to weep.

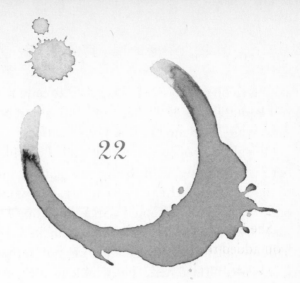

22

Mona leaned against the doorjamb, a wadded dust rag in her hand, and watched Joe as he sat on the front steps and watched the fiery sunset. He had a worn blue baseball cap propped backwards on his head, and he held his hammer in his lap while he absently rubbed Rip's ear. She lifted a tiny prayer of thanks for her handyman. *He's so much more than I expected, Lord.*

"And He will give you your heart's desires." The words buzzing through her memory made her tremble.

After their date to the dump, Joe had disappeared all day Saturday and most of Sunday. Where to, she had no idea, but she had missed him. Relief had washed over her when she heard his truck pull into the gravel drive late last night. Missing him, she realized, was a fairly significant emotion. It meant she'd made room for him in her life. She was starting to depend on him. She tried to ignore the rush of fear at that thought.

Her emotions did a tiny jig when he'd rapped on her back door this morning, just as dawn dented the sky, asking to be put to work. Liza was already painting something in the back shed, and Mona had been making a list while brewing her first pot of coffee.

One glimpse of Joe's alluring smile had sidetracked her pensive thoughts of the upcoming day, and she had to fight to keep her emotions at bay. But when he slid onto the counter, accepted a steaming cup of coffee, and said, "At your service, milady," she melted. She'd never had a problem with shyness before, but in that instant, words abandoned her. The twinkle in Joe's magnetic blue eyes didn't help.

It took a long sip of coffee before she could say, "Bruce Schultz is bringing over the bookcases."

"Great!" Joe exclaimed, as if moving furniture was exactly how he wanted to spend a Monday morning. Her face flamed, and to her profound relief, the doorbell rang just then.

Mona raced Joe to the door and met Bruce. The old carpenter, wearing a faded flannel shirt and a fraying Minnesota Twins hat, smiled through his tanned, wrinkled face. He was an old family friend with a long list of customers. She'd wisely put in her order for handcrafted oak bookcases months ago.

"Got your order in the truck. Where do you want 'em?" Bruce hooked his thumbs in his belt loops and grinned. Joe extended his hand and introduced himself. Bruce pumped it like they were old friends. Mona had to admit that Joe fit right in with the Deep Haven wildlife.

Mona directed the movers to the living room, where the sunlight glided over the smoothly varnished floors. She'd spent the rest of the day painting the final coat of varnish on her coffee bar and hanging a bright yellow,

rose, and light blue plaid swag over the newly painted front windows.

Now a heady peace swept through her as twilight polished the room in rose gold. Mona ran the dust rag over the paned-glass, oak front door Bruce had installed. She'd commissioned the oval glass picture of a pine tree, lake, and rocky bluffs from one of Liza's art buddies in the city. The perfect rendition of heaven on earth.

Rip groaned in pleasure as Joe rubbed his ear. Beyond them, the red sun painted the lake in shades of cranberry.

Mona stepped outside and plopped down beside them on the steps, hugging her knees. "Why do you call him Rip?"

Joe cupped the dog's snout. "He tried to eat me."

"You survived, I see."

Joe angled her a wicked grin. "Barely. He tore a hole in my favorite jeans. Hey, you don't sew, do you?"

Mona returned a mock glare. "Don't even think it." She found it so easy to relax inside Joe's honeyed laughter. "You seem to know your way around animals." She reached over and patted Rip on the head.

Joe caught her hand and directed it to a soft spot behind Rip's floppy left ear. "Here. He likes it right here."

The feel of Joe's hand on hers sent waves of heat through her veins. The warmth lingered long after he let go and folded his hands between his knees.

"I've had a few dogs," he added. "First one was named Stretch. He was a dachshund I picked up in Mexico . . . saved him from being a fella's lunch."

Mona swallowed a grin.

"The next dog was a cocker spaniel—blonde and

feisty." Joe cocked an eyebrow at her. Mona swatted him with her dust rag. "No, she was sweet as sugar and with me for many years. Finally died one day in my lap as I was driving through Montana."

"What was her name?"

"Olive Oyl."

"Olive Oyl?" Mona frowned at him.

"You know, Popeye's girl?"

She rolled her eyes. "So you think you're Popeye?"

He pasted on a mischievous look and flexed his muscles. "No, I'm Brutus!"

Mona giggled, then gave way to a hearty laugh. It felt good.

Joe smiled at her approvingly. "It's good to hear you laugh, Mona."

She heard her name as a melody in his voice and felt an accompanying tingle down to her toes. "I laugh, Joe."

He pursed his lips and shook his head. "Not enough. Your laughter reminds me of the breeze from Lake Superior . . . refreshing and clean."

His compliment settled over her like a soft flannel blanket. "So, you've had a few dogs. Ever had any girl-friends?"

The bold question had incubated in the warmth of his kind words, but as soon as it escaped, Mona wanted to die on the spot. Why had she asked that? It was so revealing and desperate. She felt like skipping herself into the lake surf, along with the other shards of bare driftwood, and letting the waves wash her far, far away.

It seemed to catch Joe off balance as well, and it eased her pain to see he'd turned faintly red. He swallowed

hard. She noticed that all at once he found the sunset riveting. "A few. Not many. No one that stuck around."

"Or you didn't stick around for . . . ," she added quietly. She was really going out on a limb, and her audacity stunned her. But she had to know. Did Joe usually do the leaving? Or had he been left?

"Right," he said simply, and her heart fell slightly.

"Maybe you just never found the right place to call home," she offered softly.

"Maybe," Joe whispered. He picked up a twig and threw it. Rip shot after it like it was fresh meat.

The air seemed hotter than she had thought, and the humidity moistened her skin. "I gotta get back to work," she murmured.

"Mona, wait." Joe's voice, small as it was, practically grabbed her. "I have to know something. Why are you doing this? Deep Haven is such a remote place, and you are so young to be settling down here. Why?"

The lilac tree in the front yard had just begun to bud clumps of lavender, but the breeze reaped the scent and perfumed the sunset. Mona rubbed her knees and sighed. "This has been my dream since I was a kid. It just seemed to make sense, especially after . . ." Mona let her explanation die. No need to bring it up. It wasn't any of his business, especially if he wasn't sticking around. She felt her fragile hope start to wither.

"After?"

"Nothing. Forget it." Mona sprang to her feet, shooting for a quick retreat. Tears stabbed at her eyes.

"Mona." Joe caught her wrist.

Mona paused, one foot on the upper step. *Please, don't make me tell you.*

"I think this will be a great place."

Mona bit her lip. An unguarded tear made it over the edge. She smiled weakly. "You think so?"

Joe released her. "I know a little bit of heaven when I see it."

Something like a whimper erupted inside her, and all at once she was sitting beside him and pouring out the entire wretched story.

"I was born with a headstrong streak, and as my father's only daughter, he fed the independent blaze. While I suppose it has helped me pull together the Footstep, perhaps I wouldn't even be sitting here if it weren't for my penchant to have my own way."

Mona's throat closed, but she forced words through. "It happened ten years ago, after our annual summer vacation here in Deep Haven. My mom decided to stay on for another week; she likes the early autumn and the spray of firelight in the poplar and oak along the hill. I, however, was starting school, and my pop had offered to help me move." She closed her eyes, remembering their last conversation.

"We left for home too late. I suppose neither of us could abandon the last sunset on the beach. We watched God paint the sky, turning the lake from indigo to platinum." Her eyes misted, and her voice turned ragged despite her attempts at composure. "That last sunset was magnificent."

Mona felt Joe's eyes on her but refused to meet his gaze. Steeling herself, she curled her arms around her waist and continued, tumbling over her words. "I insisted on driving, of course, even though we were both tired. The accident happened south of Duluth on I-35 around

midnight." She focused on the blurry shoreline. "I don't remember much. One second the road was a clear black ribbon; the next, headlights blinded me like lasers."

Her voice dropped to a wretched whisper. "I fell asleep at the wheel."

When she felt Joe's arm edge around her, she instinctively stiffened. "Thankfully, Pop slept through it. He never felt a thing. I swerved and the truck broadsided us." She swallowed the wool that had gathered in her throat. "I survived."

She refused to surrender to Joe's gentle nudge but was grateful for it all the same.

"My mom and dad were together twenty-five years. Three months after the accident, Mom bought a condo in Arizona." Mona knew she sounded bitter, but she couldn't erase the tone from her voice.

Joe sat silently beside her, his arm around her waist. His presence eased the brutality of the memory, and as the wind dried the tears on her cheeks, twilight slowly descended, a beautiful canopy of magenta and periwinkle.

"I don't know why the Footstep is so important to me," she finally offered, flicking a glance up at Joe. "But I feel like I've been searching for something all this time, and it was right here waiting for me."

Joe captured her gaze with his languid blue eyes that seemed more perceptive than she felt comfortable with. "Peace, maybe?"

Mona bit her lip. Maybe she had been searching for peace. It certainly wasn't an easy commodity to lay her hands on. But maybe here . . . especially sitting next to Joe . . . She wiped her cheeks. "So, Joe. In fairness, why are *you* here?"

Joe withdrew his arm, threaded his fingers together, and cracked his knuckles in a staccato rhythm. "I'm not sure. But peace, maybe, sounds okay."

Ce

"Come for a walk with me?" Mona ducked her head into Liza's room. Liza sat cross-legged on her orange carpet, a garden of pottery sitting on a plastic sheet arranged in a circle around her. "What are you doing?"

"Signing my stuff." Liza looked up and grinned. "These are going to be collector's items someday, you know."

"Absolutely."

"Where are you headed?" Liza returned her focus to the mug in her hand.

"Down to the beach. I have some stale bread I thought I'd throw to the scavengers."

"Yum," Liza said, but her attention stayed on the work in her lap.

Mona was just turning away when Liza glanced up abruptly. "I'm going to go see Brian. He's sitting in the Deep Haven jail, and I think he needs some company."

A shocked gasp escaped Mona. "Why?"

"Because he's our friend."

"He's our enemy. He tried to destroy us."

Liza's dark eyes glinted. "I know. But he needs some forgiveness, and we need to give it to him."

Mona considered her friend. Liza had a way of seeing the world through rose-colored glasses. Reality never seemed to hit her straight on. Even Brian's deception and betrayal had only skimmed her emotions. Why?

"I'm not sure I can do that. He set out to destroy me, to wreck my dream. He even tried to kill me!"

Liza set down her pot. Her face flecked with the hue of sadness, and tears edged her eyes. "Mona, honey, you call this place the Footstep of Heaven. And it will be, for both of us. I've been dreaming this particular dream since you suggested it five years ago. But for it to truly be the 'footstep of heaven,' the fragrance of heaven needs to permeate this place, not just be a sign over the door. We have to forgive, even if Brian doesn't deserve it."

The truth of Liza's words struck a soft place in Mona's heart, but everything inside her rebelled from the thought. Her face must have reflected her pain, for compassion entered Liza's expression. "I know it is harder for you, Mona. You have so much more invested in this place than I do. But think about it."

Mona nodded, unable to get words past her confusion.

"We can hardly expect God to forgive us when we don't forgive others," Liza reminded softly.

The moon hung like a thumbnail in the inky sky above Lake Superior. Mona lifted her face to the brisk wind and listened to the waves crash on shore. The air smelled wet and fishy. Mona spotted seagulls riding the rolling current.

Liza's words burned in Mona's chest. She'd never expected God to forgive her. Somehow it just seemed logical that forgiveness, like blessings, had to be earned. The grace of God simply overwhelmed her, and to be honest, she struggled to embrace it. She seemed to be constantly grabbing at reality, trying to take in the concept, afraid to settle in and be comfortable with the impossibility, the wonder, the magnitude of forgiveness. And of course, God's forgiveness meant that she should certainly forgive herself.

Sometimes that was asking too much.

Liza was right about one thing—Mona couldn't let bitterness and anger sour her future. Perhaps that was why Liza seemed to bounce back from Brian's deception so easily. She'd already wrestled with forgiveness and won. Mona had to agree that in order for God to truly bless the Footstep of Heaven, she would have to find a way to forgive Brian also.

Mona picked her way along the shore. Rocks crunched and rolled under her steps. She found a large uneven boulder, hoisted herself aboard, and gazed skyward. *Lord, I know You want me to forgive Brian. Please help me.* Mona pinched her lips together to keep her jaw from quivering. Forgiveness was a painful and soul-wringing affair, and she couldn't manage it without God's help. But He had already answered her other prayers, in ways she wouldn't have imagined.

Mona pressed her fingers against her eyes and effectively halted her tears. The image of her handyman filled her mind with such clarity, she could trace his face. Joe had been an answer to prayer. A blessing. And if her heart spoke the truth, she desperately wanted him to stay.

His words lingered in her mind. *Peace, maybe.* Why would Joe need peace? What kept him drifting from place to place? He'd certainly made the rounds—Mexico, Montana, and did he say Russia? The man was a tight-

lipped enigma, to put it in shorthand. That certainly wasn't the prescription for a solid relationship.

But she had to admit that she hadn't felt so comfortable in a man's presence since she'd sat on the beach with her father years ago. And Joe offered her more than just comfort. While her father had stood before her, guiding and advising, Joe stationed himself behind her, supporting and encouraging. When she thought of him, something inside her made her want to wrap her arms around his neck and hold him close. Forever. She'd known it this afternoon when he'd listened to her story without comment or accusation, then spoken those tender words. She'd even known it Friday, sitting at the dump, nestled against his shoulder, cherishing every minute.

Mona bit her lip. She loved Joe. And now she'd have to ask God to make him stay. Talk about *heart's desires* . . . she swallowed hard.

It seemed that God was blessing her plans, however. There had been no roaches, no floods, no poison on her grass, no fires, and no building catastrophes for nearly a week. She was setting a record, she thought ruefully. Mona laced her fingers behind her neck and kneaded a stiff muscle.

"I can do that."

Every muscle in her body froze. Joe's soft voice drifted on the breeze. "I give excellent back rubs. At least Rip seems to like them." Mona's eyes widened as she watched Joe climb up and settle on the boulder behind her. He put two strong hands on her shoulders, gently wiped away her hair, and began to work her neck muscles with his thumbs.

Mona held her breath and trembled. "Thanks, Joe." She was mortified to hear her mousy voice.

"No problem," he returned in his melodic tenor.

Silence mingled with the harmony of the waves. A seagull's song echoed in the velvet darkness. Mona relaxed as Joe worked out the tension in her neck. Rip chased birds, then gave up and scrambled up the boulder. He collapsed on Mona's feet and sighed.

"Rip likes you," Joe said.

Oh, how she wanted to ask Joe to stay. It nearly crossed her lips, but he interrupted her.

"The place is almost ready. Less than two weeks left. Amazing how time flies, huh?"

A lump suddenly formed in her throat. "Right," she croaked.

She didn't ask him to stay, didn't offer more comment on his words. He finished rubbing her neck, then scooted behind her and pulled her back against his chest. It almost hurt physically to rest against him, to feel his strong arms around her, and to let him fold his hands over hers. She kept calling herself an idiot, and even more so when he whispered in her ear. "I sure do hope and pray your bookstore is a success."

His breath was close, and her skin prickled when his whiskers brushed against her cheek. He smelled of soap, jeans, and flannel, and she let herself savor it. She told herself to pull away, but the urge to let him hold her, to trust him despite her fears and inevitable broken heart, overwhelmed her so, it felt almost supernatural.

Tears pricked her eyes. "Me too," she agreed in a broken voice.

He went quiet, as if he, too, sensed the inevitability of their relationship.

"Thank you, Mona," he murmured into her hair.

Mona turned in his arms to meet his eyes. "For what, a job?"

His white teeth and crooked grin flashed in the moonlight. "Well, that too, but I was thinking more about this afternoon." His voice dropped. "For telling me your story." His expression grew tender, and something in his eyes made her heart thump—hard. He cupped his hand on her face and rubbed his thumb along her cheekbone. "I'm sorry about your father. It sounds like he was a wonderful man."

Mona's eyes began to mist, and she leaned her face into his palm.

"My father left us when I was fifteen," Joe said. His voice hardened. "Sometimes I wish he had died. It might have been easier to know he was gone and left us against his wishes."

Mona saw a muscle pull in his jaw. He looked beyond her into the dark shoreline. Into the past. "I'll never forget the day he left. It ripped me in half. Part of me wanted to go with him. The other half knew I had to stay with my mother."

Mona hurt from the agony twisting his face. "Did he come back?"

His expression suddenly became like that of a wounded animal facing its own mortality. He seemed afraid, and she didn't understand it. A chill rippled through her.

"I don't know yet," he answered.

He had opened his heart and let her peek inside. The realization of that humbled her and filled her with hope. Joe could be vulnerable.

Mona cupped her hand over his on her cheek and

couldn't ignore the delight that filled her when he threaded his fingers through hers. "I'm so sorry, Joe."

His gaze touched hers, and she saw his emotions fill his eyes before he had a chance to hide them. Mona's mouth went dry and her pulse jumped. The moment was now. She would ask him and maybe he would stay. He brought such life to the Footstep . . . the place would be barren without him. Yes, he could stay and—

Joe slid his other hand behind her neck and entwined it in her hair.

She scrambled to find the words to voice her request. His eyes roamed her face, caressed her eyes, her forehead, her nose, and stopped at her mouth. The question lodged in her throat as she saw his intention pool in his eyes.

She surrendered without hesitation.

He whispered her name just as his lips brushed against hers. His kiss was tentative, not demanding, and devastatingly gentle. Mona melted against him. He made a soft noise in the back of his throat, making her entire body tingle. Yes, this is what she'd been waiting for—the tingle, the peace. He wound his arm around her neck, and she sank into his safe embrace.

As his kiss deepened, so did her understanding that indeed she would not have to ask him to stay . . . he was already counting on it.

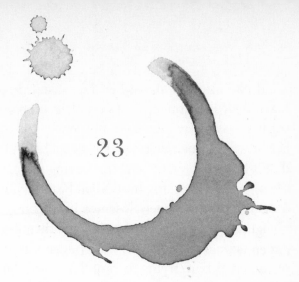

23

They're here!" Mona's delighted whoop shook the rafters, and her dash through the dining room rattled the cups Joe was stacking under the coffee bar.

How she heard the UPS truck from the kitchen was a marvel. Joe couldn't hear anything but Handel blaring through the house on her new stereo system. Anything, even Conway Twitty, would have been an improvement. But when he suggested a change, he'd been on the receiving end of one of her famous sour looks and he'd backed away, hands up.

She'd grinned playfully, however, immediately icing the bruise with concession. "I found an Alabama album at your favorite hangout—the Goodwill. We'll try it after 'Water Music' is finished."

Joe had laughed also, but it was a facade, and every time he noticed the twinkle in her eyes, shame stabbed him. He'd spied on her all morning, listening to her hum and watching a contented smile grace her face, and through it all, guilt played him like a bass drum in a parade.

He had no right to kiss her. He wasn't prepared to make the commitment that should accompany last night's passionate kiss. Commitment? He had yet to tell her his real name! He'd woven such a web of lies he didn't know where to start untangling them. He'd tossed the night away, calling himself all brands of idiot. Somehow he'd let the tender closeness of her body nestled in his arms crumble his resolve, leading them both down a path he could never journey. A condemning voice had screamed at him, trying to yank him back, but the sweetness of her kiss and the heady perfume of her unmitigated trust had drowned it to oblivion.

If he could only find a way to make the unspoken promise he'd given her through his kiss a reality and spend the rest of his life with her. If only he could find a way to confess to every lie he'd told.

She'd be furious.

And wouldn't that put a nice touch on their last days together? His deceit would surely make her jump into his arms.

If only time didn't loom above them.

If only he'd told Mona the truth the first day.

Mona skipped by him, joy written on her face as she lugged in the first box. Her green eyes sparkled. "They're here!"

Joe nodded, grinning. She looked like a kid at Christmas. And he was the Grinch. Dread's cold fist wound around him even as he walked onto the porch to help the deliverymen.

An hour later she was outside signing for the delivery when the telephone rang. Joe thumped down the last heavy box, probably filled with gold bars, on a tall

stack and leaned out the window. "Mona, your phone is ringing!"

"Answer it for me!"

He found the cord and followed it to the base. The cordless unit wasn't on the stand. The phone continued to ring as Joe sifted through papers, boxes, and eventually dove for the other phone in the kitchen. "Hello?"

"I knew I could find you."

His heart plummeted to his knees. He winced and considered slamming down the receiver, ripping the cord from the wall. The voice on the other end gave a shrill laugh.

Joe gulped back panic. "How did you find me?"

"Oh, c'mon. Who helped you hide your little brother up there in the woods? The new director seems very nice. Helpful."

"Gabe's not hiding," Joe growled. He looked around, praying that Mona wouldn't walk in.

"Yeah, but you obviously are. You're late. We expected to hear from you two weeks ago. I don't like having to track you down. That's not our deal. What's going on?" The voice turned dark. "Please tell me you have something cooked up for me."

"We'll discuss it when I see you," Joe whispered. This was not the time to face his failure . . . and the consequences. He'd done a pretty good job of dodging his responsibilities for the past three weeks. Too good. But now, showing up without the goods he promised seemed the least of his problems.

"I certainly hope you're not going to let us down. You know we invested the farm on your word."

Joe rubbed the back of his neck and stared out the

kitchen window at Liza, busy at work in her pottery shed. "Just give me a few more days. I'll be there."

"You've got one week, pal. One week. Don't disappoint me. And you keep your pretty face out of the news, hear me?"

"Like a siren."

The line clicked off and Joe pressed the receiver to his forehead, fighting back a swell of frustration. As if to add fuel to his rising panic, he looked down on the counter and noticed a brochure topping the stack of mail. *Try the Garden for fresh strawberries* it read.

He grabbed the advertisement and shoved it into a drawer just as Mona sauntered into the room. "Who was on the telephone?"

Joe shook his head, trying to force words past the knot in his throat. "Wrong number."

He lied. It seemed like such a little one in the face of all the betrayals of the past month. But this one stung, driving home the awful reality of the nightmare he'd created.

As Mona went into the living room, he replaced the phone and braced both hands on the counter. Like the climax of a bad Western, he had villains ambushing him on all fronts, and the hanging at high noon felt only minutes away.

"I'm going out for a walk," he hollered, not waiting for Mona's reply before he slipped out the back door.

The last thing he wanted was for her to see him cry.

The sun turned her hair to gold, and Mona had such a whimsical look on her face, it nearly made Joe turn right

around and head back out to the beach for another hour
of pacing and stone skipping. As it was, he barely felt
able to saunter into the Footstep with a forced smile.
"Do you plan on selling these books warehouse-style,
or are you actually going to use the bookshelves you
ordered?" he teased.

Surrounded by boxes, she looked up from her cross-
legged position on the floor. It tickled Joe to see her
startled expression—like a child caught stealing cookies.
She'd tucked her hair haphazardly behind her ear, and
she looked deliciously rustic in worn brown leggings and
a green-and-brown flannel shirt.

He felt something inside him go weak. He should
leave now—today. In a week he'd be helpless. Even
now, only his boss's voice in his ears made him sift
through fantasy to see the brutal truth: he had dues to
pay, and he couldn't do it in Deep Haven.

"What are you reading?" he asked, crouching beside her.

She grinned sheepishly. "Mitford."

He resisted the impulse to run his fingers along an
errant strand of golden hair and instead folded his hands
between his knees. "I suppose a person who owns a
bookstore would read a lot."

Mona closed the book on her lap, then rubbed the
cover gently. "I love books. They're like a piece of my
life I haven't lived yet. I could live forever on a desert
island, surrounded by my favorite authors—C. S. Lewis,
Dickens, Austen."

"What about today's authors—John Grisham, Tom
Clancy, or Mary Higgins Clark?"

Mona set the book down, pushed up her flannel
sleeves, and dove elbow deep into the box, as if digging

for clams. She pulled out a stack of paperbacks by John Grisham. "Yep, like them too."

Joe laughed. "Give me a knife. I'll help."

She'd ordered everything—suspense thrillers, biographies, military operations, even romances. Mona opened boxes and directed Joe until they had built a maze of books towering around the room. She was counting a stack of Jack Higgins spy thrillers when Joe stole up behind her, a paperback copy of Clancy's *Politika* in hand, and tagged her. "You're it," he said, cutting behind a stack of boxes.

She turned, and he recognized the expression on her face—from the beach and at the Kettle. He had started a war. Mona faked, then charged. Joe darted behind a row of Minnesota coffee-table books, but Mona snared a copy of *Lake Wobegon Days* and tagged him. Unfortunately, she also nudged a wall of books. They shuddered like a building on the San Andreas fault.

"Yipes!" Mona dove for the stack and wrapped her arms around the top layer.

Joe wrapped his arms around her. "Yipes," he echoed softly. She felt so small and tender in his arms. A perfect fit. The fragrance of soft flannel and fresh lilac surrounded him, and suddenly a feeling so right it could only be peace washed over him. Overwhelmed, he gasped and sprang away as if he'd been stung.

Mona turned with a frown, and he caught the hurt in her eyes.

What was wrong with him? One minute leading her on with gentle kisses, the next treating her as if she were covered in burrs. What a cad. Blowing out a breath, he said, "Let me help you put these away."

Mona turned her back to him.

A crisp silence prickled the room.

"Please put the coffee-table books over there," she said tentatively, pointing to the walnut table.

Joe obeyed like a servant.

Moments later, when Liza popped her clay-streaked face into the room and invited them into her studio for a look-see, Joe silently thanked Mona's best friend for the profoundly needed intermission.

Mona watched Joe's back as he followed Liza to her workshop. Minutes before she'd been inside his arms. Then all at once he'd dropped her as if she had leprosy.

Joe praised Liza's latest creation, a vase with a wilting, wide lip. He blew out a long whistle. "You're really talented, Liza."

Mona suddenly wished she knew how to do something besides read and eat muffins. When she turned back to the house, she noticed Joe did not follow. Her eyes burned, but she refused to cry. Maybe she'd been misreading Joe all this time. Was he really interested in Liza? Or was he using Mona like he used all women he rescued from floods and roaches? Maybe he was some sort of playboy, stealing kisses from every woman he worked for. A sick feeling welled in her stomach.

She had been a fool to open her heart to him. She should have known better than to let him in her life, starting with the minute he appeared a month ago, looking devastatingly handsome and dripping mud all over her dining room.

She should have known there was no man for her. At least no man in the flesh.

Cl

"Pizza on the house!"

Mona bristled, hearing Joe thump down his steps two at a time. He skidded into the kitchen.

"Pizza!" he hollered again.

Mona was curled up at the bottom of the stairs, halfway through a current best-seller. She glued her eyes to the page despite the fact that the words were blurry.

Joe clomped into the room. Out of the corner of her eye Mona noticed his clean boots. "Did you hear me? I was offering free pizza."

Mona peeked up at him, took note of his boyish, lopsided grin, and something twisted inside her. "Take Liza."

Joe's smile vanished. "I was hoping I could take you."

Mona fixed her eyes back on her book and bit the inside of her lip.

"What are you reading?" Joe hunkered down beside her.

Go away, Joe. His cheerful voice grated on her nerves. But she flipped the front cover over. "It's a book by one of my favorite authors."

"Reese Clark." Joe slipped his finger into her place and pulled the book from her grip. "One of your favorites—why?"

Mona's eyes narrowed, watching him finger her

book. He looked genuinely interested and not the least bit like she'd tried to give him an infectious disease. She sighed. "I don't know. Maybe because his main character never seems to get it right 'til the end. You know, he's not perfect, just real. And each story is in an exotic location—Texas, Russia, Mexico, the Canadian Rockies. He writes as if he's been there, and I feel like I have too."

"Sounds like a good writer."

"He is. But his stories are sad also."

"Why's that?" He leafed through the book, speed-reading.

"Because the main character, Jonah, never really finds what he is searching for. He's always somewhat discontent at the end."

Joe stared at her, and a muscle quivered in his jaw. He didn't smile. "What is he looking for?"

"Well, I don't know. I'm not Reese Clark, but I think Jonah is looking for acceptance or maybe just stability, like a real home. I feel sorry for him. Perhaps Clark is lost also and is searching for something. Peace, maybe." She gave a rueful chuckle, remembering Joe's words. He and Jonah had a lot in common.

Joe opened the front cover and studied the jacket synopsis. "Mind if I borrow it when you're done?"

"Sure, no problem." Mona reached for the book.

"Not so fast. C'mon, Mona. Come out for dinner with me. We don't have to have pizza . . . we can go exotic and eat melting trout at the Portage Resort." His eyes almost seemed to plead with her, and his crazy cockeyed smile ultimately crushed her last bastion of resistance.

The Portage Resort, located on an old voyagers' trail, featured a gourmet restaurant inside a lodge constructed of stout, clean, white-pine logs. The place was famous for its lake trout and walleyed pike. As Mona eyed the mounted trophies springing from the wall like a freeze-framed aquarium, she wondered whom she was eating for dinner.

Joe had spiffed up, looking Western in a pair of black jeans and cowboy boots, a white oxford, and a tweed sports jacket. She wondered how he had removed the wrinkles.

"You forgot your cowboy hat," she had commented when he met her at the bottom of the stairs.

"And you, your parasol," he quipped back.

She supposed her sleeveless linen dress was a little early for the season, but she had added a white cotton cardigan, and it seemed all right. Then Joe had grinned, and it felt so welcoming, she knew he was pleased. He'd rested his hand on the small of her back, sending a wave of disturbing tingles down her spine. Maybe she had been wrong in her rash assumptions about Liza and his intentions.

During dinner Joe made her laugh, told her about surfing in Singapore, cowpunching on a dude ranch in Texas, and nearly being eaten by a grizzly in Glacier National Park. Somewhere between the golden-fried walleye steaks and gooseberry pie, she knew she could never hold on to her anger in light of his distracting smile.

They lingered over coffee and arrived home late. The crescent moon glistened, and the stars blinked gloriously against an opal sky as they sat on the steps of the

porch and listened to waves scrape the shore. Their knees touched now and again, and every time they did, a little jolt would ripple through Mona. She kept fighting the desire for him to kiss her, to hold her like he had the night before. But he kept his hands glued to his knees, and Mona couldn't reach out to him, not after his erratic behavior that afternoon. Just sitting with Joe, however, seemed so peaceful. It was enough.

"So, tell me, why do you like Jonah?" Joe stared into the darkness, and his question hit her like a cold breeze. What did he know about her attraction to Jonah?

Mona scrambled for an answer. "I don't know. He's honorable, I guess. He helps people without asking for anything in return." She sighed and rubbed her arms. The wind had raised goose bumps. "But his best trait is his honesty. Jonah doesn't play games. He always shares his heart. And with his good morals, he must be a Christian. I wish Clark would write that in."

"What do you know about Reese Clark?"

Mona leaned back on her hands. "As much as anybody, I suppose. He's a recluse, only shows up for book signings. I've heard he's a little cold personally, although I wouldn't mind meeting him. Actually," she laughed, remembering, "I *did* meet him!"

Joe frowned.

"Yes, that's right. I met him in the Mall of America, several months ago. He was on a book tour." She shook her head in amazement at the memory. "He fixed my car."

Joe swallowed loudly. "Doesn't sound like too bad of a guy."

"Well, he seemed nice but a bit defensive. I offered to take him out for coffee, and it was all he could do to hold his ground long enough to turn me down. Fond of his privacy, apparently." She paused, recalling the way he'd smoothly rebuffed her in the parking garage. "Edith told me this horrible story—something about his boots getting stolen by a fan?"

"It was more than that," Joe mumbled. "I think he got his shoulder broken, and I remember reading about him being hospitalized."

"Well, whatever it is, he seemed pretty fanatical about his privacy. I don't know if I could ever trust someone like that," she mused. "I would always wonder what secrets he was keeping from me. And the whole famous thing would be hard to deal with, don't you think? What if he really did have obsessive fans stalking him?" She gave a mock shiver and cast Joe a kooky smile.

Joe didn't match it. He stayed silent beside her and stared out at the lake. Mona sensed something, a shift in his attitude, or perhaps it was just the breeze, reaping something foul from shore. Joe must have picked it up as well because he stiffened. Then he spoke in a hoarse voice, as if he had suddenly developed a cold. "I think I'll be going, Mona."

Mona felt like she had the wind knocked from her. She opened her mouth to reply, but no words came.

"I think it's time for me to move on. You've got everything under control here, and Chuck said he'd help with anything that comes up."

Mona clenched her teeth and willed the tears back. Disbelief had her reeling, and she struggled to find her voice. "Well, thanks, then." She, too, sounded like pneumonia had settled in her chest.

She saw him nod twice, as if, *phew,* that was over, and blow out a breath. Clapping his hands on his legs, he pushed up from the steps. "Thanks for a great evening, and of course, for the classy pad. Rip and I loved it." He didn't look at her.

Mona tore her gaze from him and searched the lake for anything to get a fix on. The world suddenly seemed blurry, dangerously off-kilter.

"No problem," she returned. The first tear dropped. She shot a trembling hand to her cheek, whisked it away, and bounced to her feet. "Good night, Joe." Then she turned and dove for the front door, hearing a faint ripping sound somewhere deep in her heart.

Joe left at midnight. She listened to him thump down his steps and wondered why he was in such a hurry to escape. He didn't even knock on her door for his last week's pay. Rip, at least, barked a final good-bye. Seated on her padded window seat, she watched from her darkened bedroom, tears dripping off her chin.

Joe threw his duffel bag into the bed of the truck, stared at the house for a long moment, then followed Rip into the cab. He peeled out northward, his engine coughing an oily wake.

Mona cried until sleep washed her into precious oblivion.

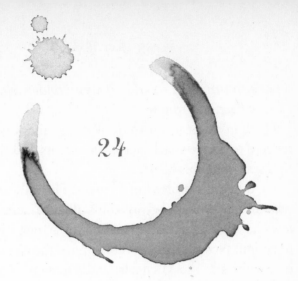

24

$\mathcal{J}$oe's knuckles blanched white as he gripped the steering wheel. He heard only the heart-wrenching echo of Mona's words as he raced north through the milky, forested darkness toward the Garden. *Jonah's honorable. He tells the truth.*

How he wished that were true of himself.

He'd been dancing around the truth all evening. He knew he had to tell her . . . either that or leave, and the thought of leaving had driven a dagger through his heart. He'd been tossing the idea around in his mind that perhaps he could start small, telling her his real name, and work into the truth as he might write a poem, one carefully constructed line at a time. He still had a week before the lies could blow up in his face, and perhaps, by then . . .

Somehow, he couldn't get the words started. They lodged in an iron ball in his throat. Back there on the porch, he'd been halfway to the truth, tripping around the subject when she'd shocked him with the Reese Clark comment. *I don't think I could ever trust a man*

*who is so private. I would always wonder what secrets
he was keeping from me.*

He didn't even want to think about the way she'd
reacted to Reese Clark's celebrity status and the threat
of a stalker on his heels.

He'd had no choice but to leave. His only comfort
was that he'd never betrayed his alliance with Gabe. At
least he'd protected his brother from Mona's inevitable
rejection. Now she would never have the chance to face
the realities of the Michaels family gene pool and run
for cover. He gritted his teeth and tried to ignore the
sick hollowness in his chest.

The wind hissed through the trees, branches lurching
in shadows across the road. Occasionally Rip would
raise his sorry brown eyes and grunt, as if he, too, knew
Joe had surrendered to a familiar history. Thankfully, he
hadn't actually voiced his feelings. *I love you, Mona.* At
least he still had his dignity.

But he'd happily swap dignity for courage. If only
he'd had the slightest inkling how she felt. Despite her
sweet surrender in his arms and the way her eyes lit up
when he walked into the room, he might be totally
misreading her warmth for thankfulness. And wouldn't
that have made his vulnerability especially poignant—
open his heart just so she could respond with a horrified, embarrassed silence? No, tonight's gut-wrenching
conclusion was best for both of them.

Then why did he feel so bereft?

Joe hit the steering wheel. *God, why did You bring
me here? To hurt Mona? To destroy me? You knew this
would happen, and You still let me walk right into
Mona's arms.* Regret seared him.

A person with any smarts would have turned and
headed right out the front door the first moment he set
eyes on Mona and her intoxicating smile. A person with
real genius would have never lied to Mona in the first
place. Even if he had a plethora of excellent reasons.

So maybe his reasons weren't so excellent. If he was
honest, he might admit they were mostly self-serving.
Joe swallowed the regret filling his mouth. Whatever his
reasons were, there was no going back.

Rip sighed and Joe put his hand on the dog's head,
working his fingers into the short fur. He slowed and
turned into the Garden's dirt drive. At least he would
have the decency to say good-bye to Gabe.

Stay, Joe. The impression blew through him like
wind, as if trying to direct him. He fought it, eyes
forward on what he had to do. Stopping in front of the
Garden's porch, he noticed the lights were out, and his
heart sank. He climbed out of the truck and shut the
door in Rip's face. The dog whined a moment, then
settled on the bench seat.

Joe sank onto the porch steps and laced his fingers
behind his neck. The birch trees were a ghostly white in
the darkness. A chill shifted through him as he considered his future. *What now, Lord?*

His answer came in the creak of the porch door. He
heard a gentle, familiar voice. "Joe? Is that you?" He
turned and watched Ruby descend the steps, clad in
leather slippers, a fuzzy gray sweat suit, and a pink
terry robe. She sat beside him. "It's a little late for a
visit, isn't it?"

Joe blew out a tortured sigh and rubbed a muscle in
his neck. "I'm leaving. I came to say good-bye."

Her silence told him how she felt about his decision.

"Ruby, you know what I do for a living. I can't stay. I have to keep moving. I don't have a choice."

Ruby harrumphed.

"My time here is up."

She crossed her arms.

"Fine. I'm going to say good-bye to Gabe."

"He's sleeping."

Joe stared at the inky sky, noticing how bright the moon shone against the black eternity of the universe. "I can't leave without saying good-bye."

"We have a sofa. It's yours 'til morning." Ruby stood up. He felt her gaze linger on him a moment. "You can take care of business then." He heard the screen door close quietly behind her.

He clenched his jaw, frustrated at having to prolong the agony. He much preferred a full-speed, midnight trip south to Minneapolis.

Joe traced the shadows lurching off the ceiling, fighting the image of Mona's beautiful face as she hid her tears, calling himself an array of truthful names until sometime near dawn, when exhaustion drove him into a fitful sleep.

Joe woke to the smell and sound of bacon sizzling in the kitchen. A small congregation was assembling breakfast when he shuffled in.

"Joe's here!" the welcoming redhead announced, and Daniel slapped Joe on the shoulder. Joe acknowledged them with a crooked grin, found a chair, and slumped into it.

Ruby marched into the kitchen, wearing the same sweat suit and slippers, but minus the bathrobe and stern look. "Good morning, Joe. Sleep well?"

Joe nodded but couldn't meet her eyes. First thing after breakfast, he was southbound.

Gabe's voice ushered in his presence. "Joe's truck is here, Ruby."

Ruby extended her hands toward Joe, as if presenting him. "So is Joe."

His brother embraced him, and for an instant, the exuberance eased the knot in Joe's chest. "Good morning, Joe. Why are you here so early? Are we going fishing again?"

It would have been so much easier to slip away last night, without the messy good-bye. Rip out Gabe's heart with one quick twist. He shook his head and met his brother's dancing blue eyes. "Not quite, buddy." He blew out despair in a breath. "We gotta talk, okay?"

Gabe frowned.

"You can use my office," Ruby said. Joe caught her disapproving look.

He ignored it, stood, and stalked out of the kitchen. "C'mon, Gabe, let's go to your room." Gabe followed without a word.

Joe stared out the window of Gabe's bedroom, watching the dawn illuminate the strawberry garden. The tiny dew-covered plants sparkled deep, jeweled green. Joe couldn't help but be constantly amazed at the talents of his brother and friends. He turned, and the pressure of Gabe's confused expression made him gulp.

Joe sat and clamped his hands over his knees. He'd grappled with this the better part of the night and decided a straight approach would be best. "Gabe, it's time for me to move on. I have work to do, and my deadline here is up." Joe noticed Gabe's chin begin to quiver so he rushed on. "But I need you to help me out. Can you take Rip? He needs a home, and he loves the Garden."

Gabe bit his lip. "Why can't you stay? You don't have to go. You can do anything you want."

Gabe's voice made Joe's throat burn. His brother simply didn't understand, and Joe didn't know how to explain that he felt trapped—in the past and the present. That it seemed easier to be alone, and most of all, that he couldn't bear the thought of failing and being failed.

Joe scrubbed a hand through his hair. It felt greasy and unkempt. So did he. "I'm sorry, Gabe," was all he could manage. He hardened his heart to Gabe's agonized face. "Can you take Rip?" he repeated.

Gabe nodded through a sheet of tears. Joe struggled to his feet and made a trail to the porch. The delicious smells of bacon, fresh coffee, and scrambled eggs sneaked toward him, but Joe knew anything he put in his stomach would be soured by the sorrow in his heart. He let the front door slam behind him.

Poor Rip was still curled on the front seat of the pickup but awoke the second Joe opened the door. The dog streaked out of the car. "Sorry, bud," Joe muttered. It seemed he was hurting everybody these days. He heard the door creak and noticed a small group gathering on the porch, led by Ruby. She had her arm around Gabe, and she shot Joe a crippling look.

Joe whistled for Rip and caught the Lab by the fraying collar. He nestled his face into the fur. "Take care of

Gabe," he whispered. Then he led the dog around the truck to the porch.

Gabe crouched beside the animal and ran a gentle hand along his back. His eyes were red-rimmed when he raised them to Joe.

Joe steeled his resolve. "Take care, y'all." Gabe stood up and caught Joe in a sudden, desperate hug. Joe stiffened, unable to let himself relax in the embrace. "Take care, buddy. I'll write." His voice cracked and he knew he had to hurry.

"You too. Write to me."

Joe had to wrench himself from Gabe's clinch. He strode toward the truck, aware of Ruby's presence closing behind him. He whirled, defensives in overdrive. He *dared* her with his eyes to mention one word about all he was leaving behind, Mona included.

"This is for you, Joe," Ruby said softly, holding out a folded note. He noticed the compassion in her eyes, and a lump gathered in his throat, replacing his defensive words.

He took the note, opened it, and scowled. "No thanks," he said, but she refused to take it back. He shoved it into his pocket.

"You're welcome here anytime, Joe. Whenever you feel like coming home."

"This isn't my home."

"That's what you think."

Joe shrugged, but her words hurt. For all her smug, intimate knowledge about him, she simply didn't understand his life.

He pasted on a practiced smile, waved, then climbed into the cab. The truck sputtered to life, a pungent cloud of gas and dust filling the air. Joe floored it and refused to look back.

Only the roar of emptiness in his heart accompanied him south to Minneapolis.

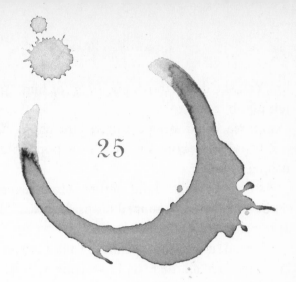

25

"You had the tingly thing for him, didn't ya?" Liza leaned over the brass footboard of Mona's bed, her ebony hair dripping down over the photograph Mona held.

"What?" Mona strove to inject surprise into her voice.

"Joe. You love him." Mona gaped, but Liza returned a stern look. "Don't argue with me. I noticed your red eyeliner this morning, and you've been bumping around in a daze all day." She took Mona's hand. "Do you know why he left?"

Mona shook her head.

"I'm sorry it didn't work out," Liza said softly.

Not as much as I am. Mona shrugged, but pain fisted in her chest. At least she hadn't told him she loved him. She thanked the Lord that her brain hadn't completely turned to cooked oatmeal. What had she been thinking—to crack open her heart and let Joe peek inside? She'd even told him about her father. How mortifying.

She glued her eyes to the picture and bit her trembling

lip. Yes, she'd had the tingly thing for him. And now she felt numb to her toes.

Liza reached down and fingered the photo. "This you?"

"Yep. I was about six. That's my pop, holding the fishing pole."

As Liza scrutinized the picture, Mona leaned forward on her knees and examined it upside down. "Ugh! Look at my clothes!"

"C'mon, it was the seventies. Tank tops and bell-bottoms were all the rage. I like your hair—that's the Meg Ryan look, right?"

"We'd just pulled in from fishing all day in some northern lake, and I, by the way, caught that whole stringer full there, and Pop handed the camera to some other fishing duo and asked them to snap the shot." Mona cracked a flimsy grin, remembering the proud smile of her father. She heard his voice, *You're my fishin' buddy, Mone.* "I thought I was really something."

Liza's voice was gentle. "You were, to him."

A familiar rawness filled Mona's throat. She grabbed her pillow and clutched it to her chest, ready to bury her face in it should any tears resurface.

"Joe reminded you of him, didn't he?" Liza handed Mona the picture and held her gaze.

Mona tucked the picture into the drawer of her nightstand. She didn't answer.

The bed creaked as Liza settled on it. "You can't bring your father back. I know you want to. But you have to stop blaming yourself. It was an accident, and I know he'd forgive you."

Mona's eyes misted at Liza's targeted words. "Yeah, I know."

Liza ducked her head, searching for Mona's eyes. Mona looked away.

"Mona," Liza said firmly, "you have to let it go. You have to stop trying to make everything perfect. Only when you realize you can't erase your mistakes will God be able to heal you. You have to trust Him to repair your life."

Mona blinked back tears. "I don't deserve His help." She winced at the despair in her voice.

Liza's silence betrayed empathy. Finally, she reached out and fingered a strand of Mona's blonde hair. "The Footstep of Heaven. You know what I think of when I say that? I think of sitting at Jesus' feet. I feel Him wrapping His arms around me, and I hear Him telling me it's okay, that I don't have to be perfect, that He loves me just the way I am. Even when I make huge mistakes."

"You don't make huge mistakes, Liza." The bitter words spurted out.

Liza dropped her hand. "Is that what you think?"

Mona wiped an escaping tear and nodded.

"I've got news for you, Mona Reynolds. I've made huge mistakes with my life. Girlfriend, you're talking to a woman who quit school in the tenth grade."

Mona blinked in shock.

"I didn't go to college, and I can't read an entire book like you can. It's only by the grace of God that I hooked up with you. If it weren't for you, I'd still be waiting tables at the Big Sub. You showed me that if I had a dream, I should stick to it, just like you did." Liza's eyes sparkled. "You idiot, have you forgotten how I met you? A double order of Italian subs down the back of your sweatshirt?" She grimaced so crazily Mona had to stifle a chuckle. "But you forgave me. You taught me how to be a friend and to receive forgiveness."

Mona cocked a finger at her. "I did get a free meal."

"Well, this is true, but at the least, it cost you your favorite outfit."

Mona shrugged; then her smile faded.

"Let it go, Mona. God's already forgiven you. You need to forgive yourself and let God love you. Be His child, and embrace His grace. You can't create your own heaven on earth. That's His job. If you try to do it yourself, you'll never experience the love of God fulfilling your wildest dreams."

Liza's eyes flashed, like light hitting an opal, and Mona heard in her words something eternal and priceless.

Mona had opened a door to her heart, let Joe enter her private world, and now the empty space inside ached as if he'd ripped out a part of herself and taken it with him. Her heart throbbed every time she caught sight of her mended ceiling or blooming poplar sapling. When she drank her coffee on the porch, she remembered the feel of his strong hands around hers when he helped her hold the jack. When she wandered into Liza's pottery shed, she thought of that first day when he'd suggested there were treasures to be found at the Footstep. Late at night, Mona longed to hear him return from his loud midnight runs with Rip. And when the waves scraped the shore, all she could think of was being cocooned happily in his arms.

She had been such a fool to fall for a rootless drifter.

If she wanted to heal, she had to expunge him from her life. She knew it, but it still required all her grit to ascend the stairs to his tiny apartment with a mop and broom.

She was about to defrost an already immaculate fridge when she found a journal wedged behind, as if Joe had set it on top, then accidentally knocked it off. It was a small, thick notebook with tattered corners, each page indented by the weight of the pencil, and perhaps the thoughts impressed upon it. Mona rubbed the cover with her palm. Joe kept a journal. That fact only added to his baffling personality. She would have never guessed that rumpled, rustic Joe, with a soft spot for homeless strays and a competitive streak, would find solace scribbling his feelings down on paper. A lump formed in her throat.

Maybe Joe's secrets were in this book, everything he couldn't tell her. Everything she longed to know about him. Answers, perhaps, to why he'd abandoned something good and maybe even lasting in the middle of the night like a bandit. She trembled, remembering Joe's crooked smile, the twinkle in his jeweled blue eyes, the fresh smell of soap and flannel that trailed him. Tears pricked her eyes. Maybe Joe's little book even held solutions.

Mona turned the journal over in her hands, biting her lip. Then she slid down to the floor, propped her back against the refrigerator, and invaded the privacy of Mr. Joe Michaels.

Joe's story peeled away the hours. Mona read until the setting sun painted long shadows across the uncarpeted floor. She discovered between the pages a man who had been around the world but always longed to come home. He'd managed to see Red Square, Winchester Abbey, and the Berlin Wall, but woven among his words she detected a desire to kill the wanderlust. He had a family—that news startled her. A brother named Gabriel.

At least he is happy, Joe wrote of his sibling, but the tone pulsed of melancholy. She also noted a spiritual quest. Joe's psalms were copied down in modern-day prose next to David's, their hearts entangled into one. Joe obviously loved God, yet he ran, like David, from an enemy. She sensed its insidious presence filtering through his thoughts: the fear of unworthiness, of rejection. Tears ran unhindered. She understood all too well.

Then on the last page she discovered her name, neatly penciled in a week after his arrival.

> *Mona is everything I want. Her determination to see the Footstep work delights me, and I am actually envious she has found her niche. I want this niche also. And . . . do I dare say it? . . . it would be nice to have it with her. Today she stood on the porch, leaning against the railing with a coffee mug in her hands. The wind teased her hair as she stared out toward the surf, and I saw in her gaze a hint of peace. I believe she will find her peace here. And mine . . . ?*

Mona turned the page, but the last page remained blank. She ran a finger down the empty space and wondered why he had stopped writing.

Joe sat in the cool grass, watching the breeze ripple over a sapphire Lake Calhoun, fingering a stick in his hand and wishing he had Rip to toss it to. He missed Mona. He more than missed her—he ached to see her. The pain was so blinding that at moments he actually thought he had a gaping wound in the middle of his chest. It didn't help that her image and the hurt written on her beautiful face when he announced he was leaving haunted him like a specter.

After his abrupt flight, he'd found a hotel room in Minneapolis. And when he collapsed on the bed, staring at the white ceiling and listening to the hum of the air conditioner, his wounded heart began to throb.

He'd left the best part of himself in northern Minnesota.

Drawing up his knees, he buried his face in his folded arms. Why had he ever thought freedom was more precious than the smell of Mona's fresh-perked coffee, the sound of her laughter, or the prospect of waking up to her smile every day for the rest of his life? Maybe if he could find the guts to crawl back to her and beg her forgiveness, he might recover from this terrible lesion in his heart. He'd even assume the role of handyman forever if only he might repair everything his cowardice had destroyed.

Right, she would surely open her arms to him after he'd abandoned her with repairs the size of Texas. She was probably singing his praises right now as she tried to hot-wire her rattletrap car for a quick trip to the hardware store.

She'd trusted him, and he'd repaid her with lies. He felt ill with shame. She deserved better. She deserved someone who wasn't afraid to love, regardless of the cost. Not someone who lit out on a run at the first hint of trouble. Yes, he'd had plenty of reasons to weave together a facade, and even better ones to escape before that facade blew up in his face like a cluster bomb. He'd categorized and rationalized those reasons in his mind during the five hours it took to race south on I-35. By the time he hit Highway 694 and the loop around the Twin Cities, he'd known he'd become a pretty good liar, even to himself.

He'd left because he was a coward when it came to issues of the heart.

Joe stared at the lake. Sailboats flagged in red, white, yellow, and sky blue skated over the pristine surface, and a squadron of ducks dodged them and scolded their impudence. The aromas of fresh popcorn, corn dogs, and french fries saturated the air, mixed with the heady perfume of blooming lilacs.

Mona's lilac tree was probably in full violet bloom right now. The thought was so vivid Joe lifted his hand to bat it away.

A gaggle of girls walked by. One peeked at him, her eyes shining. He tugged his baseball cap lower on his head and turned the stick in his hand, avoiding her gaze. He wanted to hide, and Lake Calhoun seemed just the place for it. Roller bladers whizzed by, their headsets pumping out rhythm. A Frisbee landed yards from him, and a teenager scooped it up and flung it back to his partner.

His broken heart ached.

Spearing the stick into the dirt, Joe dug the note from his pocket. Ruby, the persistent. He opened the note and read it again. She'd written an address—whose, it wasn't hard to guess—and a verse. He'd looked Isaiah 41: 9-10 up so many times over the past two days he had it memorized: "I have called you back from the ends of the earth so you can serve Me. For I have chosen you and will not throw you away. Don't be afraid, for I am with you. Do not be dismayed, for I am your God. I will strengthen you. I will help you. I will uphold you with My victorious right hand."

Joe closed the note and creased it. Tapped it against his leg. Ruby wanted him to forgive his dad. The initial step in coming home. For the first time in his life, he had a good idea of what homecoming meant. Family. Something to hold on to, someone to love, who loved the real you, not some fantastic phony.

What kind of liar was he? Mona didn't have a clue about his identity. He had to admit, however, neither did he. The real Joe Michaels lurked behind a persona he thought he needed. Perhaps, safe inside the Footstep of Heaven, the real Joe Michaels had made his first appearance in years, wrapped inside a cloak of deception, but still there, aching to be freed. Aching to be seen, to be confronted, to be loved, and to return that love.

Maybe confronting his dad, the man who'd run from his fears, could help Joe face himself, confront his own guilt, perhaps even forgive. And if he could face himself . . . maybe the real Joe could find the backbone to face Mona and unravel his web of lies, including introducing her to Gabe.

And just maybe she'd surprise him, like he hoped.

Ruby's words, spoken in the cover of twilight after the glorious fishing trip with Gabe, rushed back to him. *Perhaps, if you stood your ground, you'd find the strength to forgive and let someone in your life. Maybe you'd even find the thing you're always searching for.*

Yes, he'd found what he'd been searching for. Found it, turned, and ran for the hills. And he'd keep running until he discovered a way to fight the demon on his tail. Until he could stand his ground . . . and forgive.

He'd learned that from Gabe. Forgiveness gave Gabe power. It didn't stop the hurt, but it released him from revenge and allowed him to reach out. Gave him room in his heart to love. Until this moment, Joe hadn't realized how much space anger had occupied in his heart.

Ruby had said that God would help him forgive. Do not fear. Joe reread Ruby's script and knew she had nailed him—he wasn't calloused to his father; he was terrified of him. He'd crack open his heart in front of the old man, and out would pour a decade of hurt. And he'd be left with a gaping hole in his chest.

But didn't he already have that?

Fear had been his master for too long.

Fear had cost him a home.

Fear had cost him Mona.

There was only one way to face his fear. He had to track down Wayne Michaels and forgive him. Forgive him for abandoning his family. Forgive him for ripping Joe's world to pieces, forgive him for teaching his son that the only option to problems was to punch the gas and leave a cloud of dust.

And maybe learning to forgive would give Joe the internal fortitude he needed to unlock his heart and risk

letting God be in charge of his relationships. To risk loving and finally find a place to call home. To finally have peace.

If Joe ever wanted to be free to embrace all God had for him, as Ruby suggested, he'd have to face his past like Mona faced her home repairs—with dignity and the boldness of Joshua tackling the fortress of Jericho.

Joe sunk his head in his hands. He wasn't Mona, and she had about ten times the courage he did. Ten times? She had more tenacity in her little toe than he had in his entire body.

"Chip, no!"

Joe raised his head a second before a large Samoyed plowed him over. A teenager, dressed in a blue windbreaker and wearing a horrified expression, ran up to him and dove for the dog's collar. "Sorry, mister," he said, wrenching the dog away. The Samoyed had his treasure, Joe's stick, clamped firmly in his mouth.

Joe didn't reply. He was twenty-five years in the past, staring at the dripping jaws of Jerry Hopkins's purebred white Samoyed, Blizzard. His heart locked, just as it had then, and he saw himself raise the newspaper, whether to deliver it or throw it at the dog, he didn't know. Even now he couldn't remember what he'd done with that *Star Tribune*. What Joe did remember, in painful lucidity, was the wind screaming through his ears as he turned tail and sprinted across the yard, beating out a race with the growling beast for the next yard. Hot breath licked his neck; teeth nipped his feet. He pumped his ten-year-old legs and arms and flew over the grass until he was airborne. He ran full speed over the five-foot retaining wall, then pitched face first onto the neighbor's gravel driveway.

The next few minutes blurred into a smear of pain. Somehow he recalled the sight of the Samoyed, drooling and perhaps even laughing as he stared down at him like a king from his yard. Then Mrs. Allen had popped out of her house to inquire why her paperboy sprawled bloody and crying on her driveway. Joe had limped home, climbed into bed without washing, and sobbed until he slept.

The memory burned in his chest. The fear sent his heartbeat on turbo and felt as real today as it had twenty-five years ago. Sweat even greased his palms. He'd let terror take control and send him running.

He obviously hadn't changed much since then.

Joe wiped his hands on his pants and sucked a calming breath. Propping his arms on his knees, he clenched and unclenched his fists as the memory continued.

His father had found him curled in his bed. He'd rubbed his back until Joe awoke and poured out the story in hiccupping sobs. His father had listened, face etched with concern and determination. Then he'd tucked Joe in, kissed him on the forehead, and said, "We'll tackle it tomorrow."

Warmth spread through Joe's chest, recalling how his father had met him halfway through his paper route the next afternoon. He must have been white-faced, for his father had clamped a hand on his shoulder, squeezed, and said, "Don't be afraid, Son."

They'd walked together to the Hopkinses' house, and when Blizzard tore out of his pen, unchained and smelling fear, his father tucked Joe behind his back and lunged at the dog, crying out a thunderous roar. The stunned animal skidded to a halt, and at the second

roar, retreated into the dark safety of his doghouse. Joe peeked around his father and spied the dog cowering, blinking at him with sheepish eyes.

"Go ahead, Joe. Deliver that paper. The animal just needed to be met head-on."

Joe's mouth had felt as dry as the Sahara as he tiptoed toward the door, and he could still hear the roar of his pulse in his ears as he jammed the paper into the box. But his father stood sentry behind him, and the dog only flicked a wary eye in their direction.

Blizzard never bothered him again, and eventually, with the right number of dog biscuits, the Samoyed became his friend.

Joe gripped the back of his neck, kneading a tense muscle. If his earthly father, who failed him, could stand in the gap and help him overcome his fear, couldn't his perfect heavenly Father do so much more? Ruby's well-chosen verse trumpeted in his head. *I will strengthen you. I will help you. I will uphold you with My victorious right hand.*"

Joe rubbed both hands through his hair and stood up. Maybe it was time to let God uphold him. His jaw tightened as he considered the implications. *I don't know if I can do this, Lord.*

"*God has not given us a spirit of fear and timidity, but of power, love, and self-discipline.*" Joe frowned, shoved his hands in his pockets, and started for the truck. "*Perfect love expels all fear.*" His truck keys jingled as he fumbled through his pockets. "*Be strong and courageous! Do not be afraid or discouraged. For the Lord your God is with you wherever you go.*"

Joe looked toward heaven, eyes burning. The steady

echo of verses kept beat with his pounding heart. *"When the people heard the sound of the horns, they shouted as loud as they could. Suddenly, the walls of Jericho collapsed."*

Joe threw his hands in the air. "All right already!"

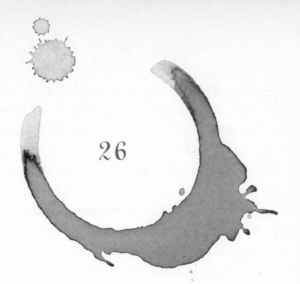

26

Five days before opening day, an aura of anticipation drifted through the Footstep of Heaven as the lilac tree, then the jasmine bush in the front yard, flowered, signaling the onset of the tourist season. Mona had planted an abundance of mums, asters, and gladiolas in the bed along the front porch, and she sang to the peonies that flanked the newly paved side driveway, in hopes they would bloom early. She packed wooden planters full of impatiens blossoming in every shade and arranged table centerpieces with dried hydrangeas, eucalyptus, and day lilies.

Inside, the buffed and waxed floor glinted delicious amber in the afternoon sun, and the green-and-navy-plaid sofa was settled regally in the lounge area, opposite the coffee bar. Mona's intimate round tables had arrived in a shipment from Minneapolis, along with a box of tablecloths and indigo-and-yellow napkins. Mona helped Liza display her current stock of earthenware bowls, plates, mugs, and serving platters on two stripped and glazed oak dressers they had picked up from one of the locals. Out of a rusty metal table Liza had unearthed in the shed, she created nouveau art with a wire brush and some navy and white appliance paint.

The bookshelves, adorned with an assortment of colorful displays and freebies from publishers, beckoned every time Mona entered the shop. She had to fight the urge to select a novel and plop onto the sofa. It was just the temptation she had hoped for.

Mona leaned on the porch rail, letting the fresh evening wind whisk away the worries of the day. She heard the porch door squeal, then Liza's light step. Mona turned, and her roommate handed her a cup of steaming cappuccino.

Liza's dark eyes danced. "The Footstep is almost ready."

Mona took the cup and gave her friend a grateful smile. Over the past week, Liza had successfully managed to avoid the topic of their absent handyman, but it hovered like grief between them. Joe's imprint embedded the Footstep of Heaven. His handiwork was everywhere—from the lush green front lawn to the gleaming white front porch, from the new back siding and the sturdy garage stairs to the hall chandelier.

But most of all, Joe's imprint was etched in Mona's heart. For she knew it was Joe who had nudged her toward believing in God's love for her, and believing He would help her build her dreams. Joe said she didn't have to earn God's love—it was packaged with His forgiveness. If only she could get that truth to settle deep into her heart and truly embrace it. It seemed too wonderful to be true, just like the Footstep.

Perhaps, if she could be successful at opening her bookstore, she would also be successful in believing that God could make fantastic dreams come true. Dreams like bringing the only man she could ever love striding back into her life.

"When will you start baking?" Liza leaned against the rail of the porch, blending her gaze with Mona's as they watched the sparkling lake.

"I have twenty dozen frozen muffins for emergency, but I have a new recipe for berry muffins I want to try for the opening."

"I heard about a place not far from here that sells strawberries. Maybe they'll have an early crop."

Mona sipped her coffee. The sharp taste of java soothed her worn body. Thankfully, it hadn't been too difficult to add the final touches to the Footstep without Joe. And each twilight, as her muscles screamed, she thanked the Lord that Joe hadn't abandoned her right after the fire. He had been a blessing to her, even if her heart writhed every time she thought of him.

She watched a fishing boat bob over waves on the horizon. Why had Joe left? The question plagued her at odd moments—when she had hung Monet prints in the dining room or when she had painted the tiny downstairs bathroom. She even pondered the question while mowing the grass. Was it something she had done?

"Where is this strawberry farm?" Mona asked, returning to Liza's suggestion.

"I saw an advertisement around here a week or so ago. I'll see if I can find it. I think it was called the Garden."

Joe expected to find a greasy garage, an echo of his impressions from childhood. He was pleasantly surprised to see that the auto shop was clean, well lit, and miraculously, not a hint of grease had snuck in from the back stalls to the reception area. The pungent smell of oil and gas, however, confirmed he'd found the right place.

An elderly woman with graying hair and a saggy round face looked up at him, her thin penciled eyebrows pushed skyward. "What do you want?" she barked.

"Um, I'm looking for Wayne Michaels," he stammered.

"He's out back. What do you want with him?"

Joe's mouth suddenly parched. Words escaped him. What *was* he doing here? *"Be strong and courageous."* He was instantly glad he'd committed that verse to memory on the drive over.

"Did one of the boys do your car wrong or something, mister?"

Joe shook his head and received a deep frown in response.

"Spit it out!"

"He's my father," Joe croaked.

The woman recoiled and went ashen. "Is it really you?"

Joe nodded.

She jumped to her feet and hustled around the desk. "Please, sir, come this way." She waddled down a narrow hall, turned a corner, then flung open a set of double oak doors. "Please wait here. I'll get him. Can I get you anything?"

Joe arched his eyebrows at her and shook his head.

"I'm very glad to meet you, sir," she said, jutting out
her hand. Joe reluctantly took it and hid his revulsion at
her sweaty grip.

When she closed the door behind her, Joe wiped his
hands on his suit pants, straightened his tie, and scanned
the office. It was paneled in mahogany, and the carpet
gleamed copper in pools of lamplight. The smell of
leather emanated from two low armchairs and the tall
captain's chair behind a glass-topped cherrywood desk.
Joe whistled low. This was no grease monkey's office.
Maybe he had the wrong Wayne Michaels.

Then he spotted his own face in a framed picture—
eleven years old and holding a stringer of fish. A side
table held a group of photos—Gabe with his strawberries, a black-and-white of their mother in college,
Joe's senior class picture, and a shot of him he'd had
professionally taken. How had his father obtained these
last two items? Anger rose like a flash flood. If his father
had cared all these years, why hadn't he bothered to
contact him? Joe was easy to find if someone wanted to
take the time to search.

Joe was simmering toward full boil when the door
opened. In walked Wayne Michaels. Shock washed over
Joe.

"Howdy, Joe." The man before him was lean, strong,
and dressed casually in blue dress pants and a short-
sleeve, hunter green polo shirt. His thin face, lined
heavily, betrayed hard years, but his blue eyes danced.

Something inside Joe cracked open. In that moment,
all the anger, fear, and accusations melted into one
emotion—regret. He'd missed his father. A fifteen-

year-old ache roared to life. He suddenly had trouble breathing.

Memory flashed through his mind in a tangle of joyous, heart-wrenching emotions: his father, grease-streaked and grinning as he taught Joe how to over-haul a Ford; the sound of hearty laughter captured in a moment of playing catch in the backyard; the smell of Old Spice and soap late at night; and the feeling of warmth as his dad tucked a little boy into bed.

"Hi," Joe returned in a weak voice.

Wayne closed the door behind him. Then he turned and met Joe's eyes. "I'm glad you came." His voice faltered, matching Joe's. "I prayed we'd meet again."

An endless list of questions shot into Joe's mind. He asked the most important, slashing through the knot of crippling images to find confidence in righteous anger. "Why, Dad? Why did you leave?"

Wayne swallowed and shoved his hands into his pockets. "I made a terrible mistake." His eyes glistened. "I was afraid. A handicapped child seemed more than I could handle. I was just starting to enjoy being with you, and then we had Gabe. I panicked and ran."

"And destroyed our family." Joe's anger, focused now, swelled.

Wayne closed his eyes and nodded.

Joe balled his fists, and once again he saw himself standing by the door, watching his father leave, listening to his mother sob in the kitchen. The urge to flee this office nearly sent his legs into motion.

His father must have sensed his struggle, for his expression changed. He shrank the distance between

them, and his voice grew earnest. "I was a coward, Joe. I can't change what I did to you and the family. I can't change the awful things you went through because of my fear. But I can change what happens from now on. Don't go. You are a better, braver man than me, and I'm begging you to give me a second chance. Please, forgive me."

Wayne reached out to his shoulder, but Joe jerked away. He teetered on the thin line between hatred and love, willing himself to land on the side that had a future. How had he ever thought he could do this, face this man, this anguish? *Lord, help me!*

Joe's prayer bolstered his courage. Forgiveness was something he'd have to learn daily—to both give and, Lord willing, accept. And it had to start today.

"I forgive you!" The words erupted from Joe in a sob. He pressed his thumb and forefinger into his watering eyes. He felt raw, near to collapse. "I forgive you," he repeated, his voice in shreds.

Then his father's arms were around him, fighting to embrace him despite Joe's reluctance. Joe froze, but his emotions crested over him. He weakened and, with a childlike cry, buried his face in his father's neck. He wept, unashamed at his tears, for the anguish his father had bequeathed, for the years he'd been betrayal's executor. "I forgive you," Joe said again, this time more to himself.

A wave of pain—sweet, cleansing pain—swept through him. It knocked his stronghold of unforgiveness to smithereens.

In its place swelled a soul-healing joy that could only be divine.

Cu

Mona followed the map printed on the back of the brochure. The pamphlet read *Best Strawberries in the North* and pictured a luscious red berry on the cover. Inside, it explained the Garden's varieties, shipping policies, prices, and services. The Garden even made its own jam. Mona itched to talk with the owners and place a hefty order for the Footstep.

She slowed as she drove under a wooden sign dangling between two fence posts. The wind toyed with it slightly and shifted the surrounding fir. The scent of pine filtered through the air, and Mona decided this place was definitely another entrance to heaven. Driving up the dirt road, she spotted a number of neatly constructed outbuildings and a stunning white-pine lodge.

A large wide porch ran the length of the lodge. *It certainly is a homey place for such a large operation,* Mona mused as she pulled up. She climbed out of her Chevette and mounted the porch stairs, searching for the proprietor.

The screen door opened. "Can I help you?" A young man with tousled brown hair and dressed in coveralls smiled at her.

Mona was warmed by the twinkle in his almond-shaped eyes. "I'm looking for the Garden strawberry farm?"

"You found it."

"Could you point me to the manager?"

The young man thumped his chest and grinned. "That's me."

Mona couldn't help but smile at his enthusiasm, but

her brow wrinkled in confusion. Certainly an operation of this size wouldn't have . . .

"Can I help you?" The porch door creaked open, and a gray-haired woman dressed in jeans and a pink floral sweatshirt stepped out.

"Yes, I'm looking for the manager of the Garden."

"Oh, you're in luck; he's right here." She gestured to the beaming young man.

Mona swallowed her perplexity and stumbled ahead. "Okay. Well, I'm Mona Reynolds, and I'm interested in your strawberries."

The man's eyes widened. "We have lots!"

The woman patted his shoulder. "I'm Ruby Miller, director of the Garden, and this is Gabriel Michaels, this season's manager. Why don't we show you our store, and you can tell me what you need." She turned to the man. "Okay, Gabe?"

Shock hit Mona with a gale force. "Gabriel Michaels?"

The man nodded, brow pinched.

"You wouldn't happen to be any relation to a man named Joe Michaels? He worked as a handyman here in town."

Ruby looked stunned. "You're Joe's Mona?"

Mona felt the blood drain from her body. As if to confirm brutal reality, a large brown dog bounded onto the porch and layered her with a kiss.

"Rip!" she sputtered, wiping her face. The need to sit down—and fast—swept over her.

Ruby must have seen her dazed expression, for the woman put a hand on her arm. "Come with me, Mona. I think Joe had a few secrets he didn't share with you."

Mona felt numb. Ruby led her through a comfortable-looking living room and a large kitchen to a back office, where she gently settled Mona into a leather sofa. "Can I get you a lemonade?"

Mona nodded.

Ruby disappeared, and Mona was left to stare at the puzzled young man rubbing his hands together and shifting from one foot to the other. He'd turned the color of his strawberries, and an arrow of pity shot through her.

So this was Joe's secret. Why had he hidden his greatest treasure—his family—from her? Was he ashamed of Gabe? Or was he afraid of her reaction? In the room, alone with Joe's brother, the deceit glared at them, and she felt just as sorry for Gabriel as she did for herself. The poor man obviously had no idea she knew Joe.

She stood up and walked over to him. "Your brother is a wonderful man. He helped me rebuild my bookstore, and because of him, it's opening in a few days." She tried a smile.

Gabriel glanced at her with suspicion in his eyes and nodded.

"I'm sorry we never met," she said softly. "Would you like to come to my bookstore sometime?"

He nodded again. "I like books. Joe sends them to me."

"Really? What kind do you like?"

"His books."

"Oh." *He must send him his castoffs,* Mona thought, wondering if Gabriel liked Louis L'Amour.

"Here's your lemonade, dear." Ruby returned and handed her an icy drink. "Now, I'm not going to reveal *all* of Joe's secrets, but I'll let you in on this one. Gabriel

is Joe's younger brother. He's lived here for about five years. Joe's visit was only the second time he's been here."

"So that's why he was in town," Mona murmured. "Do you have any idea why he left?"

"He said it was time," Gabriel answered.

Silence thickened like paste, gluing the questions Mona had to her clenching chest. What wasn't Ruby telling her? "So, this is a group home?" She forced through her agony, shifting the topic from the obvious . . . Joe's secrets.

Ruby nodded. "And a strawberry farm. Are you still interested in our strawberries? We have an early blooming variety in the greenhouse, and you're just in time for the pick of the crop."

Mona smiled.

Ruby wove a hand around Mona's arm. "C'mon. Let's see if the Garden has what you're looking for."

Stealing a glance at Joe's brother, Mona wondered if she'd already found it.

Cee

"I ordered a fresh supply for every week until the end of the season." Mona plunked down a box of strawberries and grinned at Liza. Her friend looked impressed.

"And I found Joe's brother." It delighted Mona to see Liza's jaw sag open. "Yup. He lives at the Garden, which is a group home for mentally challenged adults, as well as a strawberry farm."

"So, you think that's why he left? He feared you'd find out?"

Mona shrugged, but she couldn't hide the disgust in her voice. "As if that would matter to me. Gabe is nothing short of charming. In fact he is overseeing their entire strawberry crop this year. Joe is a fool if he thinks I wouldn't fall in love with his brother immediately."

As Mona headed out to her car to retrieve the last strawberry crate, she said, "If you ask me, Gabe has twice the sense of our mystery handyman."

Liza hummed in agreement.

Mona slammed down the telephone receiver. The unit shuddered.

"Any luck?" Liza treaded in with another load of freshly painted pottery. Her side of the house glittered with color. Mona buried her head in her arms on the walnut table and groaned.

Only three days before opening day. The plumbing had stopped up, Mona found a wandering roach under her sink, and just after her first cup of coffee a publicist called and dropped the bomb. Mona's star attraction, an author from Minneapolis who had agreed to read an excerpt from her book *Life in the Boundary Waters, a Journey of Discovery* had developed a case of laryngitis.

"I've been on the phone for two hours," Mona mumbled from the hiding place inside her arms. "The last call I made, I actually begged the publicist for a cameo, not even a reading, from *any* author. I don't care who they are. I think I might have even offered to send the publicist a dozen muffins." She looked up at her friend and grimaced.

"Want a cup of coffee?" Liza slid behind the coffee bar, where an espresso machine, cappuccino maker, and two industrial-sized coffeepots waited for opening day. The oak gleamed under the polish of the midafternoon sun.

"Make it a double," Mona groaned.

Liza added two scoops of mocha and a generous dollop of whipped cream on top. "Nobody, eh?" She set down the coffee mug on a yellow crocheted coaster.

Mona shook her head. "No one is available, as beautiful as the North Shore of Minnesota is, to make the trek on a two-day notice." She wrapped both hands around the mug, seeking something solid to hang on to. "I don't know what to do."

Liza looked heavenward. "Right about now, as my mama would say, we need a little grace."

"Who was that?" Reese Clark drummed his fingers on the linen-covered tablecloth, annoyance churning through him. A five-star, art-deco café was the last place he wanted to be on a gorgeous, blue-skied Friday. The wind was pushing a regatta of shiny white sailboats across Lake Calhoun, and he thought he'd spotted a youngster attached to a high-flying kite on the way over. He could easily kill an afternoon watching the kid war with trees, light poles, and dogs.

He narrowed his eyes at Jacqueline as she snapped her cell phone shut and dropped it into her black leather satchel. Exasperation padded her answer. "A desperate woman."

"Oh? Maybe I can help."

Jacqueline gave him a flirting look and laced her manicured finger over his arm. "Darling, if I knew desperation would attract your attention, I'd wear sackcloth and ashes."

He chuckled politely but pulled out of her grasp and leaned back in the chair. "So what's her problem?"

Jacqueline shrugged. "I'm not sure." Her crimson lips formed a confused pout. "She was a mess, really. She mentioned something about losing her main attraction for some special event she was having. I think it was her bookstore's grand opening. . . ." Jacqueline waved her hands as if shooing away a bad dream. "Anyway, she begged me to help her find an author." She scooped up her napkin and dabbed her lips. "I told her no one would want to go that far for a reading to a bunch of tourists and retirees."

"Where is this place?"

"Some sleepy little tourist town on the North Shore. Deep Haven, I think she said." She paused, then shot him a sharp look. "Reese, what's the sudden interest in this little hick bookstore? I can barely drag you to a signing in the largest mall in America."

"Did I say anything about going?"

Jacqueline pointedly ignored him while fishing around in her bag. Whipping out a tube of lipstick and a compact, she frosted another layer of gloss on her lips. While Reese watched her pucker and smear, the salmon steak he ate for lunch squirmed in his stomach. He wasn't relishing the next three months in her company.

She glanced up at him, smiled broadly, and snapped the compact closed. "Now, tell me about your next book."

Reese made a face and scanned the café for an escape route. His spent advance for his signed book contract suddenly rose, taunting, like the ghost of Christmas past. He took a sip of his diet Coke and dredged up his voice. "Ah . . . well, it's not quite . . . plotted."

"It's not done." Jacqueline pursed her shiny lips. "Is it close?"

What could he say? He hadn't even managed to scribble an opening line. "No."

"I see." She raised her eyebrows, those skinny ones that made him think of Morticia Addams. "Well, I guess we'll have to hope you get inspired—and soon—or we'll be talking breach of contract." She grinned as if she hadn't just dropped a grenade on his future and threatened to pull the pin. "Meanwhile, you have a book to promote."

Reese managed to nod, despite the fact that his bones had turned to ice.

"Listen, baby," Jacqueline said with the suave of a psychologist, "you have two days before your first appearance. I know how you love that privacy of yours. Try not to destroy it by making any unscheduled appearances. Stay low, cultivate the 'fresh from the backwoods' aura we love, and show up on Monday with a wild look and a bit of a stubble. We'll sell books like hotcakes." She winked at him. "And just maybe, if you play nice, I can get you out of hot water with the head honchos."

Reese clenched his teeth and forced a smile. "Thanks, Jacqueline. I'm sure I can come up with something with the right inspiration."

"Oh, honey, I just wish that were me." Jacqueline

batted her eyes, and for a panicked moment, he wondered if she was serious. Reese quickly scanned the room for the waiter, caught his eye, and signaled for the check.

Jacqueline was already dialing her cell phone. She snapped the bill from the waiter. "My treat, Reese."

Reese frowned, but she waggled a long finger at him. "Be a good boy," she purred, "and stay out of the news."

Reese stood up and made his escape.

"Oh, Reese," Jacqueline called as he strode away from the table. Thirty heads turned in their direction. So much for lying low. "I love your new haircut!"

He let the door of the café slam behind him.

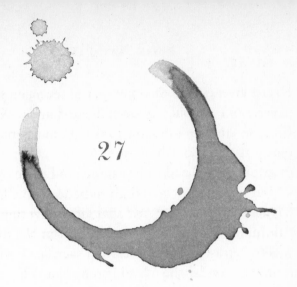

27

Mona watched the birch-tree shadows lurch across her ceiling and pondered Liza's easy words from that morning. *We need a little grace.*

Grace. Accountability and forgiveness in one shot, just as Joe had suggested so long ago on the windswept beach. God's perfect plan, worked out through the sacrifice and love of His Son. For what purpose? To show God's love to the world. To draw men to Himself, so they could worship Him, enjoy Him, *delight* in Him, so He might shower them with His unfathomable love. A love that brought the dead to life, that gave children to the barren, that reunited man with his Creator, and that resurrected hope and fulfilled dreams.

God was so worthy of her delight. Suddenly the verse Joe had spoken to her the night she'd sat crumbling at the bottom of his stairs crying over her soggy Footstep, rushed through her mind. *"Take delight in the Lord, and He will give you your heart's desires."*

The first step in delighting in God was delighting in

His forgiveness—something that in ten years she'd never, not even once, allowed herself to do. Why not? Because she didn't deserve to delight in a forgiveness that was easy. Somehow, she couldn't get past the idea that forgiveness had to be earned, had to be painful.

But hadn't she been forgiven because of Christ's payment for her sins? And that gift had certainly been painful for her Savior. To not delight in His forgiveness was to betray Jesus' excruciating sacrifice for her salvation. No wonder she felt so bereft. Not delighting in God's forgiveness was like opening up a priceless gift, setting it aside, and demanding to pay for it. It cheapened the gift and offended the giver. What she should be doing is throwing herself into the arms of her Savior.

Grace.

Mona slipped out of bed, her heart in her throat, and knelt down. The wood floor chilled her knees, and she trembled, though not from the cold. The awkwardness of folding her hands and summoning the boldness to speak aloud the secrets burrowed in her heart overwhelmed her, nearly stifling the flow of words. But she choked them out and willed herself to approach the Lord in prayer, something she'd become woefully unaccustomed to doing.

"Dear Lord, I am so sorry I haven't embraced Your forgiveness. I know I have offended You by not accepting the fullness of Your grace. Please, please forgive me."

Beloved, I've already forgiven you, long ago.

The sense of God, close and listening, pushed tears into her eyes. "But I still hurt, Lord. Why is the grief so raw?"

You have not forgiven yourself. You hang on to your

pain, wallowing in the familiarity of its thorny grip,
unwilling to accept that you cannot work your way free.
I must pluck you out of this painful place. But only if
you allow Me. Let Me heal you. Let Me lavish upon you
My love. Give Me your pain, your tears, your grief, and
I will give you peace.

Mona nodded, bunching the covers into her fists.

Delight in My forgiveness. Delight in My power.
Delight in My wisdom. Delight that I Am, and Was,
and always Will Be. Delight in Me and My ability to
free you and fulfill your dreams beyond your imagina-
tion. Delight in My fatherly, agape love.

Delight in His love, in being His child. Yes. Mona let
the tears drip off her chin. "Lord, help me delight in Your
forgiveness, believe in Your love. I need You. I know I
can't make this dream happen without You." As she said
it, the bindings holding her together for the past ten years
snapped. She dug her fingers into the bedclothes and
sobbed. "This bookstore has been my dream for so long,
I can't remember when it started. And I know You've
helped me."

She gulped. "You sent Joe." His name came out as a
moan, but somehow with it, her courage bolstered. "No
matter where he is or why he left, I thank You for him."
Her words somehow balmed the shattered pieces of her
heart. Her voice fell to a whisper. "Please, watch over
him, and bless him."

She inhaled, gathering strength. "Lord, I know
You're the only one who can make my dreams come
true." Mona forced herself to surrender the next
words. "I give You this dream, and all others, right
now into Your hands for You to handle however You

see fit." Her last words emerged on a shudder of pain. "And please, Lord, help me forgive myself. Pluck me free." She buried her face in the sheets and wept.

An unearthly stillness entered the room. Suddenly Mona imagined sitting at the footstep of heaven just as Liza had said. And next to her sat Christ, His eyes filled with tears, embracing her. Next to Him stood her father. Smiling. A glow on his face that could only be the look of rapture. For the first time Mona realized that the grief she'd harbored was for her loss, not her father's. Her father had been ready, and he'd gone home to a glory she couldn't even imagine. Living blissfully with his Savior. Unrestrained, perfectly delighting in his God.

All at once a cleansing fullness drew through her, as if God had breathed into her. The magnitude of it made her cry out. The breath lingered and filled every pore, every corpuscle, with an unearthly peace. Solid. Complete. Eternal. Then a voice rumbled in her heart: *Be not afraid, for I love you,* and she realized how much she had missed the touch of her heavenly Father.

The healing left her trembling, sobbing, and praising God until a joyous exhaustion drove her to the warmth of her bed.

Cle

Police Chief Sam Watson tapped his pencil on his desk blotter, considering Mona's plea. "Brian's not a happy man, Mona. I'm not sure this is a good idea."

Mona smiled at him, glanced at Liza, then leaned forward and placed both hands on his desk. "I know it is a bit unconventional, but I think it might be just what

Brian needs to get him to accept a lawyer and pull him out of despair."

Sam rubbed a wide hand over his chin. He squinted at her, then at Liza and back to Mona. "Okay. But I'll be right behind you. Don't forget, this fella tried to hurt you, not just burn your house down."

A wave of weakness swept over Mona as the brutal memory of her breath constricting in her lungs and her lips crunched against her teeth revived and sunk in its painful claws. Brian had confessed to attacking her and to hiring Leo Simmons to set fire to her house. Sam's reminder raked her bruised heart. It brought to mind Joe's daring rescue and waking up clasped in his arms. She thought of the way she'd treated her handyman and how he'd forgiven her. The thought bolstered her spirit. She exhaled a calming breath and forced a smile. "Let's go."

County jail visiting hours were once a week, on Saturday mornings, but there were no other visitors present in the barren room today. The breeze filtered in through a barred window. Mona sat down on a folding chair and heard Liza pull one up beside her. Mona reached for her hand and felt her confidence grow in Liza's warm grip. Sam's presence hovered behind them.

The door opened, and a shackled Brian shuffled through. Mona gasped. She could hardly believe it was the same man. The spark in his dark eyes had vanished, his skin hung sallow and dry on his gaunt cheeks. He looked like he hadn't eaten, bathed, or brushed his hair for the three weeks he'd been sitting in jail. He stared in shock at his visitors, then glared and turned to flee back to his cell.

"Not so fast, pal," Sam commanded. "You sit and listen to what these women have to say to you."

Mona noticed a muscle in Brian's jaw tense, but he kicked out a chair and dropped into it like an unruly teenager. Defense glinted in his eyes, the only evidence of life.

Mona licked her dry lips. Her limbs felt like rubber, but she'd prayed it over and knew this was the right thing to do. She had to free Brian from his prison of guilt, for his sake as well as hers. Deep inside, she could never fully embrace the joy of her own forgiveness if she harbored anger and bitterness in her heart.

"How are you, Brian?" Mona asked. She noticed the quiver in her voice and fought for control.

He glowered at her. "How do you think?"

Liza leaned forward. "Brian, it's not Mona's fault you're here. Listen to her."

Liza obviously still had an effect on him, for he softened his expression.

"I hear you won't talk to a lawyer," Mona continued tentatively.

"No need. My life is over." He crossed his arms, and Mona caught a glimpse of the flaking scabs on his forearm where she'd clawed away his skin as he'd tried to suffocate her.

Memory rushed in and filled her throat with the sick taste of fear. She gulped it back and closed her eyes. *Please, Lord, help me to say the right thing.* "That's not true. Yes, you did a terrible thing, but it doesn't mean life has to end for you. You can still have a worthy, meaningful life."

Brian sneered.

"We all do things we are ashamed of . . ." Mona's voice died.

Brian's stance was armor.

"Brian, I forgive you," she blurted. His face turned white. Mona nodded. "I know you hurt me and sabotaged my business, but I want to forgive you. In fact, I want to help you get through this. Liza and I have talked. We don't have any choice in the criminal charges, but we aren't going to sue you for the damages you did."

Mona's hope lit when she saw the tenseness in Brian's face ease. His jaw slowly dropped open.

Mona's courage mustered. "In fact, we're going to visit you every week and pray for you and bring you meals. You're not forgotten." She pushed against the tears strangulating her voice. "You're forgiven."

Brian turned away, but Mona could see he struggled against her words. She understood. Love, in the face of guilt, can be so overwhelming. The words of her favorite hymn filtered to mind: *"How precious did that grace appear the hour I first believed."*

"Why?" Brian's wretched voice broke through her thoughts.

Mona smiled. Tears dripped off her chin. The answer God had given her was for herself as well as for Brian. "Because while we were yet sinners, Christ died for us. We can forgive little when He has forgiven us so much."

So very, very much.

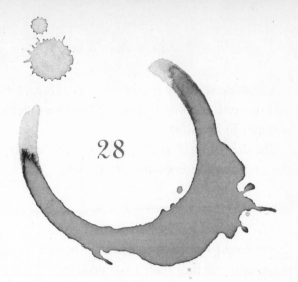

28

Opening day Mona rose early and greeted the rose-hued dawn from her perch on her favorite boulder overlooking Lake Superior. The parchment pages of her Bible rustled in the morning breeze. She'd turned, almost without thinking, to her father's favorite verse, Jeremiah 29:11, and as she let the words soak into her heart, she realized why he quoted them so often. "For I know the plans I have for you," says the Lord. "They are plans for good and not for disaster, to give you a future and a hope."

Mona bowed her head. *Lord, I do believe You have good plans for me and have had them all along. I am beginning to realize that those plans don't always mean things will be easy. You will allow roaches and floods and fires to help me realize I can't depend on myself. I have to depend on You. Thank You for forgiveness, for Your grace, and for giving me this dream. But I know now, that even if it fails, I have not failed. You love me and shelter me in Your hands. I know I can depend on a good future from You, no matter what happens.*

She peeked at the brightening sky. *Please take this day and do with it what you will.* She sighed, feeling hope whisper in her soul.

She determined to cling to that verse as she opened the doors to the Footstep of Heaven.

Cee

They would just have to open without a spectacular personality to hail their first moments. The Footstep of Heaven Bookstore and Coffee Shop would have to make it on its own two feet.

As soon as Mona returned from her devotional trek, she set up the menu board on the porch, writing the daily specials in chalk. She had made three kinds of muffins for the day—chocolate chip, bran, and strawberry, courtesy of the Garden. Maybe later she would attempt wild blueberry with the berries gathered from the hills around Deep Haven. If she lasted that long.

As the sun crested over Lake Superior lighting the lake on fire in dimpled brilliance, the aroma of brewed coffee escaped into the street. The music of Chopin tickling the ivories swirled through the bookstore, filling the shop with elegance and a hint of anticipation.

Liza descended the stairs decked out in a fringed wraparound skirt and a white leather vest. "Just thought I'd jazz up the local flavor a bit," she explained when Mona eyed her with arched brows.

Mona acknowledged that they were definitely breeds apart. She had on a decidedly conservative cashmere peach cardigan and a khaki skirt.

When Mona turned over the Open sign, she was

thrilled to see a figure on the porch, pacing as if impatient to sample a taste of Heaven.

It was Chuck, their Realtor. "How's it going?"

Mona hunched her shoulders. "We've only been open one minute."

"Right. Gimme a café au lait."

Mona fled to the coffee bar while Chuck wandered through Liza's pottery collection. He even picked up a couple of pieces and smiled. He bought a chocolate-chip muffin and a *Superior Times* and sat on the porch.

After an hour of business, Chuck was still the only customer. Mona stood on the porch and rubbed her arms, worried.

"Don't worry, honey; they'll come. It's early."

But by ten o'clock, the muffins were crusting over, and Mona was desperately clinging to the verse from her morning devotions.

Liza sat with her on the steps, biting her lip. "I know what we need," she announced and bounced to her feet. She headed to the porch and wrote on the menu board.

Mona followed her. "Why did you write that?"

"To help us keep our perspective."

Mona smiled and her heart filled with gratitude for the friend the Lord had given her. The board read *"Take delight in the Lord, and He will give you your heart's desires."*

"Amen," Mona said. No matter what happened, she would look heavenward and let God, the author of her dreams, delight her with His love.

"Good morning, Mona dear." Edith Draper's voice spliced through her thoughts. The older woman breezed into the coffee shop, dragging behind her four of her cronies dressed in their polyester Sunday best.

Mona's enthusiasm dipped. Now her mother would hear all about her failure. Perfect.

"Is he here yet?" Edith's gray eyes danced. She exchanged a bright look with a shorter woman who wore a similarly gleeful expression.

Mona blinked at her. "Chuck?"

Edith laughed. She sidled up close, as if they were sharing an intimate secret. "Why didn't you tell me? I had to find out from Mabel down at the dime store." Before Mona could stammer a reply, Edith winked. "We'll just get our coffees and wait."

The five women purchased five coffees, three strawberry muffins, a bran muffin, a chocolate-chip one, and three copies of Reese Clark's new book, *Canadian Catastrophe,* which had arrived only yesterday.

"I just love Jonah," Edith giggled.

Mona stared at her as if Edith had turned purple.

A shiny, red, antique Corvette cruised up in front. Mona watched from the window as a man, decked out in black jeans and a matching Stetson, headed for the Footstep, a sign under his arm.

Mona's breath caught when she saw the man stop and prop up the placard in the front yard, then stare at the house. She'd seen that look a week ago in the dead of night as he'd bid the Footstep good-bye. Joe Michaels. She ignored her thumping heart and strode out the door. On the steps she saw another group of women—tourists, from the looks of their *Welcome to Deep Haven* shopping bags. They seemed in a hurry to get to the Footstep.

"What are you doing here, Joe?" Mona marched down the sidewalk, shocked at her angry tone.

Joe tugged the brim of his hat as if he had never seen her before. "Howdy, ma'am. Reese Clark. I'm here for my reading."

Mona gawked at him.

"Mona, close your mouth or a seagull will fly in."

She snapped her lips shut and examined the sign. The answer was written in plain English: *Reese Clark, author of the Jonah Series, appearing for one day only at the Footstep of Heaven Bookstore and Coffee Shop.*

Words deserted her, but as she glowered at Joe or Reese or whatever his name was, anger simmered. Had she been fodder for his next Jonah story? Had he been here doing research, writing down her every mishap, her secrets? Had he been plotting the destruction of her heart as he held her under the stars? The image of his next book title, *Disaster in Deep Haven,* flitted through her mind. She hoped it was a murder mystery—who killed the handyman?

"You tricked me," she finally growled.

Joe's smile evaporated. "I didn't trick you. I just didn't tell you everything. Some things are private."

"Like your being a best-selling author and acting like a handyman?"

"I was a handyman, remember? I fixed everything."

"Well, you can't fix this, buddy." Mona turned and stalked toward the house.

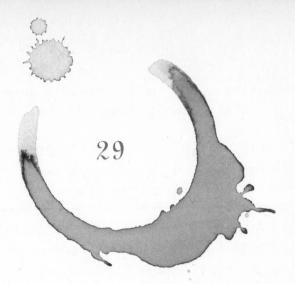

29

How could the suave, refined gentleman greeting Mona's patrons be her very own handyman, Joe? Yes, she recognized those gorgeous blue eyes and couldn't help but melt when they turned her way, but it truly was *Reese Clark,* best-selling author and handsome enigma casually strolling through her Footstep of Heaven. Bitterly, Mona sandbagged her heart and told herself the man was also a deceiver and a manipulator.

It didn't help that Reese Clark attracted business like bees to a flower. All the locals stopped by, along with a steady flow of tourists, and Mona discovered why when she read the half-page ad, in bold type, posted in the *Superior Times.* She had seen the professional picture of a guy in a Stetson leaning on a fence post a dozen times, on all his book jackets, and she felt like an imbecile.

The good news was that she sold out of her supply of Jonah books, even the ones Reese had brought in the trunk of his Corvette, and took two pages of back orders besides. Her muffins vanished at an alarming rate, and the coffeemaker gurgled like a contented baby all day.

"This is a darling place, Mona," Edith commented as she walked out, clutching a bulging bag of books. "It certainly lives up to its name. I think it is just what Deep Haven needs."

Edith's warm words only added to Mona's quandary.

Liza sold pottery like hotcakes as soon as the locals discovered her creations included a seagull etched on the bottom, as if she were a born-and-bred native of Deep Haven. As her stock dwindled, she compiled a list of orders long enough to keep her blissfully hibernated in her pottery shed throughout the winter.

When the doors finally closed, Mona and Liza dropped into an exhausted heap on the stairs.

Even Reese seemed worn out from all the admiration. "Not bad, eh?" he said, tucking his thumbs into his belt loops.

"I'm not talking to you," Mona said. She wanted to surrender to gratefulness, but the sting of his betrayal bit at the impulse. Gratitude stayed locked inside her tightening chest. She glued her eyes to the floor lest confusion unfurl in the form of tears.

Liza, however, grinned at the rogue. "I'm going to take a bath and order a pizza." She stood up. "Thanks, Joe . . . uh . . . I mean, Reese."

He smiled sheepishly. "Actually it is Joe. Or, really, Jonah."

Both women gaped at him.

"Reese is my pen name. Jonah Michaels—" he thumped his chest—"that's me."

"You named your character after yourself?" Liza
gasped.

"It seemed to fit at the time."

"I might need some chocolate-chip ice cream too,"
Liza muttered and headed upstairs.

Mona felt as if her heart had been yanked into her
throat. *Joe was Jonah.* The comparison was so obvious
now that she must have been blind not to see it. Or
perhaps she had been so obsessed with making her
dreams come true that she failed to see when God
brought one walking right through her front door.

Jonah was real. . . .

Joe toed his black cowboy boot into the shiny wood
floor, avoiding her eyes, as if he had just handed her his
heart and now waited for her to pummel it.

"I have something of yours," she offered quietly, her
anger peeling off at his palpable discomfort. Mona fled to
her room and grabbed his journal from her nightstand.
Shame seeped through her. She'd had no right to read it,
and when she handed it back to him, she saw the question flicker in his eyes. "Yes, I read it," she admitted.
"I'm sorry."

He winced. "It's okay."

They stood there for a moment, he blowing out painful sighs and she rubbing her cashmere-covered arms.

"I know about Gabe, Joe."

That seemed to knock the wind from him, for he gave
her a look so desperate, her last embers of irritation
died. He opened his mouth, but no words emerged.

"He's a wonderful man. I bought all my strawberries
from the Garden." She smiled with compassion.

Chagrin colored Joe's face in the form of a blush.

"I'm sorry, Mona. I should have introduced you to him."

"Did you think the fact that he has Down syndrome would matter to me? That I would love him any less?"

"It mattered to my father," he answered bluntly. "He left us because of Gabe."

Pity swelled inside her. "Well, I wouldn't leave. I would trust the Lord and find a way to see His blessings." She tightened her gaze. "Would you leave?"

He paused, stared at the floor. "I did. I ran away from Gabe and all the pain my father left behind." When he looked up, his agony wrenched out her heart. "I was afraid to get close to Gabe, to my father . . . to you."

She put a hand on his arm. "Joe," she said tenderly, "why did you leave?"

He stiffened. "Isn't it obvious?"

Mona frowned.

"You said you loved Jonah for his honesty." Joe's voice grew ragged. "But I was living here, deceiving you with every slam of my hammer. I knew when you said that, you could never forgive me."

His face reddened, and he looked away as he continued. "I even came here at first thinking I might be able to write another Jonah story. Something about Jonah saving a young woman's dreams. But it didn't take long before I didn't want it to be just a story. I didn't want it to be something I dreamed up, watching from afar. I wanted Joe to be your hero, and I wanted . . ." His voice trailed off to nothing, and Mona bit her lip to keep from crying. "But I know now that I was just fooling myself."

Tears pushed into Mona's eyes. Bravely, she stole closer. "If God can forgive me for killing my father, and

you can forgive me for blaming you for the Footstep disasters, I think I can forgive you for pretending you're a handyman."

"I *am* a handyman," he returned, and she caught a mischievous, grateful spark in his eye.

Mona hurled him a semi-cross scowl. "And a best-selling author—only my favorite, I might add—and you knew it!" She clamped her hands on her hips, feeling a swell of sickness in her chest. "You were probably rolling over inside with laughter when I told you my impression of Reese."

Joe shook his head. "Mona, most women I meet see Reese Clark, author and recluse, and think they know me. They know the author, the image they want, and that's whom they run after. You, on the other hand, accepted me, Joe, with all my quirks and imperfections. You didn't run after me. You just let me be who I needed to be. Who I desperately *wanted* to be." His voice dropped. "I wasn't laughing at you; I was seeing myself through your eyes."

His tender voice soothed the pain around her heart. Besides, how could she doubt the sincerity in those disarming blue eyes? "So, it was you I met last fall at the Mall of America?"

"Yep." He looked so mournful it reminded her of Rip hiding from her after he'd tracked mud through the house.

She suddenly wanted to laugh. "Did you follow me here?" she asked, stifling the urge to laugh.

"No! That was purely God's doing. But it didn't take me long to remember where I'd first met that delicious smile or seen that dirt-streaked face."

Mona glowered at him in mock fury.

"I didn't set out to deceive you," he said, abruptly serious. "I was just trying to keep things simple. I thought if you met Gabe and found out who I was, and that I had a passel of fans who might invade your life, you'd send me packing. I didn't want anyone to get hurt." He rubbed a hand behind his neck. "In fact, I prayed that when I showed up I would be a blessing to you."

"You have been a blessing, Joe," Mona affirmed softly and felt a blush creep up her neck. Staring at the floor, she folded her hands. Oh, how she wanted to pull his hand into hers, feel the gentle warmth of his touch again. But she held herself back. What if, now that he was a big star, he really *was* here for only one day? What if he'd come back out of guilt, or worse, out of pity? Tears burned her eyes.

As if to confirm her rampaging doubts, he turned abruptly. "I'm glad I could help you, Mona."

Oh no. It was just as she suspected. Pity. Her Jonah was walking right out the door, possibly forever. "Joe," she blurted, "why did you come back?" *Oh, please let me be wrong. Please let him have come back because he, too, stared at the ceiling every night, listening to the despairing groan of his broken heart.*

He swallowed hard, as if working up the truth, and she heard the echo of her fears.

Joe finally met her gaze. His eyes blazed with an inferno of unspoken emotions so warm it made her mouth dry. "I wanted to help you. It seemed you were trying so hard, and I wanted it to work for you. I heard about your problem through my publicist and knew God wanted me to come back. I realized then that He'd

given me a gift—a successful writing career. I could either hide from it or use it to help you."

"Oh." It was worse than pity. Joe had reverted back to handyman mode . . . fixing the black holes in her life, but this time doing it by flexing his author muscles. It didn't have anything to do with romance or the love she thought she'd felt emanating from his warm smile as he'd helped her build her dreams. "Thank you," she said through her knotted chest.

He tugged his hat, as if he had just walked her across the street, and turned toward the door.

Mona's heart made a tiny whimper. *Please don't go.* Her pride might be slashed to smithereens, but she couldn't let him leave. Here he was, back in the Footstep of Heaven, practically hand-delivered by the Lord, and there was no way she was going to let him stroll out of her life. Not when she thought she'd seen their future written in his smoldering eyes. So his words had stabbed at her heart . . . *Jonah had walked through her front door.* It seemed impossible, glorious, and suddenly she heard Joe's words like a siren in her head. *God wanted me to come back.*

God had given her everything—her forgiveness, her Footstep, and her Jonah right off the pages. She wouldn't let Joe run away. Not if her love could bring him home.

"Joe, did you mean what you wrote about me?"

He whirled, and the look on his face made her want to cry. Achingly raw and desperate. "I meant it."

"Then let me finish the story for you," Mona whispered. "Jonah stops running. He finds the woman of his dreams in some tiny town and decides he's going to have to risk someone invading the privacy of his heart . . . just like the rest of us."

An odd look filtered into Joe's eyes. Mona swallowed her heart, which had lodged in her throat, squarely cutting off her air supply.

A smile spread across his face. "I like it."

"I love you, Joe. Don't leave." Summoning her courage, Mona nudged closer, nearly into his arms.

Joe's eyes searched hers, piercing, intimate, testing her words. He reached out and traced her cheek with his fingers, sending a ripple down Mona's spine and igniting every nerve ending.

"I love you too." His voice trembled when he spoke. "You're all I've been thinking about this last week, you and the Footstep and Gabe. . . ." He closed his eyes, obviously fighting a wave of emotion.

Mona waited, her pulse nearly flinging her into his arms, longing to comfort, to soothe. Instead she leaned her head into his hand as it cupped her cheek.

"Mona, after I left you, I went to see my father."

She saw his face change subtly, like the effect of the sun moving from behind a cloud through a thick forest. His emotions, once hooded, began to shine. Passion swept through his voice. "I told him I forgave him for leaving us, and when I did it . . . okay, here goes—I felt like I could breathe again. Suddenly I had all these places in my heart that were wide open . . ." His eyes roamed her face. "And just waiting for you to move in." He cradled her face with both hands, causing her entire body to quiver.

"Mona, I've loved you almost since the first day I met you. Your crazy, wonderful dreams make me want to put

down roots and build a life here in Deep Haven. I don't care if I get hurt, or if something happens and you leave me. I'll take the risk if you'll let me love you. Let me fix all your broken pipes, your leaky roof, mow your lawn. I don't even have to write anymore. Not one word. I just want to be with you. I'll be your handyman. Forever." He swallowed, and she felt his nervousness strum through her. "Mona Reynolds, will you marry me?"

She went weak. "Marry Jonah?" she teased in a shaky voice. "I'd be the envy of women across the world." Her head spun. Marry Jonah . . . her dream man?

He held her gaze with those beautiful eyes that could turn her bones to jelly. "Yes, marry Jonah. Marry me. I can't promise that it will be easy. We'll always have people peering into our lives. But I think, with you beside me, I can bear it. Will you share my world and let me into yours?"

Mona nodded, unable to speak, to breathe, to do anything but let her tears flow.

When he gave her a tender smile, she could have danced to the music in it. Then Joe bent and kissed her, tentatively, lingeringly, as if the touch of her nourished his soul. Mona put a hand on his chest and relaxed against him, tasting tears in their kiss. When he pulled away, she felt his body tremble and saw in his eyes the magnitude of his love. Her heart filled with a swirl of joy.

"What about Reese Clark?" she murmured, drinking in the fragrance of his cologne and the intoxicating scent of flannel that always surrounded him. "Your book plots take you all over the world. What will happen to Jonah?" His lips were close to hers, and she longed for his strong, capable arms around her.

He entwined his fingers through her hair and smiled, those beautiful blue eyes turning rapscallion. "I was serious about being your handyman."

She laughed softly. "Well, I might employ your services occasionally. But you can't stop writing. What would your public say?"

Worry shifted into his face. "Are you sure you're ready for my public?"

"Mister, I *am* your public," Mona said, and a new wave of disbelief washed over her. *Jonah's here, kissing me.* "You can't stop writing any more than you can stop breathing."

He leaned his forehead against hers. "Have I told you how much I love you?"

"Tell me again."

"Since it's okay with you, I have one more book to write," he said. "I'll call it *Deep Haven Dreams.*"

Then Joe gave her a kiss that was so sweet, so gentle, so perfect it sent shivers to her toes. It spoke of commitment and promises that were forever. When he drew away, a lopsided smile creased his face. His incredible eyes, however, were serious. "It will be the last of the series. Jonah has finally found what he's been searching for."

He put his arms around her, drawing her close, holding her eyes with a soul-reading look. Mona barely managed to find her voice. "And what's that?"

His gaze left hers briefly, scanning beyond her and encompassing the bookstore—at the many repairs he'd completed, at her bookshelves, the coffee bar, the oak stumps, the light fixture in the hallway. When he looked at her again, tears pooled in his eyes. "Peace."

Mona traced the shape of Joe's crooked smile and wove her hands into his soft hair. Then she kissed the man upon whom she'd come to depend, to trust, to love. The man God had sent to remind her that yes, dreams do come true in the hands of the Author of happy endings.

"Welcome home, Jonah Michaels."

A Note
from the
Author

The idea of *Happily Ever After* has been incubating in my heart since childhood, when I first set eyes on the North Shore of Minnesota. It seems as though everything significant in my life has birthed from moments sitting on the shores of Lake Superior, listening to the call of the seagulls or throwing stones into the surf. I found the Lord at a camp on the Gunflint Trail, met my husband years later in Grand Marais, and began my writing dreams at a rough-hewn picnic table overlooking the rocky shoreline.

Mona and Joe—and their story—touched my heart and reminded me that God is the author of my dreams and all my golden moments. My desire in writing this story was to share how God truly is our refuge, our deep haven, and that whatever happens, whether travail or triumph, we can fling ourselves into the Father's loving arms with trust and abandon.

A good friend once told me that God doesn't give us a dream just to yank it away and laugh. We serve a loving

God who knows our hearts better than we do and longs to delight us with His love. I've clung to that thought throughout the years as my family and I have served God in challenging places, enduring difficult stages in our missionary service. Through it all, I've seen His provision, His protection, and His love, showing me repeatedly that I am His beloved child. Most of all, I've learned that the more I surrender to Him and the more I trust in His grace for every situation, the more He surprises me with His abundance. Try it! Give Him your dreams and your heart, and enjoy being loved by the Almighty.

Thank you for reading *Happily Ever After*. I hope you've enjoyed reading it as much as I've enjoyed writing it. I'm looking forward to sharing with you other romantic adventures on the shores of Lake Superior in Deep Haven, Minnesota.

God bless,

Susan May Warren

About the Author

Susan May Warren is a career missionary with SEND International, serving with her husband and four children in Khabarovsk, Far East Russia, where she divides her time between homeschooling, ministry, and writing. She holds a B.A. in mass communications from the University of Minnesota and has been published in numerous Christian magazines and devotional books.

Susan's novella "Measure of a Man" appears in the HeartQuest anthology *Chance Encounters of the Heart*. *Happily Ever After* is her first novel.

Susan invites you to visit her Web site at www.susanmaywarren.com. She also welcomes letters by e-mail at susanwarren@mail.com.

Visit www.HeartQuest.com for lots of info on
HeartQuest books and authors and more!

COMING SOON (SUMMER 2003)

An Echo of Love, Dianna Crawford

Speak to Me of Love, Robin Lee Hatcher

Love's Proof, Catherine Palmer

CURRENT HEARTQUEST RELEASES

- *Magnolia,* Ginny Aiken
- *Lark,* Ginny Aiken
- *Camellia,* Ginny Aiken
- *Letters of the Heart,* Lisa Tawn Bergren, Maureen Pratt, and Lyn Cote
- *Sweet Delights,* Terri Blackstock, Elizabeth White, and Ranee McCollum
- *Awakening Mercy,* Angela Benson
- *Abiding Hope,* Angela Benson
- *Ruth,* Lori Copeland
- *Roses Will Bloom Again,* Lori Copeland
- *Faith,* Lori Copeland
- *Hope,* Lori Copeland
- *June,* Lori Copeland
- *Glory,* Lori Copeland
- *Winter's Secret,* Lyn Cote
- *Autumn's Shadow,* Lyn Cote
- *Freedom's Promise,* Dianna Crawford
- *Freedom's Hope,* Dianna Crawford
- *Freedom's Belle,* Dianna Crawford
- *A Home in the Valley,* Dianna Crawford
- *Lady of the River,* Dianna Crawford
- *Prairie Rose,* Catherine Palmer
- *Prairie Fire,* Catherine Palmer
- *Prairie Storm,* Catherine Palmer
- *Prairie Christmas,* Catherine Palmer, Elizabeth White, and Peggy Stoks
- *Finders Keepers,* Catherine Palmer
- *Hide & Seek,* Catherine Palmer
- *English Ivy,* Catherine Palmer
- *Sunrise Song,* Catherine Palmer
- *A Kiss of Adventure,* Catherine Palmer (original title: *The Treasure of Timbuktu*)
- *A Whisper of Danger,* Catherine Palmer (original title: *The Treasure of Zanzibar*)
- *A Touch of Betrayal,* Catherine Palmer
- *A Victorian Christmas Keepsake,* Catherine Palmer, Kristin Billerbeck, and Ginny Aiken
- *A Victorian Christmas Cottage,* Catherine Palmer, Debra White Smith, Jeri Odell, and Peggy Stoks
- *A Victorian Christmas Quilt,* Catherine Palmer, Peggy Stoks, Debra White Smith, and Ginny Aiken
- *A Victorian Christmas Tea,* Catherine Palmer, Dianna Crawford, Peggy Stoks, and Katherine Chute
- *A Victorian Christmas Collection,* Peggy Stoks
- *Olivia's Touch,* Peggy Stoks
- *Romy's Walk,* Peggy Stoks
- *Elena's Song,* Peggy Stoks
- *Chance Encounters of the Heart,* Elizabeth White, Kathleen Fuller, and Susan Warren
- *Happily Ever After,* Susan May Warren

HEART
QUEST.

HEARTQUEST BOOKS BY SUSAN MAY WARREN

Measure of a Man—The last person Calli Deane expects to see trapped in an elevator in Siberia at 2 A.M. is Peter Samuelson—the man who broke her heart. Now she is swept into the past and drawn toward a future she never expected. This novella appears in the anthology *Chance Encounters of the Heart.*

OTHER GREAT TYNDALE HOUSE FICTION

- *Safely Home*, Randy Alcorn
- *Jenny's Story*, Judy Baer
- *Libby's Story*, Judy Baer
- *Tia's Story*, Judy Baer
- *Out of the Shadows*, Sigmund Brouwer
- *The Leper*, Sigmund Brouwer
- *Crown of Thorns*, Sigmund Brouwer
- *Looking for Cassandra Jane*, Melody Carlson
- *Child of Grace*, Lori Copeland
- *They Shall See God*, Athol Dickson
- *Ribbon of Years*, Robin Lee Hatcher
- *Firstborn*, Robin Lee Hatcher
- *The Touch*, Patricia Hickman
- *Redemption*, Gary Smalley and Karen Kingsbury
- *The Price*, Jim and Terri Kraus
- *The Treasure*, Jim and Terri Kraus
- *The Promise*, Jim and Terri Kraus
- *The Quest*, Jim and Terri Kraus
- *Winter Passing*, Cindy McCormick Martinusen
- *Blue Night*, Cindy McCormick Martinusen
- *North of Tomorrow*, Cindy McCormick Martinusen
- *Embrace the Dawn*, Kathleen Morgan
- *Lullaby*, Jane Orcutt
- *The Happy Room*, Catherine Palmer
- *A Dangerous Silence*, Catherine Palmer
- *Unveiled*, Francine Rivers
- *Unashamed*, Francine Rivers
- *Unshaken*, Francine Rivers
- *Unspoken*, Francine Rivers
- *Unafraid*, Francine Rivers
- *A Voice in the Wind*, Francine Rivers
- *An Echo in the Darkness*, Francine Rivers
- *As Sure As the Dawn*, Francine Rivers
- *Leota's Garden*, Francine Rivers
- *Shaiton's Fire*, Jake Thoene